Praise for
The Day After Yesterday

"Ms. Cozy has a definite gift for writing that allows the reader to intimately know her characters . . . A beautiful story by a talented writer."

—*Literary R&R*

• • •

"This novel captured both my attention and my heart. The characters are realistic, multifaceted, and endearing. I shared in both their laughter and their tears and was saddened to reach the end of their tale. Ms. Cozy's masterful look into the human condition provides a message of hope and understanding for anyone that has experienced a loss or knows someone who has. I highly recommend this book."

—*Flurries of Words*

• • •

"This book has touched me in a way I didn't expect and will never forget . . . It's breathtaking, heartbreaking, and just plain beautiful. I can't recommend it enough."

—Tia Silverthorne Bach, author of *Chasing Memories*

• • •

"I was so entranced with it that I found myself stopping and setting it aside—I didn't want it to end. By putting it down, I could enjoy it longer, savor it more . . . I got so emotionally involved with this story that I had to read it in bits and pieces just so I could absorb the thoughts and feelings of the characters. And yes, I will admit that when reading parts of this book, I did have tears in my eyes. I really am in awe of authors who can put so much into a book that the reader feels the emotions right along with the characters."

—*The Book Bag*

The Day After Yesterday

A novel by Kelly Cozy

SMITE
PUBLICATIONS

ISBN: 978-0-9851234-0-6

Love consists in this, that two solitudes protect and touch and greet each other.

—Rainer Maria Rilke

Acknowledgments

It's time to thank all the people who make this possible: You and you and mostly me and you.

But seriously, there are many, many people to thank.

The members of my Constant Reader Brigade: Karen Girard, Erik Hoard, Gerry Hoard (special thanks for the winter roses), Albert Muller, and Alyca Tanner. Their support, enthusiasm, and constructive criticism have been invaluable from the start.

As always, I must thank Scott and Alex for putting up with the annoyances of living with a writer and doing so with grace and goodwill. And deepest gratitude goes to Mom and Dad, for giving me the love of books and reading, for encouraging my writing endeavors, and most of all, for not being like some of the moms and dads in this story.

A tip o' the *chapeau* and additional thanks go to: Lauren Baratz-Logsted, Alex Broquet, Sean Carolin, Meg Gerzevske, Keith Handy, Richard Harmetz, April Hizny, Katy Hoard, Pauline Kiet, Billie Martin, Diane Molberg, Frank Moore, Speer Morgan, Alan Natale, Bret and Colleen Nelson, Lisa Schmitt, and Stanley and Janice Thompson. Thanks also go to the fine folks at Kindle Press.

Places get their due as well: the cities of Solvang and Redondo Beach in California, also Columbia, Missouri; and the Norton Simon Museum of Art in Pasadena, California.

For making research less onerous: thanks to EnglishHistory.net and The-Athenaeum.org.

Smite Publications logo designed by alanNdesign.

Landfall

Prologue

Highway 101 was a dark strand along the California coast, all but invisible in the night and the rain. On this strand like a bright pearl was the Shoreline Diner. Zack Fuller stood by the window. Even when he shaded his eyes against the diner's light and peered outside, he could see nothing. There were few lights on this stretch of the 101, and the storm shut out the moon and stars. Nothing but midnight-in-a-mine-shaft darkness and no sound save for the rain, coming down hard, and the wind's occasional lonely wail.

Zack placed one palm against the window to feel the chill. He rather liked these coastal winter storms. He much preferred them to the downpours of his native Louisiana; those warm rains smelled like wet plant life and reminded him too much of 'Nam. By contrast, California storms were soothing, even inspiring at times. Some nights like these made him think he ought to try writing a book, or maybe a short story. He'd thought of an opening line—*It was a dark and stormy night*—but now had the uneasy feeling it might have been done before.

He turned away from the window. Two hours until closing but only five customers in the place—not surprising. No one was going out in this weather if they could help it. Four of the five he knew by sight and experience. Local teens who left their tables a mess, used foul language when ladies and kids were nearby, and never tipped. They'd long since eaten and paid and were just killing time while waiting for the storm to die down. Zack ignored them and made his way to the counter, where the fifth customer sat. A redhead, she sat with an empty plate in front of her—she'd had the Evening Breakfast Special. She had a book open, but Zack had never seen her turn a page; she seemed more interested in the sketch pad she doodled on. The redhead gave Zack a quick up-and-down glance as he approached. Impossible to tell if she was pretty, for her face was half-hidden by her hair.

"Care for a refill?" Zack held up the iced tea pitcher.

"Yes, please. Is it still raining?"

"Cats and dogs."

She glanced at the windows. Zack took the opportunity to sneak a peek at her doodles and was surprised by their quality—no stick figures or meaningless scribbles, but detailed sketches of a saguaro cactus, a cat, the Golden Gate Bridge. There were words on the sketch pad, too, but he had to look away before he could read them so she wouldn't see he'd been peeking.

The redhead turned back to her sketch pad, biting her lower lip nervously. Zack could tell she didn't want to venture out into the storm, and he didn't blame her. Pitching his voice low so the local quartet wouldn't hear, he said, "Stay as long as you like. It's not safe to be driving in this weather."

"But you'll be closing. I don't want to keep you from home."

Zack shrugged. "I've got insomnia." A souvenir from 'Nam. "And I don't want to go out in this, either."

He thought of offering her a place to sleep. He had one—a tiny antechamber in the back among the canned goods and industrial-size boxes of flour and salt. An army cot with wool blankets, a space heater, and even a privacy curtain he'd sewn. He lay there on insomniac nights or when he and the old lady were going through a bad patch. But as he was about to

14

offer, he saw the way she regarded him—warily. Zack wondered how much of that was due to his admittedly scruffy appearance—bald head, tattoos, and long, white, braided beard—and how much of her wariness came from experience, from the telltale bump of her nose that told him it had been broken at least once.

She offered him a small smile. "Thank you. You're very kind. I'm from Arizona; I'm not used to driving in this kind of rain."

"Stay as long as you like."

Zack occupied himself with cleaning the grill, brewing fresh coffee and decaf, and reading a New Orleans–set mystery titled *The Jambalaya Alibi*. The local quartet had run out of inane chatter. The redhead was writing something in her sketch pad. The storm had long since become white noise ignored by them all, so when the diner's door opened with a thud, Zack started and looked up.

The man stood just inside the doorway, blinking as if dazed by the diner's light and warmth. He was so white-faced and soaked through he might have emerged from the sea—which of course was impossible given the storm-tossed tide. He must have been walking in the rain for hours. Water dripped steadily from his clothes, his hair, the backpack he wore.

Zack walked over to the man, bringing a mug and the coffeepot with him. "God almighty, look at you," Zack said. "Sit down and warm up."

The man didn't move save to look back over his shoulder. He seemed to be searching for someone. "Where did . . ." he said, but didn't finish.

"It's OK. Sit down." Zack put a hand on the man's shoulder—sopping wet and stone cold. When the man sat down, Zack poured some coffee. "Drink up."

"Thank you." The man hadn't lost that dazed look. He sat with water pooling around him, hadn't even taken off his backpack. He reached for the coffee mug, then with no warning slumped and toppled to the side, pitching headlong out of the booth. Zack dropped the coffeepot and caught the man bare inches before he'd have bashed his head a good one on the linoleum.

Zack grappled with the unconscious man's dead weight while his shoes slid in rainwater and spilled coffee. He yelled over his shoulder at the local kids: "Hey, little help here!" But they were already out the door. Useless little twerps.

"Here." The redhead helped ease the man to the floor. She checked the man's pulse, his breathing, felt his forehead with the inside of her wrist. She did it quickly and professionally. Zack recognized that from field hospitals and the VA. "When he spoke, was it clear?" she asked.

"Yes."

"He didn't slur his words?"

"No. Is it hypothermia?"

"Probably. I think it's mild, but he should go to a hospital. Where's the nearest one?"

Miles from here, he told her, and with the weather, who knew how long it would take for an ambulance to get here.

She nodded and asked if there was someplace they could get him warm.

Zack flipped the diner's sign to "Closed," and together they carried the man into Zack's makeshift bedroom. They worked with the efficiency of a nurse and a soldier and soon had the man's drenched clothes off; they laid him down on the cot with the wool blankets over him and the space heater on.

Only once did Zack see the woman taken aback—when they took off the man's shirt and saw the scars, red lines standing out angrily against the pale skin of his inner wrists. Not old scars, either. Zack knew wounds and gauged them to be a month or two old, at most. Nearly four inches long, straight and sure. The work of a determined man. The redhead paused for a moment, then went on with her work.

When they had the man as dry and warm as they could get him, she checked his pulse and breathing again. "He's getting some color back," she said as she held the man's right hand. "That's good. I'm going to stay with him awhile."

"OK. Let me take care of this." Zack gathered the wet clothes into a plastic bag, thinking he'd hang them up somewhere to dry. Lastly he picked up the backpack and took it with him to the diner's main room. He sat down in a booth and, after a moment's consideration, opened the backpack.

He expected to find the belongings a sodden mess, but they were in Ziploc bags and had stayed dry. The box of Ziplocs, its cardboard wet, was the topmost item. It seemed a recent purchase; Zack found tucked inside the box a barely legible receipt from a convenience store some twenty-five miles north. Surely the man hadn't walked twenty-five miles in the rain? No wonder he'd toppled over.

Zack reproached himself for prying, but curiosity was too strong, and the bag yielded up its contents. Two sets of clothes—jeans and shirts—not laundry fresh but not stale, either. One bag was most curious—it held a woman's gauzy blue scarf, shimmering cobalt beads embroidered on it, and a green teddy bear, most of its fuzz long since worn away. Zack shivered. He knew mementos when he saw them. The last bag was a treasure trove. House keys. A wallet. A prescription bottle—Zoloft, half-full. Papers: discharge papers from a hospital, referrals to a doctor, a sheet of notepaper from a motel with several names and addresses written on it, a letter sealed and addressed but with no stamp or return address.

Zack opened the wallet. About forty dollars or so. Standard-issue credit cards. A driver's license for Daniel J. Whitman of Los Cielos. Zack had the notion Los Cielos was to the south—around San Diego perhaps? Health insurance and library cards. Musicians' Union membership cards. A "Buy ten cups, get the eleventh free" card for a coffee house called Java Man—he had three more to go. Nothing that explained why Whitman was so far from home with little beyond the clothes on his back, sporting wrist scars, near to collapse with cold and exhaustion.

Feeling like a voyeur, Zack turned to the wallet's photo insert. A Christmas studio picture of Whitman with a pretty blonde woman and a towheaded young boy, the sort of picture sent out with holiday greeting cards. Whitman was a good-looking fellow when he wasn't impersonating a drowned rat. A picture of the boy in his preschool years, holding the green teddy bear. Zack felt a queasy thump and flipped through the remaining photos hurriedly. A group shot of the blonde woman with what looked like her siblings and parents. The boy having a toy-lightsaber duel with a bespectacled man, who turned up in the next picture, a wedding portrait with him and a brunette. *Are these people looking for you, Whitman? What happened? Why are you here?*

"Pardon me."

The voice was soft, but Zack jumped and guiltily snapped the wallet closed.

"He's better now," said the redhead. "Just sleeping. I'm going to stay up with him if that's all right."

"Sure. You want something to eat? BLT maybe?"

"Oh, yes please."

"I'm making a fresh pot of joe, would you like some?"

She cast a longing look at the pot. "I . . . I'd better not." She made a vague gesture toward her midsection, didn't seem to be aware she was doing it. Zack understood immediately. He was the oldest of six children and knew a breeding woman when he saw one.

Zack made the sandwich and brought it to her, along with a glass of skim milk. She was leaning over Whitman, examining his head by the light of a flashlight. Zack peered closely. "He didn't get that bump when he fell. His head never touched the floor."

She nodded. "He's got a laceration, too. That's why I wanted to keep an eye on him. Pupils are dilating fine, so there doesn't seem to be a concussion."

Zack went back to his booth and packed Whitman's belongings back into their Ziplocs. He picked up the backpack, intending to hang it up somewhere to dry, and as he did noticed several long green strands tangled in the backpack's straps. Frowning, he looked at them more closely. Sea grass. On the wet clothes was more sea grass, and there was sand on the jeans, shoes, and socks.

Zack shuddered. He'd ventured out to look at the sea during these winter storms and had been amazed how fierce the gentle blue Pacific could turn. More amazed now that Whitman was here and not feeding the fish. He hung the wet things over chair backs to dry, then sat and laid his head down on the table. A long day and a longer night, and it wasn't yet midnight. Zack didn't mean to doze off but jerked awake at the sound.

The cry was not loud but the quality of it—the oboe tone of fear and desperation—cut through Zack's uneasy sleep. He remembered a cry much like it, many years ago: some poor PFC stepped on a mine and wandered off mostly blind into the rice paddies, where he bled out over half the night and called for his mother most of that time.

This voice wasn't crying out for mother. It called for *Sarah*. And there was a phrase, one the unlucky PFC had used: *Help me*. Still woozy from his abrupt awakening, Zack went into the back, where he found the redhead and the man holding each other. Zack couldn't make out most of the man's words. As for the redhead, she seemed unsure of what to say and uncomfortable in the man's clutch. "Everything's all right," she said.

Whitman was having none of it. "No. Not ever."

Nothing she said soothed him. But then she sang.

Something strange about her singing. Her voice was untrained, wobbly at times, yet had a quality to it that wasn't so much comfort as compassion. It said that she understood why he'd ended up here even if she didn't know the exact reason. What she sang: it was slow and strangely old-fashioned. The sort of music you'd hear from some woman in medieval clothes, playing a lute. Or so it seemed to Zack.

She sang and held the man's hand. A different song, one that made Zack think of long-ago Midnight Masses on Christmas Eve; for a moment he even thought he caught a whiff of incense. The redhead didn't look up at Zack—all her attention was on Whitman. He'd quieted down and lay still. Zack couldn't tell if he was still awake. After a while Zack asked in a whisper if everything was all right, and she nodded, not taking her eyes off Whitman.

Zack went back to his booth. He meant to ask her about the songs. He laid his head down again, tried to remember the words she'd sung. A verse or two he could recall: *Do way, dear heart, not so. Let no thought you dismay. Though you now part me from, we shall meet when we may.* When he woke the rain had stopped. The dawn showed pearl-gray clouds and here and there a hint of blue. Whitman slept in the makeshift bedroom. The redhead was gone.

The Summer Wind

Chapter One

Five months before he entered the Shoreline Diner, Daniel Whitman woke early on a Sunday. No reason for his early waking other than that it was a Sunday—Sarah and Jake would sleep in, and he'd have time to play, undisturbed. He slipped out of bed without waking Sarah, then put on sweatpants and a T-shirt and padded through the small house. Past Jake's room and the living room, a detour into the kitchen for coffee, then on into the workroom.

One side of the room held a built-in bookshelf crammed with textbooks: Norton anthologies of literature and poetry, hardcovers and paperbacks with sticky notes poking out the tops and sides. Buried under papers was a small desk topped with a jar full of red pens. He went past the bookshelf and desk and sat at his piano.

It was the third piano he'd owned. His first hadn't even been a piano proper, but a portable electronic keyboard given to him by Sarah's uncle Jacob. That keyboard had long since given up the ghost, but he'd loved it and still thought fondly of those hours he'd spent learning chords and scales or making his first half-assed attempts at a Chopin nocturne or "Let It Be." Its best feature had been that he could plug headphones into it and play for hours without hearing his sister make fun of his playing and tell him to knock that shit off. The second had been a real piano, bought to celebrate his music degree. Most of his graduation gift money had gone into buying that piano, and it had served him long and well.

The one he sat at now, a Bösendorfer 170, had been a present for his thirty-fifth birthday. He'd thought it within his reach only if he won the lottery. Sarah had reassured him it had been an unexpected bargain, but her vagueness on the details and the suspiciously low monthly payment made Daniel certain his friend Mick had played a role in that purchase. Not that Mick would admit such a thing; for someone who'd made so much money, the man was remarkably uncomfortable with the subject. Oh, Mick would tell you (and tell you) what investments were good this year, and he had set up a college fund for Jake before he'd been christened, but Daniel still had no idea how much Mick earned in a year. Enough to chip in for more than his fair share of a Bösendorfer.

The keys were cool to the touch. Soon they would be warm from contact with his fingers, and by the end of the morning's session he'd be hard-pressed to tell where his hands ended and the keys began. By the time Jake came in, some two hours after Daniel had started playing, the keys felt like natural extensions of his hands and his feet found the proper pedals without him needing to think about it at all.

At seven, Jake was old enough to know not to interrupt his father's playing unless there was fire or blood involved. But the moment Daniel took a break, Jake zoomed into the room, holding an elaborate Lego construction overhead. "Incoming!" he said.

Daniel laughed and caught Jake, hoisting him up onto the bench. "Let's see what you've got there."

It looked like the bastard child of a lawn mower, helicopter, and submarine. The only thing Jake liked better than those Lego kits of Star Wars ships or racing cars was building his own vehicles. Last year he'd won second place in a "build your own Lego spaceship" contest, trouncing kids twice his age. Not for the first time Daniel wondered where that skill had come from; he himself could barely build a crude car out of the small plastic bricks. Perhaps it was some rogue Reilly gene—he'd ask Sarah's brothers and sisters about it at the next gathering—or a gift from his own unknown genetic background. "I like it. Is it a good-guy or a bad-guy ship?"

"Either. Or both. It's multiple-guess."

"You mean multiple-choice."

"No, Mom says it's multiple-guess; it's what the kids in her class do."

"Aha. That explains it. You ought to show this to Raf, he'd get a kick out of it."

"Can he come over today?"

"I'm fine with it. You go ask Mom and if she's fine, you can call Raf and ask him."

"All right!" Jake leaned in close and put on his most endearing big-eyed expression. "Can we play the creepy song for Mom?"

"OK, but you've got to help me so I don't get all the blame. I don't want her to spank me." With a grin Daniel positioned his son's hands on the proper keys. They'd done this before; Jake didn't need much instruction, and soon the melody of "In the Hall of the Mountain King" reverberated through the room.

It had been over a decade since Los Cielos University's Scary Black and White Movie Night at Stirling Auditorium with its feature of Fritz Lang's *M*, but Sarah was still creeped out by the melody made infamous by Peter Lorre. She squealed and ran into the room, brandishing a red pen like a murder weapon. Daniel thought the eighth-grade English students were going to get feistier-than-usual comments on their papers today.

"Still unhinged by Grieg?" Daniel asked with all the sweetness he could muster.

"That and I stepped on a Lego. Jake, come on. Keep them in one spot. This house is enough of a disaster area without Legos on the floor of every room," Sarah said, massaging the bottom of one bare foot.

"Can Raf come over later?" Jake asked, sliding off the piano bench.

"If you clean up the Legos, and if his mom can drop him off. I've still got papers to grade."

"I can pick him up," Daniel said. "After lunch. I have an errand to run anyway."

Sarah went back to the "what I read on my summer vacation" papers, Jake back to his Legos, and Daniel back to his practicing. Just another Sunday at Casa del Whitman.

Tucked into the coastal foothills north of San Diego, Los Cielos had somehow managed to thrive without sacrificing its charm. It had largely stayed immune to the encroachment of cookie-cutter development that plagued much of California. Its reason for being was Los Cielos University, and the teachers and students alike cherished the city's small-town, somewhat retro feel and strove to preserve it.

Daniel and Sarah Whitman, LCU alumni both, had fallen in love with Los Cielos, not coincidentally around the time they'd fallen in love with each other. Sarah could have found a more prestigious teaching position in a larger or wealthier city; Daniel would have had less onerous commutes to his session work in San Diego or Los Angeles. But they did well enough to have what they needed: their house was small and cluttered but well suited to their family. Certainly they'd never felt the need to follow in Mick's footsteps and dash off to New York after graduation. Perhaps the quest for the big brass ring wasn't all it was cracked up to be, judging by the way Mick had given up not just on New York but on other big cities.

Daniel pedaled along the town's streets with Jake's bike trailer in tow, singing Queen's "Bicycle Race" as he went, aided by Jake, who was not yet old enough to be embarrassed by such behavior. Their progress was slow, and not because of the Sunday tourists and loitering college students. Mrs. Craig, who ran the Book Barn, flagged them down and gave Daniel the new edition of *Fahrenheit 451* that Sarah had ordered. While Daniel paid for the book, Jean from the deli next door brought crullers for them both.

Past the surf shop and the Internet café, past the hardware store and the place that rented surrey bikes; a few bits of confetti from last month's street fair swirled in their wake. Their destination was halfway down the row of shops on Sandcastle Way. The sign was eye-catching at all times, but in the early afternoon sunlight it dazzled—a mosaic of beads, sequins, and bright-colored minerals spelled out the name: "Beaditudes." After Daniel parked the bike and helped Jake out of the trailer, and after Jake made a quick search for misplaced Legos, they went into the store.

Bells jingled as they entered. As always, Daniel blinked to adjust his eyes to the inside of the shop and its wares. Dresses, tops, and skirts hung from racks—all the clothes were dyed in jewel tones. Aquamarine, ruby, amethyst, sapphire, garnet, emerald, topaz, onyx, pearl, and more. Embroidered on the clothes or strung into necklaces, bracelets, and earrings were the same beads and baubles as found on the store's sign, reflecting the light and catching the eye.

In the midst of this finery, looking rather like a wren who'd stumbled into a peacock's nest, stood Mick, probably there to help his wife with the inventory. Though a year younger than Daniel and Sarah, Mick always gave the impression of being older. A certain solemnity to him. *He's one of those boys who was always told to be a little man when he was young,*

Sarah speculated once. *He never got to be just a kid, I'll bet; he's been a grown-up since he was eight.* It hadn't helped that in their university days Michael Kessler had been an anomaly in his chinos and oxford shirts and his librarian glasses. He'd even owned (and worn) a tweed jacket with suede elbow patches. This at a school where nearly all the teachers considered jeans to be formal wear. Even now, on his day off from financial wheeling and dealing, he retained a certain sobriety in his dress and demeanor.

Daniel gave his traditional greeting: "Hey, Professor." Mick had loosened up considerably over the years—he'd had no choice; if Mick had tightened up any more, he'd have imploded—but the nickname remained.

Mick turned, his face breaking into a grin. He pushed his glasses back up onto his face and put aside the clipboard and pen he'd been holding. "Dan the Man and Big Jake." Mick gave them each a high five. "Oh, let me see this," he said, and examined Jake's Lego creation.

Daniel smiled to himself and let the two of them be. With Jake, Mick would let his guard down in a way he didn't with anyone else. Except perhaps Rachel.

Speaking of whom. She emerged from the store's back room wearing an abstracted frown and holding a legal pad. Her dark hair was piled on top of her head and held in place with several No. 2 pencils. Rachel's dress, long and dyed a peculiarly deep shade of purple, was embroidered with beads and bright-colored threads; around her throat she wore a choker of blue and purple stones. She'd made the dress and necklace herself, as she had all the clothing and jewelry in the store. "I thought you two would be here soon," she said. "Birthday time again."

"But of course," said Daniel. He called over his shoulder: "What's the thirtieth? A Friday?"

"Saturday," Mick replied without looking up from the play area Rachel had set up in the corner.

"So says Mr. Almanac," Rachel said. "What did you have in mind?"

Daniel fished in his pocket and brought out a cameo brooch. "Mom Reilly gave me this. It was Sarah's grandmother's. Can you put it onto a necklace?"

Rachel took the cameo, hemmed and hawed, and mumbled to herself. While she perused her supply of beads and stones, Daniel walked over to Mick and Jake.

"When you heading across the pond?" Mick asked.

"Tuesday. Probably be gone a week, week and a half at most. It's just a couple of songs Reg Fletcher is doing for a charity thing."

"*Rock Around the Rainforest?*"

"That or *Babies Must Eat*. Some sort of worthy cause."

"I've heard he's a piece of work. Is that true?"

"He's mellowed out a lot."

"No longer the angry young man?"

"And they can do such wonderful things with antidepressants these days, or so I'm told."

"I'm surprised he's flying you all the way to London."

Daniel shrugged. "He likes the way I play, says I've got an affinity for minor-key work. Most of his music is still all doomy, so that works."

Mick scooped up a handful of the beads Rachel had in the play area—extras, discontinueds, and imperfect stones she wouldn't use in her jewelry but that kids could use to make their own while their parents shopped. "Why don't you play your own stuff? Make an album. If that street musician out there by the bookstore can put out a CD, so can you."

"And who'd buy it? You. Rachel. Sarah's family."

31

"And yours."

Daniel rolled his eyes. "As if they'd notice. 'Oh, Dan plays the piano?' I'll make you a deal. If I do my own stuff, you have to play on it, too."

Daniel didn't know if Mick even played his acoustic guitar anymore. The last time he'd seen Mick play was at Rachel's thirtieth birthday party, when they'd played "She's a Rainbow" for her. He'd been a fixture at Morgan Commons in the college days, tucked away in a corner and practicing Neil Young songs, and he'd seemed shocked that someone had actually noticed his playing. Daniel's band at the time had been short a guitar player three hours before they had to take the stage at the Backbeat. "Hey, Professor," Daniel had said. "Want to play in a show?" Mick had joined them, probably because he was too startled and too much of a nice Midwestern boy to say no.

Rachel interrupted the journey down memory lane. "I'm thinking carnelian and silver topaz in a choker style, with gold accents."

"Me like. Jake, will Mom think it's pretty?"

"Everything Aunt Rachel does is pretty."

"So that's a yes, then."

They said goodbyes and made promises to have dinner together when Daniel got back from London. Rachel locked the cameo away for safekeeping, for the necklace that she would not complete for Sarah's birthday, or ever.

The afternoon wind was sighing through the tall cedar at the edge of their yard when they arrived back home. Jake and Raf ran straight into the house and made a beeline for Jake's room and the trunk of Legos. Daniel put the bike and trailer away, then went inside and into the workroom.

Sarah was at her desk, grading papers. He stood watching her. The way her hair shone golden in the light of her desk lamp. Her bad habit of chewing on the end of her red pen, tapping it against her teeth. She plucked a book from the shelves and consulted it, turning her profile to him as she did so. He'd seen that profile so many times over the years: Sarah at age eight, sitting on a beach towel in the Reilly backyard, reading *Bridge to Terabithia*; Sarah at her uncle Jacob's wake, looking at the first edition of *Catch-22* that he'd left to her; Sarah at the commons on the LCU campus, frowning at *The Turn of the Screw*.

"See anything green?" she asked without looking away from her book. Then she turned and winked at him.

He went to her and put his arms around her, buried his face in her hair to kiss her neck. "Should I call London and tell Reg to find someone else to tickle the ivories in D minor?"

Sarah shook her head. "He pays well, and besides, I want some tea from Fortnum and Mason. It's just a week or so. Things won't fall apart without you."

"Sure they will. It's all about me, didn't you know?"

"So what's Rachel going to make me for my birthday?"

"A neckl—Shit."

"A necklace of shit? How avant-garde."

"Why do you do this? You know I can't lie worth a damn to you."

Sarah got up, put her arms around him. "That's why I married you. I knew I could keep you honest."

"I only lie to people I love."

"You're a liar."

"Yes I am."

"So you do love me."

"I think so. Maybe. Now I'm confused."

"Liars need to be punished. You'll have to make dinner tonight."

"I was going to do that anyway."

"And you have to tell Jake a bedtime story."

"I was going to do that, too. We're on part twenty-four in the never-ending saga of the Lego knights versus the Wiggles. This installment: *Dude, Where's My Sword?*"

"Well, then you have to make savage love to me tonight."

"All punishments should be so thorough."

He was jolted out of dreamless sleep so abruptly he needed a moment to find his bearings. No unusual sounds. No smell of smoke. Just Sarah's hand on his shoulder, her grip painfully tight. "What's wrong? Is it Jake?"

"It's OK." Her breathing was uneven.

"Did you hear something?"

"No, no. Bad dream." She let go of his shoulder.

Fully awake now, Daniel reached out to her. Sarah's hair was damp with sweat. He put his arms around her and was startled to feel her skin shivering with goosebumps. She sighed and settled back against him. Her limbs were still wire tight. "Do you want to tell me about it?" he asked.

She was silent for a moment. Then: "I can't remember much. But something happened. To you."

"What happened?"

Sarah shook her head, her damp curls brushing against his skin. "You were . . . lost. Jake and I were looking for you, and we couldn't find you."

"And you said, 'Thank God! I'm rid of him at last!' Ouch!"

She kicked at him again but missed. "It's not funny!"

Daniel ignored his aching shin and pulled Sarah closer. The dream must have been bad; usually his levity chased away her infrequent bad moods. "I'm here. I'm not lost."

She draped an arm across him. "I'm sorry I kicked you."

"Just don't make a habit of it." Daniel picked up her hand and kissed it, first the palm and then each finger. Then he turned so he could kiss her mouth, bury his hands in her golden hair, and she clung to him tighter than before, but now in passion. Her skin felt like warm silk, her voice an urgent whisper saying *I want you.* They were so attuned to each other he couldn't always tell the difference between what he was feeling and what she was. Afterward they fell asleep still half-tangled in each other's limbs, and when morning came she never mentioned her dream and he'd forgotten it had happened.

Chapter Two

Sarah's parents, Kate and Hugh Reilly, still owned the old house in Torrance. It was too big for a retired couple, but they'd kept it for their many family gatherings. Christenings. Birthdays. Thanksgiving. Graduations.

Funerals.

Daniel gazed out the window of the back bedroom. It was the least used of the spare bedrooms; aside from the bed, lamp, and nightstand there was no furniture. The closet was full of stored Christmas decorations and spare towels. He cared nothing about the room. He'd wanted the view of the backyard.

A wide expanse of crabgrass and dandelions, a pumpkin patch off at the far corner. On the other side of the fence grew an avocado tree that obligingly sent branches over into the Reilly yard. The rope ladder Hugh had put in was long gone.

If he looked hard, he might see himself climbing that tree. Six years old. The Whitmans had moved next door to the Reillys just a few days before. He'd already finished unpacking his belongings—they were far fewer than his sister had, but then Victoria had always gotten more of everything from Annie and Tom Whitman. He'd been first on the scene—adopted after six fruitless years of the Whitmans trying to conceive—but was second in everything else. Not one month after they'd brought Daniel home, Annie had finally become pregnant. It had been a troublesome pregnancy with Annie needing bed rest for much of the time, and things didn't improve much after the emergency C-section that brought Victoria into the world. She was their miracle child, the one whose needs came first and whose every whim had to be gratified. As for their son? *Oh, Daniel,* Annie said once to a friend, *he just looks after himself. Never gives us anything to worry about.*

Once his toys and books were unpacked and put away in the smallest bedroom, Daniel went out to explore the backyard. The tree fascinated him—decades old and never pruned, it sent limbs outward and skyward. No avocados yet, but the flowers gave off a musty, sweet scent that made him nostalgic for something he couldn't name. He climbed the tree and found a spot where he could sit and lean back against the tree's trunk. He soon found himself looking at the yard next door: at the pumpkin patch, the rope hammock, the sandbox and toys that gave evidence of other children.

"Hey, uglyface!"

Daniel didn't respond.

Victoria stood by the tree, looking up with her perpetual scowl. "I'm talking to you. Where's my Lite-Brite? It's not in the boxes."

He got a sinking feeling. If Victoria pitched a fit, this could get ugly. Yes, he was treed, but Victoria was as clumsy as she was mean and couldn't make it up here. Probably. "It was broken. Mom threw it away."

Victoria screamed, a sound that drilled into his ears. "It wasn't broken! You threw it away, I saw you. You're a liar! They should have thrown *you* away like your real parents did and let someone find you in a garbage can!"

She picked up a rock and threw it at him. Daniel ducked behind a branch. The thud of stone against wood was followed by another thud, most satisfying. He peeked back to see Victoria sitting on the ground, hands clutched to her bleeding nose. The rock must have bounced off the tree and hit her. Daniel grinned and quickly hid it—Annie and Tom were already heading out to see what was wrong with their precious baby.

Luckily Victoria was too surprised and in too much genuine pain to blame Daniel for what had happened. Fussing and uttering many cries of, "Oh, you poor thing!" Annie and Tom packed Victoria into the car and went in search of a doctor.

Daniel idly wondered if they would be back for dinner. No big deal if they weren't; he'd make himself a sandwich. He'd done it before. At the house next door, kids ran out into the yard: four of them, one boy and three girls. They were followed by a man who held a toddler with one hand and with the other hand pulled a wagon full of water balloons. "Now, there's enough for everyone. More than enough. Just don't splash John and—oh, hello there!"

Daniel looked to see who the man was talking to, then realized it must be him. "Hello, sir," he said. "My name's Daniel." One thing Annie and Tom had done right was raise their adopted son to have manners.

The kids were looking up at him. The boy looked to be a bit older than Daniel. The girls were his age or a little younger.

"I'm Hugh," said the man. "As for these—Mouseketeer roll call!"

"Martin!"

"Sarah!"

"Amy!"

"Theresa!"

"And that's John," said Sarah, pointing at the toddler.

Martin said, "We're going to have a water balloon fight. Want to play?"

"Is that OK?" Daniel was not ready to believe his good fortune.

"Sure," boomed Hugh. "Ask your folks and come on over."

"They're not around. Victoria got a nosebleed, and they took her to the doctor."

Hugh frowned. "You're there alone?"

Daniel could tell that the man seemed to think this was a bad thing, but he didn't understand why. He'd been left on his own for longer when he was even younger. "It's all right. They'll probably be back before dinner."

"Well, come on over then." He handed the toddler to Sarah, who held John expertly while her father strode over to the tree. "Here you go," Hugh said as he swung Daniel down to the ground and walked with him over to the water balloons. "The rules are not in the house, and no splashing me or John. Now have fun."

They were girls against boys. Martin and Daniel made up for their lower numbers by stealth—Daniel was particularly well suited to this, for he'd had lots of practice from evading his sister. By the time they ran out of balloons, they were all wet and tired and happy. Kate Reilly came out and asked Daniel if he'd like to stay for dinner, and he said yes please, and thank you very much. Later, as Martin and Daniel were sneaking up the side of the house with squirt guns loaded, Daniel caught a fragment of conversation.

". . . nice boy, and so polite. And they just left him there with no sitter? Unbelievable."

Martin was the one he ran around with that day, but after dinner and dessert, when it seemed his parents and sister were finally home and he had to go back, it was Sarah who said, "Can you come back tomorrow?"

"You want me to?" Being wanted was such a new feeling. He could learn to like it.

She smiled at him. "Why not?"

By the end of that week Hugh had put the rope ladder on the tree so Daniel could come and go at will. The Whitman place, that had been his house. But the Reilly's house had been home.

That was what kept him from going mad, now. Being home.

A knock at the door. "Come in." His voice was rusty. He'd cried, he'd protested, perhaps might have screamed a time or two. But he hadn't dared speak much. What would he have said?

The door opened. Daniel didn't turn around. He was afraid to see who might be there. *Please, not Hugh. Not Martin or Joanna.* They had been the ones to break the news to him. They would only bring more ill tidings with them, although what those might be Daniel couldn't guess. He wasn't sure what he had left to lose.

He looked around to see Rachel standing there. She was almost unrecognizable with her hair in a simple braid, wearing not her usual flowy beaded clothes but a dark suit. She'd even put aside all her jewelry save for her wedding ring and a necklace with a single black stone. She carried a cup of coffee and some cinnamon toast.

"Kate said you hadn't had anything," Rachel said. "I thought you might be hungry."

Daniel nodded and sat down on the bed. He wasn't hungry, but Rachel would only worry if he didn't take a bite or two. But he could barely force down any of it; he was waiting for Rachel to talk to him. And he wasn't ready for it, not yet, not now. There was a whole day ahead, a day full of people asking how he was, telling him they'd be there for him. It wasn't their talk that terrified him but what he would have to say. He could feel the words lurking inside, and sooner or later they would be spoken: *If I'd been here, this wouldn't have happened.*

40

But Rachel said nothing. She sat beside him, put an arm around his shoulders—no mean feat, she was such a tiny thing. Her silence gave consent to his, and it was a curiously peaceful moment. "Rachel's an old soul," Sarah had said just a few weeks before.

Before. The word that said everything.

He closed his eyes and saw nothing, listened and heard only the silence of the room. The sounds of the house were distant and could be ignored for now. *Before* was gone. *After* was here with a vengeance, but for now time was suspended. And with time frozen so, too, were grief and guilt and pain. Just silence and a friend's reassuring touch. However long this respite might last, it would not be enough.

Footsteps in the hall, and though he hoped they'd go past his door, they stopped. A shuffling sound on the threadbare hall runner, followed by a tentative knock. Rachel said, "Come in."

When Daniel opened his eyes, Mick stood there. Saying nothing, hands clasped together in a pose of helplessness. Odd, after his competence of the last few days, but it seemed that with no calls to make or matters to arrange the Professor was at a loss for actions. For words as well. Mick looked to his wife in mute appeal.

Rachel gave Daniel's shoulder a parting squeeze. The interlude was over; time and everything it brought with it resumed. She stood, took the cold coffee and toast, and put them aside. Rachel took Daniel's hands in hers. He was vaguely surprised that her hands were cool and damp from nerves. She was not as calm as she looked.

But her voice was steady as she spoke the words he'd been dreading: "It's time."

41

The plane had just touched down in San Diego, and he'd been reaching for his carry-on when a flight attendant came up to him, asked him his name, and would he please confirm his ID. Daniel had obliged, not without some bewilderment. Was this some Bizarro-World security measure, confirming your ID after the flight was over? He'd asked why, but she shook her head. "They need you to report to the gate agent as soon as you get off the plane, sir. I don't know anything beyond that." Later he'd recall that he'd seen something that looked like pity in her eyes, but at the time he was too confused and wiped out from the trip to take notice.

He'd been gone a week and everything had been uneventful. Reg Fletcher was his usual cheerfully irascible self; it took time to please him, but once you did he never failed to show gratitude. There'd been one night of partying with the band, but it was low-key, hanging around with Fletcher and his latest inamorata, enjoying food, music, wine, and a joint or two. All other nights Daniel had been in bed by eleven. The hard-partying life had never appealed to him.

He'd last talked to Sarah two nights before his flight. They didn't talk every night when he was overseas; it made the phone bills too outrageous. All had been well. Her only complaint was the ceiling leaking.

"What? Leaking?" he'd asked.

"Yes. Freak rainstorm all yesterday and the day before. And then we're supposed to get Santa Anas all the rest of the week."

"The weather gods forgot their meds," Daniel had said, and they'd both had a good laugh.

It was the only unusual thing, so unimportant that Daniel didn't even recall it as he gathered his things and left the plane. He went to the gate agent, who asked for ID. The agent made a phone call, and soon two security guards came and asked Daniel to come with them. They took him down a side hallway, through an employees-only door. Through another door and into what looked like an ordinary conference room.

Hugh Reilly was there. So were Martin and his wife Joanna. Their presence here, their faces, told him. A hollow, sick feeling inside, his heart racing and his mouth dry. He knew. But he had to ask. "What's happened?"

Martin glanced quickly at his father and seemed to know the burden of telling would fall on him. He sipped at some water, his hands trembling as he held the cup. High winds, he said. Just a few days after the freakish rainstorm. "They say the rain softened the ground, and with the wind, trees were down everywhere. That cedar by your house. It came down. On . . . on Jake's room."

His whole body gone numb, Daniel stared at his brother-in-law. Though he knew what Martin's next words would be, perhaps if he conjured up a different outcome, he could make it so. "What hospital is he at?"

"Daniel . . ."

"Take me to him, he's my boy, take me there!" His throat hurt. Had he been yelling? "Sarah, where's Sarah?"

Joanna stood up, tried to take Daniel's hand. He twitched away from her, but she didn't seem to mind it. "She was sleeping in Jake's room."

Of course. Since he was a toddler Jake had been afraid of the powerful Santa Ana winds. In the past he'd slept in Daniel and Sarah's bed, but now that he was older, one of them usually slept in Jake's room with him.

He didn't remember sitting down, but he was. He held a hip flask and took a drink from it without thinking. Whiskey burned down his throat; it was not his usual drink, but he seized on anything that might stop that free-fall sensation of terror and loss. When his eyes stopped watering he looked at the flask and recognized it. Sarah had bought it for Hugh as a Father's Day present a few years back.

"They're gone?" he managed to ask.

His next memory was of standing in baggage claim. Mick and Rachel were there with his bags and ran to him. They embraced him, but he did not return the gesture. He felt like an automaton; he'd come here because Hugh, Martin, and Joanna had said to. The service would be held in Torrance, and tomorrow he should come there, stay at the house. But Mick and Rachel would take him home tonight after . . .

Daniel watched as if from a distance as the Reillys and Mick held a quick conference. Mick seemed to be disagreeing with the Reillys about something, and Daniel supposed it was important, but he couldn't focus on it. He was trying to remember if he'd told Sarah and Jake that he loved them during that last phone call. He didn't know. He thought he had, was quite sure he had. That wasn't the same as knowing.

Rachel had been standing beside him, holding on to his arm. Now she excused herself, went and joined the discussion. She said something that made them all look at her, and she folded her arms across her tiny frame. After a moment, the Reillys nodded. Mick seemed the holdout, but after a moment he acquiesced, then stalked off a couple of yards and made a call on a cell phone.

The Reillys went home, but Mick and Rachel took Daniel in their car. Mick drove while Rachel sat in the back seat with Daniel. "We'll go home," she said softly, her voice barely audible over the BMW's sleek hum. "But first we have to go to LCU General."

"We don't *have* to," Mick said from the front seat.

For what? Daniel wondered. *They're gone.*

But he understood when he nodded to the morgue attendant. He wanted to hate Rachel and the Reillys for asking him to do this. But if he didn't do this, he'd never believe; he would always be waiting for them to come back.

It was worse than his imaginings and not as bad as he'd feared. If you ignored his pallor and the back of his head, Jake looked as if he were asleep. The attendant apologized before pulling the sheet back from Sarah; Daniel had to force himself to look at the left side of her face where the damage was less. He took their hands in his. So cold. *They're gone.*

He spent that night at the Kesslers' house and woke after only a few hours of fitful sleep. When he woke he didn't know where he was, only that something terrible had happened; instinctively he reached for Sarah but found only the empty side of the guest bed. Daniel lay feeling empty and numb. As dawn crept in he began to feel something. Not pain but the precursor to it, the way the ocean becomes calm, too calm, before it gathers itself into a monstrous wave that smashes everything in its path.

That morning he told Mick and Rachel what he needed to do. As with the night before, Mick protested, but Rachel agreed with Daniel. They went to Daniel's house. What was left of it.

If you looked at the house's eastern end, where the workroom was, you wouldn't notice anything wrong. But the living room's roof had a canted, buckled look to it, as did Daniel and Sarah's bedroom at the far end. The tree had come down on Jake's room. While Daniel was gone. He hadn't worked out the time frame yet, hadn't calculated the eight hours between here and London. What had he been doing while his wife and child were crushed? Snoozing away in his hotel room? Raiding the minibar? Or loafing around at Heathrow, getting some of those awful Violet Crumble bars for his session work agent?

It didn't matter. What mattered was that he hadn't been there.

It was early, but the crews were carving up the decades-old cedar into manageable chunks and hauling it away. The morning was bright and warm. Shaping up to be a typically gorgeous late-September morning in coastal California. The air had an unusually sweet scent. It took a moment for Daniel to recognize that it came from the work crews. Cedar.

Sarah had always loved cedar. Once, she and Jake had gone with assorted Reillys to San Diego for a trip to SeaWorld. Daniel had stayed home on a pretext and with Mick's help had lined Sarah's closet with cedar. It was a slightly clumsy job, as carpentry was neither man's strong suit, but Sarah had been surprised and delighted. So happy with it. With him.

He began to cry, and it wasn't the relief he'd hoped it would be. It was like bleeding from a wound that was not bad enough to kill him outright but would go on hurting for a very long time.

So many people at the service. Daniel had scarcely had a minute alone since his return home. Everyone thought this was a good thing. It ought to have been a good thing. After the funeral, during the reception at a Knights of Columbus hall, Daniel had sat with Sarah's baby brother, John, sprung from the seminary. "Do you see all these people?" John asked. "They loved Sarah and Jake, and they love you. They'll be here for you. You're not alone."

John was right. People everywhere Daniel looked. Reillys, what seemed like scores of them: Sarah's brothers and sisters and all their children, cousins, aunts, uncles, such a sprawling Irish clan. Teachers who'd worked with Sarah, even some students. Even a friend or two of Jake's—little Raf looking grave and grown-up in a suit. Daniel's musician friends, some acquaintances from the university. Those who couldn't be in attendance, like his old chum Eskimo Sally, had called. Even Daniel's parents had shown up, although sister Victoria was traveling on business and hadn't been able to make it.

Daniel sat, watching. Everyone seemed to have brought food or sent flowers. Some, like Reg Fletcher, had done both. He appreciated the gesture, although the scent of so many bouquets made him queasy. Not that he had much interest in food; he held a plate of pasta salad but couldn't remember if he'd eaten any of it.

It didn't matter. Nothing mattered, because this was *After*. He wanted his wife and son back, and if he couldn't have that, he wanted to be alone. Because there were so many people, and sooner or later someone would say: *Why weren't you here? If you'd been here, you could have done something and none of this would have happened. What kind of husband and father are you, leaving your family alone to die that way? This is all your fault.*

If he'd said this to John or any of the Reillys or to Mick or Rachel, they'd have denied it. But Daniel knew it was so because he'd spent all this time telling himself those very things.

Chapter Three

Mick Kessler put down the box and paused to survey the place. A studio apartment with a room for living and sleeping, an alcove that he supposed was meant to be a dining area, a narrow kitchen, a bathroom, and a largish closet. The place was so old that there was a small door in the kitchen wall for the icebox man to leave his wares. The walls were bare and beige, unevenly shaded from years of college students hanging their posters and spackling the thumbtack holes. The windows looked out on the Coral Villas courtyard, which consisted of an indifferently maintained lawn and a fountain that wasn't working and probably hadn't been for some time judging by the amount of dead, dry leaves in it.

A thud as Daniel set down the last of the boxes. Small as the apartment was, the belongings Daniel had brought took up very little space. An island of a suitcase and a few boxes, marooned in a sea of splintery hardwood floor. When the boxes were unpacked the place would have little resemblance to the Whitman house, where you watched where you sat lest you plant your rear on a CD or a book or a toy knight.

Mick had assumed that Daniel would bring more from the old house. Mick had asked, "Don't you want this?" and "Shouldn't you bring that?" and had gotten little more than a terse "No" in reply. Then Rachel pulled Mick aside.

"Let him be," she'd said.

"I was just asking if he didn't want to bring more."

She looked at him with a mix of pity and exasperation. "It's hardly been any time. He isn't ready to let go of this place yet. Let him be."

He'd understood it once she'd said it, of course. Mick damned himself for a fool and damned his father twice for making him into the kind of fool who could say such things. If he hadn't learned to use silence as a survival tool long ago, he might not put his foot in his mouth when he did speak. Oh, he could talk business with clients and partners quite eloquently. But things that mattered? A different situation entirely.

Mick glanced out the apartment window again. Across the courtyard was the other wing of the Coral Villas. Nearly every window was shut, shades pulled. The lone exception was the apartment of a morose-looking man who was eating what looked like Rice-A-Roni, straight out of the pot. Again Mick wondered why Daniel had been so adamant about not staying at the Kesslers' place on the Hill. Lord knew there was enough room and plenty of money to keep Daniel in style, though he could pay them rent if his pride demanded it. If nothing else Mick owed it to Daniel for letting him stay at the Whitman place after New York, after things had gone wrong with Gina.

But Daniel had declined all the offers. "This feels right to me," he'd said. "It's really kind of you to let me stay, and I'd like it, but if I don't start . . . I don't know. I feel like I need to move forward. This feels right."

Maybe it felt right to Daniel, but it didn't feel right to Mick. But then, nothing felt right to him. How could anything in the world feel right when Sarah and Jake were gone? Sarah was not just one of the first friends he'd had at the university, she was the first one he'd let down his guard around. Strange that it should be so, for she'd been so pretty then he had a hard time even looking at her. But somehow in conversation she'd asked if she could come by his place to pick up or drop off something, he could no longer remember what, and he'd had to reveal that he was living in his car at the time. It hadn't been poverty exactly, more a question of missed paperwork and bad timing, but he'd been ferociously ashamed of it. The very next day she'd offered him a room at that ramshackle Victorian she and Daniel and a few others lived in. What a joy that had been, having friends for the first time in . . . well, ever.

But now there was an empty place. All too familiar. Unwillingly he thought of his mother's departure. It was much the same, yet different. Then he'd had no one, except the old man, who didn't count. Now he had Rachel, the Reillys, Daniel. They'd get through this.

Mick wondered what Daniel was thinking now but couldn't hazard a guess. That wasn't unusual; Mick had spent too long masking his own feelings to be able to read others' easily. Yet he'd always been able to read Daniel to some extent. But now Daniel's face gave away little. His blue eyes seemed to have darkened to a slate color, like those of a newborn. His face had a curiously still appearance that took a toll on the good looks Mick had always coveted.

He looked again at the scant pile of possessions. *I had more than this when I moved into that old Victorian.* When he'd moved out of what Daniel had called the *Chateau de Chevrolet* until Sarah kicked Daniel in the shin and told him to knock it off.

"I think I can take it from here," Daniel said.

"OK. I heard from the insurance company, and everything's in place. It will just need time for the wheels to turn." Mick felt comfortable for the first time today. Taking care of the practicalities was his refuge, always had been. "There will be things for you to sign, but the settlement should be in by the end of the year."

Daniel nodded.

"And I spoke to the property people. After Thanksgiving is when they'll do the . . . tear down what's left."

Another nod.

"Do you need any help getting all the things . . ." Mick trailed off. What was going to happen to the family's possessions? Should they be sold? Packed away until some indefinite later? He remembered the day he'd come home from kindergarten and found his mother's belongings crammed into the trash cans.

"I'll take care of it," Daniel said. Before Mick could form the next question, Daniel answered it. "I don't need any help just now. I'd rather do this on my own."

"You're all right, then?"

He nodded. His smile seemed a trifle off, but it was there. "I'm even heading up to LA in a couple of weeks. Little more work for Reg Fletcher."

"Good. That's good. And call us anytime. Come over for dinner, or, you know, just because."

"All right."

They said goodbye. Huge though the pain of losing Sarah and Jake was, Mick felt relieved that he was able to help Daniel through all this. Taking care of these details just as he'd taken care of so many of the funeral and other arrangements eased his own pain, too. He could do something about it. Otherwise he'd be no better off than he had been at five: his father said *Your mother's gone* and hit Mick with the buckle end of a belt when he'd asked when she'd be back. Helpless.

Before getting on the freeway to San Diego, Mick took a detour through Los Cielos. He'd be late for work, but it hardly mattered. He'd started that business, and they could wait for him. He drove past the university—the students lounging at Morgan Commons between classes sported more tattoos these days, but the school itself hadn't changed much since his own days there. Look, there was Dr. Hill, still sporting the persecuted look of a lone conservative stranded among the liberals. He drove past the student housing, past the paint-peeling Victorian he'd shared with Daniel and Sarah and Eskimo Sally and various others over the years—he could even see his room, up on the second floor. Past the park where he'd sometimes take Jake for kite flying and where the city held its endearingly lame fireworks display every Independence Day. He'd brought Rachel to the Independence Day gathering, soon after they started going out, so she could meet the Whitmans. Sarah had offered Rachel some homemade sangria, Jake instantly fell in love and brought Rachel dandelions to rub under her chin to see if she liked butter, and Daniel had declared, "Well, if the Professor here likes you, we probably will like you, too." Rachel made a daisy chain for Sarah (and one for Daniel, too, after he asked). Then the Whitmans embarrassed him by singing, "We accept her, one of us" from that awful movie *Freaks*; he felt somewhat less mortified when Rachel laughed and curtsied to them.

His last stop was out by Lonely Point, where he could sit with his back to the sea and look up at the town. He'd never meant to live here permanently. The university had been a way station between the first miserable seventeen years of his existence and whatever life he would forge after. All he'd meant to do was get as far as he could from Missouri without drowning, and instead he'd found home.

It had been a charmed time; he should have realized it, and now Sarah and Jake were gone. At the thought his throat spasmed painfully, and his eyes stung—the closest he could come to crying. His one consolation was that he still had Rachel and Daniel. Together they'd find a way to recapture that charmed life. It might be copper instead of gold, but it would shine bright again. It would, by God. His face changed from sorrowful nostalgia to a stony look of determination that would have dismayed him had he caught sight of himself in a mirror, for that look made him the very image of his father.

Daniel waited until he was sure Mick had left and wouldn't come back with some other bit of information. Maybe some idea of suing the city for failing to prune the cedar properly. Daniel wouldn't put it past him. Wearily he sat down on the floor—there was nowhere else to sit, for there were no chairs, and he hadn't the energy to unroll the futon mattress. So tired. Conversations with Mick always left him wiped out these days. Such hard work to pretend that he gave a damn about the insurance settlement. It was as abstract as government budget figures.

And even harder work to face the daunting task of sorting through the household and Sarah's and Jake's possessions. How could he pack their things into boxes when some mornings he woke and didn't remember they were gone? In the murky predawn light he'd imagine they were still with him. All he had to do was turn over and feel Sarah's body next to his; if he listened hard enough, surely he could hear Jake padding down the hall to tell them to wake up, it was a weekend. Then he'd open his eyes and remember where he was and what had happened and would feel again that heart-stopping sensation of loss.

Those were the good mornings.

On the bad mornings he woke—if he'd slept at all—and knew. The fact was just there, as inevitable as the sunrise. Another day without them.

His intentions were good. Despite how difficult it was to get up and get moving, especially on the bad mornings, he forced himself to it. While he'd stayed at the Kesslers' it was important that he be up and about when they left for work so they could see he was doing well, or as well as could be expected. They didn't know that after they left more often than not he went to their balcony, with its enviable ocean view, and stared at the waves' steady rhythms as if hypnotized. For hours.

Eventually, though, he'd make his way to the house. The spectators were no longer in evidence. Everyone on the block save for old Mr. Frank and a couple of stay-at-home moms was gone during the day. He had the place to himself. The fallen tree had been carved up and carted away, leaving only a stump and the occasional swirl of sawdust in the wind. The impromptu shrine of flowers and cards and stuffed animals had also been removed. He wasn't sure by whom or to where.

A blue tarp now shrouded the smashed room. Daniel could enter the front door and get access to the living room, kitchen, and workroom; workmen had carved a doorway into what had been his and Sarah's bedroom so he'd be able to take out possessions. Scattered through the house were moving boxes, for the most part empty. He had tried to fill those boxes, honestly he had. He'd start to go through things but never get far before he would be captivated by some object—a toy, a knickknack, a book—and stare at it. Remembering. Wishing. And before he'd realize it, the day would have turned to murky twilight, and his cell phone would beep at him. Usually a text from Mick or Rachel or a Reilly or a colleague from the Musicians' Union or some other friend, asking if he'd like to be there for dinner. Usually he said yes. It was part of keeping up appearances.

But on nights when he couldn't face the thought of being with other people and waiting for them to realize what was plainly true—that if he hadn't caused Sarah's and Jake's death, he'd failed to prevent it, which amounted to the same thing—on those nights he usually wandered the beach or the streets of Los Cielos. Hoping to tire himself out enough to be able to sleep. It rarely worked. Sometimes he ended up at a bar and had a drink (or two or three), hoping for anesthesia. That didn't work often, either.

Today, he left his suitcase unpacked and went to the house. He bypassed the boxes and headed into the workroom. He'd barely been in it these last few weeks, and he hadn't played at all. The Bösendorfer sat gathering dust like some huge tchotchke. Daniel sat down, pushed back the cover. The keys felt strange under his hands. More alien than the first time he'd ever sat at a piano. He could recall that day clearly—a rainy fall day and him at the Reilly house as usual. Uncle Jacob, Kate Reilly's brother, had moved in for a few months and had brought with him ten milk crates full of record albums and an old upright piano. Daniel, Martin, and Sarah had spent hours having fun with the turntable. Uncle Jacob had a sizable collection of novelty records, even those flimsy plastic singles you could get from *MAD* magazine, and he let the kids play whatever they wanted as long as they were careful not to scratch anything. After a while Daniel went over to the upright, laid his fingers on the keys. He'd struck a few notes and after a few minutes picked out from memory the main melody to the tune from *A Charlie Brown Christmas*—"Linus and Lucy." He'd had a feeling of falling in love. Over the next few months Uncle Jacob sat with Daniel, teaching him what he knew. "But I'm strictly amateur and always will be," Uncle Jacob had said with a laugh. "You, though. You've got talent. If you want lessons, I'll pay for them." Daniel's parental units had readily agreed to the lessons, as well they should—they weren't paying, and it meant Daniel was around even less than usual, so Daniel figured it was a win-win situation for everyone.

Now he played "Clair de lune," but he'd played that to woo Sarah once, and he had to stop. He switched to Elton John, then to the Beatles, but something was wrong. The piano was in tune, his fingers were soon limber as they ever were, but it all sounded wrong. Not badly wrong. The tone a bit off, the measures a half beat too slow, his feet clumsy on the pedals. Nonetheless he persevered. Remembering his upcoming session work for Reg Fletcher, he played "Nova Express," one of Fletcher's songs from his old supergroup, The Anderson Council. He rushed through the last verse and quickly closed the cover of the piano. It all felt wrong, sounded wrong, and the notes echoed too loudly. The house's silence was louder still. He kept waiting for the silence to break, for Sarah or Jake to walk in.

At least he still *could* play. More or less. He had that much. Daniel walked out of the workroom before he could be tempted to play again, because if he did play, the wrongness would get worse. He couldn't risk that. It was all he had left.

"And he never takes responsibility for *anything*. He's always got some *total* bullshit excuse like—Danny, good to see you!"

Reg Fletcher sat tipped back in a chair, a cup of tea in one hand. He needed the other hand free for emphasis while speaking. It was Reg's tradition to begin every session with a vent, lasting anywhere from ten minutes to half an hour, in which he complained about whichever record company executive, former bandmate, or ex-wife had pissed him off most recently. Anyone who worked with Reg for a while had learned that it wasn't necessary to comment or even listen during these whinges; all Reg wanted was an audience. In fact, one of Reg's backup singers, Desiree Stone, had made up index cards printed with phrases like:

Really?

Wow.

I did not know that.

No!

And then what happened?

Yeah?

That's really interesting.

I'm not sure.

All you had to do was shuffle them and say the phrases at random intervals during Reg's rants; he never noticed a thing. Daniel had found the cards were good for conversations with his adoptive parents, too.

Reg never bad-mouthed people in their presence. Yet Daniel wondered if *he* was the one who never took responsibility and had the total bullshit excuse of being out of the country when . . .

Reg leaned forward, causing the chair's legs to come down with a loud clunk. He stood and put a hand on Daniel's shoulder, smiling perhaps a bit too broadly. Or perhaps not—Reg had a narrow face and a wide mouth, and his grin could be disconcerting. "How are you holding up?" Reg asked.

Daniel nodded. "OK," he said. "Considering."

"That's good. There's no rush at all today. Just relax, have some tea, and we'll warm up. All I need is some backing track. No, wait, you're a coffee man. Jim! Get this man some coffee. No, not that commissary stuff. That coffee's like making love in a canoe."

Daniel had heard the joke before but knew Reg liked having his wit appreciated. "Making love in a canoe?"

"It's fucking close to water. Here, get us all some espresso." Reg handed his lackey, Jim, a twenty, and Jim left on the coffee quest.

Daniel sat down. Reg sat as well, soon joined by Desiree the singer, guitarist Lowell, and Alan the long-suffering engineer. Though Daniel wasn't hungry, he took one of the offered scones and nibbled at it while Reg resumed his rant: "And so I told her, I said, 'No, I'm not mad. I was mad yesterday when I called and called and got no answer. Now I just don't care.' And then I hung up."

"Wow," said Lowell.

"And then what happened?" asked Desiree. She tipped a wink at Daniel, who felt a genuine smile coming on for the first time in weeks.

At first it was all right. They whiled away a good part of the morning with refreshments and chatter, Reg and Desiree and Jim gossiping while Lowell tuned his guitar. It was low-key, almost lackadaisical, and Daniel began to wonder if there *was* any work to be done.

"Mind if I warm up?" Daniel asked. "I'm a bit out of practice."

"Go right ahead," Reg said. "Take as long as you like."

They went into the other room while Daniel sat at the piano. Thinking it would please Reg, he started with "Nova Express." The wrong feeling was back and if no better than it had been yesterday, it was no worse, either. He played one of Reg's solo songs next and couldn't seem to get the right tone, though he knew the piano was in tune. It was as if the keys were fighting him or changing so that he hit the right ones but the sound was wrong. And then the tempo was out of joint, and no matter how hard or how soft he played, none of it was coming out right. He didn't look up to see if they were staring at him; he knew they were. Daniel ignored the flop sweat and segued clumsily into another song, hitting off notes every measure, and everything was wrong, and he slammed his fist onto the keys, somehow hoping that would make things right. Then he stopped.

In the wake of the piano's discordant jangle, the silence was very loud. None of the usual studio banter when someone screwed up royally, no comments like, "If you get near a song, let us know." Jim and Alan were in the engineer's booth, looking at him with carefully neutral expressions—by now Daniel was familiar with that look. The door opened; Reg and Desiree stood there, conferring. Debating which one was going to have to talk to him, no doubt.

Daniel excused himself and squeezed past them. Desiree put a hand on his shoulder, but he shook it off and kept on, heading to the little courtyard where smokers were banished in these health-conscious days. No smokers here today. He had the place to himself for a little while.

Reg must have lost the debate. "Hey, man." He sat down on the bench near Daniel's. Reg had quit smoking a few years ago, and now he chewed nervously on a pencil. "Are you all right?"

"No." Daniel knew he was being rude, but it was a relief to be honest. Of course it might cost him work in the future . . . if that even mattered.

But Reg didn't look angry. He nodded. "I thought so."

"I'm sorry I fucked up."

"Don't worry about it. Danny, I . . . well, maybe you figured it out. I didn't need any tracks. I thought you might need a break away from . . . everything."

Daniel's throat ached so, he could barely speak. "Thank you," he managed, and meant it. Reg had thought it would help; it wasn't his fault that it didn't.

"I'm heading up to Seattle for a few days. My daughter Jade's a photographer, they're showing some of her work at a gallery. Want to come along? Desiree and Jim will be there, keep you company. What do you say?"

He yearned to say yes. Even a weekend away from his lost family, ruined life, wrecked home, sounded like paradise. But what entitlement had he to paradise when it was his fault that his family was lost? He was grateful to Reg. Although a voice inside said Reg had played a part, too; if he'd held that last session in LA instead of London, Daniel would have been home and things would have gone differently.

Daniel didn't trust himself to speak, just shook his head. After a moment he said, "Thanks, but I need to stay close to home. Sarah's family needs me, and there's the house to deal with."

"OK. Let me know if you change your mind. Maybe around the holidays? Some of the old boys, we were thinking of renting a place on Ibiza, like we used to. Join us if you like."

"Thanks, Reg, I appreciate it. I'll let you know." He couldn't think ahead to the holidays, not when he could barely fathom how he would get through tomorrow.

They invited him to stay, but Daniel declined. He was tired, and it was a long drive back to Los Cielos. He tried not to think of how the music had gotten away from him. It had always been there. This was different from trying to learn a difficult song, when he knew that time and practice would bring it to him. Nothing connected anymore.

So lost was he in his reverie and so used to the old ways that he was two blocks from the house before he remembered it wasn't his home anymore but a shell awaiting demolition. He went to the apartment, which wasn't a home either, and lay down on the futon. He lay there, mostly sleepless, all night, and didn't stir from it the next day. He couldn't think of a reason to.

Chapter Four

Rachel sat in a plastic chair, her spine straighter than it had been in years, while Dr. Hill addressed the auditorium. Business Practices 201, a course Rachel had never taken—in fact, she'd taken only a single economics class during her college days and had mostly bluffed her way through it. But every semester Dr. Hill asked a local entrepreneur to tell the class how it was done, and this time he'd picked her. She wasn't sure how much worthwhile information she'd be able to give them, but she was flattered to have been asked. Maybe it would help get some more female faces into these classes. She wore the most professional attire from her collection—one of the reasons for her success had been wearing her wares whenever possible. You could drum up more business from a stranger's inquiry of "Where did you get that?" than from a week's worth of newspaper ads.

She scanned the crowd. Mick wouldn't be there—he'd been called at the last minute to a conference in Irvine—but Daniel had promised to attend. So far she hadn't seen him, and she didn't know how to feel about that.

Something about him troubled her. He looked far too pale and tired, and too thin, but that was the least of it. He'd smile, but sometimes the smiles lasted a beat too long. If she came up on him unawares, she'd see a look on his face that was no look at all, just blankness. And when he'd look at her there'd be a flicker of what looked like fear in his eyes.

On the surface everything seemed as right as it could be: he had a new place now, said he was working on getting the things from the old house taken care of, saw his friends and family often. Yet Rachel had the feeling, all the more maddening for its vagueness, that what she saw was not the real Daniel but the façade of a mediocre actor.

So far she hadn't confided in anyone. But if Daniel showed up tonight, perhaps she could get him on his own and find out more.

There he was. At the back, wearing an LCU sweatshirt. He waved to her, then sat down. Before Rachel had time to assess how he looked or wonder what she'd say to him after the lecture, Dr. Hill was introducing her. She stood, drew herself up to her full height, and took the podium, ready to explain how she'd turned a knack with a needle and a passion for semiprecious stones into a thriving business.

She told them, "It's not just about profit and loss. It's like falling in love."

Rachel had made her own clothes for years, tired of trying to find garments that suited her slender, short frame but didn't make her look like an old lady. She liked beauty, but she liked comfort as well, and her favorite look was flowing skirts and loose jackets, things that could be dressed up or down and suited the temperate climate of her native San Francisco. She fell in love with beadwork after attending a powwow with a friend and being dazzled by the dancers' intricate costumes. At museums, let others look at the dinosaur bones or the ancient pottery. Rachel would be in the hall of minerals, watching the way light played off quartz and topaz; or she'd be looking at the antique clothes—the everyday dresses, the elegance and comfort that could be found in the simplest things.

She'd fallen in love with what she made and wore, and like many others had fallen in love with Los Cielos. Rachel had been on her way to San Diego, had stopped in town to catch the local street fair, and that was it. When she'd seen how few clothing boutiques there were in town, she began dreaming up a business plan. It had taken some start-up money from the family, though not as much as they'd offered—the Beaumonts doted on the generation's only girl—a loan, and a year of hustling her wares, striking deals with local businesses, trying different schemes to get her name out there.

When Beaditudes had been open for a year, she entered the town's Christmas parade, driving her Vespa and flying a banner she'd embroidered herself. That holiday season she'd had almost more business than she could handle and even had to rope some friends in to help.

One reason for the store's success, she told the students, was that it had appeal not just to the tourists and the transient college kids, but to the locals as well. Trade waxed and waned, as it did with any retail business, but there was always a steady stream of townies and teachers.

Yes, love. For what she did and the place where she did it. And after she'd been open two years, the bells on her door jingled and in came a man: blond, bespectacled, with a plain face and clothes that seemed unremarkable but which her experienced eye recognized as custom-tailored. He gazed around, then came over to the counter. He spent a while looking over the cabochons and rings, the strands of beads and minerals, then settled on a turquoise bracelet. "Is this for a sweetheart?" she asked. "No, just a friend," he replied. "I'm between sweethearts." He looked at her, and his gaze lingered. He smiled, and it transformed his plain face. By the time a month or two had gone, she fell in love with him, too.

The class was the last of the day, and afterward Dr. Hill took them to the Mermaid. Rachel was not a fan of the place, which teetered on the brink of seediness. There was nothing to eat except peanuts, the drinks were expensive, the bathrooms smelled of mildew, and some of the clientele made her glad she had Daniel as her chaperone. Sarah had told her the LCU crowd favored the Mermaid because it was less than stringent about carding and gave the older professors the illusion that they were slumming, bolstering their flagging street cred.

Dr. Hill certainly seemed to feel that way, especially after a couple of drinks had given him a bonhomie that juxtaposed uneasily with his buttoned-down look. "I liked the way you worked with the other local businesses. Especially the bed-and-breakfasts. Too much grabbing for the tourist dollars here, if you ask me. Businesses need to work together," he said. "Giving the B-and-Bs embroidered pillows in trade for . . . what was it? Coupons to your store. A nice touch. Well done." He patted her on the back a little too familiarly for Rachel's taste.

Daniel said, "I thought about starting my own business, but then I figured, why would I want to work twenty-four hours a day for the biggest asshole I know?"

Rachel laughed. The old Daniel was back, and Lord, how she'd missed him. Best of all, Dr. Hill looked affronted. He took his hand off Rachel's back and went to talk to some students.

"Thanks," Rachel said.

"Don't mention it."

"I can't tell if he's being patronizing or flirtatious."

"A little of both, I think. Don't worry, you were great." He smiled, and it seemed so genuine. It didn't have that fixed quality that troubled her.

She was about to ask him how he was doing when the bartender came by. "Hey, Whitman. Here's your usual." He banged down what looked like a double Scotch? Double bourbon? Rachel had never been able to tell the difference—something amber and strong looking. Except for an occasional fruity drink at the Tiki Terrace, she'd never seen Daniel drink anything but wine or beer before.

"Come here often?" Rachel asked, hoping humor would put the right spin on what she was really asking.

"Sometimes," was the evasive reply. He didn't look at her; he looked at the drink, and there was a certain craving in that look she didn't like.

"Ms. Kessler? May I talk to you?"

Rachel turned to see one of the few female students from the class. She sat at a table with two other young women. They all looked eager to talk to a businesswoman who'd made a success of herself without having to wear a suit and play hardball with the boys. "Excuse me," Rachel said to Daniel, who nodded, and she went over to the table.

The women were all eager to know more, and their questions didn't have that slightly condescending tone of Dr. Hill's praise. Rachel started really enjoying the evening for the first time as she told the women which strategies had worked and which hadn't, about the total disaster her attempt at a radio spot had been, and how someone stole a rack of necklaces at the street fair last year and her husband and friend had chased the thief down, caught him, and tied him to a tree with a bicycle chain lock until the police arrived.

"Is that your friend?" asked one woman, pointing at Daniel.

Rachel nodded.

"He's kind of cute," said another woman.

"Seems to like his tipple," said a third. "Or not."

Rachel saw what she meant. Daniel had knocked back half his drink in one shot and done so with the wince and shudder of someone taking some particularly nasty medicine.

"Excuse me," she said to the women, and sat down beside Daniel. He had his eyes shut and didn't look at her. She put her hand on his shoulder; the muscles were like stone. She wanted to talk to him but couldn't think of what to say. *Are you all right?* was just foolish, as was *How are you doing?* After a moment he sighed, opened his eyes, and reached for his drink, finishing it off with that same shuddering wince.

"Dan," Rachel said, "Let's get out of here. Let me get you home."

He shook his head. "Can't. The power's out. No lights."

"What, at your apartment?" She knew he hadn't been working much lately. Perhaps he hadn't had money for the electricity bill?

"Not there. At home. They turned off the electricity. The water, too."

Of course. The demolition was less than three weeks away, just after Thanksgiving.

"Why don't you come over to our place then? There's plenty of room, you know." If nothing else, they could feed him; he was turning into a scarecrow.

"Thanks," he said with that slightly fixed smile. "It's OK ... just. Ever tell you how Sarah and I took Mick here once? Man so naïve he got a Long Island iced tea and didn't know until he drank it that it wasn't real iced tea. We go to the midnight show, and he's so tipsy he falls asleep in *Phantom of the Paradise*." The smile winked out as if a switch had been thrown. "We dressed up as the characters from that for Halloween that year. I got pictures ... in the house. Need to find them." Any traces of nostalgia had vanished from his face. "Have to find them. If I forget it's gone. I'll look tomorrow."

He signaled for another drink. Rachel thought of stopping him, then restrained herself, though it took a strong effort. She'd never seen him this drunk, and it disturbed her. But this was the most he'd said to her in weeks. Another glass of truth serum and he might confide in her.

The drink arrived. Daniel took a healthy sip, then sighed. "Maybe I'll sleep tonight," he said softly, as if to himself. "I shouldn't have come. I'm bad company tonight." The tension in his shoulders seemed to ease a bit, but whether that was her doing or the liquor's Rachel had no idea.

She might as well dive in. "What are you thinking about?"

He spoke without looking at her, and she thought it was a bit like old-school psychiatry, the patient on the couch and not looking at the doctor. This patient was on a barstool and swaying slightly. "My parents. The biological ones. I used to wonder about them a lot. My mom especially. What she would think of me if we ever met. Why she gave me up. If she loved me. If I'd have been better off with her than with Annie and Tom."

"The Whitmans, uh, love you." Rachel hoped she sounded more confident than she felt. She'd seen the way Annie Whitman patted Daniel on the shoulder at the funeral. Absently, the way you pat a dog.

"That's very nice of you to say so, but they don't give a tin shit about me, and I've known that since I was six years old. I used to wonder, but I never found out anything. The parental units lost all the paperwork. I asked if they had it when we were going to have Jake and I wanted to find out if there were any weird diseases hiding in my genes. But they lost it, and Jake was fine, so I didn't . . . you see, now I'm wondering. I went to a checkup last year, the doc said I'm in perfect health. And if the biologicals were . . . I might have a long time to live."

Daniel stared at his empty glass, ran a finger around the glass's lip. His eyes were dull and his gaze faraway. Despite the solidity of his shoulder under her hand, he seemed insubstantial. All the worse because he'd always been so lively. That day at Beaditudes when he'd brought in the cameo for Sarah's necklace, his face had been all alight at the prospect of giving his wife something beautiful for her birthday. Even Mick, not known for his perception where emotions were concerned, commented afterward, "How long have they been married? You'd think it was their first anniversary." When Daniel had left the store he'd made a big show of swearing Jake to secrecy, the two of them sealing the vow with an elaborate handshake ritual that was obviously the work of many years, with thumb wrestles and fist bumps worked in.

Sarah and Jake were dead, but Daniel was the ghost.

Rachel's sight blurred; tears traced warm courses down her face. She took her hand from Daniel's shoulder, reached out for his hand. He jerked away from her touch as if burned.

"Oh God," he said, looking her in the face. "I'm so sorry. I didn't mean to . . . I'm sorry."

Before she could wipe the tears away and tell him it was all right, nothing to be sorry for, he sprang from his barstool and headed for the door. Rachel ran after him, but her shoes skidded on the peanut shells that littered the floor, drunk students blocked her way, and by the time she ran out the Mermaid's door, Daniel had vanished into the night.

Rachel's Aunt Cassie had once trained to be an opera singer. These days the only arias she sang were in the shower, but her voice still carried so well Rachel was sure half the shop could hear it as clearly as if she'd been on a speakerphone.

"And you won't catch *me* near the stores on Black Friday. Some of us were thinking about going to see *The Nutcracker* that day. The local troupe's performance was lovely last year—I just wish I could stop feeling guilty about watching it, Tchaikovsky hated it so. Do you think you'd like to come?"

Leave it to Aunt Cassie to be worried about what Tchaikovsky thought. "That would be nice. Let me check with Mick and see if he's interested. I don't think he's ever been to the ballet before. And would it be all right if we brought a friend up with us?"

"Of course!" her aunt trilled. "Is it the friend you told me about? How is he doing?"

I wish I knew. "I think getting away would be good for him."

"Bring him along, then. And tell him he doesn't have to bring anything to the dinner, although if he wants to, he's more than welcome."

Rachel smiled. Traditional Thanksgiving dinner had been anathema among the Beaumonts since a long-ago incident of food poisoning. Rachel had been very young then, and her only recollection of the incident was of the grown-ups being too ill to watch the parades the next morning. Since that day, the Thanksgiving feast had been a potluck in the truest sense—everyone brought what they felt like bringing, with no coordination between the dishes. One year the feast was nothing but salads and desserts, the next it was a mix of Italian, French, and Lebanese specialties. Last year her brother Anthony had brought a huge tub of Kentucky Fried Chicken—it had gone well with cousin Leonard's blini and caviar. The first time she'd brought Mick to one of the Beaumont Thanksgivings, she'd worried it might offend his Midwest sensibilities, but he'd loved it. She felt sure Daniel would love it, too, and it would be good for him to get some time away.

It would be nice for all of them, really. Much as she loved Los Cielos, she needed the sights of San Francisco and the company of her clan to take her mind off recent events. It would be worth paying her assistants double time to manage the shop in her absence.

"I'll let you know." She and Aunt Cassie said goodbye and hung up. Not five minutes later, the bells on the store's door jingled. "How did it go?" she asked Mick.

"Fine," he said. "We met at Sandwiches on Seventh, then went for coffee."

When Mick had come back from his conference in Irvine, she'd told him about the night at the Mermaid. It had been frustrating, for she couldn't convey just how troubled she was. *Trust me,* she'd wanted to say, *I can't explain it, but trust me, there's more than ordinary bereavement at work.* But that sounded ridiculous even to her, and she knew it would carry no weight with Mr. Rock-steady, Facts-and-figures.

"He was sorry he ran out on you like that," Mick continued. "He thought it was something he'd said that made you upset. He didn't want to ruin your night or have Dr. Hill think something was wrong."

"What about the drinking?"

"It's a quick fix. He knows that. He says he's working on cutting down. It's mostly for insomnia; he's had a problem with that lately."

That all sounded fine. Nice and glib and probably said with plenty of charm.

Mick took off his glasses, polished the lenses. "I feel a bit better about things. If he'd denied it, I'd be worried. But he was honest. And he knows that he can come to us if he needs us."

"Are you sure about that?"

He put his glasses back on, gave her a look that was curious. "He's not lying. I'd know if he were."

"I hope so."

The look of curiosity turned somewhat chilly. "He's been my friend for, what, fifteen years now. I know him pretty well by now."

Rachel said nothing, but her unvoiced thought was: *No, I don't think you really do.*

Chapter Five

The windows of his apartment's main room faced the west, and on sunny days Daniel could lie on his futon all afternoon and watch the squares of sunlight make their way across the room and up the wall. He'd watch them turn deep gold, then red, then slowly fade into nothing. At night he'd watch the moonlight as it slanted in the same windows, chart its way across the floor and the wall.

He watched because it was better than thinking.

The last few days had been shrouded in clouds, unusual for so close to Thanksgiving. Clouds hid the sun but brought no rain, so he had nothing to watch. He spent those cloudy days looking through the photo albums—a dozen of them, the only things he'd brought from the house since he'd first moved into the Coral Villas. He'd been through the albums so many times, yet on each page was some small detail he'd overlooked until now that could captivate his attention for minutes at a time.

As for time itself, he'd lost all track. The only clocks were those on his phone and answering machine. He would have liked to have pulled the plug on both, but they were useful for keeping everyone at bay. The phone would ring, and he'd look at the caller ID to see who it was. Most times it was the Kesslers or one of the many Reillys or his manager or some other friend. Once Eskimo Sally had called, all the way from Fiji. He dreaded these calls and answered every one feeling queasy as he waited for someone to say they understood now that the blame lay with him. It was only a matter of time.

By now he half wished someone would say it and get it over with. At the same time he prayed it wouldn't happen just yet, because until then he still had something to hold on to. It was so hard, though. That night at the Mermaid he'd let his guard down, and for a moment it had been a relief to talk honestly to someone, to stop pretending that things were fine. Then he'd made Rachel cry—Rachel, who he liked tremendously, who was his friend, who was the best thing to happen to Mick. He'd made her cry, on the night that was supposed to be a good one for her.

A call was coming in now—from Auden Company Demolitions. This one he could ignore. He let the answering machine pick up and heard a disembodied voice apologize for disturbing him, remind him that the demolition of the house at 841 Sandpiper Street was scheduled to take place five days from now, the Monday after Thanksgiving. The voice asked that all items be removed from the premises and told him to call if he had any questions. A click and a beep and silence.

Less than a week from now? So soon. His mind struggled to engage through the rust that clogged it. Yes, it made sense now. The day after tomorrow was Thanksgiving. He knew this only because there had been invitations that he'd fended off: he'd told the Kesslers thanks, but he was going to the Reilly gathering; he'd told the Reillys thanks, but he needed a break and was going with the Kesslers to San Francisco.

Only a few days left. Less than a week to gather his ghosts around him. Daniel got to his feet, unsteadily, his limbs shaky from disuse. At least he wasn't hung over this morning (or was it afternoon?). He went into the bathroom and showered. It was the first time in several days that he'd done so, and he lingered a long time not for the chance to be clean but to turn his face into the hot spray and let the water wash his tears away; it was the only way he felt able to cry now.

73

The house was as he'd left it. The gaps in the tarps covering the smashed roof and the impromptu doorway cut into his bedroom had let air in, and the place wasn't musty, though there was a sour smell coming from the kitchen.

Daniel was reluctant as ever to pack things away, but he'd run out of time. In the bedroom he started boxing up the books from Sarah's night table. Then he emptied the table's drawer—an old lipstick, a trashy bodice ripper novel, other odds and ends. The last item on the table was a knickknack—a blown-glass Pegasus he'd bought for her when they were courting, at one of those tourist-trap shops on the pier. He picked up the Pegasus, held it carefully. He'd have to wrap this up well so it wouldn't—

It slipped from his fingers, dropped to the hardwood floor. Daniel flinched, waited to see it shatter. But when he picked it up it didn't have so much as a scratch.

He stared at the glass trinket feeling something he thought was wonder but then realized was anger—no, rage. Daniel let the Pegasus fall to the floor again, brought his foot down on it. Once, twice, three times, until it was nothing that could be pieced together again.

Daniel sat down on the bed, looking at the little mess of broken glass. Part of him wanted to pull down the whole house, the town, the world, and wreck it all. The other part felt exhausted; destroying such a small thing seemed to have taken everything he had. Both feelings were soon overwhelmed by remorse. He'd destroyed one of his gifts to Sarah, and his brief feeling of satisfaction had not been enough. What if Kate Reilly or one of Sarah's sisters had wanted it? Why hadn't he brought it with him to the apartment or given it to someone for safekeeping?

He couldn't think of it anymore. It hurt to think, nearly as much as it hurt to remember, and oh God, he was tired. He lay down on the bed. Without thinking he rolled to the left side, his side. He pulled Sarah's pillow to him, held it close. He drowsed, breathing in the faint scent of her.

Voices woke him. They were close. Right outside the window perhaps? He slid off the bed, crept to the window, where he peered through a crack in the venetian blinds.

A pickup truck with a sign on the door—"Auden Company Demolitions." Two men, one in a hard hat and one wearing a suit and holding a clipboard. Talking and gesturing at the house.

Daniel felt the same rage he'd felt when stomping on the glass Pegasus. How dare they tear this house down? The house he and Sarah had bought. The night they'd moved in, there had been no power yet and all the furniture was in disarray; they'd eaten takeout by candlelight and made love on a pile of moving blankets. The house where Jake had spent his whole life. The first day they'd brought him home, to sleep in the bassinet in their bedroom, Daniel had watched his son while Sarah napped, entranced by the rise and fall of the baby's breathing, the graceful movements of the small fingers and toes. Miracles, both of them, his wife and son, granted to him and taken away, and now these men wanted to obliterate where these miracles had dwelt.

He had a sudden urge to shout out the window at them. *Go away. Don't dare touch this house. Leave us alone.*

Except there was no *us*. Not anymore.

Daniel looked back over his shoulder at the bedroom. It was his, yet it wasn't. Something had changed, and he couldn't feel his ghosts here anymore. He couldn't feel that he belonged here, either. All the furniture and possessions he saw were like dusty relics from someone else's attic.

When the men had left and he didn't need to be stealthy, he wandered the house. Searching for some ghost, some sign of life. Gone. Like everything else.

Gone. It sounded like a fine place to be.

Chapter Six

Mick was on his way to San Diego, getting ready to brave the Monday commute. He stopped for a large coffee at Java Man—he and Rachel had gotten back late from San Francisco yesterday, and he was still tired. As he added Splenda to his coffee, his cell rang.

He didn't recognize the number, nor the voice. "Mr. Kessler, I'm Vin Gerard; I'm with Auden Company Demolitions. It's about the house at 841 Sandpiper. I'm afraid we've got a problem here."

Mick stepped outside the coffeehouse so he could hear the conversation better. "What's the problem?"

"Well, we're scheduled to demolish the house today, but we can't do that unless all the owner's possessions have been cleared out."

Mick frowned. "What do you mean?"

Vin Gerard sighed. "What I mean is, they haven't been. And I can't get hold of the owner, Mr. Whitman. I've called his home and his cell five times each this morning, and all I've got is voice mail. I found your name in our records, so that's why I'm calling you. Someone needs to get out here and sort this out."

Now it was Mick's turn to sigh. No doubt there was just a box or two that Daniel had overlooked and the bureaucracy was fouling things up. "I'll be there in just a few minutes."

As he got into his car he dialed both of Daniel's numbers. The cell went to an automated voice mail—no surprise. Daniel was always letting his battery die or leaving the phone in the car.

The answering machine was a different matter. Mick had never heard it since Daniel had moved to the Coral Villas—Daniel had always answered the phone. Now the phone rang six times, and the message was simply: "It's me. Leave a message."

Mick didn't leave one. He hung up and redialed, sure he'd had the wrong number. The weary voice on the machine barely sounded like Daniel's. Mick didn't know what else to do but say: "Dan, listen. There's some sort of problem with the house today. Call my cell, OK?"

He hung up and was just getting ready to head for Sandpiper Street when his cell rang again. Rachel this time, which was odd. She never called when she knew he'd be in transit.

"I just got a weird phone call," she said. "About Daniel."

"The house, I know. There's a problem with the demolition, I'm heading over there now."

"No, it was Kate. She can't reach him. She thought he'd been in San Francisco with us."

"What? I thought he went to their place."

"That's what he said. But he told the Reillys he was going with us. What's the problem with the demolition?"

Mick had trouble answering. His mouth felt dry, and his heart was knocking at his ribs in a nasty way, sending out a Morse code he couldn't understand. "They say they can't. That there are still things in the house. I'm heading over there now, can you meet me there?"

He arrived at 841 Sandpiper to find a few heavy equipment trucks parked nearby, along with a pickup truck with the sign for Auden Company Demolitions. A crowd of men in coveralls and hard hats stood there, eating doughnuts and looking cheerful about the prospect of an idle morning. Their supervisor, on the other hand, was not cheerful. He was dialing a cell phone, his finger jabbing at the keypad, and wore a dark scowl. Mick thought of those *Thomas the Tank Engine* videos he used to play when he'd babysat Jake, when the engines were described as "very cross."

Mick went into businessman mode. "You're Mr. Gerard? I'm Michael Kessler; we spoke on the phone."

"I'm glad you're here," Gerard replied. "I'm glad *somebody's* here. Look, if it was just a box or two I'd deal with it, and I understand the guy lost his family and all. But I've got a whole crew here, and this has been set up for weeks. Take a look for yourself if you don't believe me."

Mick had hoped that Gerard was exaggerating, but even before he set foot inside the house, he knew Gerard wasn't—even a quick glance through the window told the truth. A few boxes, none of them more than half-full. Most of the rooms exactly as they'd been the last time he'd visited. On the living room coffee table lay a book that Sarah had been reading. In the workroom there was an empty plate and juice box next to the PlayStation. The same as he remembered, except for the dust and the houseplants that were dead and brown now. The kitchen was the worst—in the vegetable basket, potatoes had sprouted and avocados had gone bad. He made the mistake of opening the refrigerator, and the stench made his eyes water: the power had been shut off weeks ago, but the fridge had never been cleaned out.

He left the kitchen and went back down the hall, out the front door, and around the back to the doorway that had been cut into the bedroom. As he stepped inside he felt a touch on his shoulder and let out a startled yelp.

"Sorry, sorry," said Rachel. She followed him in and together they looked around. Here, there were signs of activity. Several dresser drawers were open, and their contents seemed to have been raked out carelessly.

The same went for the bedroom closet. "It's like he was looking for something," she said. "Any idea what?"

Mick shook his head. "I've got to talk to Gerard. Then we'll head over to his apartment."

He stepped outside, thinking how strange it was. The outside of the house looked derelict with the lawn overgrown, weeds in the flower beds, old newspapers in a soggy pile. But it was the inside of the house, where things were unchanged, that troubled Mick. He didn't let himself wonder why things were in this state; he pushed the thought aside as he went to do what needed to be done.

Gerard was standing there looking more sullen than ever. Mick put on his best ingratiating smile and apologized profusely. He wasn't sure what had happened, but there was a perfectly logical explanation. He'd compensate the company for its time today and make arrangements to have the belongings moved out as soon as possible, contact Gerard as soon as things were ready. After a while Gerard seemed somewhat mollified; he told his men to go home, and after a few more complaints about the time he'd wasted, got into his truck and left.

Mick sighed, relieved, when they were gone. Rachel stood, staring at the house and chewing on a fingernail. She asked, "Did the Whitmans own a . . ."

"Own a what?"

She shook her head. "Nothing."

They went in Mick's car, leaving Rachel's Vespa at the house; they'd come back for it later. Rachel drove while Mick made calls, looking for someone to pack up everything and a storage place big enough to keep it until things could be sorted out. He found them in short order—one of his clients was a moving company he'd kept from going under with his financial advice, and they were happy to return the favor in any way they could. They'd start work two days from now.

"That's taken care of," he said as they made the turn onto the street where Daniel's apartment was. Rachel didn't answer. She had a lock of hair in one hand, kept wrapping it around a finger so tightly that her fingertip went white. Even after she parked the car she sat for a moment with the engine running, still twisting her hair. If he didn't know better, he'd say she was frightened. And there wasn't reason to be frightened. Uneasy, yes. Concerned. But they'd talk to Dan and sort it out, and there'd be an explanation for everything.

Rachel stood, arms folded tightly, while Mick knocked on Daniel's door. There was no answer. She knew there wouldn't be. Just as she knew that whatever was behind that door wasn't going to be pleasant. She kept thinking about the house. What lingered in her memory were the drawers and closet that had been opened, contents strewn about carelessly. Daniel had been looking for something. The question she hadn't been able to ask Mick was: *Did the Whitmans own a gun?* Because if the answer was yes, then Rachel feared what they'd find on the other side of the apartment door. She told herself not to think of such a possibility, but then she remembered Daniel at the Mermaid, when he'd said he had a long time to live.

No answer. "Maybe the landlord . . . no, wait." Mick took a credit card from his wallet, inserted it between the door and the jamb. Rachel hoped no one was counting on a locked door for security at this place; in less than thirty seconds Mick had the door open.

Her first reaction was relief. Her worst fears were for naught. Daniel wasn't here, but neither was he here with a bullet in his head or a Demerol-

and-bourbon cocktail in his stomach. But the relief was short-lived. How long had he lived here? A couple of months at least. And yet the place looked as if he'd moved in only the day before.

No furniture. Not even a bed, just a futon mattress. No decorations on the walls. No dresser, just a suitcase on the floor. Nothing in any of the rooms save the bare essentials. In the bathroom, one towel and a scant set of toiletries. A few boxes had been shoved indifferently into a corner; peering inside she saw books and a frying pan and some clothes hangers, all seemingly tossed in with no regard for order.

Signs of life nearby the futon: A stack of photo albums and the phone and answering machine, sitting on the floor. Mick knelt and pushed the button to play the messages. His own call from this morning, Vin Gerard's multiple calls. One from Saturday: Reg Fletcher asking Daniel if he was interested in that Ibiza jaunt. One from Thanksgiving day itself: Daniel's mother asking if he was all right and wishing him a happy holiday. Rachel rolled her eyes.

She went into the apartment's tiny kitchen, expecting a stench like there'd been at the house. But it was bare, almost sterile. A peek through the trash can showed that if Daniel had been eating at all, he'd subsisted on ramen noodles and microwave meals. That wasn't like him—he was a fairly good cook. He'd learned to be, he'd told her once, during all those times his parents had been off somewhere with his sister and left him to shift for himself. *It was learn to cook or live off peanut butter sandwiches and end up with scurvy,* he'd said.

Rachel walked back into the studio's main room. Mick still knelt by the answering machine. As she watched, he picked up one of the photo albums, looked at a page or two. Then he looked around the apartment, seeming to take in the emptiness of it. Rachel looked as well. The relief she'd felt when they walked in had long since faded. There was no corpse, but the place still felt like a tomb.

Mick stood, his knees cracking. The sound was very audible in the silent apartment. "We'd better call the Reillys," he said.

Sunday. Rachel carried carafes of coffee and lemonade into the living room. The room was quiet despite the presence of so many people.

Kate and Hugh Reilly sat together, holding hands. They were no longer young: Kate's fair hair was shading to silver, Hugh's carroty red locks were fast receding. Yet there was a vibrancy about them that made up for lost youth. Despite the blows of the past few months, they weren't letting grief defeat them. Hugh immediately leaped to his feet and took the carafes from Rachel. She protested; after all, she was hostess, but Hugh insisted. He passed one carafe to Kate, and the two of them began filling cups and glasses for the others gathered there that day.

Sarah's brother, Martin, and sisters, Amy and Theresa, sat on the sofa, along with Amy's husband, Carl. Martin's wife, Joanna, and Theresa's husband, Stan, had taken various children to the zoo for the day. Only the youngest Reilly, John, couldn't be in attendance, as he was unable to get away from the seminary.

The beverages were poured and pastries were distributed, though no one ate. Rachel didn't take offense; she didn't feel like eating, either. After a moment Mick took a breath and began. "I called in the missing persons report on Wednesday. It took a while to get hold of friends and anyone else who might know where he is. I wanted to make sure we had a good description of what he was wearing, things like that."

"Who was the last person to see him?" asked Kate.

"As near as I can tell, it was Sandra Cordova, his next-door neighbor. She said she saw him go into the house two days before Thanksgiving, early afternoon."

"Is she sure of the time?" asked Martin.

"Yes, her kid was napping, and she was getting ready to watch her soap opera. She didn't see him leave the house, though. And she can't remember what he was wearing beyond jeans and high-tops and a sweatshirt," said Mick, looking through his notes.

Amy laughed mirthlessly. "That's like, his uniform. Any of us could have said that."

Mick continued: "She didn't see him leave, so who knows when it was. Oh, and he must have walked there or caught the bus. She didn't see his car, and in fact it's still at his place. The car keys were in the apartment. She didn't talk to him. As near as I can tell no one's talked to him since maybe Monday of last week. No one's heard anything or received a letter. The police say there's been no activity on his bank account except for automatic billing. Nothing on the credit cards, either." He looked as if there were more he wanted to say.

At last Carl spoke up: "Does anyone know where he might have gone?"

Kate said, "It sounds like we've asked everyone who might know. I even called his parents, but they were no help at all. Annie just said, 'Oh, I wouldn't worry; Daniel always used to go off by himself.'"

"Jesus Christ, what an idiot," grumbled Martin. "He wasn't off by himself, he was hanging around with us."

"Martin, that's not helping," said Hugh.

"I filed the report and talked to Sheriff Marquez. He says that it will be distributed to nearby police jurisdictions, and they'll be on the lookout.

And we need to let anyone he may contact know, and they can call us if they hear from him," Mick said.

"We could put up a website," said Theresa. "Set it up so that anyone who googles his name finds it. Ask people to link to it from their blogs, their business sites, Facebook, things like that."

Rachel could feel the questions hanging over them. *Why did he leave? Why didn't he tell anyone? Where would he go?* "Excuse me," she said. She wasn't normally a reticent person, but she was the newcomer here. She and Mick had only been married for four years, whereas everyone else here was family save for Mick, who'd known the Reillys as long as he'd known Sarah and Daniel. "I had a thought as to why he might have left."

She waited for someone to say she was overstepping her bounds, but they all looked at her expectantly. Rachel told them about the uneasy feeling she'd gotten about Daniel, the way he'd seemed almost afraid of her and the others. "I get the feeling he might think we blame him for what happened to Sarah and Jake."

The snort of disbelief came not from the Reilly family but from her husband. "That was an act of God," Mick said. "Why would anyone blame him for that?"

"I'm not saying anyone does, I'm saying that maybe he thinks we do," Rachel said, feeling her face turn red. "I didn't mean that anyone had said that, not at all . . ." This wasn't coming out the way she'd hoped.

Chatter broke out among the siblings, and Kate held up a hand for silence. "There's no need to argue about it. None of us know why he left. We don't know what's in his heart. We do know that he's grieving, and that can do strange things to people sometimes. He needs to know that he's loved and we want him back."

Nods and sounds of agreement from everyone in the room. Rachel looked down at her coffee and her uneaten pastry. It reminded her of the morning of the funeral, when she'd brought the coffee and cinnamon toast to Daniel and how he'd sat there, just holding it as if he'd forgotten the concept of food or drink. Someone took her hand. At first she thought it was Mick, but the hand was smaller than his, and softer, the skin cool and papery. Rachel looked up to see Kate looking at her; Kate gave her hand a reassuring squeeze and smiled. Amazing that Kate could find it in her to smile, yet she did. Somehow that made Rachel sure that Daniel would come back; he wouldn't leave that kind of love behind.

Days went by. Weeks. The trees lining Los Cielos's main shopping area were strung with twinkling lights. Store owners arranged their windows to lure in the shoppers. The farmers market added poinsettias, chestnuts, and dried fruit to its wares, along with gift baskets ready to bring to holiday get-togethers. Beaditudes made a brisk trade from locals and tourists, and Rachel spent many evenings working on a custom order: a red velvet dress embroidered with gold thread and seed pearls.

She sat on the living room sofa and worked on the dress, relishing the way the detailed stitching occupied her mind. The house, too large for just the two of them, was silent. Mick was working late, something he did with increasing frequency these last couple of weeks. She'd put on music earlier, the Mediaeval Baebes' Christmas album *Mistletoe and Wine,* but the music had ended some time ago, and she hadn't put on something else. The house was brave with Christmas decorations, but they all seemed surface trappings. She didn't feel Christmas in this house. Oh, it looked the part, even smelled the part with the tree and the bayberry candles and the homemade gingerbread cookies that Martin and Joanna had brought over last weekend when they came to invite the Kesslers to the Reilly Christmas gathering.

At this time last year, they'd had Jake over a couple of times while Sarah and Daniel went to Christmas parties for the grown-ups. They'd gone to Jake's school Christmas play; he played one of the wise men. At this time last year Rachel hadn't had a week without Daniel or Sarah popping into her shop to buy something for a friend or relative, or to show her the latest gift they'd bought, or to ask what to get for Mick, who was notoriously hard to buy for, or to give her some homemade treat like candied nuts or bonbons.

Three weeks had passed since Thanksgiving, and there was still no word from Daniel. The website they'd set up had plenty of hits—Rachel should know, for Mick checked it every day—but they were all from people wondering where he was. At Kate's suggestion they'd added a section for messages to Daniel should he read it. The messages were all different, but they all came down to the same thing: *We care for you. We miss you. We want you back.*

Rachel wondered if the others felt the same contradictory way she did; that he might never come back and that he might show up at any time. Only last weekend she and Mick had gone to Los Cielos's Christmas tree ceremony, where the mayor gave the OK for the tree in the park by the library to be lit. The tree was festooned with its gaudy assortment of lights, and all the local schools had contributed ornaments made by their students. A festive mess, the ceremony itself was good-natured chaos, and standing there holding Mick's hand and sipping hot chocolate, listening to the choir from Queen of Peace do justice to Christmas carols, Rachel had felt content for the first time in weeks. And at one point she'd seen someone out of the corner of her eye: he'd seemed to have Daniel's height and hair color, his sharp nose and chin; he'd even worn a leather bomber jacket like the one Sarah had given Daniel for his birthday a few years ago. But she looked again and it wasn't him. The man was too short, too young, his hair was dark blond rather than brown, and Rachel remembered that Daniel's bomber jacket was in a storage unit across town, along with all the other possessions from the now-demolished Whitman house. She hadn't had the heart to tell Mick or anyone else about that mistaken glimpse; it had taken all her joy out of that evening.

Of course, how much worse must this season be for everyone else? She'd had half a notion to refuse the Reillys' Christmas invitation, for she dreaded seeing what toll things had taken on them. But she knew she'd attend, for they needed her company.

That reminded her. She set aside the embroidery and opened the package that had been waiting on the doorstep when she got home. Inside she found a white pillar candle and a handsome brass stand for it. And a note from Kate:

Mick and Rachel:

I can't tell you how glad I've been of your help and support—not just these last few weeks but since September. I've sent these to all the family, and I'm including you. There's an Irish tradition of placing a lit candle in the window at Christmastime. It shows a family's love and loyalty to those who are away from home. Could you please put it in one of your windows and light it? I'm looking forward to seeing you on Christmas.

God bless,

Kate

Rachel lit the candle and placed it in the window. She turned out the lights; the window faced the west and the dark ocean. She had the impression that her candle was floating in darkness. Such a little light. How easy would it be for a grieving traveler, eyes downcast, to miss that light and continue on their lonely way? Very easy, she suspected.

The front door's lock rattled, and in walked Mick. "Rachel? You here?" he asked. Before she could answer he flicked on the light. He looked at her, and the sight must have struck him as odd—her embroidery in a heap while she sat by the window and the candle. "What's that?"

She explained, showed him Kate's note. He nodded and smiled, then said, "Give me a minute," and left the room. She heard the computer fire up and knew what he was doing. Checking for any word. Rachel left him to it, went on looking at the candle's dancing flame and at the darkness beyond the window.

Chapter Seven

Their car was loaded down with presents, a few bottles of wine for the dinner, and Rachel's Gruyère cheese puffs. They drove north toward Torrance, making good time because there was so little traffic—their fellow drivers all seemed to be on the way to holiday gatherings, the cars decorated with garlands and the back seats piled high with presents. The day was as seasonal as it could be in Southern California. It had rained yesterday, and today was sunny but cool, a few cotton-ball clouds scooting along the sky.

As they turned off the freeway and onto the surface streets, Mick tried to recall the first Christmas he'd been to the Reilly's. The first year he'd known Daniel and Sarah, or the second? He couldn't quite recall. Probably the second. Yes, now he remembered. That first year he'd concocted some lie about going to a relative's house. Sarah hadn't bought that lie. Had anyone? The housemates had surely noticed that he got no mail, no phone calls, not even a care package. Hell, even Daniel got those, although his parents, true to form, couldn't remember his likes and dislikes, and Daniel ended up sharing out half the package ("Hey, Professor. You like vanilla Zingers? Take 'em all, then."). It was worse than they knew, of course. Even if his father hadn't disowned him, there hadn't been a Christmas celebration at the Kessler house in years. The last one must have been when Mick was four; his recollections of it were fragmented and mostly unpleasant. Something about the dinner had displeased his father, whose anger had been so palpable that Mick had barely been able to eat. Later that night, their voices had woken him. The familiar duet. He couldn't distinguish his father's actual words; he never had been able to, only the low tones of anger and contempt. His mother's words he could hear clearly, and they were always the same during these nighttime duets. He could repeat them now, if he wanted to. *Please don't. Please. I'll try harder. I'm sorry I made you mad. Please.* By the time the leaves turned the following year, she was gone, and there had been no more Christmases.

He'd wondered now if the fall's sorrow might have cast a pall over the holidays, but the Reillys seemed to be fighting back. The willow tree in front of the house was strung with lights and hung with ornaments, the driveway was lined with luminarias, and the mingled sounds of holiday music, chattering people, and children at play could be heard two doors down. Before they could ring the bell the door flew open and several Reillys were there to take their coats, bags, food, and presents.

As Mick stepped inside, he reflected how little seemed to have changed since the last time he'd been here. Even the tree was the same—a white-flocked artificial one (in deference to Hugh's pine allergy), bathed in colors from a rotating color wheel that was vintage 1970s kitsch. Rachel laughed when she saw it. "I thought my cousin Ethan was the only person who still had one of those."

Kate had appeared with glasses of mulled wine for them. "Oh, that thing. I swear, every year I've threatened to get rid of it and get something more modern, but the kids all squawk, and I have to keep it. And by kids I mean the grown ones."

"I *like* the color wheel," said John, who'd appeared carrying a large box. "Daniel always said it wasn't Christmas until he saw our front window glowing."

91

"Who broke our old color wheel, anyway?" Kate asked. "You kids never would tell me."

"Promise not to send the perpetrators to the children's satellite table?" John asked. When his mother nodded he said, "Martin and Theresa, Daniel, too. They thought it would be groovy if it was speeded up."

Kate sighed. "A freak-out Christmas, just what I always wanted."

Rachel went with Kate to the kitchen; Mick declined, preferring instead to see how the family was weathering the holiday.

It looked like Christmas. The way Christmas should always look. Every room had some kind of decoration, and bowls of candy, nuts, and other goodies invited gluttony wherever he went. In the backyard some of the older kids bounced on a trampoline that seemed to be Kate and Hugh's present to their grandchildren. In the far bedroom John had set down the large box he'd been carrying. "Videos," he said in response to Mick's query. "Home movie marathon all day. I think you're in a few of these. I'll let you know if I see you."

"Need any help?" Mick asked while John fiddled with cables and a VCR so old it loaded from the top. But John shook his head in reply, and in another moment the TV showed not static but an image.

"I was right," John said. "You *are* in some of these."

Last year. Sarah had been filming. Jake had gotten a double-bladed lightsaber from Santa and now stood dressed as Darth Maul and waiting patiently while Daniel and Mick argued over who got to be Obi-Wan Kenobi and who got to be Qui-Gon Jinn.

"I should be Qui-Gon," Daniel said. "Because I'm taller, and that way I get a noble and tragic death scene while you just stand there and scream, 'Nooooo!' and be all ineffectual."

"Yeah, but you're also the only guy in the saga who dies because he gets punched in the chin. That isn't exactly death with dignity. And you ask me to train the kid who's going to grow up and fubar the galaxy," Mick replied.

"Mommy, what's fubar?" asked Jake.

"Something that Mommy can't explain on baby Jesus's birthday," Sarah said.

John laughed and looked through the box of tapes. "I hadn't seen that one. Who did you end up being?

"Obi-Wan." Mick wasn't sure how to feel. Why was everyone acting like this was a normal Christmas? Were they just pretending they didn't feel the void? But maybe this was the right way to act. He'd always suspected it wasn't right during his childhood that the streets of his town could be decorated like something from a Norman Rockwell painting but inside the Kessler house it was as if the holiday didn't exist. The only concession, a year or two after his mother vanished, was his father handing him money and telling him to buy himself something. Mick wondered if his father knew that he'd spent almost none of that money; once he'd learned about colleges and that many of them were far, far away from Missouri, he'd put every spare penny into his escape fund.

Even then, it had barely been enough. He'd chosen Los Cielos University not for how well its business school ranked—surprisingly high for a small, artsy-fartsy place—but because of the scholarship. Still, money had been tight, which was why he spent his free time at the commons playing the secondhand guitar—movies and clubs were luxuries he hadn't been able to afford. It had been a way to pass the time. He hadn't supposed anyone would actually notice him or the guitar playing—why should anyone notice? His accent was wrong, he wasn't in one of the cool majors, his clothes (like the guitar, secondhand) were wrong. Even his slang was out of date. So it had been a shock when the pretty blonde girl and the funny guy in the Mr. Zog's Sex Wax T-shirt asked if he wanted to play at a gig that Friday. And somehow he'd found himself on stage as the newest member of William Howard Taft And The Undersize Bathtubs (the drummer was a history major), playing "Like a Rolling Stone" and trying not to laugh when Eskimo Sally bungled the verse about the chrome horse and the diplomat.

Laughter jolted him out of his reverie. He and John weren't the only ones in the room now. Hugh was there, along with Martin's oldest daughter, and Amy's husband, and Theresa's son. All watching the past, the memories. Yes, this was how it should be.

In the room the women come and go, talking of Michelangelo.

That line had been a favorite of Daniel's, Rachel recalled; he quoted it whenever he was faced with a kitchen full of women talking together. Strange, Sarah had been the English teacher, but Daniel was the one you could count on for a poetry quote, and Eliot had been his favorite. He'd told Rachel once that his fantasy project would be a rock opera based on Eliot's *The Waste Land*. She wished he'd done that. She'd have bought it. Might not have listened to it more than once, but she'd have bought it. She'd sometimes wondered why Daniel had never done his own songs, even just to distribute to friends and family. She'd never asked him, but it had come up once on a girls' night out, she and Sarah at the Tiki Terrace. LCU's English Department had put out its yearly fiction magazine, and as usual Sarah's name had been in the masthead as editor but she'd contributed no stories. "Oh, I wrote a few, ages ago," Sarah had said, "but it's hard when you're an English major. You write a story and think it's pretty good, then you turn around and read something by Steinbeck or Bradbury or Oates and wonder why you bothered. Then I got into some creative writing classes and learned I just didn't have it in me." She'd plucked the umbrella from her drink and twirled it between her fingers. "Someone has to be an editor."

"What about Daniel, will he ever do his own music?"

Sarah had stuck the umbrella back into her drink. "Hard to say. I think he's got it in him, but he needs a catalyst. That's why we're in awe of you and Mick. You both have your own businesses. Your work's so creative, and I think his is, too, although I couldn't tell you what Mick actually *does*. Still, moving money around is a kind of creativity."

"Rachel? You OK?" It was Kate.

"Fine. Just woolgathering. Can I help out with anything?"

In the room the women come and go, talking of Michelangelo. It was the same at every family holiday gathering she'd attended. The kids played, the men sat around and talked or played video games or ran herd on the kids, and the women congregated in the kitchen to prepare food and talk. Rachel stood in the kitchen and sipped her mulled wine. The Reilly kitchen was small—too small, at any rate, for five women, most of whom were in the final stages of dinner preparation. It was like watching a complicated dance as Amy attacked the gravy with a balloon whisk, Theresa set about carving the goose, Joanna ran dishes out to the tables while making sure the creamed corn didn't get overdone, and they tried to get Kate to relax for a few minutes before dinner.

At last Theresa put a small plate of Gruyère puffs and a glass of mulled wine into her mother's hands and pushed her to the end of the kitchen where Rachel had retreated after being told for the fifth time she was a guest and didn't have to pitch in. Kate relented and stood by Rachel.

"Thank you for the appetizers," Kate said. "We've all been eating them. I doubt there will be any left by the time dinner's on the table."

"It's my mother's recipe. I'll be sure to pass the thanks on to her," Rachel said. She watched as Kate took a sip of wine, then glanced toward the front door. Rachel understood—she'd been doing the same thing all day.

"I keep looking for them. All of them. But mostly him," Kate said, softly so the other women couldn't hear. "It's different with Sarah and Jake. I miss them so much it hurts, but I know they're with God now. But Daniel . . ."

Rachel nodded. On an ordinary Christmas Daniel would have been in the thick of things, handing out presents, probably out bouncing with the kids on that new trampoline or teaching the little ones the *Jingle bells/Batman smells* song.

Kate said: "Maybe we all remind him too much of what he's lost. He's not as strong as he seems. Maybe if his family hadn't treated him as baggage all those years, or maybe if Sarah or Jake had lived, he'd be better able to handle this. But I'm afraid he's lost too much and can't bear it. Why else would he have left?"

Only one thing left for Rachel to ask. "What do we do now?"

To her surprise, Kate smiled. "We celebrate the family we have and keep our hopes up."

After dinner, and it was getting late. A long drive back to Los Cielos, but Mick couldn't find his wife. "Have you seen Rachel?" Mick asked. He hadn't been able to find her in the kitchen, nor was she watching videos in the spare bedroom.

"I think I saw her with Kate and John," said Hugh. "Try outside."

Mick stepped out into the dark backyard. It was clear, and cold for December in California. He heard the murmur of voices from over by the hammock and headed that way. As he approached he heard the sound of a lighter and caught the whiff of smoke. That struck him as strange, for none of the Reillys smoked, and Rachel had quit two years ago. He stopped, peered through the yew bushes, and saw Rachel's face illuminated by the cigarette's glow. She took a drag and then coughed harshly.

"Are you all right?" asked John.

She nodded. "I shouldn't have gone back to Gitanes after so long. *Mea culpa.*"

"Te absolvo."

Silence. Mick was about to go around the bushes and greet them when Kate said: "I hoped he'd come back."

No need to ask who she meant. Mick peered more closely through the hedge and saw John and Kate sitting in the hammock, Rachel standing nearby and taking tentative drags on her cigarette.

"There's always the Epiphany parade," John said, but his tone was dispirited.

Rachel coughed, then said, "Mick checks the site every day, calls the Los Cielos Sheriff's Department every week. Nothing."

Kate sighed. "Caitlin asked me today where Uncle Dan was. I told her that he was feeling very sad because Aunt Sarah and Jake died and he'd gone away for a while. She asked when he was coming back, and I told her I didn't know. She said she hoped it was soon because he was fun and she missed him. And then Robby asks *if* he's coming back, and what could I say to that?"

"It's hard on the kids," John said. "Most of them are old enough to understand about Sarah and Jake, but this is different."

Kate sounded close to tears. "I wish I knew how to feel. It wears you down, not knowing."

"I don't check the answering machine," Rachel said. "I let Mick do it. I come home and think today's the day we hear from some hospital saying they've got him and need us to ID him. I'm sorry, I shouldn't have said that."

"Don't feel bad." John patted her on the arm. "It's what most of us are thinking."

He'd heard enough. Mick turned and walked away, finding a deserted spot along the side of the house. He couldn't go back in the house just yet, and he didn't want to stay near the three by the hammock. He'd expected better from them: Kate, who was a better parent to Daniel than his adoptive ones; John, who should have had more faith considering he was going into the priesthood; and Rachel, well . . . he'd thought she would be more understanding.

They all seemed to think Daniel had abandoned them forever. If he didn't know better, he'd think Rachel was implying that he might have . . . but that was unthinkable. How could they talk that way? Didn't they know that with uncertainty there was hope? Unreasonable hope, perhaps, but hope nonetheless. He'd forgotten those months after his mother had gone when every day he'd woken up hoping that he'd go downstairs and she'd be there in the kitchen, smiling at him, ready to send him on his way to school—and when he hadn't seen her there, had seen only his father looking at him coldly and impatiently tapping his foot, feeling the disappointment and loss all over again. What he did remember: the resignation he'd felt when he finally accepted she wasn't coming back. Daniel had gone off the rails—who could blame him?—and was elsewhere. What or where that elsewhere might be, he couldn't say. It came down to faith, and if he had enough of that, surely it would work out. It hadn't before, with his mother, but this time it would be different. It had to be.

Chapter Eight

Rachel arrived at the shop well before opening time. February, and the Valentine's Day rush was approaching, but that wasn't the reason for her early arrival. The atmosphere in her house was the sort you sometimes felt before a rainstorm, the kind her weird cousin Ethan claimed he felt before earthquakes. It had been that way off and on since Christmas.

Of course she knew the reason for it. It was losing Sarah and Jake, but most of all it was not knowing where Daniel was. Mick seemed angry that Rachel was able to face what was an unpleasant but unavoidable fact: since Thanksgiving there had been no word at all, and it didn't seem likely there ever would be.

Not that he would say this to her. Heavens, no. The man was steady as a rock but often silent as a rock as well. She'd known that from the beginning, but she'd thought she might be able to bring out the best in him, the way the right cut and polish can bring out the beauty of an agate.

The silence had broken a few nights ago. He'd come home, kissed her hello, then gone straight into the office to check on the computer. She'd continued on with dinner preparation and didn't even hear him return. "Don't you want to know?" he asked.

"Not if it's nothing."

"You don't think he's going to come back, do you?" Phrased as a question, voiced as an accusation.

Rachel had never been much of a liar and wasn't going to start now. "No, I don't."

"I don't know how you can think that."

"I don't know how you can't."

Maybe he was right, and she was being too negative. Maybe Daniel wasn't coming back, but did that have to be a bad thing? What if he'd started over fresh, forged a new identity and started his life over again in some small town? These last few days she'd tried to envision that. Daniel at the piano in some bar. She wasn't sure where. Some place with inclement weather, perhaps? In her imagination the patrons had umbrellas they put away before sitting down at the bar, while Daniel played Tom Waits's great song "The Piano Has Been Drinking (Not Me)."

It was a good daydream. But intertwined with it was her memory of Daniel at the Mermaid. He hadn't looked like a man taking a bold step into a brand-new life.

She busied herself until it was time to open the shop, then spent the morning helping customers and working on new items. The day was quiet for so close to Valentine's Day. No doubt the rush would happen on the weekend, when men all over town looked at the calendar, panicked, and ran in looking for something to buy the girlfriend or the wife or the mistress. Rachel smiled. Those days could be amusing. Frantic men walking in, looking around the place, and saying, *Do you have anything my girlfriend would like?* Well, what sort of jewelry does she like to wear? *I don't know, shiny stuff.* What colors does she like? *Blue, she likes blue, I think.* She seldom got many returns after Valentine's, so either the men were better at remembering their women's tastes than they thought, or Rachel was good at suggesting things.

At noon her stomach rumbled, reminding her that breakfast had been scanty and a good five hours ago. Rachel picked up the phone and dialed Casbah Falafels three doors down; she asked for the three-hummus special.

The proprietor, Tony, was one of her best customers, always buying jewelry for a never-ending stream of girlfriends. "I'll send it over in about ten minutes," he said. "That sound good?"

"Fantastic, Tony. Thanks much." Rachel went back to her work. The necklace was a complicated one—an elegant choker of silver and moonstones. She always broke out the white around this time; wedding season was a few months away, but it paid to be prepared and have the wares ready. One less thing for the bride to worry about. She'd barely threaded a needle when the bells on the door jingled. Without looking up she said, "Hey, Tony, that was quick. Be with you in just a moment."

"Rachel?"

She dropped her needle, heard the faint rattle as beads fell to the table, looked at the doorway. A jolt of adrenaline made her fingers tingle, her heart pound. She got to her feet but couldn't seem to feel the floor beneath her.

Daniel stood just inside the doorway. He fidgeted nervously, the cuffs of his too-large sweatshirt pulled nearly down to his knuckles. He was still too thin and needed a haircut badly, but it was him.

You don't think he's going to come back, do you? No, she hadn't.

Her expression must have been one of utter disbelief. "Rachel?" he said again. "It's me."

Rachel wasn't aware of walking over to him. She was just there, looking up at him. He'd been gone months, and now he just walked right in? Before she knew what she was doing, she slapped him in the face. It couldn't have hurt much but she saw pain in his eyes. And she saw that he half expected her to send him away.

Instead she embraced him. He returned the embrace; when he spoke his voice was shaky with emotion. "I'm so sorry I left." He drew a deep breath. "I want to come back. I want to be home again. Please."

She reached up to take his face in her hands. Yes, he'd been gone, and she was angry with him, but more than that she was glad he was back and glad that he wanted to be back. "You're home now," she said. "But . . . where have you been?"

The Ghost Soldier

Chapter Nine

"Where have you been?"

Daniel tried to think of what to say. His face stung from Rachel's slap, but he was more undone by how shocked she'd seemed at his return. *She thought I was dead. Maybe they all did. Dear God, what have I done?*

His wrists sent out a phantom throb of pain. In his mouth a strange aftertaste that seemed to be partly the ocean and partly the sedatives they'd given him those first few days at St. Jude's. His mind groped for something to hold on to. *A talisman,* Dr. Howard had said. He found it. The song. What the woman had sung to him the night he'd collapsed in the diner, the night . . . he wouldn't think of that now. The song was enough. *This poor youngling for whom we do sing / Bye bye lully lullay.* It calmed him enough to tell Rachel . . . not the truth, but a story that would set her at ease.

The day he left Los Cielos he waited until late afternoon, when the neighbors would be busy getting kids to do their homework or putting dinner together. By that time he had everything he needed in a backpack. A few changes of clothes. A scarf of Sarah's, blue with beads and embroidery, bought at Rachel's shop of course. From the keepsake box, the green teddy bear that had been Jake's constant companion until he was five or so. In the closet, he dug until he found a blanket—thin but wool, so it would keep him warm. He rolled it up tightly and put it into the backpack with the clothes and the mementos. Lastly he hunted through the sock drawer until he found it—an orphan argyle sock, full of money. It was the emergency fund that he and Sarah had contributed to over the years. Daniel didn't bother to count the money but stuffed the sock deep into his backpack. The day had turned chilly, so he tossed in an Irish wool cap and put on a jacket.

There wasn't much left in the kitchen that wasn't spoiled or stale, but he found a few bottles of water and some granola and candy bars. He considered leaving his wallet—after all, he wouldn't need it—but habit won out. Besides, it had pictures of Sarah and Jake.

He left the house, taking no particular precautions to hide his departure. Someone would see him or they wouldn't. It didn't matter. He wasn't coming back. As he turned the corner and walked toward the beach, he glanced back over his shoulder at the house. Dark, derelict, it looked as though it had been abandoned for a year. A place for ghosts. No, if there had been ghosts he might have stayed, but even the ghosts had fled.

Time for him to do the same.

When he reached the beach, the sun was near the horizon. In the distance was a jogger, but aside from that the shore was deserted. North or south? He flipped a coin and north he went. He walked, paying no heed to distance, only taking care not to get his shoes wet as they were his only pair. With each step that took him farther from Los Cielos, he felt lighter. Freed from grief and guilt. Daniel walked until after the sun had gone down and the moon rose. When he tired he found a niche in the rocky cove, well above the tide line and out of the worst of the wind. He ate a PayDay bar, drank some water, then wrapped himself in the jacket and the blanket, put on the wool cap. His sleep was the dreamless oblivion he'd been craving.

He woke to a bright morning and walked north all that day and all the next, not hurrying, not thinking. Content to let the shore take him where it would. He rested when he was tired, ate from the supplies in his backpack when he was hungry. He did not tire of his surroundings; the sameness soothed him. He saw people—beachcombers and joggers mostly—and if they waved to him, he waved back, but he didn't stop to talk to anyone. It was a kind of bliss, this silence and not having to think about anything.

When the scant supplies in his backpack ran out, he unearthed the stash of money and finally counted it. Nearly $1,000. At a state beach he showered and changed clothes. Nothing to shave with, but he decided he liked how he looked with a beard coming in—it made him not just look but feel like someone else. He stopped at a small grocery store and bought some food, also some matches in case he wanted to start a campfire one night. Then he went back to the beach and resumed his walk north.

Soon he had to detour—he'd reached the marine base at Camp Pendleton. Daniel went to the highway on-ramp and thumbed a ride from two marines on leave who were heading up to San Juan Capistrano to catch a concert. "At the Coach House. Have you ever been there?" asked one of the marines.

Yes, he had. He'd even played there a few times. "It's a fun place. Good acoustics. Be sure to get their potato skins."

"That's good to know. Thanks. We're going to see this band called Chekhov's Gun. You heard of them? Oh . . . sorry, I didn't catch your name?" said the other marine.

He gave them his middle name. "James." He was friends with nearly everyone in Chekhov's Gun—Kenichi, Vic, and Athena had all been in the bands that formed and disbanded back in the college days. They'd recognize him. Would want to know what he was doing here and why he'd left Los Cielos. Maybe Kenichi would be the one—he'd say *anything*. Maybe he'd say something like *Well that's what I expect from someone who gads off to London and lets his wife and son get killed.*

"You heading all the way to Capistrano?" asked the marine who was driving. Even though they'd introduced themselves, they looked so much alike with their military haircuts that Daniel had a hard time remembering who was who.

"San Clemente's fine."

He felt relieved when the marines were on their way and he was alone once more. It had felt so strange to talk to people, almost as if the English language had altered slightly, or as if words were a song and he was half a beat behind. No matter. He made his way to the beach and resumed his northward walk.

Days went by. He was never sure how many. Nor did he have much sense of place. Looking at a map of the state would have told him nothing about his trek. He remembered little of the days, they were so much the same. Most nights he slept on the beach or in an empty campground. He liked the isolation. Some cloudy nights he woke and might have been blind—no moon, no stars, no streetlights. *Now it's dark.* No one could find him here.

There came an evening when he happened upon a group of college-age stoners who invited him to share their campfire, cheap wine, and good pot. For a while it was all right. He sat there saying little, just enjoying the kids' chatter, mostly about music. Once he could have said, *I played on that song.* But he mostly let their conversation wash over him like the sound of waves, let the wine and the smoke wrap his mind in a pleasant haze. As the fire burned low one of the girls, a doe-eyed brunette with her hair in a Louise Brooks bob, sat beside him. They passed the wine bottle and a joint back and forth and talked for a while. He said something that amused her and she laughed. "I like you," she whispered, and kissed him. She tasted like wine and smoke and strawberry lip gloss; her kiss roused in him not desire but a sadness so deep it was like physical pain. How long had it been since he'd felt another person's touch? The girl frowned, concerned, and put a hand on his cheek. "What's wrong?" she asked, but he couldn't answer. What would he tell her? That he wanted nothing more than to be close to someone again, but the only people he wanted to be close to were his wife and son and friends and family and they were all lost to him, one way or another? He took the girl's hand from his cheek, gently, and turned away from her. He looked out at the night-black sea as tears burned his eyes. Grief had finally caught up with him.

Chapter Ten

"You going to be OK?" asked the driver. In the gray drizzle she looked pale and tired. "I'd stay until your friend comes, but I've got to check in on my mother, she's not well."

"No worries," Daniel said.

"Well, here." She plucked a dog-eared paperback from behind her seat and tossed it to him. "In case you have a long wait. There's a diner down the block. It's across the street from the coin laundry; you can't miss it."

"Thank you."

"Oh, and stay out of the north side of town. It's gone straight to hell in the last few years."

"I'll be careful," he said, and waved goodbye as she drove away.

Daniel stood with the paperback in his hand, idly wondering where he should go first, the diner or the coin laundry. Probably the latter. He wasn't hungry, and his clothes could do with a wash. It wasn't dire, he could still get rides, but the opportunity was here.

And he didn't have anywhere else to go.

The beach had lost some of its appeal for him after the night with the stoner kids. That section of the coast, Ventura and Santa Barbara, had always been one of his favorite places. And that was why he couldn't walk that shore anymore, at least not for long. Too many memories. Memory was not his friend these days. Sometimes he'd let himself think of Sarah and Jake; it was always painful to do so, but he couldn't keep from it.

Trying not to think of them did no good. In fact, it was worse, for occasionally there were times when he couldn't recall their faces precisely, and he'd have to fumble for his wallet and its photo insert, so horrified at the thought of losing his memories that he couldn't feel relieved at seeing their pictures (and realizing that his recollections had been exact, he just no longer trusted them).

So he'd alternated walking the beach with hitching rides. He'd never done any serious hitchhiking before and was surprised at how easy it was and how friendly many of the people were. The marines down by Camp Pendleton hadn't been an exception; nearly every rider who'd picked him up had bought him some food or coffee, and now this lady had given him a Stephen King book.

He shrugged on his backpack and walked over to the coin laundry. It occurred to him that he didn't know what town he was in. He'd lost track after Santa Barbara. He supposed he'd recognize San Francisco if he got that far. But he'd paid little attention, other than to bypass Monterey and its resemblance to home. Destination didn't matter. Grief had caught up with him, but he still hoped he could outrun it.

So he'd kept on: walking the shore or bumming rides, sleeping in inexpensive motels if the weather was too cold for the beach. What he'd do when he ran out of money for food and shelter was a vague concern. He'd worry about it when it happened.

The coin laundry was only half-full, and he found a washer with no problem. Daniel took the clothes from his backpack and tossed them in, then took off his shoes and socks, both grimy from travel, and tossed those in as well. He held the paperback in his lap but did not read it, instead preferring to watch the tumble of clothes and suds through the washer's glass door.

The clothes took a long time, and while the food at the diner was good, the cooks were shorthanded and the service slow. Daniel didn't mind, but when he stepped out of the diner it was full dark already.

His aimless walk took him toward the center of town, where he saw official-looking buildings. Perhaps there'd be a library there, open late, and he could while away some time. It must be close to the holidays, judging by the Christmas decorations he'd seen in the towns he passed through, but then most of those had probably been up since Thanksgiving. When he got to the library, the librarian was just locking up. "Sorry," the librarian said. "We're closing early. Tree lighting ceremony tonight, didn't you know?"

No, he didn't know. He didn't know what day it was, though he wasn't about to say so. Against his better judgment Daniel tagged along to the small park on the other side of the library. And stopped, transfixed by what he saw.

Home. I'm home. The scene reminded him so much of Los Cielos he half wondered if his aimless wandering had brought him back. A fat Douglas fir stood in the center of the park, festooned with lights and with paper chains clearly made by children's inexpert hands. A choir stood in front of the tree, singing. At the far side of the park a vendor sold hot pretzels and candy apples. Everyone looked happy to be there.

Yes, it might have been home. This park was smaller, its occupants a few rungs down the economic ladder, but otherwise it might have been Los Cielos with its feeling of small-city camaraderie. For the first time in who knew how long, he allowed himself to think of home and those he'd left.

In Los Cielos, all the trees on Sandcastle Way would be strung with lights. The surrey bikes would have garlands pinned to their canopies. There would be parties—Jake's elementary school, the middle school where Sarah taught, the local Musicians' Union. At least once a week Mick would come by, loaded down with food gifts from his clients, begging everyone he knew to take something or he'd have to eat it all and none of his clothes would fit anymore.

And at the Reillys' Christmas party, in the evening they'd gather around the willow tree in the front yard, join hands, and sing the Whoville song from the animated *How the Grinch Stole Christmas!* On Epiphany they'd have their Feast of Fools parade.

Last year Jake had begun to doubt Santa Claus, and Daniel, remembering how his sister Victoria had broken the truth to him when he was about Jake's age, assured Jake that Santa was indeed real and told him to ask his uncle John if he needed confirmation. After all, Uncle John was going to be a priest, and priests don't lie. And John, who had always considered Daniel an honorary older brother, had been happy to continue the deception. "I just asked a future priest to lie. I am *so* damned," Daniel had said, and they had both laughed about it.

He stood there for a long time, until the crowds had dispersed and there were just a few people left. Friends of the food vendor, it seemed. Daniel saw backslaps and friendly greetings, food handed out for no charge, and a flask being passed around. He sat down on a bench and gazed at the lights. From the food vendor's direction he heard music—one of the friends had brought out a boom box. Sinatra singing "I'll Be Home for Christmas."

Home. He thought he'd left it forever. After all, what was left for him now that Sarah and Jake were gone, the house no doubt demolished, and his music lost? By now everyone knew that everything was his fault and were no doubt saying good riddance to bad rubbish.

Yet if he could transport himself back to Los Cielos this moment, he'd do it. Just to be home again, for even a few minutes. Leaving had seemed the right thing—the only thing—at the time, but whatever he'd been looking for when he'd fled, he hadn't found it.

Was it possible? Could he go to the nearest on-ramp and say, "South, and I'll go as far as you're going"? Could he go back? The thought of all those miles was daunting. He seemed to have gone further than mere distance.

And it wasn't the place he missed, so much. There were many places, a world of them, and surely he could find one. But home wasn't a place. It was people. When he was twelve and his adoptive family had moved from Torrance to Riverside, he'd still thought of Torrance as home. Riverside had just been where he lived. This Christmas party in the park might have reminded him of Los Cielos, but it was the people he wanted to see again. His family—the Reillys, not the Whitmans. His friends. Even if they didn't want to see him, it might be worth it just to stand outside a house and peer in, see how they fared.

He sat for a long while until he was startled not by sound but by silence. The park was empty now save for him. No sign of the vendor and his friends. Not even a cop nearby to tell him to move it along. It was probably too late to call anyone in Los Cielos, but he had to do it now before his nerve failed him.

Daniel stood up and went in search of a pay phone—no easy task, and harder to find one that was working. He walked at least ten blocks before he found one, in a seedy-looking strip mall, between a dry cleaner's and a vacant store. He fished through his pockets for enough change to make a call to Los Cielos, absently noting that he'd made it all the way up to the 510 area code. Thinking he could feel some change in his jacket pocket, he reached inside, and as he took out the change a wad of his cash fell to the ground.

He knelt down to retrieve the money; a hand snatched it away.

"What the . . ." Before he could finish, hands hauled him upright, spun him around, and slammed him against the wall. He bit his tongue and tasted blood. An arm held his shoulders pinned; Daniel tried to see his attacker and caught only a peripheral glance of gray sweatshirt. Then a face leaned into his field of vision. Bloated and moonlike, topped with dead-straw hair. "Shut up, and don't make me use this." The face's owner held up what looked like a box cutter, its blade gleaming in the moonlight. Another set of hands went efficiently through his pockets, yanked the backpack from his shoulders.

I'm being mugged. Nothing like this had ever happened to him. And just when he was considering going home, too. What else could go wrong now? He couldn't help it—he giggled.

"Knock it off, fuckface!" Something hit the back of his head, hard, and Daniel's forehead connected with the wall. The pain wasn't bad, but it took all the laughter out of him.

"Jeez, Clay, let him alone," said the one with the box cutter.

"I don't like people laughing at me. Turn him around."

The arm holding him against the wall released, and hands spun him, pushed him back against the wall. Now he could see them both: Moon Face in a skanky-looking hoodie, and the one named Clay—eyes like marbles and a meth addict's rotten teeth. Well, Daniel's last ride had told him to stay out of the north side of town; now he knew why.

The box cutter was still near Daniel's face, so he didn't protest as he watched Clay go through his backpack. "You holding?" asked Moon Face.

"No."

"Waste of time," said Clay, pawing through Daniel's belongings. For a moment Daniel feared Clay would take Sarah's scarf or Jake's teddy bear, but apparently all that interested Clay was money and dope.

Clay pushed the backpack aside with a snort of disgust, then grabbed it again and unzipped a small pocket he'd overlooked before. "Payday."

His wallet. With the pictures of Sarah and Jake. "Give that back," Daniel said.

They both laughed.

"Look, take the money, take the cards, take it all, just give me back the wallet." It was crazy to be arguing with two meth heads, one of whom could carve up his face if so inclined. But all he could think of were the pictures. *You can't take those, they're all I have left.*

"This wallet's quality shit, I ain't giving it up," Clay said. "Let's go."

Rage, the same he'd felt when he smashed the glass Pegasus. As Moon Face sheathed his box cutter and Clay turned away, Daniel lashed out at Clay. He'd never thrown a punch in his life, but his clumsy hit connected solidly with Clay's ear. Clay let out a screech of pain, and the next thing Daniel knew he was back against the wall.

Looking at a gun.

"You're gonna die for that, shithead," said Clay, but Daniel barely heard him. The gun was less than a foot from his face. It was a revolver, and he could see the bullets in their chambers, waiting for Clay to pull the trigger.

So this was how it ended. Not what he'd expected. Much like the last few months. A random quirk of fate had taken his family from him, and now a quirk just as random would take his own life. Not the end he would have liked, but at least it would be quick. Even a tweaker like Clay couldn't miss at this range. An instant of pain at the most, and then . . . perhaps he'd be with Sarah and Jake again.

He waited for Clay to pull the trigger. And waited. Then Moon Face spoke: "Clay, he isn't . . ."

Isn't what? Daniel wondered.

"I know, I know!" snapped Clay. He brought the gun closer to Daniel's face. Now Daniel could smell the gun's oily metal, and still he waited. Why was this taking so long?

Clay seemed to scan Daniel's face with his marble-like eyes, looking for something and not finding it. Then he lowered the gun, handed it to Moon Face. Clay opened Daniel's wallet, took out the cash, and stuffed it into his pocket. Then he tossed the wallet back to Daniel.

"Let's get out of here," he said to Moon Face. Clay gave Daniel that searching look again. "Something's *wrong* with you." Then they were gone.

He stood there, feeling empty, wondering if they might come back. Daniel checked the wallet. Only the cash was gone. The pictures were there, and they were all that mattered.

He walked back to the park, remembering after a little while that he had planned to call someone in Los Cielos. No matter. It didn't seem to be important anymore. At the park he sat down on a bench and watched the Christmas lights. All night he sat there. No one troubled him. He saw not a single person until dawn came. He sat and wondered why Clay hadn't shot, and what they had seen that troubled them so. It wasn't until the stars were fading from the sky with dawn's approach that he finished Moon Face's sentence: *Clay, he isn't afraid.*

Chapter Eleven

Faber was the name of the town, its raison d'être seemed to be lodgings for people who missed the turnoff to Monterey or were too impatient to wait until San Francisco. Perched at the end of a peninsula, it was scenic enough; if you kept your back to the east, you might think yourself on an island.

Daniel supposed one hotel was as good as another, but the Marina Inn caught his eye—*"Every Room an Ocean View!"* boasted the sign. He walked inside, found the lobby cheerfully done up for Christmas. A tree was covered with seashell ornaments; a fireplace blazed, making the room festive if a little overheated.

The girl at the lobby desk seemed unaffected by the holiday spirit. Her sweater was black, as were her hair and nails and eyeliner. She wore a silver necklace that sported many different religious symbols: a cross, a star of David, an ankh, a yin-yang. He wished he could tell Rachel about it; it was the sort of thing she'd like.

When the girl saw him she took out her iPod headphones, and he could hear the music clearly—not festive tunes but Sleater-Kinney.

"Not exactly seasonal," he said.

"I know, but it's been all Christmas all the time since Halloween, and I've been dying for something with a backbeat." The name tag said she was Tamara. "Need a room?" She smiled prettily despite crooked teeth.

"If you have one."

"You're in luck, we were no vacancy until five minutes ago, but I just got done entering a cancellation. How many nights?"

"One." He surreptitiously crossed his fingers, hoping the cost of a night's lodging wasn't prohibitive. Moon Face and Clay had missed some of the stash, but there wasn't much left, and he still needed to buy a few things.

His luck was in. The amount she asked for was within his means. He handed over cash, and she seemed a bit surprised but took it in stride. While she got the key ready he filled out the information form; for the address he wrote down that of the house on Sandpiper. Not the apartment—he couldn't remember that exact address anymore.

Tamara took the form, seemed to frown slightly. Perhaps she thought it odd that he had no car. "Any bags?"

"No, just this." He gestured to the backpack.

She put a map of the hotel in front of him. "Here's your room, 201. Ocean view, just like it says on the sign. Ice machine's here. Jacuzzi's here. Any questions?"

He asked her where he could find a good restaurant, preferably something that served breakfast at any time, and if there was a drugstore nearby. She told him; he said goodbye and went on his errand.

When he got back, there was a different person behind the desk—an older fellow who didn't even glance up as Daniel entered—but Tamara sat in one of the lobby chairs. Her headphones were draped loosely around her neck, and she held a CD in one hand—Reg Fletcher's album from a few years back, *Glass Eye*.

Tamara stood up when she saw him. "Did you find what you needed?" she asked.

"Yes, thank you." He was careful not to let her see what was in the bag.

"Good. I, uh, don't mean to pry," she said. "But can I ask you something?"

His heart gave a thump; he must have given himself away. Still, he nodded.

She held out the CD. "You're on this, aren't you?"

He'd played on all but one of the tracks, and on the West coast leg of the tour. A career high point for him. Daniel remembered the tour's last night at the Hollywood Bowl—*the freaking Hollywood Bowl!*—a stage he never thought he'd be on. At the end when the band took their bows, he'd seen Sarah there in the front row, holding Jake, who wore hearing protectors, both of them cheering, and he'd blown them a kiss.

"Guilty as charged." No use denying it. What harm could there be? Despite everything, he was pleased.

She pulled the booklet out of the CD, held out a pen. "Could you . . . ?"

"Of course." He tucked the bag under one arm, then took the pen and booklet. This was a rare occasion. Session musicians got all the work and none of the glory.

"You'll think it's weird," Tamara said, "but I always read the liner notes and see who the musicians are. I used to play guitar."

He signed it: *To Tamara: Keep reading the liner notes! Daniel Whitman.*

"Thank you," she said when he handed it back to her. She seemed to regard it the way she'd looked at his check-in information, with a slight frown. As if she doubted its authenticity, or perhaps she was trying to remember something. But the next moment she was all smiles, wished him a good afternoon, and left the lobby.

Room 201 was clean and pleasant. Pale, weathered pine in the bedroom; white tile and a big claw-foot tub in the bathroom. And it indeed boasted an ocean view—quite an enviable one. Daniel regretted not knowing about this place before. It would have made an ideal getaway for a long weekend. Drop off Jake at the Kessler house or with the Reilly grandparents and drive up here for lazy days of beachcombing and reading. Have dinner out, share a bottle of wine in the Jacuzzi, and find out if the four-poster bed was as accommodating as it looked.

He set his backpack down on the bed, then went over to the desk and chair. He took his drugstore purchases out of the bag, putting the legal pad and the envelope on the desk. The package of razor blades he set aside for now.

Daniel sat at the desk with a hotel pen in hand and the legal pad in front of him. For a while he wrote nothing, looked from the blank yellow page to the view of the sea, then back again. He'd thought the note would be easy to write. His reasons were really quite simple. He was just finishing a job that had somehow been left undone.

Yet there were important things to decide. To whom should he send the note? And many important things to say. That he was so sorry for it all. That no one should think they'd failed him; he was the one who'd failed Sarah and Jake and everyone else. That he hoped no one would be angry with him.

At first he thought he might send the note to the Reillys, but then knew who the right person was. *Dear Mick,* he wrote, because Mick was his friend, had been Sarah's friend as well, and was as good as a flesh-and-blood uncle to Jake. He'd been through dark times himself; Daniel knew that even if Mick didn't talk about it. He would understand, and might even be able to forgive. Daniel wrote: *By the time you read this, you'll probably know what's happened.*

It took a long time. It seemed harder than it should have been to find the right words. As the afternoon waned the wastebasket filled with balls of wadded-up paper. From time to time he looked out at the ocean view. The afternoon sun had painted the seascape with a golden hue, and it was a lovely sight, but it was as if it were a photo of a painting, under glass. It didn't touch him; nothing touched him anymore, and nothing would unless he could have his wife and son back. There was only one way to have that—he'd understood that when he'd looked at Clay's gun and felt no fear.

By the time the note was finished, sunset had nearly arrived. He put the note into the envelope and addressed it to Mick, realizing only then that he'd forgotten to buy stamps. He really could do nothing right. He took the pen in hand again and wrote a note to the hotel people: asking their pardon, apologizing for the mess, asking them to mail his note. He hoped they would do it; he hoped that girl Tamara wouldn't be the one to find him. She seemed so nice, and it was bound to be an ugly sight.

Daniel sat at the desk and watched the sun set. He watched the sky turn the deep blue shade of twilight. Strange that this should be the last sunset he'd ever see. Strange that his life should be ending so soon—he was only thirty-seven. He'd never once imagined it ending this way. He'd loved his life and for the most part would not have changed a moment of it. He'd loved his life, and it should have ended with Sarah and Jake. Together.

Wrapped in a cocoon of pleasant warmth. Steam in the air, carrying with it a coppery scent. The pain in his wrists a distant throb, much more bearable now. It had been bad at first, he'd almost balked, then understood that it was the last pain he'd ever have to feel. That had made it much easier.

The metallic scent stronger now. The water warm around him, but inside he was cold, as if his lost blood was being replaced with ice. How much longer? He opened his eyes, tried to raise his head so he could see the picture of Sarah and Jake he'd propped nearby. But his head was too heavy, and he let it fall back against the tub. His eyelids heavy now, too, and he tried to think only about the warmth and the ringing in his head almost like music, something he'd heard long ago, a forgotten lullaby. Soothing. Perhaps this wasn't an ending after all but a beginning.

A voice cut through the sound in his head and the room's silence. "Sweet mother of Christ!" said a man. Then a woman's voice, distantly familiar: "Call 911 and help me get him out of there." He wondered who they were talking about, and then hands seized him roughly, ripped away the warm cocoon. Lying on the floor now, white tiles that looked like ice and felt like it, too, so cold and no warmth left anywhere in the world. If only he could speak he could ask them to put him back into the warm cocoon, but his voice wouldn't obey, and his teeth chattered from the cold. If only he could catch someone's eye. He forced his eyes open to find them blind. Fog had rolled in thickening so fast it turned the world to night, and the voices were gone, too. Nothing left in this place but him, and it was dark here, and cold, and so lonely.

Hours later—he had no idea how many—and he sat in his hospital bed. He'd woken to find his forearms wrapped in stiff white bandages and secured by some sort of restraint. Daniel had wanted to tell the nurse who was in the room, keeping watch, that they needn't have bothered. He felt too tired and numb to get up to any further mischief.

He nodded and made the appropriate responses when the doctor came in and talked to him about how lucky he was, that there seemed to be no major nerve or tendon damage, that he'd be required to spend some time at a psychiatric hospital for observation. The doctor was a friendly sort but just a kid, really, and what did he know about any of it? Every word out of the doctor's mouth meant nothing, for Daniel wasn't lucky: he'd lost the music, so it didn't matter if he'd done damage to his hands, and whether he spent days or months in some bin, it wouldn't fix the wreck of his life.

He was staring out the window without seeing anything, not just because there was nothing to see beyond an anonymous skyline, when the knock came at the door. Daniel turned and was unsurprised to see Tamara from the Marina Inn. She wore black, same as yesterday, but had left aside her makeup; she looked very young. From the way she looked at him he knew she'd been one of the voices he'd heard. One of the people who found him. Saved him.

"Is it OK if I sit down?" she asked, looking from Daniel to the nurse and back again.

The nurse nodded and immediately stood up. She seemed to assume Tamara was a friend. "I'll leave you two alone to talk," she said, and left the room.

Tamara remained standing, looked at Daniel. "It's OK," he said.

She sat down, pulled the chair closer, then pushed it back to its original position. She carried what looked like a case for a laptop computer. "How are you doing?"

He wasn't sure how to answer because he didn't know what he felt. So he said what he did know: "I'm sorry you had to see that. I'd hoped it wouldn't be you."

"Are you mad at me?"

Again he wasn't sure how to answer. He'd thought he'd found the way out, but she'd stopped him, and he honestly didn't know if it was for good or ill that she'd done so. More than anything he felt empty. As if he'd lost something aside from blood, something that couldn't be replenished. "I don't know how to feel about it."

She nodded, as if this was the answer she'd expected. "It wasn't just knowing your name from the liner notes. I'd seen it somewhere else. All day it was nagging me. When I got to class I googled you and . . . I had a bad feeling about things, so I got Bernie to let me in with the passkey when you didn't answer the knock." Tamara looked away. "I understand why you did it."

So she'd read some news story. But she didn't know what it had been like. One of those flares of anger seized him. "No. You don't."

But she did. He saw it now. In her eyes. Strange to be able to recognize someone else's grief. "Who?" he asked gently, to make up for his anger.

"My little brother. Car accident. A long time ago." She fiddled with her necklace and its polytheistic charms, fingered the ankh, then the cross. "There's something else, though. Something you need to see." Tamara pulled the laptop from its case, started it up. "Your friends and your family are looking for you. They want you to come back."

It was the last thing he'd expected. She drew her chair close to him and propped up the laptop. "I wasn't sure if they had wireless in here so I took screen captures. But I tried to get every page. See?"

He saw. Several pictures of him, but he looked right past them, looked at the words. His name and identifying features, height and weight, brown and blue, when he'd last been seen. And below that, the messages. From every Reilly he knew. From Mick and Rachel. From his neighbors on Sandpiper, Mr. Frank and the Cordova family. From the townspeople in Los Cielos: Ariel at the Chez coffeehouse and Mrs. Craig at the Book Barn, Eli the bartender at MacHeath's, and others. Clive his session work agent and Reg Fletcher and Reg's band and other musicians. LCU teachers and some old college friends; Eskimo Sally had written, too, saying that if he needed her, she'd row a canoe from Fiji to California if she couldn't afford a plane ticket. So many messages, and they all said the same thing: *Come home.*

One message in particular caught his eye. From Rachel. *No one blames you for what happened,* she'd written. *No one ever would. Please come home if you can. You're loved, and you're needed.*

His sight blurred; he tried to speak but couldn't. It seemed something had broken inside him. Some poison that had been slowly killing him was now being counteracted. Oh, the antidote had its work cut out for it, and some trace of the poison would always linger, but he might be able to live. He might want to live.

Daniel wanted to thank Tamara for showing him this. But hope and remorse had struck him dumb. He looked at Tamara, and she seemed to understand. "Do you want me to tell them you're all right?" she asked.

He didn't answer right away but looked again at the messages. He knew that if she told them, they'd come and get him. But he needed to heal first—not just his physical wounds but the damage that the poison had done to him. At last he found his voice. "I need to get better first. If something goes wrong, I'll be worse off than I was." There might be no help and no antidote the next time. "I'll be going to another hospital soon," he said. "When I get out, I'll go back."

Tamara nodded. "After I lost my brother, I didn't want anyone around me. I felt like no one would understand and nothing they said could help. That's the worst part. Even when people are there for you, sometimes you can't be around them." She sighed, fingered her necklace again. He saw that among the religious symbols was a circular locket.

"May I?" he asked.

She nodded, opened the locket. A little boy around Jake's age, with Tamara's dark hair and eyes.

"I'm sorry," he said.

"Thank you." She closed the locket. "What hospital are you going to?"

He tried to remember the name. "Saint Jude's."

Tamara smiled in her off-kilter way. "You'll be all right there. My mom was there for a couple weeks, after . . ." Her smile went away, she looked at him keenly. "I have some of your things. The pictures, and your wallet. I can bring those to you tomorrow. Should I throw away the letter?"

His letter to Mick. There wasn't a need for it now. No reason for her not to throw it away, but he said, "If you could put it somewhere safe. I'll come by the hotel when I get out and say hello, you could give it to me then."

"I will. And I'll print these messages out, bring that to you when I bring your wallet." Tamara put her laptop in her case and stood up. "I'll see you."

"Tamara." It was important to say her name. "I'm sorry. And thank you."

That night he dreamed he was walking—not on the beach, he heard no sound of waves. In the dark, no moon or stars to light his way. Yet he somehow knew that if he took one more step, and the next, and the next, something would appear to guide him. It would be some tiny candle flame, so small that it might go unnoticed. But it would be there, as long as he kept searching.

Chapter Twelve

Later, when Daniel told people about those lost months, he rarely mentioned Saint Jude's. He was not ashamed of having been a patient there—he had needed help, and that's where he had gotten it. But some people seemed to think he should have been ashamed of it. And some thought the place had been some horrific bedlam out of bad horror movies. It wasn't, although he was apprehensive when he arrived. The hope Tamara had given him was still fragile, and on the drive to Saint Jude's he sat very still, his hands cool and sweaty and clamped together tightly despite the pain it caused his healing wrists. Perhaps he feared they'd toss him in some nineteenth-century dungeon where the incurable loonies were locked away. And there was the name of the place to consider—his adoptive parents hadn't been churchgoers, but he'd absorbed a smattering of catechism from the Reillys and recalled now that Saint Jude was the patron of lost causes.

He was surprised to see the place. He'd been expecting a generic medical facility, but it was a large, old house that had been renovated. Save for the security gate it might have been a retirement home, with its broad, green lawn and willow trees that reminded him of the Reilly house. There was a wide veranda with wicker chairs; in one chair sat a woman wearing pajamas, a robe, and slippers. She was chatting with another woman who wore a nurse's scrubs and stood leaning on the veranda's rail.

It looked pleasant enough, but he couldn't help his trepidation. His life had gone beyond his control, and the only help for it was to put it in others' hands. He had to take it on faith that their hands would be kind ones. Well, he'd gotten this far on strangers' kindnesses—all those people who'd given him rides and bought him meals, Tamara at the Marina Inn. He might as well go a little further.

The hospital's inside was pleasant as well. He'd been half expecting people to look at him askance or treat him like a criminal, but no one did. Then again, the fiftyish nurse who checked him in had probably seen all manner of sights in her time; the bandages he wore were nothing new to her.

They took him to what was to be his room. A Spartan affair with a bed and a lamp. There was a small dresser, but he had nothing to put in it— they'd provide him with things to wear, and in the meantime his backpack and clothes and wallet would be kept safe for him. He'd asked to keep the photo insert, though, and they'd allowed that. He sat down on the bed and gazed around the room. Up in one corner of the ceiling, a small camera. The room had a door, but it was a thick screen rather than wood—it could not be barred against help. A glance at the windows showed they were plastic, not glass, and had bars. Decorative bars, but bars nonetheless. They knew what sort of person they were dealing with. It was oddly reassuring.

Daniel lay down, intending only to rest for a little while. But he was more tired than he knew—not surprising, for he could hardly recall the last good night's sleep he'd had—and fell deeply asleep straightaway. He woke only once, when the room was murky with twilight, and could not remember where he was or why he was here. For a moment, had trouble remembering *who* he was. But someone was there in no time to give him a shot, and he slept dreamlessly until morning.

Never having been to a place like Saint Jude's, he was unsure of what his doctor would be like. After breakfast in the communal dining room—though he sat apart for now, which no one seemed to mind—he was led to a room with comfortable chairs and a big aquarium. Daniel settled himself in one of the chairs and watched the fish glide around their silent world.

He wouldn't have been surprised to see the ghost of Sigmund Freud come in, or perhaps Jung. But the person who walked in was a woman, probably in her midfifties. A handsome brunette, she reminded him of Rachel—they might have been distant relatives.

She came up to him. "Mr. Whitman, I'm Dr. Susan Howard." She put a hand on his shoulder; he understood it was in lieu of a handshake, to spare him any strain on his healing wrists. Daniel found the gesture unaccountably touching. At the same time, her name triggered an odd flicker of nostalgia. It must have shown in his face; once she sat down she regarded him and asked, "Have I said something funny?"

"I was going to make the 'Dr. Howard, Dr. Fine, Dr. Howard' reference, but you probably get that a lot."

To his relief, she smiled. "Actually, you're the first this month. The Three Stooges aren't the cultural touchstone they once were, sad to say." Her face became more serious, though there was still a trace of a smile in her eyes. She held a folder—his file, presumably—in her hands but didn't look at it. Instead she looked at him.

There was something about her gaze that left him unsettled. He had the feeling she could *see* him—not just his outward appearance but his mind. Maybe even more than that?

Before he had a chance to let that idea distress him, the intensity of her look faded. She spoke; her voice was low and though not loud, carried well. "I know it's an adjustment, coming here. Are you comfortable so far?"

"With the place, yes. With this . . ." He looked around the room, back at her. "I'm not sure."

"Why so?"

The doubts that had been creeping in over the last couple of days were in full force. "I'm afraid it's all for nothing. It won't change what's happened." That was true. Nothing they did here, no treatment or pill, no words no matter how kind from this doctor, would change it.

He expected denial, but she said, "You're right. We can't change what's happened. No one can. What we can do is help you find your way. If help is what you want."

For a moment he was tempted to say that what he wanted no one here could give him. But then, nothing could give him what he wanted—the past reversed, the dead resurrected. Escape had brought no relief; isolation had only made grief fester. His wrists ached, and the stitches itched, but what troubled him now was the dark loneliness he'd sunk into—was that what he'd been chasing after?

He made himself think of what Tamara had shown him. The messages from his friends and family. He owed them a return. And now that he knew they didn't blame him, he yearned to see them again. To go home.

"Yes," he said. "That's what I want."

She asked him to tell her why he was here. That struck him as strange, for she had his file right there. But he spoke, haltingly at first, unused to talk after his long isolation. Told Dr. Howard the whole story, and she sat, listening. When the tale was told he again felt that sensation of poison being drained from him, and when he looked at Dr. Howard and saw her regarding him with the same keen compassion as before, the spark of hope in him flared a little bit brighter.

He expected Dr. Howard to ask him why he'd cut his wrists, or why he was so far from home. He went into their session the next day full of dread at having to explain these things, not least because he couldn't think of an answer that didn't make him look guilty or crazy.

But Dr. Howard asked him to tell her about Sarah and Jake. He started to tell her about the tree and how he could have changed things had he been there. "No," she said. "I'd like to know about *them*. Can you tell me?"

He complied. Reluctantly, for he knew the memories would hurt. And they did. At first. He told her about meeting the Reilly family and how they'd welcomed him in a way his adoptive family never had. For five years he spent as much time next door as he could. Martin was his first friend among the children, and Daniel doted on baby John, who sometimes was left in the dust by his older siblings; Daniel was the one who made sure John got his fair share of treats and let him tag along on trips to the park and the beach. Yet Sarah was his friend, too, probably because she was a tomboy who preferred to climb trees and catch lizards with her brother while the twins Amy and Theresa occupied themselves with the Easy-Bake Oven. It was one of those memories that had become a tableau in his mind: him and Sarah and Martin on a blanket under the willow tree reading comic books or *The Chronicles of Prydain* while John scribbled in the coloring books Daniel had brought over for him; a beat-up old boom box played the local classic rock station, and as the afternoon grew hot Kate brought out Kool-Aid and Fig Newtons for them. When he was twelve his family moved to Riverside; he'd been only half joking when he said he should stay behind at the Reilly house. It wasn't as if the parental units would have noticed, and Victoria would have been glad to be rid of him. But he'd gone, and it had not been as bad as he'd feared—the Reilly kids wrote, he managed to meet up with them at Disneyland once or twice, and Kate sent him presents and several packages filled with cookies and candy each Christmas. But that old magic had never really come back until, of all times, Uncle Jacob passed away.

Daniel had known for years that Uncle Jacob hadn't been well, but the end itself had come quickly, too quickly for the Reillys to let Daniel know. But they'd invited him to the wake. By then Daniel was starting his senior year in high school and had his license. Rather than ask permission from the parental units, who paid less attention to him than ever, he simply left a note saying he'd be gone for a few days, wheedled a friend into loaning him a car, and took off for Torrance. He'd felt guilty on arriving, happy to be back where he belonged but sad about the reason, but the warm welcome he received banished all guilt from his mind. Which was fortunate because it left him absolved and free to bask in the realization that Sarah had transformed from a gawky tomboy into a beautiful girl. But still the same Sarah—the first thing she did was hug him and thank him for coming, and then she made fun of his tie. That evening they'd sat in the hammock, drinking the wine coolers Kate let them have on the condition that neither of them drove anywhere that night, and talked. About the old days. About Uncle Jacob. About how school was going, where they were heading for college. Sarah talked about the colleges on her list—no Ivy League, the Reillys couldn't afford it—and asked about his list. He hadn't thought much about it yet, and his parents hadn't thought to remind him that time was approaching. But he made a mental note of Sarah's list and later on applied to any of them that offered a music major.

After the wake he was making ready to leave when Hugh and Martin came over, lugging milk crates full of record albums. "Jacob wanted you to have these," Hugh said. He and Martin ignored Daniel's protests and loaded the crates, all ten of them, into Daniel's borrowed car. Then it was just he and Sarah standing by the car, and he'd protested one last time, said, *I'm not family.* And she said, *You are. But only a little, which is good because I want us to go on a date next time you visit.* He knew then he'd do better than that, by hook or by crook he'd go to the same school so they could be friends even if the date didn't work out. He'd never forget the first sight of her on the LCU campus, sitting on a bench by a tacky modern art fountain, wearing her Austen 3:16 shirt—how she'd smiled when she'd seen him.

He told Dr. Howard about Jake. He and Sarah had held off on having a child until both their careers were established—in the early days of their marriage there had been more than a few breakfast cereal dinners when they were strapped for cash, though they never went hungry. (Also, Kate had a knack for showing up at their door every few weeks with casseroles or with "extra" bags of groceries.) But there was more to it—he'd worried that he'd treat a child with the benign neglect his parental units had shown him, treat it the way a spoiled child treats a pet whose novelty has worn off. He'd confided this fear to Mick once, when Mick was visiting from New York. It was strange to see his friend's face, usually almost preternatural in its calmness, get a look of sadness that was somehow childlike. *You won't act that way. How do I know? Because you're worrying about it. If you weren't worrying about it, that might be a problem. You'll do fine.* And he had. While there were many things he was unsure of, one thing he did know was that his son knew he'd been loved; Jake had never had to wonder, as Daniel always had, why he'd been given up, why his adoptive parents did not care for him, and when the Reillys would come to their senses and push him away as well.

Late at night after one of these early sessions, and Daniel lay awake. He wondered when Dr. Howard would ask him why he'd run away, and then realized she'd been asking this, and he'd been telling her, all along.

He didn't have to wonder if the talks were helping. Many nights he thought of his losses and grieved—the sorrow was painful, but there was something clean about it. He allowed himself to think of Sarah and Jake, and to remember. Such a relief to finally be able to mourn.

He expected to find help at Saint Jude's, and he found it. He also found two things he did not expect.

He discovered the first thing several days after his arrival. Daniel was beginning to feel at ease with the place. Every day seemed a bit easier. He was in the common room, trying to find something in the woefully inadequate selection of books, when one of the nurses summoned him in to an exam room.

The doctor, a portly fellow with a breezy manner, removed the bandages and checked on the stitches. He made no comment about how the cuts had gotten there but treated them like any other injury. "Healing up nicely," the doctor said. "Any pain?"

"Not anymore. There's some itching."

"That's to be expected. We'll probably take the stitches out in a few days. But first let me do this. Hold out your hands." The doctor removed a pencil from his pocket and ran the tip of it over the backs of Daniel's hands, over his fingers. "Any place you can't feel that?"

"Here," said Daniel. "The left hand, the little finger."

"OK. Now try touching each fingertip to the thumb, one at a time. Very good. You play piano, don't you? I can always tell."

Everything seemed to be working well, save one thing that Daniel had noticed over the last few days—along with some numbness, a peculiar stiffness to the small finger on his left hand. "Is that permanent?"

The doctor regarded it for a moment, asked Daniel to do the finger exercise again. "Hard to tell. There's been some damage to a tendon or a nerve. I'll give you some exercises you can do, just take it easy at first. And there's a piano here, did you know? I'll talk to Dr. Howard about that."

Yes, he knew about the piano in one of the rec rooms. It was used infrequently at best, and every time he saw it he hungered to feel that smooth, cool ivory again.

The next day he sat down at the piano, Dr. Howard standing close by. She watched as he pushed back the cover, laid his fingers on the keys. Oh, he'd missed this. Yet he was afraid to play, afraid that he'd hear that same off-tone, off-rhythm jangle that had put an end to the session with Reg Fletcher. He struck a few notes, and it was amiss but not his doing. "It needs to be tuned."

Dr. Howard smiled. "I'll take your word for it. I'm tone-deaf."

"Really?"

"If you'd heard me sing, you'd be in no doubt."

He started in on scales at first, taking it easy, getting reacquainted. Strange that it should come back to him so easily. He began to play songs then, nothing too complicated. There were mistakes and missed notes, but they didn't matter; he recognized them as blunders that came from lack of practice. Daniel closed his eyes, opened his mind to the music, and forgot everything else. The music was a drug, better than any liquor or dope, and when he finally stopped, his hands aching and his scars itching, he was dazed. His pleasure collapsed into dull disappointment; for a few moments he'd almost believed he'd open his eyes and find himself back in the house on Sandpiper and that he'd turn around to see Sarah standing in the doorway, smiling at him.

But there was only this empty room—Dr. Howard had left, he knew not when—and no one to listen to him. He closed the piano cover and left, went to the other rec room where the sounds of the TV and patients' chatter helped him put the music out of his mind.

Yet he couldn't keep away, and the next day went back to it. He'd never thought he would want to play again, not if he couldn't have Sarah and Jake to hear it, but he needed the music as much as he needed his talks with Dr. Howard and the medication they'd put him on, as much as he needed sleep and food. Daniel soon spent as much time in that room as the hospital's schedule and his healing wrists would permit.

And that was how he found the second unexpected thing: a friend.

He hadn't done more than engage in small talk with the other patients so far. He felt uncharacteristically shy—in the old days he'd chat with people in the grocery store lines about the high price of tomatoes and the ridiculous tabloid headlines. But he felt unable to make conversation those first days at Saint Jude's; the people for the most part seemed the same as he, which paradoxically made him more nervous. Who knew what pain lurked underneath the exterior and what he might say that would inadvertently deepen that pain and set somebody back?

One afternoon he was playing; he'd left scales behind some days ago and was now into songs. Old favorites that brought back memories with nostalgia and melancholy, bittersweet. He thought of Uncle Jacob, who had set this in motion not just with his lessons but with the music he'd introduced Daniel to so long ago. Folk, progressive rock, the blues, classical—Uncle Jacob had been nothing if not eclectic.

Daniel wondered where the albums were, now that the house was surely demolished. He shivered—he wanted to go home, but not for the first time he wondered what he'd find there.

He pushed the thoughts out of his mind, played the first song that came to mind. Elton John's "Goodbye Yellow Brick Road." And when the last note had faded there was silence in its wake.

"I liked that song a lot better after I figured out it's about a man whore."

Daniel was taken aback as much by the sentiment as by the voice. He turned and saw leaning in the doorway a fellow probably in his late twenties, with long, lank blond hair and what looked like a Dead Kennedys T-shirt under his standard-issue robe and pajamas.

"I'm serious," the newcomer said. "Listen to the words, man. Fucker's a kept boy, finally got tired of servicing some old broad and putting up with all her shit."

Daniel laughed. It was the first genuine laugh he'd had in months.

The blond guy grinned. "Right? Tell me I'm fuckin-a right."

Daniel found himself grinning back. It reminded him of the time he and Mick were driving somewhere and one of Daniel's mix CDs cued up The Who's "Squeeze Box." Halfway through the song, the Professor said, "I don't think this is just about an accordion."

"Mind if I play some more?" Daniel asked.

"Shit, no, man! I was hopin' you would. I was gonna ask, but I've *seen* you, and you're carrying a fucking heavy load. Didn't want to bother you or anything. I'm Wayne."

"I'm Daniel." They shook hands. "Good to meet you."

How long had it been since he'd talked with a friend? About nothing serious, just the things friends talk about? Too long.

They talked about music mostly. Wayne didn't play any instruments, but he had an appreciation for musicianship, if not always the vocabulary to express it. Rock was his favorite genre, but he liked reggae also, couldn't get into folk but had a surprising recognition for classical music, primarily from movies and Warner Brothers cartoons. He'd been impressed by some of the people Daniel had played with.

"No shit, really?" Wayne asked about one middling-famous person. "What's he like?"

"Kind of a cheapskate. Pays your fee and that's it. Doesn't even spring for coffee or beer or take you out when the album's done," said Daniel.

"Well, that sucks. I shouldn't be surprised. I worked at this Johnny Rockets once, and the worst tippers were always the fancy-dressed people and the hipster douchebags. Best customer was some old fucking geezer, looked like some kind of professor with the tweed coats and shit, but he always said please and thank you and tipped thirty percent. Awesome dude."

They were sitting on the veranda, watching the rain. Ordinarily they'd have been upstairs—by now Wayne had gotten Daniel hooked on *Days of Our Lives*—but the TV was on the fritz. "Just our luck, on Wednesday— that's sex day," lamented Wayne, just in time for Dr. Howard to overhear as she joined them on the veranda.

"Ah yes," she said. "And Friday is cliffhanger day. I haven't watched soaps since they took *The Edge of Night* off the air, but nothing's changed. Wayne, you're wanted on the second floor."

"Whoa. Already?" Wayne bowed to Daniel. "I must dash. See you at dinner, dude."

"Don't be late this time or there'll be nothing but vanilla pudding left for dessert," said Daniel as Wayne headed off to his appointment.

Dr. Howard lingered on the veranda. "I see you and Wayne have hit it off."

"I like him. He reminds me of people I knew in school." Daniel paused, looked at her. "You're surprised?"

She shook her head. "Not really. You two will have a lot to talk about."

The chess set was missing three pawns and the white bishop. They substituted checkers for the pawns and a salt shaker for the bishop. Wayne had never played before but took to the game quickly; he had a knack for seeing patterns and strategic thinking that Daniel, who never cared if he won or lost so long as he had fun playing, lacked.

"Too bad it's not like the wizard chess in those Harry Potter movies," Wayne said as he captured one of Daniel's knights. "Wizard chess fucking owns, man."

Daniel regarded his chess pieces without seeing them. He'd wanted to ask for some time now. What Wayne was doing here. And something else. "Can I ask you something?"

"You want to know why I'm here? Nah, it's OK. Shit, yeah, I'll tell you. We're here for the same reason, you and me."

So that's what Dr. Howard had meant by *you two will have a lot to talk about.*

Wayne casually rolled back his pajama sleeve to show not razor cuts but track marks. Daniel had seen such marks before, but none so fresh as these.

"I'm in narco recovery here. That's why you don't see me around some days. I'm on methadone now, and boy does that stuff fucking suck. Shit, we can put these awesome Hot Wheels on Mars, why can't they make meds that taste like Flintstones vitamins—man those owned, I miss those—and don't block you up so bad. I get cranky if I go too long without taking a shit, and it ain't good for your system, either.

"Ha! I got you smiling. I rule. Guess it's pretty Goddamn funny coming from me, but except for hooch and weed I was straight edge till a few years ago. That's when I met Linda. Oh, she was fucking beautiful, man. Like an angel or a doll, real pale with these big eyes. Wonderful ass, too, best I've ever seen. So I'm ass over teakettle in love with her, and I find out she's into heroin. She snorted it, didn't shoot up, so I didn't catch on at first. Well, that shit was scary, but she kept saying, 'Come on, Wayne, try it, you won't believe how good it is.' Then she started saying how it was so sad that she had to get stoned by herself, that if I did it with her we'd be so much closer. So I did it. You want to know how good that shit is? Don't ever fucking try it, that's how good it is. There's only been one thing better than it, but I'll get to that. So one thing leads to another, and I'm trying to keep a lid on the habit and all I can get are shit jobs, so we're living in this fucking dump. Linda didn't care but, man, I loved her, and I wanted to set us up someplace nice. I knew that shit wouldn't happen until I got clean, but Linda didn't want to, and she'd say that if I did, it was like I was leaving her. So after a while this friend of hers from high school, Jack, crashes with us, and it turns out he's a dealer, and pretty soon he's got Linda dealing, too. I'm scared, man, because some of the customers can be really fucking twisted, and I'm scared Linda's gonna get robbed or some dude's going to mess with her, and then I'd have to kill him, and I don't want to do that. Even junkies got morals, man. So one day someone rats us out, and the cops come. Jack'd moved out by then. Linda's starting to freak cause the stash isn't hidden so good and she doesn't want to get busted. I say I love her and don't worry, and when the shit goes down I tell the cops it's mine, all mine. So they send me to the fucking big house; I got off light because I've never even jaywalked before this, and they put me into rehab, too. So I'm in there trying to get along and not get ass raped, and every week I write to Linda. And she writes back, every week, then every couple weeks, then every month, and by the end she isn't writing at all, and I'm fucking panicking, man. I'm thinking she got busted or OD'd or some guy attacked her. So just before I'm ready to get out this guy who used to hire me for odd jobs and shit comes to visit and tells me Linda's shacked up with Jack now, has been for, I don't know, maybe a month after I went to jail.

"So when I get out I find Linda, and sure enough it's true, and she doesn't even apologize. Just like that. And here I'd been thinking that I was clean, I was going to turn it all around now and give her everything she ever wanted. 'Cept I wasn't one of the things she wanted. So I'm there with forty bucks to my name and no place to live, my parents have fucking disowned me, and I'm sofa surfing with friends or people I thought were my friends—I can't go back to my friends I had in my straight days, 'cause I'm thinking who'd want a broke ex-junkie whose girlfriend dumps him? My Uncle Bob comes by and—no, it's not a joke or anything, he really is my Uncle Bob. Anyway he comes by and tells me he'll help me out if I stay clean and stay in NA and go to church, man. Tells me not to waste my life now that I'm clean and out of jail. And I'm thinking, clean, schmean, I don't think I've ever given less of a fuck about anything in my life, ever. All I want is the old days with Linda back. So I tell Uncle Bob I'll think about it and that night I go to this dealer I know and score as much as I can. I take it to where I'm staying and think about Linda and all the stuff that's gone now, and I try to think about what might happen the next day, and it's like looking into a big black hole, just a lot of fucking nothing, you know? So I say, fuck it, I've had enough of this shit, and I cook up and shot the whole thing.

"It feels all right at first, and then I'm laying there, and it's like I'm made out of rock or something. Everything's really fucking heavy, and I can't move except for, you know, breathing and blinking, shit like that. I'm starting to get scared because this is no Goddamn fun at all, and then one of the roomies comes in; I didn't think he would till later. So he freaks the fuck out and calls 911, and the whole time it's like I'm sinking into a grave or something. I'm going down down down into the dark, and for a while I'm scared, and then it's like the world's way far away from me, but I'm not scared, just kind of sad, man. Like, is that what my whole life was? That's it? Thinking how fucking pathetic it was and how I'd do things different if I had the chance, and wondering if my mom and dad will miss me, or my Uncle Bob. And then it's like everything just stops. Next thing I know I'm watching myself in the emergency room, and these doctors are all messing around with CPR and other stuff, and I'm wondering why the hell they're bothering. I'm fine. I'm better than fine. I'm free, man. You don't know what a drag it is carrying around your body until you don't have to.

"I get this feeling like, yeah, this is kind of interesting to watch, but what's going to happen next? It was kind of like being a little kid, going to Grandma's house for Christmas, feeling like ... what's the word?

146

Anticipation. That's it. What happens next is I go kind of zip down this tunnel, and that's when I saw the light, and oh man. Never, ever did I see anything like that. Take the most beautiful thing you ever saw and the best feeling you ever had and multiply that by a hundred, and that's what it is. And it loved me. Me! Fucking loser that I am. And I was thinking, oh man, this is so wonderful, this can't be for the likes of me. And it's like I don't hear it, but I feel it, like God saying, 'It's OK, Wayne, you made mistakes, but I still love you.' I'm not saying it right. But kind of like that. And I'm thinking, well, it's kind of too bad that I can't fix any of those mistakes, and I'm sorry that my life was so lame, but here I am now, and everything's better, and I hear something like, 'No, you still have work to do,' and then—BAM! I'm back in my lame-ass body, and all these doctors are looking like, 'Oh ho, look at us, we brought you back, and don't we rule.' And when I could talk again I said, 'What the fuck did you do that for?' I was super pissed for a while, but then I got to thinking that it was right. I've got work to do. Not sure what it is, but I know I'll figure it out." Wayne took a long swig of orange juice, then pointed at Daniel's wrists. "How about you? You see any awesome shit like that?"

Daniel shook his head. "No. I guess I wasn't far gone enough." Nothing but darkness and cold, so lonely. He shivered as an unpleasant thought struck him. "Or maybe I was headed to the other place."

"You?" Wayne guffawed. "No way. You've got a good soul. I can see it. Ever since then I can see stuff about people."

"What? Their future?"

"Like *The Dead Zone*? That movie kicks ass. Walken fucking *owns*, man. Nah, not that. I can tell if someone's got a good soul. Like some people seem nice on the outside, but you can see that they're just doing nice shit because it'll make them look good, not because they want to be nice. Or like my Uncle Bob who's all square and has this big stick up his ass, but he really does love me and wants to help me. He's paying for me to be here, you know. If it weren't for him I'd be stuck in some shitty place, not here with awesome people like Dr. Howard."

"She's got a good soul." Daniel already knew that.

"Hell yes. And you do, too. You're just lost. It's OK. It'll work out, you'll see." Wayne looked at the chess pieces. "Castle captures the white salt shaker. Check. Your move."

Late that afternoon, while Wayne was in rehab, Daniel went to the rec room. He sat at the piano but didn't play yet. His head was full of the things Wayne had told him, full of his own story. *You're just lost.* That was true. He'd been lost since the day he'd gotten off the plane and walked into the conference room where the Reillys had been waiting with their awful news.

He closed his eyes and for once did not try to fight back against the memories but let them have free rein. His hands went to the keyboard seemingly of their own accord. Music filled the room, a melody that accompanied the memories. Halting at first, then strong and sure.

Sometime later he stopped. The notes rang through his head, the melody etched there now forever. He didn't need to write it down. His hands ached, and his eyes were wet.

"Daniel," Dr. Howard said softly.

He turned to look at her. As he turned he saw the clock—he'd missed their afternoon session. Before he could apologize she asked, "Whose song is that? I've never heard it before."

"It's mine." The first thing he'd created in years. He could still hear it in his mind; his hands felt the power of its creation. He thought it might even be good.

"It's so . . ." She paused, regarded him. "What is it about?"

"About me."

"I thought so."

The days turned into weeks. On a morning when the willows were sparkling with frost, Dr. Howard told Daniel he'd be ready to leave in a couple of days.

"Of course, you still need to see a doctor," she said. "You can think of us as intensive care, but you need someone for the long term. I've referred you to a doctor down in Los Cielos. Duncan Levinson—I've known him for a while, and I think you two will be well suited to each other."

Daniel got up and looked out the window. For the last week he'd been truly hungering to go home. He missed his friends and his in-laws, and he wanted nothing more than to meet Mick and Rachel at MacHeath's Tavern where they could eat some sweet potato fries and just be with one another. Yet now . . . he'd gotten used to Saint Jude's. Everything here was safe. If he got lost, there were people like Dr. Howard to help him find his way back. "I'm not sure I'm ready."

"If you said you were, I'd know you weren't." She stood up and put a hand on his shoulder, the way she had at their first session, though his wrists were long since healed. "You have people there who will help you. You know that now. And you can always call me. I'll want to hear from you and find out how you're doing."

"What do I do when it gets bad?"

"Play your music. I've heard the songs you're writing. Creativity is a powerful medicine. And when that's not possible, it helps to have a talisman. Something, whether it's an object or a thought or a prayer, that lets you hold on when things are bad."

Something to keep him from getting lost. "I understand."

A couple of days later, Wayne said, "You out of here?"

"Looks that way." Daniel had his backpack on, full of his belongings and a few new things—his referral papers to Dr. Levinson down in Los Cielos, his medication. "How much longer for you?"

"About another week or so."

"Where will you be after that? I'll want to drop you a line."

Wayne shook his head. "Not sure yet. Write to me at my Uncle Bob's place for now—he can send it on if I'm not there. Here." He scribbled an address down on a scrap of paper. "If you turn those songs into a record, send one my way."

"I will."

"Good stuff, man, even if it does make me weepy as fuck."

Daniel laughed. "I'm going to miss you. Come down and see me any time. *Mi casa es su casa.*"

Wayne high-fived him. "*Vaya con Dios*, daddy-o. Shit, I've been hanging around you too long, I'm even talking like you. Get out of here."

They said goodbye, and Daniel went to the ride that was waiting for him. Wayne called out one last thing to him; he smiled and waved back his reply.

"What did he say?" the driver asked.

"He said, 'Don't get lost,'" Daniel replied.

The driver shook his head, apparently figuring it was something crazy people said to one another. "Where to?"

The lobby of the Marina Inn looked sparse without the Christmas decorations, but Tamara looked much the same. He'd called to let her know he'd be coming, and she smiled shyly when she saw him.

"I'm glad you came back," she said. "You look much better now."

"I've still got a long way to go."

"You're going home now?"

He nodded. A long road ahead, and not just in terms of distance.

"Is someone coming to get you?" she asked.

"No, I'll just get there when I get there." He didn't admit that he still feared no one would come if he called.

"Let me know that you get home safe. I'll worry." Tamara wrote down her address on a sheet of Marina Inn stationery. She glanced around. "Oh, and here. Don't tell anyone. She handed him money—sixty-three dollars and change.

"I can't take your money." Especially after what he'd put her through.

Tamara grinned. "It's not mine. I cleaned all the coins out of our fountain, and that's what it came to. Usually the owner takes it and plays the ponies, but you seem like a surer bet."

"Let's hope so," he said, and they laughed. He leaned down and kissed her cheek. "Thank you." For hope. For his life.

Tamara gave him the things she'd kept for him—his note to Mick, a few odds and ends from his backpack. He put them away, and though she invited him to stay the night, on the house, he wanted to be on his way.

The day was clear and cold. He could smell the sea. At the highway on-ramp he caught a ride. "South," he said. "As far as you can take me."

Chapter Thirteen

He almost didn't make it home.

He should have caught a train and let Amtrak do the heavy work. That option didn't occur to Daniel until he was well on his way, and by then it seemed easier to thumb a ride. But the strangers' goodwill that had helped him on his northward journey seemed to have vanished. Few were willing to pick him up, and fewer were making trips of more than twenty or thirty miles. More than once he wondered if his progress heading south was slower, or if it only seemed that way now that he actually had a destination. It couldn't be helped, so he made the best of it, and made his halting way down the coast.

Night on Highway 101. Ride-wise, his luck had run out shortly after noon. That morning a perky old lady had picked him up, told him he reminded her of her son, and then proceeded to try and sell him Amway for the duration of the ride. Just as he was about to try rolling back his sleeves to see if his scars would shut her up, she stopped at a gas station, and he took the opportunity to escape.

"Be careful of the weather, dear," she trilled as she drove off. She had a point. The sky to the north and west looked like a tidal wave of dark gray. Rain, and a hell of a lot of it. Already he could feel the temperature dropping. Daniel went into the convenience store next door to the gas station and bought a package of gallon-size Ziplocs. He methodically unpacked his backpack and put everything into the plastic bags. Surely he could get another ride before the rain hit, but it seemed best to be prepared, the way his luck was going. His belongings safeguarded against the rain, he went in search of someplace to eat lunch.

Either the storm was faster than he'd reckoned on, or he'd dawdled too long over his Quarter Pounder and fries (he could blame that on the dog-eared copy of *Flowers in the Attic* he'd swiped from Saint Jude's bookshelves, for he'd been reading it over lunch). When he finished eating it was already raining, though not hard. Daniel shrugged, left the book on a table, and walked to the nearest highway on-ramp in search of a ride.

But no one stopped, and as the afternoon waned, the air grew colder and the rain came down harder. He'd spend half an hour at one on-ramp, holding his thumb out for a ride that never came, then walk to another one, not because he thought his chances would be better but because motion eased the cold settling into his bones. His feet in their sodden canvas sneakers felt like chunks of ice.

When night fell he decided to chance it and thumb a ride on the highway. It was illegal, but if the cops busted him, they might at least put him up for the night; a jail cell wasn't the Hilton, but it would be reasonably warm and dry. But there were no cops, scarcely any drivers at all. For ages he walked south, getting more and more discouraged as headlights came and went without slowing, much less stopping. Only the fact that there were no pay phones to be seen kept him from dialing area code 760 and saying, *Hey, Professor, it's me. I'm on the 101 somewhere between Bumfuck and East Jesus; any way you can come and get me?* That, and the fear of getting no answer but the click of a broken connection.

153

A flare of headlights, a douse of cold runoff, and when Daniel wiped the water out of his eyes he saw an eighteen-wheeler truck creeping along the highway. The passenger door flew open, seemingly of its own accord, and a voice from inside the cab shouted, "Get in if you want, I'm in a hurry!"

Needing no further invitation, Daniel ran to the truck and hoisted himself in. The truck sped off before he was scarcely inside the cab, and if he hadn't had a good grip on the seat belt, he'd have tumbled out. Gaining his balance, he flung himself into the seat without bothering to take off his backpack and pulled the door closed. The truck accelerated with a roar, the force of it pushing Daniel back against the seat. He tried to ignore the queasy feeling he got as the truck fishtailed on the wet road, and quickly put on his seatbelt.

"Where you headin'? I'm bound for San Diego and I'm really Goddamn late so I'm not stopping. Figure you can talk, help keep me awake; if I take any more NoDoz my frickin' heart's gonna explode. Put on the radio if you want."

The words were said in a monotone rush, and Daniel felt a chill that had nothing to do with the rain. He looked at the driver's hands—as he'd guessed, white-knuckle tight. Speed freak. He wondered how many pills the guy had popped, how long he'd been without sleep.

To take his mind off it, Daniel put on the radio. He recognized the song instantly and for a moment relaxed. The Grateful Dead's "Brokedown Palace." One of his old favorites. Perhaps it was a good omen. He felt in need of a good omen.

"Goddamn hippie shit. I hate that hippie shit, don't you?" The driver snapped the radio off, turning the knob so hard it flew off, landed somewhere on the floor.

Daniel actually liked that hippie shit a lot, but he wasn't about to say so. Glancing down where the radio knob had vanished, he saw a mess of energy drink cans and NoDoz boxes. The oddest feeling came over him: he was afraid. It had been a long time.

Through the headlights and the rain Daniel could just make out a rest stop sign. One mile ahead. "You could let me out there. I've got some stuff to . . ."

But the sign went by in a blur. How fast was this guy going? "Toldya, I ain't stopping." Daniel was afraid to look at the speedometer, just as he was afraid to see the trucker's eyes; the pupils would be black moons. Instead he looked out the window, though he could see nothing for the rain and the night. And all that lay out there were bluffs of sandstone and a sharp drop to the ocean.

Daniel sat, one hand holding on to a backpack strap, the other on the armrest of the truck's passenger door. Let there be a roadblock, a fender bender, anything that would slow traffic down. The truck didn't have to come to a complete stop, even ten miles an hour would do. He'd take his chances, as long as he was out of here.

But there was nothing, only the nearly deserted highway. Well, maybe that wasn't so bad. If there were no other cars, how much trouble could the driver get into? Daniel let himself relax a little bit. He just had to wait for the caffeine in this guy's system to do its work, and there'd be a stop to piss. He watched the road, glancing from time to time at the driver, who seemed all right in spite of his too-fixed stare at the road and his death grip on the truck's wheel.

When it happened, it was quick. "Fucking shit!" The driver stomped the brake, trying to avoid something in the road that Daniel never saw. A sickening sensation like free fall as the truck swerved, jackknifed, seemed on the brink of tipping over. From the back of the truck was a sound of scraping metal, then a flat snapping sound. The guardrail—Daniel grimaced, knowing that the bluffs would be like mush in this rain, nothing left to support a truck this heavy. For a moment they were still, but before Daniel could get control of his shaking limbs, undo his seat belt, and leap from the truck, it slid backward down the bluff toward the rocks and ocean below.

Daniel braced himself for a hard landing—from a distance he heard the driver scream and swear. Heard the engine's roar, the way the dinosaurs must have sounded as they sank in the La Brea Tar Pits. It didn't seem to be real, any of it. *Like this? Now? But I was on my way home. I was going to—*

The smashing sound of impact, and the world went upside down. Daniel's head hit the passenger side window; he had time to see the starry shape of the cracked glass lit up by lightning, had time to note how pretty that looked, and the world went away.

Wake up.

Something wrong.

Daniel. Wake up.

Sarah calling him. He fought to wake up, wondering vaguely why it was so cold. Raining. He must have left the window open. Needed to get up and shut it. If he could only wake up, he'd do that. He'd—

DANIEL!

He jerked, let out a startled cry. Not just Sarah's voice, not just that she was screaming, but her voice was *in* his head, in his *mind*. Not physically painful but so loud that he clutched at his head, and that *was* painful as he touched where he'd hit the window. It came back to him then.

The truck had spun out and wrecked, gone down the bluff, and he was alive but in what sort of shape. Daniel shook his head to clear it and looked around.

The truck lay on the driver's side; all the windows had broken, and rain poured in. No sign of the driver; he was dead or fled. The only light was from the truck's dashboard and the headlights that glared out into the rain with idiot brilliance. Daniel couldn't hear his own breathing, it was drowned out by the sound of the storm. Waves crashed on the rocks where the truck had come to rest. He saw empty energy drink cans bobbing in the water.

Sarah screamed his name again, not so loud this time, but her cry and a wave that doused him brought him to full awareness. Now he heard the sounds of straining metal, felt shudders as the truck began to lose its uneasy grip on the rocks.

He fumbled for the seat belt, his fingers cold and clumsy, and as he pressed the release button the truck slid into the water.

The headlights and dashboard stayed lit for just a moment after the truck went under, then they winked out into blackness. *Now it's dark.* The truck hit the bottom, and he wriggled free of the seat belt, struck out toward what he hoped was the surface. He swam blind, with nothing besides the lessening pressure in his ears to tell him he was headed in the right direction. It wasn't enough—he couldn't be that deep so close to shore. He tried not to think about steep drop-offs or that he might be swimming at an angle instead of straight for the surface; he tried to ignore the demand for air that made his lungs ache and the cold that made his limbs sluggish. Daniel clamped one hand over his nose and mouth, swam harder than he ever had. Dying at the Marina Inn would have been one thing; dying here in the cold darkness where he'd never be found was much different. His lungs seemed to be on fire now, his strokes were panicked thrashings. Not now, not this way—

He broke the surface, breathed in a great draught of air that tasted of rain. He'd barely gasped in that breath and another when a wave slammed him. He coughed and gagged, swallowed seawater, and struck out for what he hoped was shore, instinctively following the direction of the waves. Lightning lit up the beach enough for him to see that he was heading in the right direction and was far closer to the shore than he would have thought.

Still, it was a near thing. By the time he was having trouble keeping his head above water, his feet struck bottom. Daniel dug in against the undertow and made his way to shore, crawling the last couple of yards. Once on shore he let out a grateful sob, embracing the wet sand and rocks like a lover before he had to lurch onto hands and knees and retch up what felt like a quart of seawater.

Daniel lay on the beach, too cold and weary to move. The rain poured down, a wave occasionally washed over his legs. He knew he had to get up and get someplace dry and warm, but he couldn't. He felt half-frozen, and so tired. Besides, where would he go? He was on a deserted beach with nothing in sight; no lights for miles around, not even the moon, and he couldn't see his way to the bluffs, let alone find a way to get up them. *Please. I need help.* Sarah had helped him, screamed his name and roused him to consciousness; if she hadn't, he would have still been dazed when the truck went under. *Please. Help me. I have to get home.*

"Give me your hand."

The voice startled him nearly as much as Sarah's had. But it wasn't in his head—he *heard* it. A man's voice, low yet clearly audible over the storm.

"I'll help you. Give me your hand."

There was something vaguely familiar about the voice, yet he was sure he hadn't heard it before. Perhaps it was the quality of the voice— almost fatherly. Or the way he'd imagined a father should speak. It wasn't the voice of Tom Whitman, nor quite the voice of Hugh Reilly.

Blinded by darkness and rain, he reached out with one hand. The owner of the voice took his hand, helped haul him to his feet. Only now did Daniel wonder if he'd been hurt in the truck's wreck, but he'd been able to swim, and he was able to walk. His backpack hung heavy on him; he hadn't thought to leave it behind. No wonder he'd almost drowned.

A lightning flash gave him a glimpse of his benefactor. A tall man, bearded, wearing a long coat and a dripping fedora. With his right arm he supported Daniel, with his left he carried a stout walking stick. When the lightning had gone, the world was in darkness once more, yet the man seemed to know where he was going; he never once stumbled, and kept secure hold of Daniel's arm.

"We'll get you someplace warm," the man said. "You can't stay here, the cold would kill you. And if the tide caught you, you wouldn't last five minutes. My name's Pete, by the way."

Daniel stammered out his name. His jaw was clenched against the cold, and he had trouble speaking. He felt half in a dream. Nothing seemed real, save for the arm he held on to. He could feel the wet tweed of the man's coat, the arm beneath the coat, what felt like a wristwatch or a bracelet.

They walked a short way down the beach, then to the bluff. No stairs for them to climb, but Pete guided them up a footpath, the sort worn by hikers and beachgoers, a twisty trail through the wild anise and brambles. Daniel thought of other beaches and other paths like this one. A beach in Santa Barbara: he and the Reilly kids making their way to the shore. Or back in Los Cielos on spring break: him, Sarah, Eskimo Sally, Mick, and Mick's then-girlfriend Holly all with boogie boards and surf mats. The warmth of the sun, the scent of sunscreen, the laughter of the people he loved. It was all so far away, and he'd never get back to it.

He wasn't aware of speaking, but he must have given his thoughts voice, for Pete said reassuringly, "You'll get back. You're nearly home. Help's close."

Up and up the bluff. Through what looked like a campsite closed for the season. Back on the highway, and Daniel instinctively put a thumb out. "No," said Pete. "Just a little farther."

"I can't," Daniel said. "It's too hard."

"You've come this far. Just a little more." They walked, and then Pete said, "Do you see?"

Glittering like a bright jewel on the dark highway was a diner. Only two cars in the parking lot, but the place was open. It would be warm there. It looked like . . . well, like that heaven light Wayne had described.

Pete laughed. "Oh yes, rather like that."

Daniel walked into the diner, hearing Pete call out something, some word of farewell perhaps. Strange, he couldn't recall letting go of Pete's arm. He blinked in the bright lights. The diner's owner was talking, but Daniel barely heard him. He started to ask where Pete had gone but stopped. He had to sit down. He was so tired. The world was swimming, everything bleaching out to white, then to gray. He felt the world spin, tilt, and he fell away from it into darkness.

He'd have the dream only once in his life. That was enough.

He was back in the wrecked truck, and this time Sarah didn't call his name. He woke as the water was closing over his head, had no time for a breath before he went under. The lights went out, and he sank, full fathom five and no way he'd ever make it to the surface, and none of that mattered because he couldn't get free. The seat belt wouldn't release, and the more he pulled against the seat belt straps, the tighter they bound him. Time and breath ran out, and when the pain was gone and his limbs ceased their struggling—when it was over—he waited for release or oblivion, and neither came. No hell either, but he realized that this was hell, to be imprisoned in this body forever. No voice to call with and no one to hear him, yet he called out: *Help me. Sarah. Jake. Someone. Please.*

"Help me." Daniel looked for something or someone familiar, but there was nothing; he was lost again, and what if there was no being found this time?

A gentle hand on his shoulder. "Sarah." He sat up and held her close, repeated her name.

"I'm not her," said a voice, and it was true. The voice wasn't Sarah's, this person didn't feel like Sarah, her scent was not Sarah's. "Everything's all right."

She was just saying that. It wasn't true. "No, not ever."

"You'll be all right," she said. "You're safe now," she said, but he didn't believe her. He could tell she didn't believe it, either.

She sang to him.

Her voice was untrained, shaky. Yet there was meaning in her voice and what she sang that had not been in her words. This she believed in.

Whereto should I express
My inward heaviness?
No mirth can make me fain,
Till that we meet again.

Do way, dear heart, not so.
Let no thought you dismay.
Though you now part me from,
We shall meet when we may.

She sang, and he knew her for another lost soul. Her voice spoke of loneliness and of hope. Faint and fragile, but hope nonetheless.

Then woe is me, poor child, for thee,
And ever mourn and say;
For thy parting, neither say nor sing,
By, by, lully, lullay.

She stroked his hair, and her touch was not Sarah's, but it was welcome nonetheless. Daniel closed his eyes, let his mind sink into her songs the way a body sinks into a warm feather bed. Safe. He'd be safe as long as she kept singing.

He woke to find himself on an old army cot. Wool blankets, slightly musty but delightfully warm, covered him, and a space heater ticked close by. He saw a curtain that seemed to be made of flour sack dish towels stitched together. Behind him was a set of shelves crammed full of restaurant supplies: boxes of pancake mix, salt and flour; jugs of cooking oil and maple syrup. By the foot of the cot was a small bookshelf with a pair of reading glasses, a lamp, and some beat-up paperbacks that seemed to include everything Ken Follett had ever published.

This is the weirdest bed-and-breakfast I've ever stayed in. It was good to feel his sense of humor returning; it had been gone for too long. His faint smile vanished as he wondered where he was. And whether the woman who had sung to him last night was here.

"'Scuse me." The curtain was yanked aside, and a Latino man in cook's whites casually reached over and plucked a jug of maple syrup from the shelves, barely glancing at Daniel. He left as quickly as he'd come, and Daniel heard him say to someone else, "That guy's awake."

"Good timing," said another voice. Footsteps on the other side of the curtain, and this second voice said, "You all right?"

"I think so," Daniel replied.

The curtain pulled aside again, and the diner's owner stood there. A tall, bald fellow whose white beard had been plaited into braids here and there. He wore cook's whites, had military dog tags around his neck, and held a plastic laundry basket. Inside the basket were Daniel's clothes, neatly folded. "We had to get those wet things off you last night so you didn't get hypothermia," he said. "My old lady took the liberty of doing your laundry—I hope you don't mind."

"Please tell her thank you," said Daniel.

The diner owner nodded. "Get dressed, and I'll make you some breakfast. You look like you could use a good meal." He set the basket down, pulled the curtain back, and left.

Daniel pulled the basket near and picked out some clothes. They'd been laundered, yes, and the old lady had ironed them as well, even the jeans. He dressed and went into the diner's main room. It seemed the breakfast rush was over; there were only a few patrons, and the Latino fellow did the cooking while a buxom woman brought plates and poured coffee. She nodded and smiled at Daniel; perhaps she was the old lady.

The diner owner sat at a booth and gestured for Daniel to join him. Daniel sat, and almost immediately food appeared before him: biscuits and gravy, orange juice, coffee. He fell to at once—he hadn't realized how hungry he was until the food was before him.

"My name's Zack," said the owner. "You gave me a hell of a fright last night. What happened?"

"I'm Daniel. I was hitching a ride last night and got in an accident."

Zack stopped with his coffee cup halfway to his lips. "One of my regulars is in the CHP, told me about an eighteen-wheeler that went off the road and into the drink. Was that it?"

Daniel nodded.

"Jesus, man, you are lucky to be alive. Driver's OK, he managed to bail out, but he didn't say anything about a passenger. You could sue the balls off him—pardon my French—if you wanted."

"I don't care about that," said Daniel. "Right now I just want to get home." He glanced around the diner for the woman who'd sung to him but saw no likely candidates. The patrons were all men, and the buxom waitress's voice wasn't the one he'd heard last night.

"You mind if I ask, were you in the service?"

"You mean the military? No."

Zack pushed his empty coffee mug aside. "I went through your stuff last night trying to figure out what was going on and didn't see anything about that. Still, when you first came in you reminded me of some guys I saw in 'Nam. Guys who'd seen way too much and it was like their bodies were here but their souls had gone someplace else. We called them ghost soldiers."

Ghost soldiers. Daniel shivered. "No, not the service." He told Zack what had happened, from walking into the conference room at San Diego International to how he'd come to stagger into the diner last night.

164

Zack whistled. "You've been through the wringer, and there's no denying that. Go ahead and rest up, crash here another night. It's on the house, and the food, too. I'll see what I can do to help you get home."

Daniel thanked Zack profusely. Not for the first time he wondered how he'd have made it this far if not for strangers' kindnesses and vowed to extend the same kindness to anyone in need of it for the rest of his life. "One more thing," he asked. "The woman. The one who sang to me. Is she still here?"

A deep sigh from Zack. "I thought you'd ask. She's gone. She'd left before I woke up this morning. I think she was a nurse—she knew just what to do when you passed out. She's a redhead, maybe thirty years old. She never told me her name, and she paid cash so I don't have a credit card record. I think she said she was from Arizona. Must have been just traveling through."

"Must have been." Disappointment took away what remained of Daniel's appetite; he'd planned on asking for another helping of biscuits and gravy but instead pushed his plate away. He'd wanted to thank her for her help; he wanted to hear her sing again. He wanted to talk to her. Perhaps he was mistaken, but he'd gotten the feeling she was a bit lost, like him. He thought of what Dr. Howard had said about he and Wayne: *you two will have a lot to talk about.* Daniel shook his head. Probably he was just imagining it—the woman, whoever she was, had just been in the right place and time and had a voice that had touched him. By now she was at some happy suburban home with a husband and two kids and a yard with a white picket fence and had forgotten all about the ghost soldier.

He wouldn't forget about her, even if he never saw her again. She'd given him what Dr. Howard said he had to find—a talisman. He got through that day all right: he let Christiane, Zack's old lady, fuss over him and feed him; he helped out with the dishwashing and fixed the jukebox. But when night came he lay on the cot, unable to sleep, unable to push unwelcome thoughts aside. Most of all he couldn't stop thinking of how Sarah had screamed his name. It was a cry of fear, not for herself but for another, and he'd only heard that tone from her once before—when Jake was three and had dashed into the road. She'd screamed Jake's name, and Jake had been so startled his feet had tangled in each other and he'd fallen onto the edge of the road, instead of straight into the path of Mr. Frank's truck. This should have reassured him—she wanted to save his life—but it didn't. If Wayne was right about what he'd seen after his OD, then Sarah was in a good place now; why didn't she want him there with her? It wouldn't have been a pleasant end, but what was a minute or two of suffering if he could be with her and Jake again?

These were dangerous thoughts to have. He should have stayed at Saint Jude's. Dr. Howard had been wrong—he wasn't ready for this yet. But there was no help for it. He had to be ready for it. Daniel closed his eyes, conjured up the woman's voice, her songs. Peace washed over his mind. He was wondering if the songs were her own or something she'd learned—he didn't recognize the words or the tunes—when he fell asleep.

After the breakfast rush was over, Zack drove Daniel to the Amtrak station. Daniel had his faithful backpack by his feet, and a bag Christiane had packed for him, full of oranges, sandwiches, candy bars, a bottle of ginger ale, and even a couple of paperbacks.

"My buddy Jackson owes me one, he said he'd comp you for the ride down to Los Angeles. After that you'll have to pay. It's not a sleeper, but it's better than what you've been used to, am I right?" Zack said.

"You are, sir."

"Make sure you drop us a line when you get home. Christiane wanted us to drive you down there, and I said, woman, you are nuts. We'd have to close the whole diner down while we did that, and he'll be safe as houses on the train. You'll have to excuse her; she's going through the change, and she gets maternal sometimes."

Daniel smiled. At the Amtrak station he thanked Zack once more for all his help, and soon he was sitting at a window seat, looking out at the coastal view. The train lurched, shuddered, and gathered speed. He'd never been on a train before and was surprised at how quiet it was, save for the rushing click of the wheels on the tracks and the occasional announcement of a stop ahead or that refreshments were available.

Almost home. He felt anticipation and dread. It would never be the same as it had been before, and not just because Sarah and Jake were gone. Everything was going to change, and not all for the better. But it was home, and it was where he belonged. Daniel leaned his head back against the train's seat. The clickety-clack of the wheels soothed him. He thought of Jake and Sarah—he could do that now. He thought of Los Cielos—the sweet ocean breeze and all the places there he loved. He thought of his friends and family and of how good it would be to see them; he hoped they wanted to see him again.

Winter Roses (Part One)

Chapter Fourteen

Rachel stood in the Reilly living room, watching the siblings and biting her lip so she wouldn't laugh.

It shouldn't have been funny. Outside on the porch Daniel was talking with Kate and Hugh. The Reilly parents had been waiting on the porch when she and Daniel and Mick had arrived in their two-car caravan. That in itself had been odd; Rachel had assumed they'd all ride up to Torrance together, but this morning Daniel had asked if they could drive separately—in case he stayed overnight, he'd said, but from the way he'd looked when they'd seen Hugh and Kate waiting on the porch, Rachel thought it might be in case things didn't go well.

She couldn't tell how it was going because she couldn't see. There was a small window that gave a view onto the porch, and now the four siblings were jockeying for position, whispering at one another: *let me see, what do you think Mom's saying, my turn now, move your ass.* John was the one to make this last remark, which Rachel thought was a bit inappropriate for someone in training to be a man of God.

At last Amy, always the least competitive of the siblings, gave up and sat down on the sofa. "Well, from what I was *able to see* . . ." She threw a withering look at her brothers and sister that went completely unnoticed. "Mom looks kind of severe. But I know that look. It's the 'you'll get in less trouble if you tell the truth about what mistake you made than if you lie and try to cover it up' look. Be interesting to find out what he . . ."

Amy was interrupted by the sudden arrival of Theresa, Martin, and John. They raced in and sat down, trying with very little success to look casual. Hugh walked in and shut the door behind him. "They'll be in—give them a few minutes," Hugh said.

"Did he tell you where he really was, or is it still that bullshit story?" asked Martin, his tone one of curiosity rather than anger.

A nervous bubble of laughter escaped Rachel's lips. Beside her she felt Mick twitch—she couldn't tell if it was in response to her laughter or to Martin's blunt but correct assessment. The bullshit story: Some musician friend, no you wouldn't know the name, real hermit type, had this cabin up around Big Sur, and Daniel had gone there to grieve and get his head back together; no phone there or TV or Internet, so he hadn't realized everyone was looking for him until he got back into town. Rachel hadn't believed it the first time she heard it, the day Daniel came back. Mick had been there, too—she'd called to let him know, and he'd driven up from San Diego in record time (earning himself a speeding ticket, she found out later). Daniel had told them both, his eyes going from Rachel to Mick and down to his hands, which were nearly swallowed up by the cuffs of his sweatshirt. No, she didn't believe it. She didn't even think Mick believed it. Not that Mick had said anything. Quite the contrary: he was more of a clam than ever since Daniel had returned; it didn't seem to have sunk in that his friend was back. The next night, Rachel had caught him trying to check the site, only to find that Theresa had taken it down.

Hugh folded his arms. "His story's the same. Let's not question it now. I think he'll tell us the truth when he's ready to."

"But . . ." said John.

Hugh shook his head. "Give him time. You didn't see how he looked when he arrived here. He thought we were going to send him away. Let him get used to being back home again."

The siblings nodded, as did Rachel. She glanced at Mick but didn't see him nod. He had a distant sort of look in his eyes, as if he was trying to remember something. Before she could inquire, the door opened, and in came Kate and Daniel.

Rachel watched Daniel be welcomed back by the people who were more his family than those who'd adopted him. She saw the relief and the remorse and the happiness clearly in his face, and the last of her anger disappeared. Only terrible pain could have driven him to flee from this.

It wouldn't be a visit to the Reilly house without a fine spread of food, and today was no exception. The day was one of those unseasonably warm ones that grace February with summerlike weather and earn California the enmity of the rest of the country. So it was barbecued chicken and fruit salad, with root beer floats for dessert. For Rachel, it all tasted better than any food had since Thanksgiving.

Throughout the meal she regarded Daniel. Now that he'd gotten his hair cut and she wasn't distracted by its length, she was able to see the gray in it. Not a large amount, but noticeable. His eyes lingered over them all, taking in the sight of people he'd been away from, and he gazed longest on the nieces and nephews who were Jake's age, and on John, who had the strongest resemblance to Sarah, with his blond hair and pointy chin. The only thing that seemed off was his clothing. With the day so warm she'd have expected him to be in a Hawaiian shirt (as long as it wasn't the gold one with the purple crabs, which hurt her eyes). Instead he wore a long-sleeved shirt that looked oddly formal with everyone else in short sleeves or summery dresses.

After the meal Daniel tried to help clear the table, but they refused. Then he tried to help with the dishes, but no one would let him do that, either. So he settled for loitering in the kitchen. It was overcrowded; Martin and Joanna were out in the yard running herd on the kids, but everyone else was piled in the kitchen, talking or doing dishes. Rachel sipped a root beer; she ran a hand along Mick's back, then laid her hand on his shoulder. He leaned into her, looked at her and smiled. It was the most relaxed she'd seen him in ages.

"OK, Dan," Theresa said. "You really want to help?"

"Yes, please."

"Here." She handed him the bowl the fruit salad had been in. "Top shelf, Mr. I-don't-need-a-stepladder."

He laughed. "You're just jealous 'cause you're not a pituitary freak." He reached up to put the bowl on the high shelf of the cupboard, his shirtsleeve pulling back.

Rachel was never sure who saw it first. "Holy Christ," was said in a flat voice that could have belonged to anyone, and someone else gasped. Mick's shoulder muscles tensed, felt like he'd been carved out of stone.

Silence in the kitchen save for the faint gurgle of dishwater running down the drain; from outside came the faint sounds of Martin, Joanna, and assorted kids jumping on the trampoline. Daniel stood frozen in the act of putting the bowl on the shelf. He seemed to regard his sleeve and the bared scar for a moment, then set the bowl down gently. Turning back to face them, he looked over all of them as if committing their faces to memory.

He spoke, and this time it was the real story. Rachel wondered what the others thought of it, but she didn't want to look and see, didn't want to take her eyes off Daniel.

"I shouldn't have lied to you about where I'd been," he said. "Being back home, and being with you, that's what I need. It's what I want . . . if you'll still have me. I understand if you don't. Just know that it was good to see you all again. It gives me hope, and hope is . . . for a long while I'd lost it, and that's a terrible thing. All I can do now is say that I'm sorry. I didn't do this to hurt any of you. I truly didn't. And . . ." Daniel stopped. His voice had grown rough as he spoke, and it was clear he was fighting back tears. He turned and slipped out the side door—after a moment Rachel could see him through the kitchen window, out in the yard, sitting in the hammock.

She turned to Mick to ask what he thought and only then realized that he'd left the kitchen as well. Rachel started to look for him, but was stopped by a touch on her shoulder.

"He didn't tell you any of this?" Kate asked.

Rachel shook her head. From the other end of the kitchen the siblings and Hugh were in murmured conversation that she couldn't hear. "No, we'd heard the same story you did. But I never really believed it." She fumbled for a cigarette but didn't light up. "It's strange, I'm not surprised by what he said. Shocked, but not surprised."

Kate nodded. "I'm going to go out and talk to him. You might want to check on your husband. I don't think he's taking this very well."

Rachel went in search of Mick, but he was nowhere to be found in the house. Nor was he in the backyard where she could see Kate, Hugh, and the siblings talking with Daniel. Where she found him was by their car. He stood leaning against the side, drumming his fingers on the roof impatiently, staring at the Reilly house with a lack of expression she found alarming. "You've got your things? Let's go," he said.

"I'm not going. I'm staying here; they might need us."

They, she said, but Mick knew what she really meant. "Need? He doesn't *need* us. Takes off with no word, leaves no trace, could have died and never a word to anyone. Fuck that. We don't need his bullshit."

Rachel stepped back, uneasy. At the harsh sentiments. At the profanity—what did Dan tell her once? *That's our Professor. Never says "fuck" in mixed company. Or any company, for that matter.* Most troubling was the accent she heard creeping into his voice—a flat Midwestern twang that she'd heard only rarely, when he was very tired or very drunk. But he was neither, and the accent changed his voice in a way she didn't like. He didn't even sound like himself.

He opened her car door. When she didn't approach he looked her over and let out a chuckle with no mirth in it. "You're staying."

"Be angry later."

"I'll be angry now, thanks," he said coldly. "You're taking his part. He ran out on all of us, on you, too, and you're taking his part."

She saw that nothing she said would change his mind, not now. "Call it that if you want. I'm staying."

He nodded. "I suppose you are." Mick slammed her door, got into the car, and drove off.

She stood alone on the peaceful suburban street. From here it was impossible to see what was going on in the backyard. Rachel wanted to know but didn't want to intrude. She'd find out sooner or later. She sat in the shade of the willow tree and waited.

After what seemed like a long while she heard the sounds of farewells from the front porch, and then Daniel came walking down the drive. He carried a grocery bag in one hand and in the other held a covered casserole dish. Despite everything, Rachel smiled.

She watched him set down the bag and the dish and lean against the roof of his car. The sigh he let out was deep and had many emotions in it. He straightened up, glanced to where the BMW had been parked, and sighed again.

Rachel stood and brushed herself off. "Dan, I'm here."

He jumped. "Where . . . I heard you leave."

Had he heard the argument or the car roaring off? Or both? "I'm still here."

"I see." Daniel turned and looked south, the way home lay. Then he smiled crookedly and opened the passenger door and bowed. "Your chariot awaits."

"Thanks." She took up her purse and climbed into the car.

They didn't talk much on the drive to Los Cielos. Rachel started to speak but noticed how tired Daniel looked. He must be wiped out emotionally and physically. She let him be and busied herself with looking out the window and listening to him hum. One or two of the melodies sounded vaguely familiar, but the others were new to her.

"What's that one?" she asked after one.

"Oh. It's, uh, mine. I haven't named it yet." He sounded a trifle sheepish.

"I like it," she told him. "I didn't know you were writing any songs."

"I started when I was in the hospital up north." Daniel seemed less embarrassed by having been in a psychiatric hospital than he did to be writing songs. "It helped a lot."

It was late afternoon by the time they got back to town. Rachel expected Mick to be home already, but he was nowhere in sight. "I know it's been a rough day," she said. "But do you mind talking a little bit? Have some coffee? I've got some baklava that Tony gave me."

He looked tired, but he nodded. "Sure thing."

Inside, she made a pot of coffee and brought it to the living room along with the baklava. Daniel took a bite of the pastry, and his eyes closed in pleasure. "You don't know how good this tastes. The hospital food wasn't bad, but bland. Really bland."

She sat down next to him. "How did it go with the Reillys?"

"I think it's going to be OK. Maybe it's good that the truth's out now. Keeping secrets, it wears you down. I hated lying. And I don't think I'm that good at it."

"You're not." She smiled, remembering a girls' lunch out with Sarah, who'd lamented that Daniel never could pull off any surprise party or present because it was too easy to catch him in a lie. *It keeps him honest,* she'd said. *You don't have that problem, though, married to Mr. Stone Face. Mick could be a serial killer and none of us would know until they found the bodies in the crawl space.* Rachel's smile faded.

Daniel went on: "It's going to take a while for everyone to get past this, but I think they understand that I didn't mean to hurt anyone. Martin took me aside and said that what I did wasn't right but if he'd lost Joanna and the girls he might have done the same thing."

Rachel inclined her head toward his hands. "May I see?" It seemed an odd request, she knew, but that quick glimpse she'd caught in the Reilly kitchen scarcely seemed real. She had to know she'd really seen it.

He didn't seem to mind. Probably a direct question was easier to deal with than a hundred furtive glances. He held out his left arm, and she took his hand in hers, turned it palm up. A thin red line, slightly raised. She was surprised by the length of it, and the straightness. It must have been hideously painful. Rachel tried not to think about what would make this kind of pain seem like a good idea.

"It didn't hurt as much as I thought it would," he said. "And I was lucky. I could have really damaged my nerves and not been able to play anymore. There was a bit of trouble, but that's mostly gone now."

"Were you scared?"

Daniel didn't answer right away. He took his hand out of hers but didn't roll down his sleeves. It must be a relief to not have to hide it, at least from her. "Not scared, exactly. More sad than anything. It all seemed such a waste. Not just me but Sarah and Jake, too. What was it all for? I still don't know. One more thing to talk about with the doc."

"You're seeing one?"

"First appointment's on Monday. I'm on meds, too. What I mean is that you don't have to worry. About me. I'm not going to go off again."

Before she could reply there was the sound of a car, very much like Mick's BMW. Daniel quickly rolled his sleeves down.

"It's not him," Rachel said. "The lady next door has the next year's model." What she was going to say next might not sound pleasant, but it was the truth. "Several of us, and I was one of them, we didn't think you were coming back. I don't know what that says about us. But it's true. Mick, though, he'd check that site every day and call the sheriff's office every week. I don't know what he believed you were doing, but what you told us today . . . it hit him hard."

Daniel sighed. "I didn't think that would happen. Well, lots of things I didn't think about." He drank down the last of his coffee. "I should go. Only thing more tiring than lying is telling the truth."

Rachel took a breath. "While you're telling the truth, can I ask you something?" When he nodded, she asked: "I was the first one you saw when you came back. Right? I'm curious. Why me? Why not Kate or . . . "

179

He was a long while answering. "I thought . . . well, I wasn't sure how everyone was going to take it. I told myself I hadn't known you as long, so if you didn't want me back, it wouldn't be so bad.

"But that wasn't it. When you hugged me I knew that it wasn't too late. I guess I knew that somehow you'd understand. I wish I'd known that sooner. I should have. That night at the Mermaid, if I'd told you how it was, things would have gone a lot differently."

Rachel smiled and said: "I don't know if I actually said this, with everything that's been going on. But I'm glad you're back."

He sat by the Coral Villas fountain, waiting. It had been a while, but Mick didn't care, much. He was a pro at waiting. He'd waited nearly three months for Daniel to come back. He'd waited for his eighteenth year to arrive so he could flee the Midwest and his father's dominion. He'd waited his whole life to find out what had happened to his mother. Another couple of hours of waiting was trivial.

It was close to dusk when the blue PT Cruiser pulled up. Moments later Daniel came ambling up the walk, looking as if he didn't have a care in the world. It seemed Kate had forgiven him—he was carrying one of her big CorningWare dishes. No doubt she'd sent him home with a casserole. It was almost funny. Kate and Rachel were the ones who'd given up on Daniel; they were probably too happy he'd come back to understand what a horrible thing he'd done.

"I thought you'd be back before now." Mick's voice sounded strange in his own ears and yet distantly familiar, too.

Daniel nearly dropped the CorningWare dish. "Sweet Jesus," he breathed. "You scared the crap out of me."

Well, that was appropriate. Mick had been scared for months now. He stood up, knees popping and muscles stiff from his long wait on the stone bench. "Everything all right now? Peachy keen?"

Daniel just regarded him with a wary look.

"That's good. I figured it would be. I figured you'd make your big puppy-dog eyes and say that you were sorry and that would be enough for them. And maybe it is. But it's not good enough for me."

Mick took a step closer. He didn't feel angry at all. Rather calm, in fact. "You know why that's good enough for them? Because they gave up on you. I heard them. Kate and John and Rachel, at Christmas, saying they thought they'd never see you again. They didn't come out and say what they meant, but I knew. I thought they were wrong, because I knew you'd never do anything so . . . so hateful."

"That wasn't—"

"Shut your mouth when I'm talking to you! I filed the missing persons report. I got all your stuff moved into storage and took care of the insurance settlement and paid the rent on your apartment all the time you were gone. I took care of everything."

Daniel took a deep breath. He held the casserole in front of him like a shield. "I know, and I'm thankful for all of that. I'll pay you back for . . ."

"That is not the point. I never gave up on you. Not even when Sheriff Marquez said it was pretty weird that they couldn't find a paper trail, said maybe you didn't *want* to be found. Oh, I was sure there was an explanation—why would you do something like that? But he was right, wasn't he? You didn't want to be found. They might have stuck you in some potter's field, wouldn't that have been perfect? Or maybe you thought they'd ship your body home as a big fuck you to all of us. Was that it?"

181

"I wasn't thinking of—"

"Oh, you were thinking all right. Rachel always said you'd had some kind of breakdown, but I call bullshit on that. If you'd gone crazy, you wouldn't have covered your tracks so well. You wanted to hurt us, and you know what? You did. And I thought I knew you, but I don't."

The apologetic look had faded from Daniel's face. He smiled, not his usual grin at all but something off-balance. "I guess we're even, right? Because I thought you, of all people, would understand. Don't give me shit for running away. That's all you've done your whole life."

There was a jump cut, and he saw Daniel half sitting, half sprawled on the ground, rubbing his jaw and looking up at Mick with an expression of astonishment. *Didn't know I had it in me.* Mick flexed his aching hand, where the knuckles were already swelling, but he didn't feel the pain. Instead there was a strange, empty sort of elation. He started to speak, but the words were *Look what you made me do*, and he bit them back because for a second it wasn't Daniel sitting there, it was himself when he was a child, looking up at his father; he blinked and it was Gina, looking at the hole he'd punched in the wall.

Take it back, an inner voice urged him. *Take it back. Clean slate for both of you.*

A passing tenant of the Coral Villas observed the scene and smirked. "Looks like the honeymoon's over."

Daniel laughed. It was more a nervous giggle, but all Mick heard—all he let himself hear—was laughter. *That's it.* He turned and stalked off to his car, ignoring the sound of Daniel calling his name.

He drove away, at first heading for home, but he remembered how Rachel had taken Daniel's part. And there was Gina. Mick didn't let himself think of her often, but the memory was fresh now, and he needed to let it fade back again. He ended up at MacHeath's—the place was packed with a Saturday night crowd, but he managed to snag a stool at the bar.

As he sat down, a basket of fresh-cooked potato chips, one of the house specialties, appeared in front of him. "Here you go," said Eli. "Chips are on the house, Mick. Anything to drink?"

"Bombay and tonic." That caught him by surprise. It was his New York drink, the one he'd thought would make him look sophisticated. The gin and tonics, the fancy neckties and shoes, having Gina on his arm. Before he could change his order Eli was making the drink, and it seemed rude to have something else.

"Here you go." Eli set the drink down, then leaned forward and grinned. "I heard Dan's back. He doing all right?"

"Yes, fine." He couldn't tell if it was the words that tasted bitter or the gin.

"That's great. Tell him to come in soon. You know, I've still got a picture Jake drew for me, one of the last times they were all here. It's hanging on my fridge—me and Indiana Jones fighting Darth Vader."

Mick had many pictures like that on his own fridge. And why not? It wasn't like he was going to have any kids of his own whose pictures would go on the fridge. "I'll tell Dan you said hi."

"Appreciate it," Eli said, and went down to the other end of the bar.

He nibbled at a few chips, but the fine meal the Reillys had served sat in his stomach like a rock. The Bombay and tonic went down easier, and it was hard to restrict himself to one. He had to drive home, sooner or later. But not just yet. For now he'd sit here, alone in the crowd as he'd been for so much of his life. Sometimes that wasn't so bad. The noise distracted him from his thoughts, and yet no one noticed him enough to ask him for things he couldn't give. *Running away, that's all you've done your whole life.* Yes, but it was different for him. He'd had no reason *not* to run.

It was too noisy here. He paid for his drink and left a tip, waved goodbye to Eli. But he didn't drive home just yet, for he didn't know what he'd say to Rachel. How surprised he'd been when he'd gotten the call from her telling him to come home right away, Daniel was back. He'd half wondered if it had been some not-at-all-funny joke. Even when he walked into the house and saw Daniel sitting there, he hadn't known what to believe, and it only got worse when he heard Daniel's cockamamy story.

Well, now he had the truth, and what was he going to do about it?

Music drifting through the air.

Mick stepped on the brakes. His aimless driving had taken him to First Street Storage. There, in the biggest unit, were all the Whitman family possessions. He'd kept everything that wasn't broken or obviously garbage.

Music coming from the storage unit.

Mick pulled over, shut off the car's engine. The piano notes rippled through the air, echoed yet muffled by the storage unit's acoustics. There were no words, but the music spoke clearly. Told of loss and sorrow. Mick shut his eyes. For a moment he was five years old again, the first night after his mother had vanished—lying in the dark, aching from the beating his father had given him, listening for any hint of his mother's return. For a moment he was in New York, the day Gina had told him: that she was leaving, about the affair, about the baby.

He could imagine what it must look like in that storage unit. A family's life and possessions piled up, stacked, and arranged—waiting. The light would be dim and the place would smell like an antique store, the sad scent of dust and unused possessions. Rachel's weird cousin Ethan had once told them that he never bought antiques because they kept spirit attachments to their owners and could be haunted. If Ethan was right, there'd be powerful ghosts in that storage unit tonight.

Maybe that's who Daniel was playing for. The ghosts.

All Mick had to do was get out of his car, walk over to the unit. Knock on the corrugated steel door. And say ... what? There were too many things he wanted to say. And words would fail him. They always had.

The song ended. The spell broke. Mick started up the car again and made his way home.

Chapter Fifteen

The courtyard housed seven bungalows—all had been converted to health-care offices. Your insurance willing, you could get your back cracked, eyes checked, hearing tested, braces fitted, blemishes scrutinized, lungs listened to, and head shrunk all in one day. But it was only the latter that interested Daniel. He walked to the third bungalow on the right. The shingle was simple and discreet: "Duncan Levinson, MD."

The lobby was small and unoccupied. The walls were a very pale blue, and the venetian blinds had been opened to let in the morning sun. The walls were mostly bare of decoration save for a large print of the town's signature picture-postcard shot, taken out by Lonely Point and making Los Cielos look like a tiny bit of paradise. At the far end of the room, a small stone fountain gurgled endlessly.

He peered into the receptionist's area but didn't see Renee there. Daniel signed in, then took a seat. Leaning his head back, he closed his eyes and listened to the fountain. He didn't mind waiting; he liked it here. Though he'd been nervous on his first visit, nearly a month ago. Surely he wouldn't get lucky twice and have a doctor he liked as much as Dr. Howard. But he'd felt reassured the moment he walked into the lobby, with its soothing blue and its picture of home and the fountain. And his nervousness had vanished by the end of his first session with Dr. Levinson, who reminded Daniel strongly of Dr. Howard, though the two looked nothing alike. Dr. Levinson was a tall man, shambling and starting to be portly, something like Frankenstein in stature, but though he ducked through doorways and chairs creaked beneath his weight, he moved with a grace that was almost serene. Like Dr. Howard, he seemed to have a way of looking past the exterior and seeing a person clearly.

"Mr. Whitman?"

He opened his eyes and saw Renee back at the receptionist desk. She still wouldn't call him by his first name, no matter that he'd said several times it was all right to do so. Office protocol no doubt. But she smiled and tipped her head toward the office. "He'll see you now."

In the room where they had their sessions, nothing matched. The desk was a large mahogany thing, possibly antique, but the chair behind it was one of those mesh ergonomic ones that Sarah had always coveted. On a built-in bookshelf the volumes seemed to be arranged by color rather than by author or title. On the desk rested a computer—Daniel had never once seen it in use—and an electric typewriter. Daniel hadn't seen one of those outside of the LCU faculty halls. The office had no couch, but it did have several chairs of varying styles. Daniel sat in his favorite, an old leather sling chair.

He liked the office's scent as well: the leather and wood of the chair he sat in, the coffee and tea that Dr. Levinson always had on hand, the faint aroma of pipe tobacco. Most of all he liked the feeling of safety; it reminded him of Saint Jude's.

Speaking of Dr. Howard. "I heard from our mutual acquaintance up north," said Dr. Levinson as he handed Daniel a paper cup full of coffee. "Susan said you're sending some books up there?" He sat down in his session chair—not the fancy ergonomic one but a plush armchair.

Daniel nodded. "The book selection up there wasn't so great. I've been going through the things in storage and set aside some I thought might be good." It seemed the right thing to do—after all, he didn't need four copies of *Pride and Prejudice*. He'd keep the one that had been Sarah's teaching copy; it had her notes in the margins. The rest he'd send to Saint Jude's, along with all those historical novels with *Darcy* and *Boleyn* in the titles.

Daniel fell silent, thinking of the books. They had been one of the first things he'd gone through. Part of him hadn't wanted to give anything away, but he'd realized that trying to replicate the old house was as sick in its own way as the stark emptiness of his apartment at the Coral Villas. *What do I keep?* he'd asked Dr. Levinson. The answer: *What you need.*

Going through the stored items had been easier once he'd found the new house. There had been the option to build on the old lot, but that was something he could never do. He could scarcely stand to go back there— had only done so once since he'd come back. Nothing left of the house itself save for the foundation, and he supposed in time even that would be gone. The grass had gone to weeds, and the flower bed had been trampled by the wrecking crew. The only thing salvageable was the climbing rose that had once scaled the trellis outside the bedroom—a strange rose, pale lavender in some lights, faintly blue in others. He couldn't remember the name of it. He'd always called it a winter rose for its color. It had been hacked backed to a stub, but now it stubbornly sent out new branches. He borrowed a shovel from Mr. Frank and dug up the rose, gave it to Rachel to tend until he had somewhere to plant it.

"Are you moved in to the new place yet?" Dr. Levinson asked. As always, when he asked questions his voice was quiet. Daniel might almost have thought the questions were coming from inside his own head.

"Nearly," Daniel replied. "The movers will bring the piano this afternoon. I thought it best to leave that to the experts. Especially now."

Yes, now. A few months back he wouldn't have thought the piano mattered. Now he knew how much he needed it. Especially after the reunion with the Reillys and the fight with Mick. Nothing had helped soothe him after that day save for the piano. In the dim storage room with its single fluorescent bulb for illumination, he'd sat among the relics of his old life and played. As long as he was able to play, he could keep going.

"Good. Keep up with that." Dr. Levinson paused, and his tone of voice changed. "You said you were writing some of your own songs. Is there any chance I could hear them?"

Daniel sat up straight. "Are you asking me as my doctor or just asking me?"

Dr. Levinson laughed. "Do you want me to talk about how they relate to your care, or do you want me to tell you if you're rhyming *moon* and *June* too often?"

"I don't know. Which is worse—to be crazy or to write crappy lyrics?" Or with his luck, both. "Let me think it over." He knew Dr. Levinson wouldn't be offended if he said no.

"Fair enough. How are you sleeping these days? You look more rested."

"Better." It was odd. He'd slept fairly well on that ratty futon at the apartment. But when he'd moved into the new place, he'd found he couldn't sleep in the bed he'd once shared with Sarah. Even in his sleep he was aware of her absence, would wake up startled if he rolled on to her side or reached out and found no one there. He'd had to buy a new bed, and since then he'd been sleeping much better. It made him think of that old song by the Police—"The Bed's Too Big Without You." And of that time when he and Mick were talking, had gotten on the subject of things you hated to buy because they were both expensive and boring. "Like tires," Daniel had said. "I hate buying tires. All that money and you don't notice a damn difference."

"Same thing when you buy a mattress," Mick had said.

"No, when you get a new mattress there's a difference. No sex trough."

Mick shrugged. "Not an issue for me. I always do it on the floor."

"What are you thinking of?" Dr. Levinson asked.

"Old times. And that I'll be really glad when the piano's moved in. And . . . it feels strange to enjoy something in life again."

It was indeed a strange feeling, but he was getting used to it. After his session he rode his bike back to the house he was renting.

It was on Cove Street, in a cul-de-sac on the bohemian side of town. Well, more bohemian than the rest of Los Cielos. *A deranged English cottage,* Rachel had called it when she helped him move some boxes in, and she wasn't far wrong. There was no lawn, just red bricks for a yard. The house itself seemed made entirely of shingles, and none of the doorways lined up. Like the front yard, the backyard boasted no lawn but instead was filled with overgrown lavender bushes. A red brick walkway meandered through the lavender until it reached a gazebo, almost entirely shrouded in bougainvillea, that housed a hot tub—not one of the fiberglass spas but a wooden one, very old-school. The house was at the end of the cul-de-sac, and behind it was an empty lot. The first time Daniel had been to the place he'd stood by the gazebo and heard no neighbors or traffic, nothing but the bees buzzing through the lavender.

The owner's name was Arnie, and he was retiring after forty-five years of chartering fishing boats. He was a spare man with a deeply tanned face and hands, his eyes keen despite his age. "Bet you're wondering about the flowers. My wife, Bess, God rest her, she planted all this. Her back wasn't up to the lawn mowing, and I'd always forget, so she said the heck with it, I'll put in flowers, and the things just took off. We tried keeping them in check but decided it was better to just let 'em go. All you have to do is come out here with some clippers every so often and keep the path clear and get any weeds that come through the bricks. Some people don't like it, want grass instead, but I'd rather keep it. Reminds me of her. You know what I'm saying?"

"Very much so."

"Figured you would. I checked your references, you seem all right. Just don't do any crazy rock-and-roll shenanigans, and you can do as you please. I'm moving to San Diego to be near my kids, so I won't be far if you have any problems."

Over the last few weeks he'd slowly moved in some of the things he needed. There was still plenty in storage he needed to go through, but the essentials were here, save for the piano. He checked the mailbox: a couple of bills, an ad or two, a postcard from Eskimo Sally, and a letter from Wayne. He read the postcard first: *Big hugs from me! Sorry I woke you!* Daniel smiled. Eskimo Sally had called a few weeks ago to say she'd gotten word he was back and was so glad that he was safe—unfortunately she'd miscalculated the twenty-hour time difference between Fiji and California. ("What do you mean, you were asleep? It's two, you lazy bastard! In the morning? Oh, shit!")

He took the mail inside and opened the letter. It wasn't the first he and Wayne had exchanged since they'd both left Saint Jude's. Wayne was doing all right, it seemed—he was working in a hardware store now, thinking of going to vocational/technical school. On the bad side, his Uncle Bob dragged him to church each week, which was "boring as shit, no blasphemy or anything intended," but on the good side he'd met a girl there named Beth and was thinking of asking her out. Daniel smiled again. Good for Wayne.

After lunch, while he was in the middle of writing his reply to Wayne (which boiled down to encouragement on the job and school front and a hearty "Go for it!" on Beth), the movers arrived with the piano. They were pros and did the job deftly. He was glad he'd spent the extra money on them, but then, he could afford it. From Mick he'd received the paperwork for the settlements—the property insurance, the life insurance. That was one thing he and Sarah had both been diligent on, knowing that her job didn't pay a lot and his income could be feast-or-famine. Neither of them had wanted to leave Jake with nothing to his name. Daniel cared little about the money, but at least he could afford the piano movers.

They soon had it set up in the room at the rear of the house. The room's light had a faint purplish quality from all the lavender and bougainvillea outside the windows. After the movers left Daniel sat at the bench, pushed the cover back from the keys, and started to play, testing the acoustics of the room. It was different than it had been at the house on Sandpiper; the sound here was louder, with more echo, but he liked that. It went well with the purple-tinted light.

He was still playing—one of the new songs, his songs—when Rachel arrived. He heard the doorbell's ring and opened the door to see her standing there with a little red wagon by her side. In the bed of the wagon was the potted rose he'd left with her and bags full of carryout Chinese. "This work for you?" she asked.

"Sure thing." He took the food and set things up for them in the living room—the kitchen table was covered with boxes—while she went to see the piano in its new home.

"I like it," she said when she returned. "I wasn't sure I did at first. It seems a bit claustrophobic with the plants hiding the windows, but it's growing on me." Rachel sat down, dished herself up some General Tso's chicken. "I'm glad you're out of that apartment. That wasn't a good place for you."

"I agree." He still got chills thinking of the place: its emptiness, the stink of stale air and despair. When he'd cleared out the last of his stuff, he'd half wondered if he should get some of those white sage bundles from Earth Sun Moon, the New Age hippie-dippie store. You were supposed to light those and wave the smoke around, chase the bad juju away. Looking at the empty rooms, he'd remembered the days he'd spent unmoving, imprisoned by grief, and had shuddered.

"How are you doing?" she asked.

"I'm OK. One day at a time, as my friend Wayne says."

"You hear from Mick lately?" she asked, looking at him over her tea.

"He sent me the paperwork for the insurance settlements, that stuff." Daniel looked down and spent an inordinately long time picking the chili peppers out of the spicy orange beef, avoiding Rachel's eyes in case she mentioned the letter he'd sent in return.

"No, I meant has he spoken to you?"

He shook his head. "Not since we had the blowup. I called his cell the next day to let him know that he hadn't done any damage to me or the CorningWare."

"He hit you?"

"Just clocked me in the jaw. Knocked me down and made me drop the casserole, but that's it. My sister throws a better punch than—what's wrong?"

She didn't answer his question. "What happened after that?"

"He just stood there looking at me. It was . . . he looked freaked out, like he couldn't believe he'd done that. I couldn't think of what to say. I think . . . maybe he was going to apologize, or maybe I was. Then some person walking by made some remark and I laughed. I don't even remember what they said, it wasn't all that funny, but I was nervous. Then he just turned and left. Like that was the last straw." He shook his head again. "I never saw him get mad like that before. I didn't know he could."

"I see." She pushed her plate aside; she'd barely touched her food.

He wanted to ask about the letter. But he'd only made things worse by sending it. "It's nothing to worry about, Rachel. Let me and him work it out. It's between us."

She looked as if she were going to say something, then nodded. "Let me know if you need any help with the house."

"I think it's under control. But thanks."

After she left, he sat in the living room, absently drawing designs in a plate of fried rice and thinking about the letter.

It was because of the insurance paperwork. He'd received it a couple of days after the fight. It had been there, all complete. Everywhere he needed to sign was indicated with highlights and tape flags; there was even a sticky note pointing out where things needed to be notarized. No complaints on that score. It was the impersonality of it. No personal note. Just a terse letter on company letterhead telling him where to mail the forms. He'd even shaken the envelope, hoping some sort of note would fall out, but nothing did.

Who does he think I am? One of his clients? One of those quick-flaring rages had come on him, and before he could think it through he'd dug up the suicide note, which was still sealed and untouched since the day he'd written it. He put it in a manila envelope and, to show that he was in the right, included a personal note: *I'd thought you would understand, but it seems you still don't, so here it is.* He'd put it in the mailbox and half an hour later realized how stupid he was being, turning this into a passive-aggressive pissing contest. Anger deflated into shame, and he'd run out to the mailbox, but it was too late, and the letter was on its way.

He'd heard nothing, though. And had no idea how to interpret that. Daniel was used to people who blustered and stomped and yelled when they were angry. He *was* one of those people. And once the blustering and stomping and yelling was done, whether it took one minute or one hour, the anger was over for the most part. The cold rage he'd seen in his friend's eyes was different; he'd actually been relieved when Mick hit him. But that relief was long gone. Daniel set down the chopsticks, rubbed his hands against his forehead. He wished he knew what to do. He wished he hadn't sent that letter. What if Mick read it and it only made things worse? That was possible. Daniel wasn't entirely sure what the letter said anymore. It wasn't as if he'd been in his right mind when he wrote it. And God knew how Mick would react. Bad enough if he forswore their friendship forever. Daniel felt he'd earned the punch Mick had thrown him; that was the least of his grievances. But what if Mick did something like that to Rachel?

Daniel had thought everything would be OK once he'd returned to Los Cielos. Some things were, some were just different, and some were a kind of wrong he hadn't expected. And this time it wasn't a rogue wind to be blamed—some of it could be laid at his door.

He wished Rachel had a cell, but she despised them and never carried one. He left the message on the Beaditudes answering machine, making his message vague in case one of her assistants opened shop and listened to the playback. "If our mutual friend unloads on you the way he did on me, call me. First thing. Promise me."

After he hung up, Daniel became aware of how quiet the house was. Most of the time that quiet didn't bother him, but now it made him restless. This had happened before—on a few nights he'd prowled the house, circulating through the rooms again and again. Save for that interlude at the Coral Villas, he'd never lived alone in his life. There had been home, whether it was the parental units' or the Reillys. There had been the dilapidated Victorian at LCU—there had always been people there. And then it had been he and Sarah, and later Jake, too.

For a while he busied himself with unpacking, put on music. He knew his cul-de-sac well enough to know that he could play *Cheap Trick at Budokan* as loud as he wanted and no one would care. Yet it was a façade. It couldn't hide that there was no one else to fill the rooms with their sound and presence. It couldn't keep away the knowledge that no one would live in this house except for him.

It was full dark when he stepped out, locked the door behind him. Daniel walked the six blocks to the Chez coffeehouse. Proximity to the Chez was one of the reasons he'd leased the place. He pushed open the door and descended the nearly vertical staircase, stepped into the familiar scent of coffee, clove cigarettes, and dusty old furniture. From behind the bar, Ariel waved to him, bade him sit anywhere. He found himself a corner table and sat with his beverage, occasionally watching the would-be balladeer who sat at the Chez's tiny performance area, nervously picking out Simon and Garfunkel tunes on his twelve-string. Daniel occasionally let his gaze rove to the old guys playing chess over in the far corner, the girl who stood perusing the shelf of loaner paperbacks, the LCU students studying or talking together.

Mostly he sat and thought. He could do this in peace here. Ariel and the other workers would only come by if he asked them to; none of the patrons had reason to trouble him. He could sit here in the familiar scents and the memories—more of them welcome than painful these days. He could be by himself yet not alone. He could think about what he'd lost and what he might regain one day and what he still had, and his spirits would lighten, for a while.

Chapter Sixteen

After two bounced e-mails and three phone calls, Daniel finally got hold of Reg Fletcher.

"Danny!" Reg sang out. "Good to hear from you!"

Daniel moved the phone away from his ear. The years had not been kind to Reg's voice, and these days it didn't so much resonate as penetrate.

"How are you doing? You had us all pretty worried there for a while," Reg continued.

Daniel had answered the *How are you doing?* question so many times that he had his answer rote. But he did his best not to sound rote. "It's getting better. One day at a time, that's how I'm taking it."

"That's good. I'm glad to hear that. I want to see you again, but I'm stuck here in Switzerland for a while. The last divorce royally fucked up my taxes, got to sort all that out."

"Well, when you're in the vicinity, feel free to drop in. And I have a question for you." Daniel took a breath, knowing his request could seem odd. "That last session. The one . . . after. Did you tape any of that?"

A protracted silence on the other end. Reg was notorious for taping *everything* in his sessions; back in 1976 or so when he was guitarist for the Anderson Council, a perfect solo he'd laid down had somehow gotten erased. Never mind that the drummer and the bass player at the time had both confided to Daniel that the solo had not been all that great, Reg still taped everything so no more magical solos would be lost.

"Um. Well. You see." Reg lost for words was a rare thing indeed.

Daniel was tempted to let Reg squirm for a while but was merciful. "It's OK. I was hoping you did."

"Really?"

"Yes. Can you send it to me?" Daniel knew Reg never threw anything away. "I might use it in something I'm working on."

"You're doing your own stuff now?"

"Yes. It's just for me, though. It helps to work things out, you understand?"

"I've been there, my friend. I'll have it overnighted to you. But . . . if you don't mind, I'd like to hear what you're doing. If you don't want to, that's OK."

"No, I can do that. Let me rip some MP3s for you, and I'll send them to you. And Reg? Thanks for that session. Even though it didn't work out, I really appreciated your help."

"You're welcome, Danny. I'll let you know what I think of the songs."

After he hung up and sent the samples to Reg, Daniel gathered his wallet and keys together. He was due in San Diego to see Clive, his agent. There was some paperwork he was behind on, and he wanted to let Clive know that he was ready for session work again, though he wouldn't be able to take on tour gigs or anything else that would take him away from home. He didn't want to be away from his piano and his own songs.

Songs was probably too strong a word for them yet. More like bits and pieces of melodies that captured his feelings about everything that had happened. One or two were close to being proper songs with beginnings, middles, and ends, and one even had lyrics. Though he still couldn't decide if he liked the lyrics. Sometimes he thought they were good, then two hours later he'd look at them and think they were ridiculous. If Dr. Levinson didn't give him an honest assessment, Reg certainly would. Reg was nothing if not blunt. Still, quality aside, the songs helped him. Sometimes he'd wake in the night, from either a bad dream or just a feeling that he was going to get lost again. When that happened, first he'd think of the songs the woman had sung to him in the diner. That always calmed him down enough to function. And from there he'd more often than not go to his piano and play, and more often than not it was one of his songs. He'd started incorporating the melodies the woman had sung to him into one of his songs. So far it was the only one he'd given a title to: "Winter Roses."

Traffic between Los Cielos and San Diego was lighter than he'd expected, and he arrived at Clive's office well ahead of schedule. In other circumstances he'd have swung through downtown, by the Convention Center, poked his head into Kessler Financial Services, and said, "Hey, Professor. I'm in town. Want to get lunch?" But the war of silence was still ongoing, and Daniel wasn't sure how to make peace, so he went to Clive's office.

Roxanne, Clive's admin, looked startled but pleased to see him. "I'll tell him you're here," she said after looking him up and down. He'd seen that look on a few faces since returning home. It was a look that wondered if he was OK, and if so, how OK he was. Daniel supposed it was to be expected.

But it was still a surprise to see that look times ten on Clive Smith's face. Clive was an English expatriate, a balding, chubby fellow in his late fifties. Though he'd lived on the West Coast for more than a quarter century, his English accent was as strong as ever. In fact, it seemed to have gotten stronger over the years. Daniel suspected this was a conscious effort on Clive's part to woo attractive admins. Roxanne was no doubt the latest to fall for Clive's dulcet Cambridgeshire tones.

"Daniel. Hello there." Clive rose from behind his desk but didn't extend his hand in a greeting. Instead he made an awkward nod and then sat down.

"It's good to see you," Daniel said as he took a seat.

"Likewise," Clive said, and Daniel could tell that Clive didn't mean it. Clive seemed relieved to look down at the paperwork he had arranged on his desk; he kept up a steady stream of chatter, and every time he had to look at Daniel for more than a few moments, he fiddled with his pen in a staccato burst of clicks that sounded like a metronome gone mad.

Gone mad. That's what Clive thought of Daniel. The other day Dr. Levinson had asked Daniel about the people in his life and how they'd reacted to Daniel's return. He hadn't understood why Dr. Levinson had asked that. *Not every friendship can survive events like these,* Dr. Levinson had said. At the time Daniel thought it meant his broken friendship with Mick, but maybe that wasn't so. Maybe he'd meant people like Clive, who was so uncomfortable in Daniel's presence that even a blind man could have seen it. Or his old neighbor, Sandra Cordova. Last time he stopped by, to give her his new address should she want to get in touch, she'd kept a distance as if she thought loss or grief or madness might be catching. He got the same feeling from Clive. Or maybe it wasn't that; maybe they just didn't know what to say or do.

Did it matter? Things wouldn't be the same. Daniel said, "Thanks, Clive. You know, I'm happy for any work, but I'm also busy with some new stuff of my own. So just feel free to e-mail me with any new gigs. That sound good?"

The relief was visible on Clive's face. Yes, e-mail would be fine. Daniel gathered his papers, didn't offer to shake Clive's hand. He abandoned any idea of going into the Gaslamp district or Old Town for lunch and instead went home.

He found a message waiting for him on his answering machine. He expected to hear Kate Reilly, who'd asked him to come up to Torrance this weekend. But it was Reg, uncharacteristically terse. "When you get in, call me. I don't care what time it is. Call me."

He was in for it now. Might as well get it over with. Daniel calculated that it was still a reasonable hour in Switzerland and dialed. "Danny," Reg said. "You're sooner than I expected."

"I got things done in San Diego early." He licked his lips, took a breath. "Did the MP3s come through all right?"

"They did. Just let me ask, what in the *hell* have you been doing?"

Losing my family, having a nervous breakdown. The usual. Instead he said, "It's that bad, then? I'm sorry."

A pause so long that Daniel wondered if they'd been disconnected. "You don't know, do you?" Reg said in a wondering tone. "How could you *not* know?"

"Know what? Just tell me."

"It's good. No, it's better than good. Even when it's rough like this I can tell. And what's more, it really grabs people. Hasn't anyone told you that?"

"I haven't played it for too many people."

"Well, take it from me, you've got something special here. Those bits you sent me, they take you someplace."

Daniel knew Reg well enough to know that this wasn't an empty compliment. "Thank you. I'm glad you like it."

"I'll produce it if you want. See, you want to keep your vocals and the piano the focus of it. That's where the heart of it is. Something like what Tori Amos did with her first few albums. You'll need some backup, but nothing too fancy. Like I said, you don't want to detract. Get yourself a good, no-nonsense engineer—I'm sure Alan can recommend someone if he's too busy or if you can't afford him. No, stick with Alan. If the bastard quotes too high a price, let me know. I'll blackmail him if I have to, Lord knows I have enough dirt."

"Wait, wait. Slow down. I wasn't going to go whole hog on this. I'm just doing these for me."

Another pause. "Are you sure? That would be a bloody shame. I mean, if you're really not comfortable with that, I understand . . . Oh hell, Danny. You and me, we both grew up with music. It's saved our lives, or at least our sanity once or twice. What you've got here, that could do the same for others. It could really be something special. And I think that—ah, well, I shouldn't."

"No, go on."

Reg's voice dropped a bit. "I think Sarah would want you to do this, Danny. She told me that you'd do your own work one day and it would be good, it was just a matter of when."

Daniel had no answer to that. He'd told Reg and Dr. Levinson and even Dr. Howard that he was just doing this for himself, but it had been for Sarah and Jake, too.

"Danny, you there? If I spoke out of turn, I'm sorry."

"No, it's OK. I hadn't . . . You're sure about this?"

Reg laughed. "I'm more sure about this than I am about what *I'm* working on. Think on it. And if you decide you want to and need any help finding players, let me know. But you've got plenty of connections. You've even got that friend of yours that plays guitar."

It was hard to say the next words. "We've had a falling-out."

"Well, if he doesn't come round, I'll help you beat the bushes for some players. And if you need a girl singer, there's Desiree. She'll probably waive her fee—she fancies you. But I mean it. Keep up with this, and let me know when you're ready to record. Don't hide your light under a bushel."

He thanked Reg and hung up. It was past lunchtime, but Daniel wasn't hungry. Instead he went into the piano room, where he sat down at the bench, pushed the cover back. He didn't play but ran his fingers over the keys, feeling the smooth ivory. He'd never intended to turn those songs into an album. Yet now that the idea was here he could see it coming into focus. A themed set of songs that would express all the feelings of those months. It would be painful, going back, but perhaps if he could capture some of that pain, put it into a song the way you capture air in a bell jar, he might be able to let it go.

Abruptly he stood up and went to the living room where the CDs, tapes, and albums were on the shelves. They were organized by artist, with no respect for genre, so that Johann Sebastian Bach was next to Bachman-Turner Overdrive and Fats Waller was next to Wall of Voodoo. He sat down and looked at the albums and tapes for a long while. Most of them weren't just about their music. They held memories as well. Most any time, good or bad, that he could recall since he'd been a kid, there was some sort of music associated with it. Reg had been right—music had certainly saved his sanity a time or two. He thought about that last summer before going to college—listening to the albums Uncle Jacob had left for him, counting the days (hell, counting the hours) until he would be at school, away from his family and close to people who wanted him around. The first time his session work had taken him away from Sarah, he'd found a mixtape she'd made for him tucked into his overnight bag. Titled *From the Sublime to the Ridiculous*, it started with songs like "My Funny Valentine" and "I'll Be Your Mirror" and got progressively cornier until it ended with "Dream Weaver." He'd laughed so hard the people in the hotel room next door banged on the wall and yelled at him to shut up.

There had been no music after Sarah and Jake died. Maybe if he'd let music comfort him then, he might not have gone off the rails so badly.

He sat there all afternoon, didn't play anything but looked at the albums and the mixtapes and thought about all the music he'd loved and what he'd loved best about it. That evening he ate his dinner without really tasting it, instead listening to the bits and pieces he'd composed already, looking over the lyric fragments he'd scribbled in a composition book. He turned to a fresh page and began jotting down ideas. No melodies or lyrics yet. More of a mood association.

Late into the night he worked, sitting and thinking for long periods of time, then writing down ideas. From time to time he'd raid the music library, searching for something to inspire him. The night went on, and he had pages scribbled with notes, and the floor was piled high with records, tapes, and CDs, artists from every genre. He finally fell asleep lying on the floor, the dust jacket for the Rolling Stones' *Their Satanic Majesties Request* lying on his chest, with his head between the speakers, which were on the fourth replay of "2000 Light Years from Home." He woke to hear his own music in his head and could barely force himself to have breakfast before he went to the piano. He could feel the songs in his head. Clamoring to be let out, to be created. All that day and into the night the music rang through the house.

Daniel ran into Rachel's store five minutes before closing, the day before Easter. Not only was he due at the Reillys the next day and still had to buy candy for all the nieces and nephews, but it was Kate's birthday dinner as well, and he had to get a present. "Hi, Rachel," he said, winded from his fast bike ride. "I need—"

She didn't look up from her cash register tallying, just held up a gift bag. "The choker is garnet, rhodonite, and moonstones. And a bracelet with birthstones for you, Sarah, and Jake. Sapphire, tourmaline, and emerald, respectively."

He couldn't have chosen better if he'd tried. "Thanks, Rachel. I'm sorry I'm such a dolt."

"No worries," she said, and looked up at him. "I like being given free rein. Speaking of which, I made something for you as well." Rachel handed him a small flat box.

Daniel opened the box. Nestled inside on cotton batting was a silver bracelet with oval stones. He slipped it onto his left wrist, and the metal was cool against his skin. "What are the stones?" His knowledge of crystals and minerals was minimal.

"Black onyx to release sorrow. Mahogany obsidian for protection. Fire agate for spiritual fortitude. Sodalite for peace and harmony. Howlite to relieve stress. Quartz crystal to kick it all up a notch." She winked at him. "Mind you, I don't know if they actually *do* these things, but I thought it couldn't hurt. And besides, I feel bad because I didn't get you anything for Christmas last year."

Daniel smiled. He was glad that Rachel felt comfortable saying that to him. And the bracelet really was striking, though usually the only jewelry he wore was his wedding band and the Saint Christopher medal Sarah asked him to wear whenever he traveled. "I'll be sure to show it off tomorrow."

She walked over to the door and flipped the sign to "Closed." "Want to get some dinner?"

"That would be good. I forgot to have lunch today." He'd been in the throes of songwriting and, despite the alarm clock he'd set for noon, had completely overlooked lunch. It wasn't the first time this had happened.

"I figured you'd been a slave to the keyboard. You look very distracted. Plus you have Alfalfa hair, and your shoes don't match."

"Oh." He raked a hand through his hair, but there was nothing to be done about the high-tops, one black and one blue.

They drove in his PT Cruiser to MacHeath's, where the dinner rush was just getting underway. At first Daniel wasn't hungry—he'd just made arrangements for studio time in LA a month from now, and his nerves were ajangle—but when the bacon cheeseburger and sweet potato fries were in front of him, his appetite came back with a vengeance. He told Rachel how the music was going, about Reg's encouragement, and about the session players he had lined up.

"You sound excited," she said.

"And I'm nervous as hell. This time I'll be the boss, and everyone else will be covertly rolling their eyes at my clichéd melodies. Up to now I've always been the eye roller."

She laughed. Daniel was happy to see her laugh; she looked different lately. Not tired, exactly, but under strain. He said anything he could think of that might amuse her, even a truly awful joke that Eskimo Sally had e-mailed him the other week. She smiled and giggled, but the strain was still there. Maybe in the old days he wouldn't have been able to see it, but now he understood more about what people could be hiding.

Rachel was absorbed in the dessert menu when he blurted out, "Did you get my message a while back? The one I left at the shop?"

"Yes," she said. Putting down the dessert menu, she looked at him levelly. "He hasn't been taking it out on me. Not in that way."

In what way, then? "Has he been fighting with you? Or . . . yelling at you?" Daniel wouldn't have picked Mick for a yeller but he also hadn't expected the man to punch him in the jaw.

Rachel laughed, but not her happy laugh. "He doesn't fight or yell. In fact, he barely says anything to me at all. I knew he was the quiet type, but I didn't think I'd married a mute."

Daniel found himself thinking of Mick when he'd first moved into the old Victorian by the university. Daniel and some of the other housemates had tried everything they could think of to get their new guest to speak, but met with little success. Sarah had finally corralled all of them and said, *Let him alone, he'll come out of his shell when he's ready to. Pestering him will only make it worse.* She'd been right, of course.

What was fresher in Daniel's mind, though, was a more recent time and a different silence from his friend. It had been the proverbial bolt from the blue: seven a.m. on a Saturday morning and the Whitmans had all been in bed still, when Mick called from LaGuardia and said he'd be in San Diego later that afternoon. He apologized for the short notice, but there were no rental cars available, and could one of them pick him up and give him a lift to a hotel? There'd been a strange tone in his friend's voice that couldn't be attributed to the distortion of the long-distance line. When Daniel picked him up at the airport it was as if they'd gone through a time warp. Despite the Brooks Brothers tie and the Louis Vuitton luggage, Mick looked much the way he had when he'd first moved in with them. As they were loading the luggage into the car, Daniel had asked if Gina would be joining them later. *No,* Mick had replied, and before Daniel could feel relieved (he and Sarah had never liked Gina), Mick said *We're getting a divorce.* Daniel hadn't taken Mick to a hotel but rather to the Whitman home. Despite Mick's protests that he'd be an inconvenience, he'd seemed happy to sleep on the fold-a-bed couch, and the only thing that truly brought him out for the first couple of weeks was Jake. Daniel and Sarah had gone out to dinner one night and had come home to find the kitchen a shambles with cookie dough everywhere and Jake laughing hysterically as his Uncle Mick did a frighteningly good impersonation of the Swedish Chef.

"He's done this before. He goes behind his wall. But he's always come out, given time." Daniel understood it better now, for he'd done it himself.

"I hope so." Rachel looked serious, almost sad, and he didn't know what to do. He wished she would ask him for something. But Rachel never asked. She gave—not things or presents but of herself. God knew he was the benefactor of that, and he could never thank her enough for being his friend these last few months. But he didn't know how to return that gift. Nor did he know how long she could keep giving without asking for—or needing—something in return. He just hoped that when she did, Mick wouldn't give her only silence.

Chapter Seventeen

Daniel parked his car in the studio's lot and picked up the pink pastry boxes from the passenger seat. Before he stepped inside he took a deep breath and savored the feel of the early-morning sun on his skin. It was LA air and sun, none too fresh, but he might not see or feel it again for a while, depending on how work went. He didn't keep people in the studio all day without a break—in fact, Alan had told him he was too generous with his breaks. But now that the album was taking shape, he found it hard to tear himself away from the work even when he knew time away would be good for him.

For three weeks now he'd been at work with the musicians. *His* musicians, he sometimes thought of them. Not possessively, but as if they were fellow travelers. Most of them were session players he'd worked with in one capacity or another over the years: Camille McIntire on bass, Brent Taylor on synthesizers, and the two Terrys on guitars—Terry Simmons on acoustic and Terry Apodaca on electric. On drums and percussion was Reg's old stalwart Jesse Winyard. There'd been another player, a soprano saxophonist he knew from his work with Juliana Rael, but Daniel wasn't sure if he liked the horn—there was nothing wrong with the playing, it just didn't sound right for the album. He wasn't the only one to think so. Last night he'd gotten a text from Reg, who'd been doing his producing via e-mailed MP3s until he could get free from Switzerland: *Sax is too Kenny G.*

Need something else. Don't panic—let me ring up some friends and see who can help. Daniel knew Reg would come through.

It had been such an odd time. So strange and yet pleasant to hear the songs taking shape. What he'd heard in his head when he was writing them didn't always match up with what he heard in playback, with Camille and Jesse, and Terry S. and Terry A. and Brent all doing their parts. He'd tried not to be a dictator, benevolent or otherwise, but it was hard. These songs had been his alone since Saint Jude's, and more than once in the first day or two he'd been tempted to let the musicians go (with their full fees paid of course) and play the songs for no one but himself.

But he'd kept on, and he was glad. Because once he got past the initial *But it's MINE!* reaction to any of the session players' suggestions, he found that for the most part their ideas were good and made the songs better. That was no surprise. It was the way it always had been, but he was on the other side of the songs this time.

Daniel set the pastries in the break room, where they would be ready and waiting for the first arrivals (usually one of the Terrys and Alan the long-suffering engineer). Not hungry himself, Daniel sat down in the booth and played back the songs.

Ten of them so far. Desiree Stone was coming in to put vocals on "The Sparrow," "Ghostwalk," "Bitter Wine," and perhaps on "Memento," though he hadn't made up his mind yet about that song. Two more still needed to be laid down, and then he and Alan and Reg would finesse the details. It wouldn't take long now. This shouldn't have surprised him; Camille had taken him aside early on and asked him how long he'd been working on them. She was shocked when he'd told her how new they were. "They sound like something you've been working on for a long time," she said, and then blushed because anyone who knew him also knew he could never have written these before the events of last fall. The man he'd been before couldn't have written them. The man he was now had to.

He skipped the opening instrumental, "Sirocco," because Reg had been right, the sax was too Kenny G. "Winter Roses" was next, still his favorite. It was the longest, too, at nearly twelve minutes. Camille and one of the Terrys had suggested splitting it and using the parts to bookend the piece, like Pink Floyd's "Shine On You Crazy Diamond." He'd ask Reg about that. Then it was "The Low House" with its synth notes so deep they were almost subliminal and the off-kilter piano he'd played at that ill-fated session. A seamless segue into "Ghostwalk," which just needed Desiree's vocals to be complete. "Bitter Wine" was what he half jokingly called the hit single of the album, with a steady, driving beat that made you sit up and take notice—Jesse had actually broken a drumstick on that one. "Bitter Wine" ended with an abruptness that had been accidental but now sounded purposeful, especially when followed by "The Kiss," a solo piano piece. He wanted to redo his vocals on "Memento," and if he figured out what to do about the saxophone problem, he'd use that solution on "Lost" as well. "Heart of Light" gave him goosebumps—he, Terry A., and Brent had managed some truly eerie harmonics, and he still wasn't sure how they'd done it. It was a happy accident, like the slightly out-of-tune piano work on "Landfall." "The Sparrow" just wanted Desiree's vocals—she'd be singing one of the tunes the woman in the diner had sung to him. The words weren't fresh in his mind anymore, but the melody was, so he would have Desiree sing a wordless melody. Whenever he listened to the playback on that, he wondered: Would the woman from the diner ever hear it and know it was about her? Would she hear "Winter Roses" and recognize her melodies? He hoped so; it was his only way of thanking her.

For the most part he liked what he heard, but it lacked something. It didn't end properly. The individual songs were good, but the whole thing needed some grace note. Daniel tried not to worry about it. It would come to him, most likely.

It was well past time to start the day's work, so he went into the break room to find, of all people, Reg standing there, looking travel rumpled but otherwise his usual self. He was holding forth while he doctored his tea with five sugars and a Splenda. ". . . and his evil team of miscreants, wouldn't know a cross-fade if it bit him on the bum, I'll tell you that much. I say, are there any cinnamon rolls?"

Daniel wasn't surprised. Reg was the man who once stomped out the door of his London manor after an argument with his second wife, with nothing but a five-pound note in his pocket, and two days later had somehow made it to Kashmir—all this without a passport. Switzerland to LA at the drop of a hat was nothing unusual.

Standing next to Reg was a gangly scarecrow of a man with the most shocking orange Irish hair Daniel had ever seen, twisted into dreadlocks that reached the middle of the man's back. He crammed an entire blueberry muffin into his mouth and then waved hello at Daniel.

"This is Seamus York," said Reg. "The help I spoke of. He's engaged to my daughter, Jade. I told him I wouldn't pay for the wedding unless he came out here."

Seamus swallowed the muffin and nodded. "He spent the whole flight rabbiting on about your tunes, said you needed some pipes. I'm your man for that. Just so long as we're agreed on the payment."

"What's your fee?" Daniel asked.

Seamus grinned. "Don't need a fee. I want to go to Disneyland!"

Daniel laughed. "Tell you what." He stood on a chair and addressed the musicians. All of them present now along with Alan the long-suffering engineer, and Desiree Stone had just come in. "When we're done, I'm taking us *all* to Disneyland. My treat."

They applauded. After breakfast and after a round of greetings and backslappings, Reg said, "Enough tomfoolery. Seamus, play something for Danny here."

Seamus, serious now, nodded. He unlocked a narrow black case and took from it a wooden flute. "Future Dad 'ere told me about you, had me listen to your songs. I hope I can help you out." He put the flute to his lips. The sound was softer than that from a metal flute, with a sort of ethereal melancholy to it. Daniel shivered, remembering that night on the beach when grief caught up with him, remembering the taste of that stoner girl's kiss. This was the sound he'd been searching for.

The next few days were all about Seamus's flute and Desiree's voice. Daniel was glad Reg was on hand because after hearing what they added to his songs, he was often transfixed, unable to do much save for nod. "That's good," Reg would say. "One more like that." At times Daniel felt a bit like Dr. Frankenstein—his creation had gone beyond his control, become something else. It had just started as a few piano meanderings, as a way of undoing whatever damage he'd done to his wrists and hands.

By the time Friday evening came and he called it quits for the weekend, Daniel felt drained. It was the way he'd felt when he first started playing seriously at Saint Jude's or those days at his house when he'd been so absorbed in the music he'd forget all about trivial things like food or sleep. He was thankful when he arrived at the Reilly house and received his usual warm welcome. Here was his haven, a safe place to decompress from the work and the emotions that the music sessions put him through.

That night he was up late despite his weariness, long after Kate and Hugh had gone to bed. When he did sleep his dreams were a confused jumble of images and music; through it all he had the sense of trying to reach someplace. A place where he'd find safety and love and be forever sure of both. Home, or what home should be. It was veiled, out of his sight. He could hear it, though, and had the vague recollection he'd heard something like it before.

Daniel woke with music in his head. As soon as the stores opened he ran out and bought an electronic keyboard—much like the one he'd owned long ago. All that day he sat with the keyboard on his lap and headphones plugged into it so he wouldn't bother anyone or feel self-conscious. He returned to LA a day early, and when the musicians and Reg and Alan came in for the final sessions, he told them he had one more song, the one that would end the album: "Homecoming."

The day was overcast and pleasantly cool. Not at all like the last time he'd been here. To the best of his recollection that day had been bright and hot; southern California didn't pay much mind to the calendar when it came to seasons and still thought September was summer—last year had been no exception. He couldn't recall any thoughts from that day, just sensory impressions. How hot it had been in the sun in his dark gray suit and how he'd shivered in the heat. How he'd had to keep swallowing though his mouth was dry and how it seemed he'd had to remember to breathe. How any person's touch felt muffled, as if it were through layers of cotton, yet made his nerves crawl. How tired he'd been.

Daniel told Dr. Levinson once that the grief was like some serious illness that had gone unchecked, festered into infection, and even now, when the worst of the infection was banished, had left its mark on him. *Of course,* Dr. Levinson had said. *That's exactly what it is. No one expects to get over a life-threatening illness in a month or so, but people expect to get over a loss in no time. It takes as much time as it takes, and every person does it in their own way.*

He supposed some people would say he'd been derelict in his duty, not coming here sooner. Maybe that was true. Now that he was here, he was surprised and relieved to find that he didn't regret coming.

Daniel wondered if he looked odd carrying his burdens: two bouquets of blue-lavender roses and a portable CD player. Probably, but he didn't much care. It was his grief, his to own and deal with as best he could. He wondered if anyone besides Dr. Howard and Dr. Levinson understood that, really.

Here. He didn't recognize the surroundings, but here were the graves. No, nothing familiar nearby, and his memory offered no vision of anything but the caskets and the flowers. He couldn't even recall any of the mourners' faces because he'd been too focused on the sight before him, too afraid to look at others' faces and see accusation there.

Side by side. The grass long since grown in. There were flowers here, relatively fresh. Kate said she came twice a month, once on the date of Sarah's birthday and once on the date of Jake's. He added his winter roses. He sat down and for a long while said nothing, just looked at the flowers, the graves, the names and dates. Not yet a year but it seemed like so much time had gone by. It frightened him a bit, the way time had gotten out of joint. Sometimes it seemed like another lifetime ago and sometimes very recent.

"Hello." Daniel's voice seemed loud, but he was in the one place he could talk out loud to no one physically present and no passerby would care. "I'm here."

Now that he was here he wasn't sure what to say. Or if he had to say anything.

"I should have come sooner," he said. "I know that. I just . . . wasn't ready before." No, he had to say something because he was saying this for himself. Sarah and Jake probably already knew everything he was going to tell them.

"I'm all right. I mean, as much as I can be. It's just that . . . without you in it, the world's changed, and I . . ." How was he to say what he felt? He wanted his old life back but knew that was impossible. He wanted to know why Sarah had called to him, saved him from drowning—he'd never told anyone, not even Dr. Levinson, about that. Because if he told, he might get the answer he feared more than anything. She didn't want him with her and Jake because he was to blame for their deaths. And though he knew it was ludicrous to think he was at fault, at times he still felt he was. Because these things could not just happen for no reason. Someone had to be responsible.

This wasn't going well. He set the CD player between the graves. After a moment Seamus York's Irish flute began, so softly at first that it was almost inaudible, gradually rising as the song gathered strength. Daniel relaxed. Everything he needed to say was in the songs. This was what he'd wanted from the moment he started writing: to say what mere words couldn't.

It was odd to think that the music that had been solely for his own solace was going to belong to others. Literally. After the sessions were over, when the work on final mixing was well underway, Daniel had made good on his promise to take the musicians to Disneyland. It was when they were all gathered for dinner at the Blue Bayou that Reg announced that the label he was signed with, Troubadour, had heard Daniel's album and were going to send him a contract. "They want you in the stores by Christmas," Reg said. Daniel had been dumbfounded; he'd sat there with his bowl of gumbo turning cold, unable to quite believe what he was hearing. Yes, he'd told Reg to run the album by the A&R man if he wanted, but he'd just said that to make Reg happy. Daniel hadn't supposed it would amount to anything. But it had, and in a few days a contract came for him to sign. Reg had complained that the advance wasn't big enough, but Daniel had been pleased enough and promptly signed. It wasn't the money that persuaded him, or the prospect of fame. The former he didn't care about and the latter he didn't want. "Tell them I won't tour it," Daniel told Reg. The thought of playing all those songs before an audience didn't appeal—oh, perhaps a charity gig or two, but to do an extended tour and play the songs so often that they lost their meaning? Never. "And I don't want to do any press except a local thing. If they want more, they'll have to do it without me." There was some grumbling from Troubadour, but in the end they went along with it.

Why he signed: he wanted to stay busy. He had no illusions that the album would sell many copies. But it would probably give a boost to his session work, and that would be welcome. It would fill up the time. That was something to think about. He was done with the album, and now ordinary life—so much of it—stretched out before him. Work would fill the void, somewhat. He understood that: as annoyed as he was with Mick, Daniel didn't blame the man for burying himself in his work the way Rachel said he was doing. The difference was, Daniel didn't have a marriage to jeopardize with incessant work, and Mick did.

Never mind it. Those were all concerns for later. Now he lay back and looked up at the cloudy sky, breathed in the scent of grass and roses, and let the music wash over him. Now it was part one of "Winter Roses." He'd had a surprise about that song just the other week, when he'd stopped to visit Rachel at her shop. Daniel had been looking through the mail Rachel had been picking up for him while he'd been in LA, was half listening to the music Rachel had playing in the background when he'd heard it. One of the melodies the woman in the diner had sung to him. He'd gone cold, inside and out, had felt his breath catch. He'd immediately run over to snatch up the CD case from its "Now Playing" stand Rachel had set up by the register. It was The Mediaeval Baebes' album *Salva Nos*. Rachel, looking at him as if she thought him more than a bit nuts (not that he could blame her), told him it was track seven—"The Coventry Carol." "A very old song," she'd said. "It goes back to the sixteenth century." A Christmas song, though not a happy one; it was about the slaughter of the innocents by King Herod. She'd looked at him keenly, asked him where he'd heard it before. He'd avoided giving her an answer. He'd heard it when he was lost.

Whatever else would happen, he wasn't lost anymore. He'd made his album, and it said everything he wanted it to say. Daniel knew that for certain as he played it for Sarah and Jake and there was nothing he'd left out or wanted to change or felt he had to take back. He lay there for a while even after the music was over. Thinking and remembering. Then he stood up, picked up his CD player, made sure his roses were arranged properly. "I miss you," he said. "And I love you. I always will." He sighed once, then turned and left the cemetery.

He'd hardly been home in the last month, but it was all as he'd left it. Daniel flung open the windows; the stale-air smell when he'd first opened the door was too much like that dreary apartment at the Coral Villas. Restless, he changed into old jeans and one of his more disreputable T-shirts and set about wrangling the backyard into shape. He'd been so busy with his music that he'd let the weeds get rather out of hand, and the lavender bushes nearly hid the walkway.

The doorbell's ring came in the early afternoon. He set down the trimmers and glanced at his watch. No one he knew was home at this time of day, the UPS man had come and gone, and the mailman wasn't due till teatime. The one downside of his cul-de-sac was that it seemed to be inordinately popular with the Jehovah's Witnesses. He yelled out, "No thanks, don't need a *Watchtower*. I am a high priest for Cthulhu!"

That usually did the trick, but the doorbell rang again. Grumbling, Daniel went to answer the door. He wished he had the guts to emulate his college buddy Kenichi Hirota and answer the door naked when he knew it was the JWs come to call.

He flung the door open, and whatever witty thing he'd planned to say vanished. Mick Kessler stood there, his weekday business attire rumpled, almost looking slept in. He was pale, and there was a tightness to his face that spoke of too many late nights at the grindstone. But it was the appeal in his eyes that took away any words of welcome or rebuke or simple surprise that Daniel might have spoken.

"If it's a bad time, I can come back later. But I need to talk. Not about . . ." Mick drew a breath, took off his glasses and gave the lenses a quick polish, then replaced them. "It's about Rachel."

Chapter Eighteen

She was up the same time as the sun. Rachel rose from her bed and padded into the kitchen. To say that Mama had left the guest house's kitchen well stocked would be an understatement. Three kinds of coffee: decaf, mild morning blend, and put-hair-on-your-chest French roast. Both skim milk and half-and-half in the fridge. The fruit basket was fully loaded, as was the bread box. Pantry and refrigerator were full of all the ordinary staples, plus most of Rachel's favorite treats and guilty pleasures: tins of paté, several kinds of cheese, strawberry-rhubarb jam, a bottle of apple schnapps, and a homemade spinach lasagna. All this on just a few days' notice. Mama hadn't lost her touch.

A week ago she'd made the call and asked if the guest house in Carmel was free. "Yes, it is," Mama had said. "Your Aunt Cassie and her new beau will be staying there for a while, but not till next month. Are you and Mick planning a getaway?"

Rachel had glanced around her store instinctively, but the help had gone home. "It'll just be me."

She didn't know if the brevity of the reply or the tone of her voice gave her away. "What's wrong, *Bebé*?" Mama asked. "Are you two going through some trouble?"

"Yes, Mama. I just need to think about things alone for a while."

"I understand. And maybe I shouldn't say this, but I'm not surprised. I could tell things weren't right—you never talk about him these days."

Rachel clamped her lips together to suppress a giggle. It seemed Mick wasn't the only one not talking much lately.

Her mother continued: "Just tell me when you'll be here, and I'll have the place all ready for you. And I promise I'll stay out of your hair, but I would like to take you to dinner one night."

"Ta, Mama. That sounds perfect."

She'd said nothing about the trip to Mick until just before she left. This was easy, for he was never around long enough to hold a conversation. It would have been easy to leave without telling him where she was going, and part of her—a small part, thank goodness, but part of her nonetheless—had wanted to do just that, and then say, *You noticed!* when she returned and he asked where she'd been. But she realized how mean and petty it was. That sort of thing wasn't going to solve any of their problems.

She'd guessed he would be surprised, but she wasn't prepared for his look of shock when he saw her packing her suitcase. He swallowed and said, "Is it your family? Is someone sick or . . ."

"No," she replied. "I'm going up north for a week. I need to get away from everything and think about us."

"Us? But . . . why?"

"Because I'm tired of being married to a ghost. I want a husband who's around, who talks to me."

He drew a breath. "I know, and I've been buried in work."

"You buried yourself. Maybe that made you feel better, but it's done precious little for me."

"I've done that for us, so I could give you things."

Rachel turned and opened her closet door. There, in a stack taller than her, were the boxes that came for her once or even twice a week. Presents.

By now her Amazon wish list must be depleted. "I don't even open them anymore. And you didn't notice." She laughed, and regretted it as she saw a strange look on his face. She wasn't the first person to laugh at him this way, but it was too late now.

She went back to packing her suitcase. "I'll only be gone for a week. Lilah and Marie will hold the fort down at the store."

"Where will you be? At your parents'?"

"No." She could tell why he was asking—so he could send flowers or even show up with a peace offering. "I'm not going to tell you where."

She'd never seen his face so still, and that bothered her. What bothered her more was his right hand, which was rising slowly, as if he was unaware of it, loosely curling into the beginnings of a fist.

Daniel may have written that off with a jest—*My sister throws a better punch*—but Rachel couldn't do that. Wouldn't. "Lay a hand on me, and I won't come back. Not even for my things."

"I don't . . ." He saw his half-raised, half-formed fist, and a look of genuine horror flashed across his face.

For a moment she wanted to comfort him, scrap her plans and stay. But then her resolve hardened.

He lowered his hand, looked away from her. His expression didn't change, but his eyes showed sadness she hadn't seen since Sarah and Jake died. Mick's voice was quiet when he spoke, and gentler than it had been in a long time. "Take as long as you need. And I'll be here if you come back. And if you don't . . ." He took off his glasses, put a hand over his eyes. "Let me know if you need help with the suitcase, if it's too heavy."

She'd meant to leave the following morning but it was just too tense in the house; Rachel left Los Cielos that afternoon, spent the night in a nondescript hotel in Ventura. When she arrived at the guest house the next day, it was fully provisioned, and there was a vase full of flowers on the table, along with a note from her mother urging her to take as long as she pleased and to let them know she arrived safely and when she wanted to go to dinner.

Rachel got up when she felt like it, usually had a leisurely breakfast, and then spent the days hiking or beachcombing. She'd brought books but didn't read much, preferring to sit outside and listen to the night or soak in the bathtub. It was quiet here, but the quiet was comfortable. In Los Cielos she'd spent too many nights rattling around in that too-big house; not for the first time she'd wondered why Mick had bought such a barn when there wouldn't be kids to fill those rooms.

She spent a lot of time at the beach, particularly the seventeen-mile drive. She'd park at a random place on the drive and walk along the shore. Beyond scouting for sea glass she didn't do anything but think.

The beach reminded her of her first date with Mick. The day they'd met at her shop, he'd asked if he could call her sometime; she'd said yes. Yet it was two weeks before she'd heard from him. When he did ask her out, judging by the expensive clothes he'd worn when they met and a certain reserved quality to him, she'd expected him to invite her to dinner at Bella Notte, Los Cielos's swankiest restaurant. But their date had been at the pier—dinner at the Crow's Nest, where they'd eaten fried clams and hush puppies. Then they strolled through the shops and went to the arcade. He'd trounced her at the shooting gallery, but she handily beat him at Skee-Ball; they pooled their tickets afterward and got her a plush tiger (Hobbes lived on her dresser now, keeping watch over her jewelry box). He'd given her many gifts over the years—one could never say he was not a generous man—yet it was that tiger that she treasured most.

Everyone leaves.

They were the words that had clanged through Mick's mind all through the night. Every time he woke, feeling that something was wrong but not sure what that might be, and reached out for her and found nothing, the words came back. And yet he couldn't blame Rachel for leaving. How many nights had she spent alone in this bed, waiting for him to come home?

At half past four he gave sleep up as a lost cause and padded through the house. It was so quiet. It always was up here on the Hill. The Kessler house shared a block with a TV news anchorman, a couple of wealthy divorcées, and some nerd who'd sold his patents to one of the big software companies and now spent his days writing *Doctor Who* fan fiction. Los Cielos's moneyed crowd. If he had to do it over again, he'd have bought something smaller, something closer to the beach. But old habits had died hard, even after New York. Buying the house on the Hill had been his last gesture—his last conscious one, at any rate—of competing with his father. *See it, old man? A bigger house than you'd ever dream of, and with an ocean view.*

But a bigger house just meant more rooms of silence. It shouldn't have been so silent, but it was, especially when morning finally arrived and Rachel's alarm clock didn't go off. He didn't hear her singing in the shower or running to the kitchen in answer to the teakettle's whistle. Everyday noises he wouldn't have thought he'd miss. Mick wondered how much worse it had been for Daniel, who not only had two people to miss but hadn't even had the comfort of familiar surroundings.

Mick didn't want to feel charitable toward Daniel. Not after the letter. Mick had opened the manila envelope; the note had puzzled him. *I'd thought you would understand, but it seems you still don't, so here it is.*

Before he could sort out what that meant he opened the sealed envelope, unfolded its yellow, lined pages filled with Daniel's handwriting. He'd only gotten as far as the first sentence: *By the time you read this, you'll probably know what's happened.* Mick knew exactly what he was reading. Skin cold, stomach churning, he furiously stuffed the note back in the envelope. It went into the bottom drawer of his home office desk. Where he kept his divorce papers, Gina's Dear John letter, the letters addressed to a small town in Missouri that were marked *Return to sender.* All the things he couldn't bear to look at but couldn't throw away.

The morning after Rachel left, he'd gotten dressed for work, then drove not to San Diego but all over Los Cielos. On and on he drove, and it wasn't until after noon that he realized he was on the lookout for Daniel.

They hadn't spoken or met for months, but Los Cielos wasn't a large town, and sooner or later you ran into everyone whether you wanted to or not. He'd last seen Daniel about six weeks ago; Mick drove past the Book Barn while on a Saturday errand and saw Daniel chatting with that homeless guy who was always playing his out-of-tune acoustic guitar for spare change. On the way back from his errand, nearly an hour later, Daniel was *still* talking to the homeless guy, and Mick even caught a fragment of conversation ("Yeah, he thinks he's such a socialist, but he buys Twinkies at the grocery store just like everyone else."). Despite his anger, Mick couldn't help feeling grateful for those glimpses, or for the reports he occasionally got from mutual friends. And of course Rachel kept him up-to-date; to his surprise, she never pressed him to mend the breach. Mick was secretly relieved, for if she did, he might have to explain not just about the note, unread save for that first line and now languishing in his desk drawer, but the real reason he couldn't bring himself to reach out. Everyone leaves.

226

But now Rachel had left.

"It's about Rachel," he said as he stood on Daniel's doorstep. "She's gone." His old friend's face had been uncharacteristically still at first, but his eyes widened in what looked like dismay. "Not gone, like … vanished." *Like you,* he'd nearly said. "She's left me."

"Oh no." Daniel looked away for a moment. "Oh, hell." Mick waited for Daniel to tell him he'd brought it on himself and he was on his own now. Repay him in kind.

"Come on in. Place is a bit of a mess, but have a seat. Give me a minute to change, and we'll talk. You want something to drink? Iced tea?"

"Yes, thank you." Soon he was sitting on the sofa, a glass of iced tea in hand. While he waited for Daniel to change out of his yardwork clothes, he looked around. The sofa was the same blue one from the old house on Sandpiper. He recognized the lamps as well, clear glass bases filled with seashells; he recognized the framed one-sheet for *A Hard Day's Night.* Framed pictures everywhere. Of Sarah and Jake. The Reillys. He and Rachel.

Yes, here was where he'd needed to come. And there wasn't anywhere else to go or anyone else to turn to anymore.

He was a quiet man, Rachel knew that, had always known that, uncomfortable with words save for in his business dealings. She'd seen Mick put on his businessman persona and find the words he needed. It puzzled others, but she understood it. He was like her brother Stephen, who stammered when he was young and could be paralyzed by shyness, yet who'd gotten into acting as a way to be another, more outgoing person. Stephen was now a full-time actor, doing commercials and made-for-cable movies.

But quiet did not mean uncommunicative, and sometimes Mick could say more with a small smile than others could say in a hundred sentences. Moreover, he was interested in her and respected her business success; never once did he try to tell her how to run things or treat her work as inferior to his own. In fact, he seemed to regard it more highly than his own, which he described in a dismissive tone as "moving money around on the map." His work impressed her, though, for Lord knew she found her own accounts enough of a challenge; no way would she have presumed to fiddle with someone else's money.

It hadn't been until after this past Christmas that he'd started to shut down. Even losing Sarah and Jake hadn't done that to him; he'd told her stories about them, shared memories. But though she would never say it to him, Rachel wondered if Mick hadn't in a way been grateful for the destruction of the Whitman home and for Daniel's disappearance. They gave him things to work with. He could take action, even if those actions changed little or nothing.

Perhaps like the rest of them he'd thought Daniel would be back by Christmas. Because when that holiday had come and gone, Mick had started taking more and more refuge in silence. Not quiet but silence. That's when there had been more frequent nights when she came home and heard his voice on their answering machine saying he'd be working late, not to hold dinner for him. She'd thought, as those weeks between Christmas and Daniel's return in February dragged on, that things had gotten as bad as they'd get.

She'd been wrong.

Rachel sat on a flat rock, idly tossing stones into the sea. Below her the waves endlessly crashed, foaming white over the shore; overhead the sky was so blue it nearly looked purple. She'd taken off her hat to feel the chill breeze blow through her hair, and already she sported a stripe of sunburn across her nose, but she didn't much care.

She picked up a small stone; tumbled smooth by countless tide washings, it nestled comfortably in her palm. The sun had warmed the stone and it felt almost soft to the touch. Yet when she pressed the stone with a fingernail, it left no impression. The softness was an illusion. A rock, that's what Mick's friends called him (save for Daniel, who still called him the Professor). Yet Rachel had always thought of him as a pearl. He seemed solid enough, but she sensed it was a fragile strength, one built by layer upon layer. What lay at the center of that solidity she didn't know; as far as she could tell, no one did.

Not even Sarah had known; Rachel had asked her about it once. Rachel and Mick had been dating for six months by then, and the night before, in bed, they'd talked about moving in together. She was living in a tiny walk-up over her store at the time, and the size of his house on the Hill was still welcome—it reminded her of her family's house in San Francisco. Yet it troubled her sometimes that she could have stories to tell dating back to her earliest memories. Sibling rivalries and family vacations. Getting lost at the farmer's market when she was four but not minding because the woman at the lost-and-found booth gave her pumpkin bread and hunks of honeycomb. When she was sixteen and had just gotten her driver's license, driving past the Napa wineries, rolling down the window so she could shout, "Grow, little grapes, grow!" to the vineyard plants.

All Mick's stories began at Los Cielos University. Nothing before that.

"He says he's an orphan," said Sarah on that long-ago day. She and Rachel were in the Whitman dining room. Sarah was making a pitcher of her sangria. "None of us believe it. I mean, what is this, a Charles Dickens novel? Back then, he'd sometimes get letters returned to him. They were to a Kessler in Missouri, so I'm guessing that was some sort of relative. And he'd made a few calls to Missouri, too, but they were never more than a minute."

"Like the time it takes for someone to get the call and then hang up." Rachel had said.

Sarah nodded. "Daniel wanted to get all Woodward and Bernstein and call the number. I asked him how he'd like it if someone called *his* family, and that put the kibosh on it." She'd looked out the window, where Daniel was grilling burgers while Mick threw a whiffle ball to Jake, who swung the oversize bat so enthusiastically that he spun around completely, lost his footing, and landed on his backside. "I always thought he might tell us about it, someday. But someday hasn't come yet."

The first person to leave was his mother. Mick found it hard after all this time to remember her face. What he did recall were her hands, always moving nervously, smoothing down invisible wrinkles in her skirt or picking at her cuticles. He remembered her forearms, their pale skin often marred by bruises. And her voice, always so low. Even when she cried or pleaded with her husband. She had learned the same lesson her son would: no matter what happened in the Kessler house, you neither spoke nor cried in a voice that might carry to the houses next door.

One morning she'd woken him for kindergarten as usual. She'd made him his breakfast: orange juice, toast, and Cream of Wheat. (Even now he could never see a Cream of Wheat box without remembering he'd had it for breakfast that day.) She'd sat at the table with him, drinking her Constant Comment tea, and then she'd said the thing that still haunted him. *You're growing up,* she said, and smoothed down his hair. *You look so much like your father.* Later he wondered if that was why she hadn't taken him with her.

She walked him to school and kissed him and told him to be a good boy, and when kindergarten ended that afternoon she did not come to get him. He waited for an hour, reading Dr. Seuss books while the teacher prepared the next day's lesson and gave uneasy looks at the clock. Finally she walked him home, and there at the curb were all their garbage cans, and boxes, too, overflowing with his mother's belongings. Her sewing basket and her clothes and the bone china tea set she only brought out on Sundays and her carnival glass vase and her Betty Crocker cookbooks. As young Michael stood there, staring at it all and trying to comprehend, the teacher let go of his hand. "There's your father," she said, and then she was gone, walking quickly away.

His father didn't greet Michael but dumped another load of possessions into one of the trash cans. "Get inside."

"But . . ."

"Now."

There was no idea of questioning that voice, let alone disobeying it. Michael went inside, where the house had a strange, half-plundered look. Here and there on the walls a dark square where a picture had been. Some rooms were nearly untouched, but the small sewing room had been stripped bare. Even the braided rug was gone.

The creak of the floorboards, and his father stood there. "Your mother's gone. I've gotten rid of her things."

Something tore in the fabric of the world then, and the rent was never fully mended and never would be. How could it? "When will she come back?" Michael foolishly asked, as if gone did not mean gone.

He didn't see the blow coming. There was just pain, a searing flame on the side of his face, and he was lying on the floor. Blood in his mouth from where he'd bitten his lip. Michael was dazed; he'd been hit by his father before, but always in the guise of discipline.

"She's gone," his father said. "You do not speak her name. Not here, not anywhere. If anyone asks you about her, say nothing."

"Where—"

He got no further. A hissing sound, and the belt came down. Once, twice, a third time, and then he lost count. Pain outside and emptiness inside.

"Don't make me do that again," his father said.

The next day half of Michael's face was covered in a livid bruise. His classmates stared, but his teacher said nothing, nor did any other grown-up because Michael's father was a big man in a small town. He owned the paper mill, the drugstore, and the coin laundry; he had been on the city council for years. The right word from him could cost someone their business loan or even their job. No one remarked on his mother's disappearance or about the times Michael sported fresh bruises. He soon became familiar with the way grown-ups looked at him and then quickly looked away, their gaze taking on that distant look of people trying not to see something. At school, his classmates mostly took the safe path and ignored him. A few, at the urging of their parents, befriended him in hopes that their families would gain favor with his father. But it wasn't long before Michael saw through those machinations and forsook friends.

No one spoke of his mother. Countless nights he'd lain awake listening to the wind blow through the oak tree next to his bedroom, wondering. If she'd fled, where had she gone, and why hadn't she taken him? Was it possible she wasn't even alive? Perhaps she'd gotten in an accident or succumbed to some bolt-from-the-blue illness like a stroke. And once or twice—after particularly bad beatings that were always followed by his father saying *Look what you made me do*—he wondered if she might have been murdered.

He'd never recall when the idea of escape came to him. He only knew, very early on, that it had to be practical and permanent. Not for him the doomed romance of simply fleeing in the middle of the night. He'd seen those kids brought back in short order, disgraced. That would not do. Early on he began to save his money, and to do what he could to earn more. While other kids were playing Little League or doing Boy Scout activities, he was delivering the weekly shopper or collecting bottles to bring in for the deposit money. At the earliest possible age he got a work permit; his industriousness pleased his father, who assumed that Michael would one day take over his businesses. Michael was careful to keep his true purpose secret, going so far as to have his college applications sent to a post office box so his father would not see that the schools were as far from Missouri as one could get without crossing a national border or falling into the ocean.

One August night when he was eighteen he waited for his father to go to a city council meeting. When he judged the time ripe he moved quickly, flinging boxes and a suitcase into his mud-brown Chevrolet. Like the suitcase and the tweed jacket and the acoustic guitar, the car was secondhand. A castoff, unwanted, rather like himself. He drove west, craving to floor it, but he feared a cop would not just give him a ticket but send him back to his father. Michael had already seen how his father reacted to his mother's disappearance and had no wish to see how he'd react to Michael's.

"Did you ever find out what happened to your mom?" It was the first thing Daniel had said since Mick started telling his tale.

"I told myself I would, one day. Lord knows it would be easy nowadays with google, or I could hire a PI. But I never did." Mick took a sip of iced tea; he'd barely drunk any, and after talking so much, he probably needed it badly.

"Do you think you ever will?"

Mick shook his head. "I used to think it would be because I didn't want to find out that she'd died. But I've been thinking about her a lot lately and . . . maybe I don't want to find out that she's fine. That she's happy now and never missed me at all."

Familiar thoughts; Daniel had them himself over the years whenever he wondered about the mother who'd given him up. But he said nothing. Partly he didn't know what to say. Partly he was emulating Dr. Howard and Dr. Levinson. They had to do this all the time. How on earth did they do it? Glad as he was to help, relieved as he was that his friend had come to him, Daniel felt the responsibility for doing and saying the right thing weigh heavy on him. But he'd carried heavier loads in his day; he'd carry this one.

"I wouldn't have picked LCU first," Mick said. "But I didn't have a whole lot of money. I knew I couldn't go back again and ask the old man for it. It gave me the best deal. I figured I'd get in, get my degree, then head east to some big city where I could . . . I don't know. Lose myself. I didn't expect to find a place like this.

"But I almost didn't stay. I didn't fit in. The first day I was on campus, kids kept asking me if I was a TA. I wasn't one of them. It was a lot like being back at home, in a way. There I walked around with a big sign hanging over me: here's the Kessler kid. Here I had a sign saying, here's the new kid. And I didn't have a place to stay. I missed the deadline for the student housing, and I didn't know apartments would cost so much more out here. So I was living in my car. I know most people didn't guess that, because I dressed nice. I had to tell Sarah; I don't even remember anymore how it came up. I thought for sure she'd laugh at me. But she didn't. She was someone special. But I guess you know that."

Daniel smiled. "You bet I do."

Mick didn't smile, but there was a hint of one in his eyes. "I'm preaching to the choir. But when I moved into the house with you guys and Eskimo Sally and the others . . . I belonged. I wrote to the old man and told him I was OK, but he sent all the letters back. I called and he hung up. So I guess I was as dead to him as my mother was. It hurt more than I thought it would, but it didn't matter because I had friends now. People who liked me for what I was, not because it would help them get a sweet business deal. You guys didn't care that I had to live in my car for a while or that I was from some hick town or that my guitar was secondhand. That sort of stuff didn't matter. I was so happy for that then, but the trouble was . . . somewhere along the way, I forgot it."

Rachel wasn't expecting her mother to be enthusiastic about dinner at the Hog's Breath Inn, but Mama was all for it. It wasn't until they were seated on the patio with glasses of cabernet poured, the appetizer before them, and their dinner on its way that Rachel guessed the reason. She might have known it from the way Mama was dressed in her best Beaditudes outfit, the chocolate-brown dress with the amber beading and the tiger-eye necklace, and the way Mama kept looking around expectantly.

"I don't think Clint's going to be here tonight," Rachel said.

"I'm sure I don't know what you mean." Mama looked somewhat crestfallen.

"Is that why Dad's not here? Jeez, Mama, you spend our dinner date getting slutty for Clint?"

"Rachel Harmony! Such a thing to say." Mama laughed, then her face became more serious. "I thought this should be a girls' night out. There are some things I wanted to talk about with you."

That was probably best. "Thanks for letting me have the house. Getting away was just what I needed." Rachel told her mother about it all. It took longer than she expected; by the time she finished, their main courses were in front of them.

Mama sighed, poured them both some more wine. "You always did have a yen for the quiet ones, the shy boys. Your cousin Ethan used to say, 'Here comes Rachel with another of her broken-winged birds.' He may be a bit . . ."

"Weird?"

"Eccentric. But he was right about that, I think. I'm not criticizing. Most women have their soft spots and better yours than a weakness for bad boys like your Aunt Cassie. I always thought she was born too late. She'd have gone for Byron: Mr. Mad, Bad, and Dangerous to Know."

Rachel thought it over, knew her mother was right. In high school she had never been one for the cheerleading squad, and her only sport was softball, which she enjoyed despite being a benchwarmer at best. Instead of the drill team she worked on the yearbook, and instead of sports she joined the croquet society, which was more an excuse to socialize and eat scones than anything else. Letterman jackets and fast cars didn't do it for her; give her a pleasant-looking fellow with a nice way about him who could hold a conversation about something beyond the surface, and she was perfectly happy. Shy guys were the best; bringing them out of their shyness took time but was rewarding.

"But some birds' wings can't be fixed," Mama said. "Or you can spend your whole life trying to fix them."

Rachel nodded.

"What you have to ask yourself is whether it's good for you in the long run, to fix them."

"That's what I came up here to think about."

She hadn't reached a decision yet. Most of the time she thought she would try to fix things; yet she would remember the way he'd started to raise his hand to her. That was one thing she would not tolerate. Ever. She hadn't told her mother about that. "I want to get things back on an even keel," Rachel said. "It should be a partnership. But it isn't. I feel like an emotional vending machine."

"Or the Giving Tree. I always hated that book."

Rachel hadn't minded that book when she was little, but a couple of Christmases ago she'd babysat a niece and read that story. It had taken on a meaning she wasn't sure she liked, now that she was a grown-up.

"What are you going to do?" Mama asked.

"I don't know yet."

At first New York was everything he'd hoped it would be.

Mick had never been to any place that was so energized. It wasn't alive in the way that Los Cielos was, but had a constant thrumming no matter what time of day or night. No quiet moments. Even the weekends didn't have the lazy indolence of sun-kissed California. Not while there were things to do, places to go. Money to make.

He started out as one of many small, new fish in the big pond of a major investment firm, throwing himself into the work with enthusiasm. Numbers, facts, figures, careful gambles—all things he understood and which had never let him down. It wasn't long before he was a rising star with a reputation for taking small-time, lackluster fund groups and transforming them into profitable ones. What's more, he did it with as much caution as he could, refusing to make a big maneuver if it could backfire, riding out the everyday ups and downs and surviving major downturns relatively unscathed. When people asked how he did it, he told them it was because he remembered what it was like to have to make every penny count. The Kessler family hadn't been poor, but Mick himself might as well have been, the old man had been such a tight-fisted bastard. And he never forgot, as many of his colleagues did, about the people whose savings were tied into these funds. When he'd see a risky but enticing gamble, Mick would think about Daniel and Sarah, socking away nickels and dimes so they could afford to have a child one day. He thought about Mrs. Amos, his next-door neighbor in Missouri: her husband left her when they lost all their money in an S&L collapse, leaving her to swallow her pride and clean houses for a living (including the Kessler house).

Before a few years had gone he made the leading trade paper's list of people to watch. Life was good. He was where he'd always wanted to be. Always comfortable to talk business, he seemed freed from being the quiet boy. He had like-minded colleagues and relished the chance to talk shop and relive the day's triumphs. (The one downside to Los Cielos had been that most of his friends weren't in his major. Sarah studied English, Daniel of course majored in music. His girlfriends, first Holly and then Lyanna, were sociology and art history majors, respectively. Vic studied animal science, and Eskimo Sally didn't seem to *have* a major but took whatever courses suited her fancy. Only Kenichi shared any classes with him, but Kenichi's focus had been on getting the savvy to run his own auto repair business one day.) Sometimes he'd catch a glimpse of himself in a mirror and wonder if anyone from his hometown would recognize him now with his suits and ties and his gold-frame glasses. And every once in a while, usually late at night, after some party where he'd had one Bombay and tonic too many, in his head (never aloud) he'd invite the old man to take a look at what he'd become.

When he met Gina, she was the admin for his firm's senior vice president. The man was a senior VP in name only; he'd more or less retired but put in appearances at the firm a couple of days each week. Like her boss, Gina was largely decorative. She spent much of her time doing what she called networking but seemed to be gossiping with a wide range of people. However, she always carried important-looking papers with her when she did this, and looked good in her Chanel suits.

Even after the memory of her became painful to him, Mick would always remember when he first saw Gina. She stood by a window, looking out over the city, and there was a pensive quality in her face that struck a chord with him. Then she turned away from the window, looked at him and smiled. Her cobalt-blue suit brought out the color of her eyes, and the afternoon sun slanting in through the window turned her hair a particularly rich shade of gold. As she passed by he seemed to feel the very air shimmer around her.

Even then he knew he was dazzled by her beauty, her glamour. She was like his work, his apartment, like New York itself—everything he'd dreamed of having back when he'd been drudging his life away in Missouri. She didn't mind that he didn't talk much; she loved the presents he showered on her. It satisfied something deep inside him when he'd walk into a social gathering with Gina on his arm and see envy on other men's faces. He didn't even mind if she danced with someone else at one of these gatherings, because he knew once they got home and into bed she'd be his. All his.

Except she wasn't.

He'd flown Daniel and Sarah out for the wedding; Daniel was to be his best man. When he brought them into his apartment he saw the admiring looks. "It's a far cry from that place we had at school, I'll say that," said Sarah.

"Yeah, and way better than the Chateau de Chevrolet. Ow—what?" Daniel winced as Sarah administered a sideways kick to his shin. "I mean, look at you now. To the manor born."

Gina bustled in then. She was on her cell, arguing with the caterer. Once she hung up she quickly said hello to the Whitmans, then dialed the florist and began arguing with him. On every table in the place were lists of things to be done, people to call, even lists of lists. Mick thought about Daniel and Sarah's wedding. A small ceremony at the Catholic church, followed by a reception at the Reilly house with barbecue and beer and one of those inflatable bounce houses for all the kids (more than a few grown-ups, including the bride and groom, joined in the bounce house fun). Then the local ice cream van driver showed up, and everyone in attendance got a free ice cream. Mick had told Gina about that and she'd laughed, but he'd sensed something condescending in that laugh.

Daniel and Sarah seemed to be thinking about their wedding, too, as they looked over the preparations and waited for Gina to get off the phone so they could say something beyond a bare-minimum greeting. "If you decide you don't need all these trimmings and trappings, let us know," said Sarah. "Do it the old-fashioned way. You've got us for witnesses, you've got the rings, the license. We just find a justice of the peace, say the words. Yadda-yadda-yadda, 'I do.' Then we go out on the tiles and commence drinking until people are standing over us saying, 'Are you guys OK?' What do you think?"

It sounded like a fine idea, and when he got Gina alone for a moment, he floated it by her. Her face went still, and her eyes took on a glacial hue; she said nothing. It was that moment he remembered two days later, after the rehearsal dinner when Daniel produced two cigars and led Mick outside for what was at first a celebratory smoke. "Are you sure you want this?" Daniel asked.

"What do you mean? Of course I do."

Daniel's face as somber as he'd ever seen it. "As long as you're sure. It's only . . . I thought when someone finally made an honest man of you, it'd be someone like Holly."

Holly, Mick's first girlfriend. The first girl he'd even kissed—well, except for that mistletoe incident with Eskimo Sally. Holly the Texas expatriate with her waist-length brown hair and her cute overbite, who wore cowboy boots *everywhere*, even to the beach, and hooked Mick on pulp science fiction novels. *Cowgirl in the Sand*, he'd called her, after the Neil Young song. He tried to imagine bringing Holly to the same places he brought Gina and couldn't. "I'm a different guy now."

"That's cool. Just don't be *too* different. You'll always be the Professor to us. And don't forget, *mi casa es su casa*."

He'd remember that several years later, the day he left work early on a Friday. That wasn't like him, but it had been a rough month for him and Gina. Well, the last six months she'd been increasingly distant and snappish, but he'd bring her jewelry or a new pair of shoes or some perfume, and all would be well again. She did love her presents. But the

241

last month had been bad; she'd had a miscarriage. That had been a shock, for she hadn't even told him she was pregnant yet. He'd reassured her that it was all right, he didn't want kids. He'd always told himself that; he was terrified he'd be like his own father. Yet he hadn't been able to stop thinking about the child that might have been, especially when not a week went by that he didn't get pictures or e-mails from the Whitmans about what Jake was up to. He picked up flowers on the way home, intending to persuade Gina to take a weekend away. It seemed they hadn't done that in forever, and it would surely do them good.

When he opened the door he saw the suitcases. His first thought was that she had somehow anticipated his impulsive plan. Then he saw the number of suitcases. Gina was far from a light packer, but even she couldn't wear this much stuff in one weekend. She came into the room, saw him looking at the suitcases. In one hand she held an envelope with his name written on it.

"Michael," she said. "You're home early."

What he remembered most: the punched-in-the-gut feeling. The way he felt cold inside and out, his body numb and his mouth speaking seemingly on its own. How she stood there with her arms folded, not angry or defensive. Simply stating facts. She was leaving. There was someone else. No, she wasn't going to change her mind. As the talk went on she became more honestly cruel or cruelly honest, however you wanted to look at it. She didn't love him. Had she ever? That was hard to say. At any rate, he bored her now.

He wished she would scream and yell, because that might mean she had cared once. Anything was better than this detachment. He'd suited her for a while, but now he was being discarded like last season's shoes.

"It's been hard," he said "I know that. The miscarriage . . ."

"That wasn't a miscarriage."

He was a moment in understanding what she meant. There was a blank spot, a gap in his recall. Then he stared at a hole in the wall, blood smeared on the plaster and wallpaper, his hand cramped into a painful fist with its knuckles scored and bloody. Gina staring at him, edging toward the door. "Go," he'd said. She left. Everyone leaves.

Mick didn't look at Daniel; he was looking down at his hands, which were clamped together. "I didn't sleep that night; I just kept thinking. Sometimes I thought about what you asked me, if I wanted to marry Gina, and what you saw about her that I didn't. But mostly I thought about when my mom left. How my father put all her stuff out by the curb. I kept wanting to do that, and every time I did I'd give my hand a good whack on the armrest, let it hurt a little bit. Because I'd really wanted to hit her. I'd never felt that before. I always told myself that I'd never do that to my wife or kid."

Daniel remembered Mick's abrupt return to Los Cielos. He remembered talking about it with Sarah one night, the two of them speculating on what might have happened. They'd always thought something had gone badly with Gina, but then again, they'd never liked her much. They supposed he'd tell them about it when he was ready to, but he never did.

"I figured nothing bad could happen here, and even if it did, we'd all help each other out. What happened to Sarah and Jake was terrible but . . . I don't know. It just happened, it's nobody's fault. That's easier for me to understand than when someone leaves." Mick looked at the ceiling, his hands, everywhere but at Daniel.

So it was Daniel who said, "Like me."

Mick nodded. "When it looked like you weren't coming back . . . I supposed it was safer to shut down. I didn't think that it would hurt things between me and Rachel, you see, because . . . I've always needed her more than she's needed me. I thought I could give her things to make up for that and . . . when she told me she was leaving I could tell she thought I was going to hit her. And I wasn't even thinking it, but I'd done this." He held his hand up halfway, half-formed into a fist. "It scared me then, so bad. And I remembered how I'd decked you that time . . ."

Daniel interrupted: "I don't hold that against you."

Mick's eyes flashed behind his glasses. "But you should. It wasn't right. I don't . . ." His well of words seemed to have abruptly run dry. "I don't know what to do."

He looked so resigned when he said this. Daniel felt the last of his resentment fade away. They'd let each other down, that was true. But was that so surprising? Both of them damaged goods in their own way. Yet it wasn't too late to try and mend things.

"I know where you need to start," Daniel said.

Rachel's first stop when she returned to Los Cielos was the shop. It seemed to have neither burned nor been burgled in her absence, and Lilah greeted her calmly. "Hi, Ms. K.," Lilah said. She'd only recently been broken of the habit of calling Rachel *Mrs.* K., which for some reason had always made Rachel feel old as the hills.

All was well. Lilah gave her the rundown, showed her the register numbers. Then Lilah opened the register and took out an envelope. "Mr. K. brought this over the other day, told me to give it to you when you came back."

As Rachel took the envelope, Lilah said, "Is everything OK? He looked really down. I'm sorry, that's none of my business."

"That's all right." Rachel excused herself and went into the back room, where she opened the envelope. The letter wasn't long, yet she spent a long time reading it over. She kept coming back to one line: *I don't know if we can fix things, but I want to try. If that's what you want.*

After a moment she picked up the phone, dialed his work number. She knew that's where he would be, and he was. "I'm back," she said. "Let's try," she said.

When Daniel knew he wouldn't be able to restrain himself from calling one of the Kesslers to find out how things were going, he left his phone at home and walked to the Chez. It was just after sunset, and the night was still warm. As he walked he occasionally heard the sounds of kids at play in the yards, their mothers telling them to come in *now*. The sounds made him smile, for a moment took his mind off his friends and what was going to happen with them.

"Tell Rachel what you've told me," Daniel had said. "She needs to understand why things have been this way. That's the only way you're going to fix things."

"What if we can't fix it?" Mick asked. "What if she doesn't want to come back?"

Daniel wasn't sure what to say. In the old days he'd have blithely reassured his friend that of course Rachel would come back. But he couldn't do that now. She might not. Or she might but things wouldn't last. He hoped those things wouldn't happen, but now he had to accept that they might. He'd said something to Dr. Levinson, and in one of his songs: that you could get what you wanted most, but there were no assurances how long you'd keep it. Five minutes, fifty years, who could say? What you had to do was cherish it, nurture it.

And if it was gone, let it go.

In the end Mick answered. "I want her to be happy. If that means we're apart, so be it." He sighed and then said, "Thank you for listening to all this. I know that there's still a lot to say with us . . ."

"One thing at a time," Daniel said. "Get you and Rachel back on the rails if you can. Then we'll sort out the other. I'm not going anywhere."

Mick nodded. "I'm sorry I hit you."

"I'm sorry I sent you that letter."

For the first time in a while a smile ghosted Mick's face. "I didn't read past the first line."

"Throw it away, then."

Mick let out an odd little laugh. He got up, walking with the stiff-limbed gait of someone who'd sat for a long time. His voice, when he spoke again, was rough around the edges. Daniel was familiar with both symptoms from those early marathon sessions with Dr. Howard. "Rachel tells me you made an album. I'd like to hear it, if that's OK?"

"Sure." He nodded. "When I get the advance copies in I'll send you one."

"Thanks." After an awkward moment they shook hands.

Daniel knew Rachel was back in town now, but he hadn't heard from either of the Kesslers since then. He didn't know if that foreboded good or ill.

It was full dark by the time he descended the Chez's staircase. He took a moment to breathe in the familiar aromas of coffee, cinnamon, and cloves, then headed to the bar. Ariel glanced up from the espresso machine.

"Hey, Daniel." She cocked a thumb toward the far end of the room. "Your friends are still here."

Mick and Rachel were tucked into the farthest corner of the room. They seemed deep in conversation. Empty cups and plates were beside them. "How long have they been there?"

"Quite a while. Want your usual?"

He nodded. As he watched, Rachel leaned forward, took Mick's face in her hands, and kissed him. Daniel looked away, not wanting to intrude; he smiled, and yet his eyes stung. "To go, Ariel, if it's no trouble."

"You're not staying?" She was used to him whiling away hours there.

"Not tonight." He got his beverage, paid, and left. Outside, he raised his cup in a toast to his friends and wished them luck.

Chapter Nineteen

"You have to admit, this looks rather compromising."

"Just hold still."

"But think of it! Someone walks in, gets an eyeful, and the scandal gives me free publicity. Ow!"

"I told you to hold still."

Daniel glanced at his watch. The signing would start in fifteen minutes, cause enough to make him nervous. But Rachel had noticed that the cuffs on the trousers of his sharkskin suit were rolled, not hemmed. Deeply offended, she'd bullied him into the bathroom of Blue Angel Records, and now he stood on the toilet while she wielded needle and thread.

"I can't believe you never had these hemmed." Rachel bit off a thread, tied a knot, then went to work on the other cuff.

He started to shrug.

"Don't move," she said.

Daniel tried not to fidget. It wasn't easy. He could hear the faint murmur of people. The indistinct noise was familiar: the sound of a crowd. He'd caught a glimpse of the line already and was surprised at its length, though he supposed he shouldn't have been.

He'd gotten the first e-mail before the album was even released. The advance copies had gone out to radio stations and were getting airplay; he'd been startled the first time he'd tuned in to the college station, KLCU, and heard "Winter Roses (Part 1)." After that not a week went by that he didn't hear one of his songs—usually on KLCU or Internet radio, but more than once on the big LA or San Diego stations.

But it was the e-mail that brought it all home to him. Theresa had set up a website for him. Very simple: just the album's cover and credits, the list of the song titles and sample MP3s. There were only four links: one to Troubadour Records, one to a page with the song lyrics, one to a page with brief bios of the session musicians, and one to send e-mail. That was how the message had come. It hadn't been long, just a few lines, but they'd moved him all the same. *Dear Mr. Whitman*, the e-mail said, *I heard your song "Winter Roses" on the radio. I've been going through a bad time lately, and your song really helped me. I play it all the time. Thank you so much.*

There had been more like that, many more. And the album was selling better than he'd thought it would. It hadn't really sunk in, though, until his publicist said she was arranging the signing here at Blue Angel. He'd agreed—partly to give his poor publicist something to do, and partly because he felt he owed it to the people who'd been buying his album, and who'd been writing to tell him how much they liked it and, more often than not, how much the songs meant to them.

Now that the time for the signing was at hand, his nerves were ajitter. He'd written those songs to keep from going crazy because he didn't have the answers then and still didn't. What if people asked him for answers to their questions? He couldn't find the answers to his own.

Don't worry, Dr. Levinson had assured him. *Nine out of ten people will just want to thank you. Just be nice and thank them back.* It seemed the right thing to do. That, and remember that he'd been on the other side of this situation many times; he'd be kind to anyone who turned into a gibbering fanboy.

"Hold still," Rachel admonished him again. "Haven't you ever been to a tailor before?"

"No. I still think a scandal would help me out," Daniel said.

"It would go over like a lead balloon in couples counseling."

After a moment, he asked, "How's that going?"

She knelt back on her heels for a moment, gave the hems a critical eye. "It's going really well. We're talking about lots of things we should have discussed a long time ago. It's good for us."

"I'm glad."

Rachel tugged on one cuff. "It'll do. No one's going to be looking at your feet. At least your high-tops match, for a change. Hop down."

As Daniel jumped down, Rachel said, "Thanks for the referral. I like the counselor we're seeing."

"*De nada.* Dr. Levinson gave me the name. You can thank him if you want, he said he'd try to make it here today." Speaking of which. "So Mick couldn't make it?"

She shook her head. "He wanted to. We got the CDs you sent. He's been playing his a lot but hasn't said much to me. Unfortunately he's got an off-site today." She paused, regarded Daniel. "And it's not an excuse. That's been on his calendar for weeks now."

"It's all right." He'd only seen Mick once since the day of their big talk. Mick had come by the house and told him that he'd talked with Rachel, they were going to work on putting things back together, and was there any way Daniel could get a referral to a counselor from Dr. Levinson. Daniel hadn't minded the quiet—he could wait. But he wanted to know what Mick thought of the album. They'd always talked about dream musical projects, back in those college days, he with his electronic keyboard and Mick with that old acoustic guitar. A rock opera about the Three Stooges, with a ten-minute jazz fusion instrumental titled "Moe, Larry, the Cheese!" had been their favorite of those dream projects. Daniel laughed softly when he thought of it.

"What's funny?" Rachel asked.

"Old times."

They went into the store's tiny break room. As green rooms went it wasn't much, but Daniel had shopped here for years and was much happier at Blue Angel than if the signing had been at the Borders over on Second Street. As soon as he and Rachel sat down, one of the store employees came in. "You're on in five minutes," he said.

Daniel sighed. The nervousness was coming back. Out in the store was a table set up with CDs for sale and a big poster of the album cover. He still wasn't sure how he felt about that cover. He'd wanted just a simple shot of himself at his Bösendorfer, but the woman from Troubadour had other ideas. At one point she had him lie in a rather uncomfortable way, across the piano's lid. "Great," she'd said. "Now turn your head and close your eyes. Like you're asleep. That's perfect." She'd snapped pictures for what felt like ages, but that shot was what they'd used for the cover. Sometimes he thought it made him look like a poser. But everyone else seemed to like it.

And for the next hour, what he liked didn't matter. What mattered was that his music had touched people, and some of those people had come to see him.

It was one of the stranger hours of his life, as a steady stream of people came up to him and asked him to sign their CDs. Many of them were total strangers. Some he knew by sight—there was one of the clerks from the local liquor store and a little old lady he recognized as a tenant of the Coral Villas. There were a number of friends and acquaintances—from Rachel, who grinned and said, "Nice suit by the way. Who's your tailor?" to Mr. Frank from Sandpiper Street. As for family, none of the Whitmans had come: he'd dutifully sent the parental units and his sister each a copy but had only gotten "Oh, that's nice, dear" from the former; the latter's husband had sent a thank-you note, but there was no word from Victoria herself. There were a few Reillys present, although they'd all gotten their signed copies weeks ago. Kate and Hugh were there, as was Amy, and also Martin's oldest daughter.

But it was the visitors from up north who moved him the most. Dr. Howard was the first to greet him. She smiled almost shyly, looking ten years younger as she did so. "I'm so proud of you," she said as he waved aside her handshake and instead stood up and embraced her.

"Thank you," he said. "I couldn't have done this without you." She denied that, but he knew it was true, remembering St. Jude's, playing that old piano and finding his way back.

Daniel would have loved to spend a while talking with Dr. Howard, but there was still a long line. And maybe ten people later, another visitor from his lost days.

Tamara still wore her silver necklace with its locket and its multiple religious symbols. Her smile was as he remembered it, crooked but pretty. "I still read the liner notes," she said.

He embraced her as he had Dr. Howard. "Thank you. For everything." She knew what he meant by that.

It wasn't until the last few minutes of the signing that he saw the visitor who made him smile the most. "Welcome to Crazytown. Population: us!" Wayne's hair was shorter but otherwise he looked just as

Daniel remembered him. He was accompanied by a strawberry blonde with a Midwestern farm girl look to her.

Daniel laughed and shook Wayne's hand. "This is Beth," Wayne said, putting an arm around the strawberry blonde. "She didn't believe I knew you from Saint Jude's."

Beth had a slightly wicked grin that lent spice to her all-American looks. Daniel could see why Wayne liked her. "Well, if you believe Wayne, you two bunked with Brian Wilson on one side of you and Elvis on the other."

"Don't worry. I won't tell her that it was really Lawrence Welk and Tony Orlando. Wait, did I just say that out loud?"

Like he had with all the people he knew, he invited Wayne and Beth to join him at MacHeath's later. They wouldn't be able to make it—they had to catch a train back north—but Wayne made up for that with his parting words, delivered at top volume so that the entire store heard them: "Well, make sure you stay out of trouble, man. Prison's not as nice as the psychiatric hospital!"

My friends. Daniel shook his head, smiled, and turned his attention to the next person in line.

"Susan tells me it went very well." Dr. Levinson paused to squeeze three lemon wedges into his Diet Coke. "I'm sorry I got delayed."

"That's all right," said Daniel. "I was surprised Dr. Howard came."

"She's proud of you. Not just how far you've come since you were in her care but your music. She gives it to some of her patients, did you know?"

"She told me that. But . . . when she told me, and half the time today, I felt like a fraud. I just did this for me. I wouldn't have even made an album if Reg hadn't lit a fire under me."

"Do you regret it?"

"Hell no. But people are thanking me for it when I did it just for me."

Dr. Levinson shook his head. "But that's all any art is. Something done just for the artist. Whether it's a song or a story or a painting, it starts as something done for the self. If it touches other people, that's a blessing. Accept it graciously."

"I'll try." Daniel looked around. Still a couple of hours till MacHeath's closed. His publicist had left after he'd caved in and said he'd play at Coachella next year as a tag-team effort with Reg Fletcher. Tamara and Dr. Howard had left for their long drives home. The Reillys had gone and so had the local crowd.

Yet there was one person he'd hoped would come, though he wouldn't have known how to recognize her.

As he did so often, Dr. Levinson seemed to guess his thoughts. "She didn't come?"

"No." The woman from the diner, who sang to him. The one he'd nicknamed the Sparrow and thanked as such in his liner notes. Several people had asked him who the Sparrow was, but Daniel had told no one save for Dr. Levinson. To the others he said that she was someone he'd met while he was wandering. Only Dr. Levinson knew about that night, and even he didn't know everything. "I suppose it's ridiculous to hope that she'd hear the album and know she was who I meant. I guess it's my way of thanking her." For that night, and for all the others—fewer of them now, thank God—when he woke from bad dreams or was simply brought low by the dismal prospect of the years ahead without Sarah and Jake and the only

254

thing that consoled him was the memory of her voice. How soft it was, the compassion he'd sensed in it. How good it had been to not feel so alone in the world. "It would be nice to thank her in person. But it's a chance in a million that she even hears *Winter Roses*, let alone knows it's referring to her."

"It's the best you can do," Dr. Levinson said. "So for now, it will have to do." He finished his Diet Coke. "I'm expected at home. Congratulations, Daniel."

"Thank you. I couldn't have done this without you, too, you know."

After Dr. Levinson had left, Daniel considered going home. He'd thought the peace of his house would be welcome after such a hectic day, but now the thought of all that silence just seemed depressing. He lingered over his iced tea, ordered another round of potato chips. But what came was not potato chips but a root beer float, delivered by an exasperated-looking Eli.

"Gentleman over there ordered this for you," Eli said. "It's supposed to be a—wait, I wrote it down. A double-pasteurized milkshake with a swami yogurt chaser. This is the best I can do. Tell me that's all right so the gentleman will leave me the fuck alone."

"It's all right. Tell the gentleman I'd like to thank him in person."

"Will do."

Daniel wasn't at all surprised when Mick came and sat down. "I thought you weren't back till tomorrow night," Daniel said.

Mick shrugged. "I blew it off. They weren't telling me anything I didn't already know. How did it go?"

"Well. Very well. It still all feels a bit unreal."

"That's kind of appropriate," Mick said with a dry sort of laugh. "Maybe you don't know, but when you listen to it all the way through, it leaves you feeling unreal. That last song, especially. 'Homecoming.' It takes you somewhere." Mick folded his hands, spoke mostly to them. "I've been thinking about things a lot. And playing your album a lot. I understand things more now. Not everything. I still don't see why you left. It would be one thing if you didn't have anyone who cared, like . . . anyway, I can accept that you weren't doing it to hurt any of us.

"It probably makes me a pretty crappy friend, not coming around sooner. But I'm trying to be better. My best probably won't be much to write home about. What I'm saying is that I'd like to be friends again."

Daniel almost fancied he could read Mick's mind and know what he left unspoken: *I understand if you don't want to be friends any longer.* Probably it was within his rights to refuse the peace offering, but that thought never crossed Daniel's mind. Because he also understood things better now. Understood that his friend had spent so long trying not to break that he found it difficult to bend; despite that, he was trying to bend, for Rachel's sake and for Daniel's. And Daniel understood that if he hadn't had the Reilly family's love when he was young, he could have ended up that way.

He made his voice as serious as he could. "On one condition."

"Yes?"

"Let me buy you one of these." He pointed at the root beer float.

God knew what Mick had been expecting, but his relief was so obvious it sent Daniel into giggles. After a moment Mick joined him, and the two of them laughed at nothing very funny, but the laughter felt more right than many things had for a while.

Chapter Twenty

Another Christmas.

The presents long since unwrapped, the stockings emptied, the dinner and dessert consumed. The Reillys and the Kesslers were in the traditional end-of-holiday wind down. Younger kids had collapsed into bed, older kids drifted from present to present. Grown-ups were dawdling over their own presents or indulging in a last nibble of the feast.

As holidays went, Daniel rated it a roaring success. Certainly better than his Thanksgiving had been. For some reason he'd taken it into his head to see his adoptive family. Guilt perhaps? It had been over a year since he'd seen them, and he honestly hadn't missed them at all. It had sunk even lower than his already diminished expectations. Annie and Tom had been their usual pleasantly detached selves. Victoria had scarcely looked at him and had spoken even less. That left Victoria's milquetoast husband, Lester; at first Daniel and Les had a rather pleasant time talking about that autumn's Oscar-bait movies. But between the appetizer and the meal Daniel overheard Victoria admonishing Les. "I don't want you talking to him. The man's nuttier than a Christmas fruitcake," she said in a furious whisper. "Yes, it's true, don't look at me like that. For Christ's sake, didn't you see his scars? I don't know why Mom and Dad even invited him; it's not like he's family anyway." After that Les hadn't said anything beyond, "Please pass the gravy" to Daniel, and even that was said with a skittish look, as though Les expected Daniel to flip out and start flinging candied sweet potatoes at the walls. Not that this wasn't a half-tempting idea, but instead Daniel stepped outside between dinner and dessert and called the Reillys, told them he could probably make it from Riverside to Torrance in about ninety minutes if he floored it, and would they save some pie for him? He'd arrived to find not just pie but a drumstick, a huge helping of dressing, an even bigger helping of creamed corn, and half a bottle of Riesling. He felt like Max, returning from where the wild things are to find his supper, still hot, waiting for him.

But now it was Christmas, and he was where he should be.

Mick had brought a fine bottle of port as his gift to the hosts. Daniel now lay in the hammock with a glass of the port in one hand. He'd barely sipped it; he already felt half-drunk on food and good company. And melancholy.

September had come and gone but it hadn't been until this holiday that he'd felt he'd passed the anniversary. He'd lost track of the calendar during his lost time, but after looking over the paperwork from the Faber hospital and from Saint Jude's, he'd determined that the night at the Marina Inn had been on the winter solstice. Longest night—that seemed appropriate. Christmas had been at Saint Jude's. He couldn't recall any mention of the holiday then, so either he'd still been out of it, or celebration was kept on mute lest it trouble the patients.

If it was the latter, well, he could understand that. Certainly he was feeling the loss more tonight than he had when the actual anniversary had come. Christmas was an anniversary, he supposed, of when he'd started living again. It was a life not without its good moments, but it was not the life he would have chosen.

Yet it was the only life he had.

He'd told no one, not even Dr. Levinson, that he did not look forward to the coming year. Hard as this last year had been, he'd had the album to help himself heal. And more importantly than he'd expected, to keep him busy. But now, lying there in the hammock and looking up at the stars, he thought about the years ahead and his life with something that was not quite dread and not quite acceptance. Resignation, perhaps.

"Daniel?" Kate's voice.

"Here in the hammock."

"Of course. Where would anyone in this family go off to without it?" She came and stood nearby. "If you want to come in, there'll be eggnog soon. Oh, and Joanna's making hot chocolate from scratch, with peppermint schnapps if you want it."

"I'll be there with my jingle bells on," he replied.

"Whenever you're ready."

He'd thought he was ready, but he wasn't. It was what he'd said. *I'll be there with my jingle bells on* was a Sarah-ism, one he'd heard her say so often that he'd forgotten when he'd first heard it. He felt the familiar pain, like a knife taking tiny nicks out of his heart. His scars itched.

"A little while longer," he said.

She said nothing, for which he was grateful. Kate leaned down and touched his shoulder, the way Dr. Howard had at their first session. Daniel took Kate's hand in his for a moment, then she went inside.

Daniel looked up at the night sky. For a second he had the impression that someone was watching him, but when he looked around he saw only the empty backyard. He looked back up at the sky, remembering those nights when he'd been wandering. Nights spent on beaches or in campgrounds, looking up at the stars, searching for solace and finding none.

He saw no solace in the stars now, but he knew what he had. His music. His family. His friends. Were they enough? They would have to be.

Laughter drifted from the house. The clink of glasses. A chord strummed on an acoustic guitar—Mick had brought it out of storage, was attempting "Greensleeves." A poor job of it, but judging from his laughter he didn't seem bothered. Daniel lay for a little while longer, looking at the sky and listening to the sounds from the house. He sighed, wiped his eyes dry, then got up and went inside.

The Sparrow

Chapter Twenty-One

The song was "Without You"—written by Badfinger, covered memorably by Harry Nilsson. An old favorite, veteran of a dozen "songs of heartbreak" mixes. When that song was done, he segued into Nick Cave and the Bad Seeds' "People Ain't No Good." He hadn't planned a set list but went with whatever seemed appropriate for an anti–Valentine's Day concert.

Less than a week ago he'd gotten the call from Kenichi Hirota, the drummer for Chekhov's Gun. Daniel's session gig for Juliana Rael had fallen through when Juliana decided to deal with her latest breakup not by recording an album full of man-hating songs but by running off to Baja with a handsome surfer dude half her age. Daniel didn't mind, though it had been tedious languishing in the recording studio for two days waiting for Juliana to show. No sooner had he gotten home from LA and opened his door when he heard the snarky drawl of Kenichi's voice on the answering machine.

"—the *third* time I've called and you're not around. I think you're lying about not having a social life. Anyway, it's—"

"Kenichi," Daniel said as he picked up the phone. "How goes it?"

"Hey, round eyes. Wait. What? No, not you, sir. My buddy here on the phone. Sorry about that, customer heard me and probably thinks I'm going to rig his car to go all kamikaze."

Daniel grinned. Kenichi was only one-eighth Japanese but liked to play up that part of his heritage, going so far as to legally change his name from Kyle. "Tell him not to worry, you're twice as white as I am."

"Fuck you, gaijin. Listen, are you locked up for anything on Saturday? Me and the rest of the Gun are doing an anti–Valentine's show, and all our special guests have reneged for one reason or another."

"So I'm your last resort?" Daniel meant it as a joke.

But Kenichi's voice became serious. "No, man. Not at all. Tim and me, we wanted you in from the get-go. But Athena and Vic and Jerome, they said ... I mean, I know it's been a while but still. You know. Valentine's Day and all."

He and Sarah had never been big on the holiday, but they'd always done *something* for each other. The first one after they'd married, when money was tight, she gave him a handful of Hershey's Kisses, then laughingly confessed that she'd stolen them out of the candy dish in the teacher's lounge. Holidays you'd never cared about took on meaning when there was no one to share them with.

"Count me in," Daniel said. "Just tell me where I need to be and when."

Where was the Backbeat, LCU's oldest and best music club; *when* was Valentine's Day of course. But it was the *who* that sealed the deal for Daniel. He'd known all the band members for ages, roomed next door to Kenichi, shared a stage with one person or another back in the college band days. The real treat, though, would be his old friend Eskimo Sally attending the show. She'd moved back to the States from Fiji under somewhat mysterious circumstances and had shown up on Daniel's doorstep the spring after *Winter Roses* came out. He'd teased her that she'd only returned in time for the Coachella music festival and to finagle backstage passes so she could meet Reg Fletcher, but in truth it was good to have another friend relatively nearby. He wished she'd have settled in Los Cielos, but she was now in Santa Cruz, working at a New Age store called the Dancing Cat. She'd been most annoyed when he'd told her he would be in LA on session work during Valentine's. Surprising her would be the most fun he'd had in ages.

Now that he was here at the Backbeat, he realized afresh how much more affecting a small, intimate gig could be than something large-scale. Not that Coachella hadn't been fun, despite the heat. On day one Reg had been the headliner and Daniel in his backing band. On day two Reg and the band had returned the favor for Daniel, and they'd played the *Winter Roses* album in its entirety. It was the only time he ever had done that. The songs were like an old music box; he was afraid to play them too often lest they break somehow, lose their power. Coachella hadn't been his only gig that year. Far from it. Over these last two and a half years he'd kept busy—if nothing else, the cult success of *Winter Roses* put his session services in high demand. But lately his time at the keyboard felt more like duty than passion.

Not tonight, though. Tonight the keys felt alive under his fingers in a way they hadn't for quite some time. Perhaps because he was surrounded by friends, perhaps because this stage was so familiar to him. Almost before he realized it, he began playing "Winter Roses," both parts. He hadn't played it in months but didn't miss a note, for it was not just a song to him and never would be.

Daniel mused that when you went bowling with Eskimo Sally, you could count on a few things. She would always have her own ball; the latest one was blue paisley. She would bowl nothing but strikes and gutters. She would sing Camper Van Beethoven's "Take the Skinheads Bowling" at least once. And she would forget to bring her own bowling shoes and spend half the evening worrying about how germ-infested the rented shoes were.

"I still can't believe you didn't tell me you'd be there," grumbled Eskimo Sally when they took a break from flinging balls down the lane. "Bastard."

"I was hoping if you called me a bastard, there'd be 'magnificent' in front of it, but I guess not," he said with a grin. "Besides, I wanted it to be a surprise. You didn't tell me you'd be showing up on my doorstep that time."

She laughed, raised one hand in an *I surrender* gesture. "Point taken. Say, I keep forgetting to ask. Why weren't Mick and Rachel at the show?"

"Romantic getaway. They went to Carmel." After that bad patch they'd gone through a couple of years ago, he figured they needed to keep relations happy.

"Bummer. I did want to see them. And their new place. What's it like?"

"Nice. Much better than that big barn on the Hill. And it's got a pool."

"We'll have to crash it for a barbecue or something this summer." Eskimo Sally took a healthy swig of her beer, then settled back in her chair. She had a look that Daniel recognized: lazy body language but her eyes keen and taking in everything. "Speaking of Valentine's Day and all that, how's your love life?"

"My what?"

"Your love life."

"My what?"

"I see." She eased off her shoes, wriggling her toes in apparent disgust. "How come? You've been alone a long time. Three years now."

"About that." Three years and five months, not that he was counting.

Eskimo Sally shook her head. "It's not right. You're telling me there isn't a woman in this town you'd like to date? Or some fangirl you can take to watch the submarine races?"

"Well, *Winter Roses* isn't exactly a Barry White album. Though I did get an e-mail from this girl who said she wanted to give me lots of consoling hugs."

"There you go." For a moment he thought she'd let the matter drop. "But I'm serious. You really should go out on a date sometime."

Daniel said nothing. It wasn't the first time this had come up. Back at Wayne and Beth's wedding last October, Wayne had pointed out which bridesmaids were single. "Can't have you dying on the vine, dude," Wayne said.

"I don't want to butt in," Eskimo Sally said, her face unusually serious. "But Sarah wouldn't want you to be alone for the rest of your life."

"I know that."

"Then why don't you—"

"Just let it go!" It came out more harshly than he'd intended. "I'm sorry," he said. "It's . . . I can't lose anyone again."

"I understand," she said softly.

She meant it. Eskimo Sally had a knack for understanding. If she'd been around when he was going through his bad time, she'd probably have done an intervention—lured him into a cab and taken him to the nearest psych hospital.

"I wouldn't bring it up if you were happy," she said. "But you're not."

"I'm OK."

"You're not unhappy, true. But you're not happy."

He had no good answer. What could he say? That he wasn't sure he had it left in him to be happy again?

Instead he said, "I'll try. I promise."

Eskimo Sally grinned. "Good! And be sure to give me the full scoop—name, age, vital statistics."

"Oh please. The most I'll do is ask someone out to a movie."

She was undeterred. "—astrological sign, if she's into leather."

Daniel smiled, let her go on. He'd give it a try, if not for himself then to please his friend.

When he called Eskimo Sally a few days later, she answered on the first ring. "Did you score?" she asked without preamble.

"Went down in flames. We're talking Hindenburg. Oh, the humanity!" He slammed his palm into the water for emphasis.

"Where on earth are you calling me from?"

"The hot tub."

"Oh."

On Thursday evening he'd met with a reporter—local, from the *Los Cielos Weekly*. Margo Danayan had buttonholed him at the anti–Valentine's Day show and asked for an interview. He'd agreed, for he liked both the *Weekly* and Margo's stories. She was a good interviewer—she knew enough details about him and the album to ask interesting questions. Also, she was rather fetching, if not his usual type. Near the end of the interview she'd asked what his next project was, and he'd joked that he'd be writing a book: nonfiction, titled *KaChunk! The 8-Track Story*.

She'd laughed heartily, and then he'd asked her if she'd like to go to the Tiki Terrace sometime for a drink and some karaoke.

"Oh, you didn't," groaned Eskimo Sally. "She probably heard about your infamous rendition of 'MacArthur Park' and got scared."

"No, it was because I was wearing my *Namaste, motherfucker!* T-shirt." He'd also been wearing his wedding ring, but Eskimo Sally didn't need to know he'd overlooked something so obvious. "Actually, she said it would be a conflict of interest."

"A journalist with ethics. What'll they think of next?"

After some more chitchat they said goodbye. Daniel hung up, cranked the hot tub up to boil, and lit up a cigar Eskimo Sally had left him as a parting gift. He leaned his head back and closed his eyes; it was dark, no light save for his cigar, and the only sound besides the hot tub was the tap of rain on the gazebo and the bougainvillea. He sighed, relieved. Not just because she had let the matter drop gracefully.

Margo's rejection had stung, but only a little. He didn't take it as a reflection of his physical attractiveness. Then again, as the seven deadly sins went, vanity was low on his list and always had been. People, and not just Sarah, had told him he was good-looking, but he'd never much believed them—he never saw it when he looked in a mirror, just saw himself. Nor was the rejection much of a blow to his ego. Once the initial disappointment was over he felt as if he'd dodged a bullet.

True, he was lonely. He didn't lack for friends, and while he hadn't seen the Whitmans for a long while now, he had the Reillys, and they were all the family he needed. But his loneliness was for something neither friends nor family could give him. What he needed was not a companion for an evening or a month, but someone to share his life. Someone to be with through the good and bad times—even something as simple as spending a rainy day indoors or arguing about whose turn it was to make dinner.

Daniel tilted his head back, blew smoke into the air, and knew it would never happen. He'd only asked Margo out to satisfy Eskimo Sally and others who told him that he ought to start dating again. He'd no intention of asking anyone else.

It wasn't because he felt it was disloyal to Sarah. No one could replace her—how could they? He'd known her almost his entire life. And she would want him to find someone new. They'd talked about it once, a long time ago. "If something happens to me, I don't want you to mope around forever. Find someone, promise?" she'd said.

"Sure!" He'd put on his most ingratiating smile. "I'll sing the piña colada song at your funeral, that should work."

She'd punched him in the shoulder. "You do *that,* and I will haunt the fuck out of you. At least wait until I'm cold."

"Well, if you insist."

It had been especially funny to him because he'd always assumed he'd be the first to go. In a plane crash, or getting brained by an errant piece of stage equipment. It never occurred to him that he'd be the survivor.

He set the cigar down, touched the wedding ring. He'd taken it off to forestall any more nagging from Eskimo Sally, and it was now on a chain around his neck. A plain gold band, no engraving. Yes, Sarah would want him to find someone new, and in the past he'd usually done what she'd wanted. No hardship, for most of the time it had been what he'd wanted as well. But he couldn't do what she wanted now. For if a woman was first his date and then his lover and then his wife, how wonderful that would be. And if there was a child, he'd have everything he wanted once more.

Everything that could be taken away again.

I can't lose anyone again. People could say that such a thing wouldn't happen till they were blue in the face, and he wouldn't believe it. If it had happened once, it could happen again.

Daniel closed his eyes, let the hot water soothe him; without thinking of it he hummed the old comforting melodies. He was lonely, yes, and longed for what only a wife and child could give him. But he could never go through that hell of loss again. He'd rather die. Better to let things be. After all, his life was fine. If he didn't have everything he wanted, well, who did? He hadn't lied to Eskimo Sally. He was OK. Mostly. Most of the time.

Chapter Twenty-Two

It was because of the Valentine's Day show that he ended up at the Chez.

There were the usual notices from Clive about session work, but Daniel said he was going to take a break. It didn't appeal, and he was comfortable monetarily for a while. What he wanted was not to sit in a windowless studio and play the same melody over and over again but to be among people who wanted to listen.

The upright piano was a new addition to the Chez and how Ariel had gotten it down the steep, narrow stairs he'd never know. "Sure, you can play," she told him. "I've been meaning to ask you, only you've been so busy lately, haven't seen you around much."

"What night would be good? I don't want to impinge on anything you've already got going."

She turned and consulted the calendar. "Hmmmm. Thursday—no, wait, the book club meets here. Tuesday. Nothing goes on then. You'll be a nice chaser to Open Mike Mondays, seeing as you've got actual talent."

"Thanks. And how'd you get that thing down the stairs in one piece, anyway?"

"Wasn't easy!"

Every Tuesday that he wasn't away on session work, he was at the Chez. He showed up roughly around seven and stayed as long as he felt like, playing whatever suited his mood. After some fussing between the two of them, Ariel comped him beverages and snacks; she'd wanted to pay him, but he refused. After the first couple of weeks she set an oversize brandy snifter on the piano for tips and protested vehemently when he tried to pour the earnings into her cash drawer. After that he gave the week's tips to whatever worthy cause seemed right at the time. Sometimes he put it into Queen of Peace's poor box; sometimes he gave it to the Safe Haven Women's Shelter. Once he saved up several weeks' tips and sent sixty-odd dollars up to Tamara, telling her he was finally paying her back and that she could keep it or give it to her old boss to play the ponies.

It never mattered much what he played. It was about giving back something to one of the places that had been his refuge these last couple of years. It was about loving music again instead of just using it as an anodyne. It was about connecting to people—that warm glow he'd feel when someone applauded or when a person dropped some change into the brandy snifter and told him thanks.

Before long he knew the Tuesday regulars by sight if not by name. The old guy who brought in a handful of paperbacks each week to donate to the shelves—heavy on pulp sci-fi and trashy mysteries. A motherly looking woman knitting an afghan that looked big enough to cover a double bed. Dr. Hill from LCU, who looked askance at Daniel as if remembering the C minus he'd earned in Econ 102. A red-haired woman who was always busy with her sketch pad and colored pencils.

Every Tuesday it was the same. He'd arrive, order something from the bar, and take a seat at the upright. It wasn't as fine a keyboard as his Bösendorfer, but he liked it all the same, even with its chipped keys and the cigarette burns where a previous owner had missed the ashtray. He'd play, and sometimes people would applaud and sometimes they wouldn't. Occasionally he got requests, which he always played with goodwill.

Oddly enough it was on the nights when only the hard-core regulars were present that he got the least applause; yet that didn't bother him. It made him feel part of the place, as comfortable as the squashy chairs or the mingled aromas of tea, cinnamon, and coffee. He knew he was one of the regulars the night a crowd of kids in town for a game somehow mistook the Chez for a Starbucks and were being obnoxious. "Hey, Vladimir Horowitz! Give it a rest!" one yelled.

Daniel didn't miss a note of *Clair de lune*; he was trying to think of something appropriately witty in reply when a woman's voice sternly said, "Hush!"

That *did* make him miss a note, for it wasn't Ariel or the woman with the afghan. It was the redhead with the sketch pad. He'd always assumed he was just background noise to her; every time he saw her she was looking down at her sketch pad, her face half-obscured by her hair, and he'd never once seen her glance in his direction or heard her applaud.

Daniel almost wondered if he'd imagined her shushing the kid. A few times that night he looked in her direction, but she might as well have been glued to her sketch pad. When he left that night, as he walked by her table he said, "Thank you." She nodded but said nothing and didn't look up, and he went on his way.

That spring and summer went on. He took a few session jobs, but for the most part every Tuesday he played at the Chez. In a strange way it reminded him of Saint Jude's, that feeling of ease among people who were virtually strangers to one another. Though what he played varied—one week it might be classical, another time it might be all Beatles tunes—the routine itself was the same, comfortingly so.

As summer waned there was a month when the redhead and her sketch pad weren't there. Daniel inquired with Ariel, who shrugged. "I see her, doesn't mean I know her."

He'd gotten so used to his small circle of regulars that he couldn't help wondering, and worrying. It was a relief one hot Tuesday when he arrived and she was there, sitting at her usual table; as a concession to the heat she had an iced tea before her instead of an espresso drink.

After getting his own drink he glanced her way—for a change, she was looking at him. Perhaps she'd missed him, or perhaps his admittedly gaudy Hawaiian shirt had caught her attention. Daniel smiled at her and waved hello.

The next night he sat in the bleachers at LCU's gym. The place was packed, as it always was for the Los Cielos Morays' preseason exhibition basketball game against Stanford, but Daniel's mind wasn't on the game. *Afraid of me. She was afraid of me.*

"Yoo-hoo. Daniel, you in?" sang out Rachel.

"Pardon?"

"We're going to jinx Stanford's next free throw," she said in between mouthfuls of cotton candy. Rachel had a weakness for game food. "See, when the player's getting ready to shoot, we all say 'Jumanji!' at the same time."

"Get ready for it. Here he goes," said Mick.

"I'm telling you, it works. Now. *Jumanji!*"

Stanford's score went up a point.

"Huh. Most of the time it works." Rachel shrugged and devoted her attention to the cotton candy.

Daniel went back to looking at the action on the court without really seeing it. His mind kept showing him the redhead and how she'd looked at him when he'd smiled and waved at her, the way her hands had gone white-knuckle tight around her sketch pad and pencils. He'd never seen her before he started playing at the Chez, and beyond saying thank you that one time, he'd never even spoken to her. Why was she so frightened of him?

"Dan? You OK?"

Mick's voice was serious, his look one of concern. Both went oddly with his *Go Morays! Snap!* hat with the lurid green eel.

"Sorry. Woolgathering." Down below, the Moray mascot chased Stanford's tree around the court while the band played a disjointed version of "Land of 1000 Dances." Halftime already and he hadn't even noticed.

"You seem really far away tonight. What's up?" Mick's voice was casual, but there was something in his eyes. Daniel had seen it before, that look that wondered if he was going to vanish again. Mostly that look was a mild irritation—it had been years, after all—but tonight he wondered if Mick saw something Daniel himself didn't know about.

They knew he played at the Chez on Tuesday nights. He told them about the redhead and the extent of their interaction so far and how she'd looked at him when he'd waved hello.

"How did you look at her?" Rachel asked.

"Like I'd look at anyone. I didn't make a face. Just . . . you know, normal."

They leaned in and scrutinized him for a moment, then glanced at each other.

"Normal being a very subjective term," said Mick.

"I don't know, he's not that scary. Has nice hair," Rachel said, ruffling it up.

"It's because he uses Suave."

"Really? I'd have pegged him for an Alberto V05 man."

"Could use a little Grecian Formula on the sides, though. Uh-oh, we're annoying him. Look at his face."

"Yes, it's like he's trying to swallow his lips."

My friends. "Will you two knock it off?" He knew they were trying to cheer him up, but he wished they'd take this seriously. "This is important."

They looked a trifle shamefaced. Apparently as a peace offering, Rachel passed him her cotton candy. "Sorry," she said, "but I think you're overreacting. You're one of the least spooky guys I know, and I can't imagine you scaring someone."

Mick nodded emphatically. "She's probably a fan. Got all flustered when you talked to her. Like when Eskimo Sally met Tom Petty at Coachella."

Daniel said, "Probably that." But he didn't mean it. He had the uneasy feeling this woman's fear might be connected to his lost time. Perhaps he really *had* lost time, gone into some sort of fugue state and done something terrible. He couldn't recall any such thing happening, but wasn't that the whole point of fugue states? This morning he'd even called Dr. Howard to find out if she thought such a thing was likely, given what she'd seen of his mental state at the time. But she was away, the receptionist at Saint Jude's said—gone with her husband to Vancouver for a vacation. The receptionist said if it was an emergency she could have Dr. Howard paged, but Daniel declined. It wasn't worth interrupting her well-earned respite. There was Dr. Levinson, of course, but they were down to monthly visits now, and the next wasn't for two weeks yet.

He came out of his reverie to find the Kesslers still looking at him. Daniel put on his best smile. "Yes, probably that," he said, not liking the lie or the way it felt—too much like the bad old days.

When he arrived at the Chez the next Tuesday, the usual regulars were in their usual places, including the redhead. She didn't glance his way as he walked past and sat down at the upright.

Except that everything wasn't as usual. Even down here, he could hear the wind. The Santa Anas—hot and dry, stinging the eyes and blowing the smog out to the coast. The winds had started up last night, and he hadn't slept. He'd lain and listened to the lavender bushes thrash and the bougainvillea leaves rattle. Daniel had hated the sound but couldn't listen to anything else. *It happened on a night like this.* The goddamned wind. *And I wasn't here.* He didn't expect that to still hurt after all this time, but it did.

He shook his head, put his hands to the keys, and started to play. Halfway through "Hey Jude" he stopped. He could still hear the wind. It seemed to be getting in the way; the piano notes sounded subtly wrong. No, not this again. He went ahead with that old chestnut "Canon in D" and that was better. Nothing wrong.

Except that it wasn't what he wanted to play.

When he was done with Pachelbel he sat at the piano, not playing, just thinking. After a while he caressed the keys with one hand. Why not? If he couldn't play these songs now, when could he?

"Sirocco" was first. Of course. From then he went into "The Kiss." Yes, now was the right time to play these. It's what he'd written them for, nights when nothing else assuaged. After "The Kiss" he paused to take a drink but didn't look to see what anyone else thought of his playing. He'd take no requests tonight; these songs were for him.

Then it was "Winter Roses." Always his favorite. He didn't sing, just let the music reign. How many times had he played this song? It seemed different tonight. When he was well into the second verse he knew why; he could hear the redhead humming along with the song, with the main melody he'd lifted from "The Coventry Carol" that the woman had sung to him, and it was her voice he heard humming the melody now, her voice. *Her* voice.

Cold. It was so cold in here. Bone-deep cold because he'd fought his way out of the black sea and could still taste the water that had tried to drown him. Darkness of a midnight, moonless beach and he was lost, would never find his way back, not this time, not unless he could hear her voice; she had to guide him, but he couldn't hear her anymore. Couldn't hear anything but a roar in his ears that might have been the wind or rain or fathoms-deep sea. The sound of the lost.

"Drink this."

Instinctively he obeyed and then recoiled at the tasted of hard liquor. Like the whiskey Hugh Reilly had given him in that airport conference room. It was starting again. He'd come full circle and would have to go through it all over—

"You OK? Daniel?"

He blinked, shuddered, looked around. He sat in one of the Chez's squashy chairs. The piano bench was overturned. Ariel hovered over him, holding a glass of something alcoholic, looking worried. "Here," she said. "Little brandy might help."

"No, no. I don't . . ." He looked around but couldn't see past Ariel's ample form.

"What happened? You went white as a sheet and kind of backed away from the piano. I thought you were going to faint." Ariel looked over her shoulder. "Huh. That's weird."

"What?" The redhead. He couldn't hear her anymore. "Where'd she go? The woman who was sitting there, where'd she go?"

"She was right here—wait." Ariel turned, and Daniel looked to where the redhead had been sitting. The table was empty now.

Daniel jumped to his feet, though his limbs felt none too steady. Ignoring Ariel's pleas to sit down and rest some more, he ran for the stairs. His shaky legs betrayed him, and he stumbled twice on the stairs, banging his knee a good one. He paid it no mind, just ran up the stairs as fast as he could and burst through the doors where he found—

Nothing but the parking lot. Nothing but the night, and the wind blowing a few leaves and the occasional bit of trash.

No one there. He started to go inside. Then turned back to the parking lot and said:

"It's you, isn't it? From the diner. You sang to me. I always wanted to thank you for that. You see, I'd lost people I loved. And I was lost, too. But not that night. Not when you sang. I still can't explain it, but that was the safest I'd felt in a long time. And later, whenever things were bad I'd think of that, and it helped. I put them in my songs. You're the Sparrow. I always hoped that someday . . ." Daniel remembered how she'd looked at him. "I'm sorry if I scared you. I never meant to. Just . . . thank you."

No sign of life in the parking lot. No sound save for the damnable wind. He wanted to say something more but could think of nothing, and besides, she was probably long gone and he was only making a fool of himself.

Daniel went inside, back down the steps. His legs still trembled, and for the first time he noticed how much his knee hurt. "What the hell happened?" Ariel asked, but he didn't answer her. Instead he went over to the table where the redhead had been sitting.

It seemed she'd left in a hurry. Her cup had tipped over, spilling the dregs of her drink into the saucer. She'd left her colored pencils as well, and her sketch pad. The pad was closed. On impulse he opened it to a random page and felt cold all over again. She'd drawn the cover of *Winter Roses,* the image of him lying as if asleep on the piano lid. It was a very good drawing. He closed the sketch pad abruptly.

"You want to tell me what's going on?" Ariel asked. When he shook his head she said, "At least sit down. You still look freaked out." Ariel gathered up the sketch pad and pencils. "I'll keep these in case she comes back for them. It was weird. She was the one who got you over to that chair when you looked like you were going to faint. But she backed off the instant you started coming back to yourself. You have any clue?"

"No," he lied.

Chapter Twenty-Three

Elaine Cahill sat in her car. Her faithful little Honda had carried her far since she'd fled Arizona. After Greg, after Isabelle. Up and down California. It was like childhood all over again, only with hospitals instead of Air Force bases. Living out of boxes and suitcases.

Until she'd reached Los Cielos.

She should never have stayed. Certainly not after learning who lived here. What had the clerk at Blue Angel Records said? *He's a local, didn't you know? Come back often enough and you're bound to run into him.* She hadn't gone back to the store, not often anyway. And she'd made her visits brief, keeping her head lowered and eyes focused on the racks of CDs, hoping Daniel Whitman didn't share her taste in music.

The door of the Chez beckoned. If only there were windows so she could see who was inside. She listened but heard no sound of piano drifting up the stairs. He might be there, or perhaps not. Elaine wasn't sure which she wanted it to be.

She should have left once he started playing there regularly. What a shock that had been. Elaine felt sure she'd given herself away. Surely someone had noticed that she'd been nearly frozen—her pencils unable to make more than meaningless scribbles, her latte untouched. She'd been more grateful than ever for her ability to blend in with the wallpaper. For two weeks she stayed away, then missed the place too much and decided to chance it. That was the only reason, she was sure of it.

Though she was certain he didn't recognize her, she was careful to steal glances at him only when he was deep in his playing. As time went on she began to look forward to those Tuesday nights, and once or twice this summer she'd even had to restrain the urge to say hello.

The notion of talking with him about some inconsequential thing like the weather, or of requesting a song for him to play, was pleasant. But that had been dashed when he'd smiled and waved at her. There was no way he could know her, yet she'd gone cold with fear the likes of which she hadn't felt since fleeing Arizona. Her fear was not of him personally—all she'd gleaned from watching him, from town gossip and that article in the *Weekly,* told her he was a decent sort. But what would happen if he knew about their connection? Nothing good, most likely. At the very least, nothing safe. And safety was the only thing she had left.

She should stay safe. Go home and send out her résumés. There'd be a job out there somewhere. There always was. It didn't matter where. Yet she found herself getting out of her car, heading toward the coffeehouse. *My stuff,* she told herself, *I just need to get my things.* The pencils could be easily replaced, but there was good work in that sketch pad, not that anyone saw it.

Down the stairs she went, slowly. She didn't see him, nor did she see the hostess who'd been there that night—there were a few LCU students scattered at tables, and over in one corner a group of about ten women that seemed to be a book club—they all had copies of *The Shipping News.* Elaine had tried to read that but hadn't been able to get past the first two chapters; the writing was lovely, but the protagonist's loneliness was much too familiar.

All she had to do was ask the lanky fellow tending the espresso machine if he'd seen a sketch pad and pencils left here the other night.

Once she did that, she was free to never come back here, to leave Los Cielos, to never see Daniel Whitman again. She walked up, and when the fellow smiled in that vaguely flirty way common to all baristas and asked what he could get started for her, she asked not for her sketch pad and pencils but for an iced tea. When it was ready she sat down at her usual table. *What are you doing?* her mind asked, but she didn't have an answer for it yet.

Nor did she have an answer at first when Daniel came over to her table. "Hello," he said. His voice hesitant, the way it had been in the parking lot the other night. She'd heard him coming up the stairs behind her and had known she'd never make it to her car unseen, so she'd ducked around the corner of the building and heard what he'd said to her.

Now Elaine took a deep breath and looked up at him. He gazed at her, seemed to be searching for something; she should have found the scrutiny intrusive. It was disconcerting, yes, but it didn't feel like he was trying to find the chinks in her armor, the way Greg would have. The way Greg did.

"May I sit down?" He held her sketch pad and pencils, halfway extended to her, as if giving her the opportunity to take them back and send him on his way.

She didn't trust her voice yet, so she just nodded. Daniel sat down, laid her pad and pencils down on the table. They regarded each other for what seemed a long time. He was different from the man who'd collapsed in the diner from cold and exhaustion, who'd clung to her fiercely and had only been soothed when she sang. And yet it was the same man, no question. What was he seeing? What had he imagined her to be?

"My name's Elaine," she said. "Elaine Cahill." What was she supposed to say next? *Pleased to meet you?* "I'm sorry about the other night. I didn't mean to . . ." To what? To sing? But he'd asked her to. *Sing to me, Sparrow. Please sing.* It would be so much easier if he wanted to forget her. But she suspected he couldn't—any more than she could forget him.

"It's all right. I just wasn't expecting it. When I first did the album I'd wonder if you'd heard it and if we'd ever meet again. But that was so long ago that I figured . . . I'm sorry, this is all probably sounding very strange," he said.

Elaine thought of the sketch pad, wondered if he'd looked through it. There were a few—more than a few—drawings of him. If anyone had to worry about coming off as strange, it was probably her. "No, not so much."

He smiled. He did have a very nice smile; it made him look boyish. The smile faded, though. "When I waved at you that time, you looked scared. Was it something I'd done?"

"No. No, it's not you at all. It's . . ." Where could she even start?

Daniel looked troubled. "Do you want me to leave?"

"I don't know." If he left, she'd be safe. She'd go back to her life. The life that seemed dingy and faded, like a Southwestern blanket she'd seen—it had been gorgeous once, all vibrant sunset hues, but it had been left out in the sun and had dulled to a dreary beige.

Was that what she wanted?

She wanted to talk to him. It seemed she'd been waiting to talk to someone her whole life and there'd never been anyone to listen. And he would listen, she felt sure of that. As to what would happen afterward . . . well, what did she have to lose? Absolutely nothing.

He smiled, but it was a sad smile, not the boyish one he'd given her earlier. "I'm glad I got the chance to thank you. That night . . . it meant a lot to me. It still does. Please take care." Daniel got up and started to leave.

Elaine reached out and caught his wrist; like that night at the diner but their roles reversed. "If it's OK, I'd like to talk." Trying not to think of the last time she'd taken a chance, she said, "Please stay."

She was an air force brat; home was everyplace and nowhere. Texas. Georgia. Nevada. Kansas. Oklahoma. New Mexico. Tech Sergeant Brian Cahill went where the work was. Elaine's earliest memory was of her mother packing boxes for yet another move. The earliest feeling she could recall was of uncertainty. Wondering what the new house would be like. What the new school would be like. What her new friends would be like.

Before long she stopped wondering. Because the houses were always the same: drab military housing with the smudges and scuffs of those who'd lived there before. The houses were always surrounded by crabgrass or gravel; there was always a layer of dust on every surface, thumbtack holes in the walls, dead flies on the windowsills.

Likewise, the schools were the same. As for friends, she always arrived too late, after the friendships had been formed, and she never knew how to reach out. The few times she did, it came to naught, for her father would be assigned to a new base and the friendships would end. A few letters would be exchanged, but inevitably time and distance did their damage, and Elaine would be on her own again. After a while she stopped trying. It was safer to remain the new kid and spend her free time in the school library or art room. Those were always the same, too, but it was a sameness she cherished: the smell of paint and wet clay, the musty old LPs in the library's AV section, the quiet of the library and its rows of books. These things were her refuge. The books took her into other worlds— sometimes scary, sometimes amusing, but most of all somewhere else. Likewise the music. Classical called to her, and she'd let it take her away;

she liked Baroque best with its delicacy, and Renaissance-era and medieval music as well.

Art was the best refuge of all. Elaine lost count of the times she'd sat in the school library, paging through the art history books. Or sat with pencils and paper, making her own drawings. They were clumsy at first, crude, and at times she grew frustrated when she could not put on paper what she saw in her mind or with her eyes. But she kept on. Occasionally there would be something to encourage her. A teacher might single her drawing out from all the other projects in the class, declare it a fine example. And the other boys and girls would turn, look at her as if seeing her for the first time. *Who did that? The new girl. The redhead.* She would always look down at her hands when this happened, uncertain how to face the attention and the eyes turned toward her. Yet fleeting as that regard was, she'd cherish it, hold it warm in her heart all the way home.

Home. Whether it was Texas or Georgia or Nevada or Kansas or Oklahoma or New Mexico, it was always the same. She'd wend her way through the rows of identical houses until she found the one assigned to the Cahill family. Step inside to the sounds of dinner being cooked and the talk radio her mother always listened to. "You're home? Good," was Marjorie Cahill's traditional greeting, occasionally adding, "What took you?" Marjorie would come out of the kitchen, look her daughter up and down, then assign a chore and make a criticism. "Go set the table. And get your hair out of your face, you look like something the cat dragged in." Sometimes, for variety, she'd make the criticism first. "Honestly, Elaine, did you even think to look in the mirror before you left this morning? Not that it matters. Go hang the clothes on the line." At six they'd eat dinner whether or not Elaine's father was home because his presence didn't matter much either way. If he was home, he'd say hello to Elaine and ask how her day had been but took no further interest. He'd sired her and passed on his red hair and green eyes to her, and seemed to consider his fatherly duty fulfilled. As for the dinner, it was sustenance. Marjorie hated to cook but made home-cooked meals nearly every night because she couldn't seem to resist the bitter pleasure of martyrdom. When Elaine went to nursing school and ate in a hospital cafeteria for the first time, the bland institutional food was so like home it was as if she'd never left. After dinner and dishes she'd leave her parents to fight for control of the TV remote and go to her room. There she'd put on music, the volume very low so her mother didn't yell at her to turn that crap down, *now*. She'd finish her homework and then draw. It didn't matter what she drew. Sometimes it was something she could see. A saguaro cactus outside her window. The neighbor's birdbath. The African violet she kept on her windowsill. Sometimes she drew something that wasn't right in front of her; it was difficult, but her pleasure in the results was greater. She drew castles, gardens filled mysterious flowers, and people—distant figures whose features were indistinct but whose postures suggested they would be happy to befriend her. Hours she'd spend, bent over her pad and her case of colored pencils, trying to capture the details, absorbed in the world on the page. Forgetting the world she lived in, the world she'd never found her place in.

When she was sixteen she found a place she wanted to call home.

Her father was transferred to Moffett Field in California as part of a joint project with the navy. Elaine had never been near the ocean before and was soon in love with the cool coastal breeze and the fog. She'd gone to school on the first day expecting nothing, and this scarcely troubled her; by now loneliness was as much a part of her as the freckles on her nose. She'd gone with her mother's parting words for the day still reverberating in her head—seeing Elaine checking her outfit in the hallway mirror, Marjorie had said, "That's not going to help, so you might as well not bother. Get going before you miss the bus." Her mother's criticisms had been getting worse these last few years. Oddly, they'd increased once Elaine had escaped the ungainly preteen years and occasionally thought she might be halfway pretty. She'd probably been mistaken about that; if her mother's barbs were true, Elaine *definitely* was mistaken.

But that first day of school was different. She knew it the moment she walked into her humanities class and the teacher, Ms. Jordan, didn't just drone names and dates from a textbook but talked of field trips and the projects they'd do. At the end of class Ms. Jordan had passed around a small wooden sculpture of a cat and asked them to not just look at it but feel it—the texture of the wood, the curves of the sculpture. Oh, some of the students had scoffed and just passed it along, but Elaine had held the sculpture, noticed the whorls and grains in the wood, the way it became warm in her hands and felt almost like a real cat. She also noticed she wasn't the only student doing this. After class, one of those students introduced herself as Lorelei and invited Elaine to join the after-school art club. "Nothing special," Lorelei said. "Just to, you know, hang out and talk about the stuff we're doing and bounce ideas off each other. What do you say?"

She planned to say no, but the ocean air must have done something to her, for she said yes. The next afternoon, she went back to Ms. Jordan's classroom, and while the teacher graded papers the club members sat around and played music and showed their latest projects to each other. It became the thing she most looked forward to. Every Tuesday and Thursday afternoon, to hang around with Lorelei and Aaron and Jenny and Walt and Rudy, to nibble some of the snacks Ms. Jordan brought in, and to be with people who liked the same things she did. It was a fine thing, belonging, and finer still when she plucked up the courage to show her drawings to the club. Their praise gladdened her. But what mattered more, strangely, was when Ms. Jordan looked long and thoughtfully at the pictures, then asked her to stay for a few minutes after the club broke up for the week.

Ms. Jordan had two of Elaine's pictures side by side. One drawing was of a dog she'd seen in the side yard; the other was one of her castle pictures. Ms. Jordan asked, "Did these both come from memory? Or were you drawing from a model?"

"The dog was something I was looking at. The other . . ." Elaine shrugged, felt herself blushing. "Just something I made up in my head."

"Interesting," Ms. Jordan said. She tapped the castle picture. "This one's better. The other one's more detailed, more accurate."

"That's not a good thing?"

"Oh, it is. But the perfect is the enemy of the good. The other one has more life to it. It feels more real because you're creating, not re-creating. The dog is more correct technically, but that can be cold." Ms. Jordan looked at Elaine searchingly. "They're both good, don't get me wrong. But the life is what makes this one more interesting."

Elaine hadn't been sure what surprised her more; what Ms. Jordan said or that someone had noticed what she'd done. Her father had never said anything beyond *That's nice*, and her mother had seen it all as a waste of time. Someone taking notice of her work—of her—was a new thing, exhilarating and a bit frightening at the same time.

Later that same month, she came home.

A field trip to the Fine Arts Museums of San Francisco. Half a day touring the galleries. She could have spent all week there. She stood in front of Monet's *The Grand Canal, Venice*, drinking in the beauty of it and wondering how he'd captured the quality of light. Even the still lifes fascinated her. How did Van Gogh paint a bowl of pears so that it was not a reproduction of the real thing, but *better* than the real thing? More *there*. As they were leaving the museum she had half a mind to be like the girl in *From the Mixed-Up Files of Mrs. Basil E. Frankweiler*, run away from home and live at the museum.

As if the museum weren't enough, after their trip Ms. Jordan took them to an outdoor cafe. It was afternoon by then, golden sun slanting down on the city as the fog loomed on the horizon. Elaine sipped her first cappuccino and nibbled her first biscotti and felt something strange happen to her. The knot of tension at the base of her neck, the ever-present strain of being apart, had eased. She'd come home. The hilly streets, the cool, damp breeze, the people living their own lives in their own way, the street musicians, the grubby-looking artists in the park; she could belong here. She sensed it was a haven for people who'd fled places they didn't belong.

A few weeks later, armed with information she'd gathered from Ms. Jordan and pamphlets from the school's guidance office, Elaine broached the subject of college to her mother. After dinner and the dishes, Elaine delivered the spiel she'd thought out so carefully, had even rehearsed a time or two in front of her bedroom mirror. Marjorie said nothing through the spiel, just smoked while Elaine talked of pursuing an art degree and of getting a job in commercial illustration or working in a gallery or museum. Elaine talked, and her mother still said nothing, so Elaine kept on about scholarships and financial aid, well aware that she was running off at the mouth but unable to stop herself. Finally she said, "What do you think?"

Marjorie stubbed out her latest cigarette; she didn't even glance at the pamphlets Elaine had set on the table. "No."

Before Elaine could protest, Marjorie said, "And don't whine, that's not going to change my mind. I'll only pay for something sensible, like accounting or nursing."

"But that's not what I want."

"Life's not about what you want."

Before San Francisco, Elaine might have left it at that. But now she studied her mother, seeing her not with the eyes of a daughter but of an artist. Marjorie had been pretty once—Elaine had seen pictures—but life had scoured away her prettiness, turned her hair the dull black of an old shoe and etched lines in her face. Elaine tried to remember seeing her mother smile and couldn't; nor could Elaine imagine such a thing happening. It was not a face that invited questions, yet Elaine asked, "Why?"

Marjorie glanced over her shoulder to the living room, where her husband sipped his six-pack and watched TV. Turning back to her daughter, she jerked a thumb back toward the living room. "That's why."

"I don't understand."

Her mother lit another cigarette. As always, the menthol smell made Elaine slightly queasy. "You have a brain, Elaine. Use it for once. I dropped out of high school to marry him. I fell for a pair of pretty green eyes, and look where it got me. Oh, he was full of big dreams then. Always had his head in the clouds, just like you. It was all going to work out just fine, according to him. He'd rise through the ranks, and it would all be good. And now look." She gestured to the drab house, the half-unpacked moving boxes. "I paid for it once. I won't do it again."

"But . . ." Elaine began, but her mother got up and went into the living room to sit in front of the television's blare.

That night she lay in bed, hot tears of anger trickling down her face. She knew what she should do—what Ms. Jordan and the kids in her art club would have advised her to do. Say the hell with her parents' help and do it on her own. Get whatever scholarships she could—she had the grades for it, despite changing schools so often. Scrabble for financial aid and any deals for military brats. Rent a room someplace, live off peanut butter sandwiches, and work part-time to pay the tuition. It wasn't like she'd be giving up a life of luxury, and she'd be doing what she'd always loved. She might make some friends. Might even get a boyfriend.

She might have done it. But less than two weeks later the word came down that Tech Sergeant Cahill and his family would be transferred to Utah. A month after the visit to San Francisco, Elaine was unpacking her bags and boxes in yet another military housing bedroom. She'd kept the brochures, and the calendar and book of postcards she'd bought at the museum, but soon it all began to seem faded, like a picture left out in the sun.

Later, she was about to drop applications for nursing schools into the base's mailbox—by now they were in New Mexico again—and stopped, her hand frozen on the box's handle. Was she signing on for a lifetime of dreams deferred, like her mother had? Or was she going to take a chance on what she wanted? She wished for advice, but there was none, only an impatient voice behind her saying, "Hey, move it along, I haven't got all day." So she dropped the applications into the box.

She met Greg Buchanan at a Christmas party.

She'd started work at Phoenix's third-largest hospital four months earlier, and though the work was going well, she still didn't have a handle on the complex politics of the place. They were a web of friendships and alliances that switched to conflicts at the slightest provocation, and after a few missteps she avoided them altogether; she spent her lunch breaks reading a book and skipped the after-work gatherings to attend a life drawing class at the university.

Elaine hadn't wanted to go to the party. She'd wanted to stay home and watch *White Christmas*. But she was young enough to think she might get in trouble if she didn't go, so there she was, off to the side, standing near the tree, sipping a glass of punch and wondering when she might be able to leave.

"Are you having a merry Christmas?" asked a male voice on her right.

She glanced around to see to who he was talking to, then realized it must be her. "Oh, yes," she said automatically as she turned to face the man. He looked to be in his early thirties, with the bland good looks of a soap opera actor. "And you?"

"I am now," he said. "Greg Buchanan, I'm a sales rep with Andover Pharmaceuticals." He held out his hand.

She shook his hand; it was smooth, like his voice. "Elaine Cahill. I'm a nurse."

"Have you been here long? I'm usually at the hospital a few times a month, but I don't think we've met."

"Not long. Four months."

He smiled; his teeth were very white and even. "I should be ashamed of myself, not remembering someone so pretty."

Elaine didn't reply at first; she was too astonished. Later she would understand that it was a salesman's smile. Selling himself, selling her a bill of goods she didn't need. But at the time she was dazzled by his smile and his words. All through that evening he stayed by her side, told jokes that made her laugh, even danced with her a time or two. She forgot all about sneaking out of the party early, and when the evening ended, Greg walked her to her car and asked if he could call her; she said yes. She was too excited to sleep that night. She sat with her sketch pad in her lap, doodling aimlessly. Her life was about to begin, finally.

No misgivings at first. She had no time or energy for second thoughts, for when she wasn't working she was out with Greg. He took her to movies, to dinner; he brought her flowers; he called her every day. The attention was intoxicating—at times she could almost taste it, like some fine liqueur. So giddy was she that she seldom noticed that there was something impersonal about his attention. He did the things and took her places he wanted to—not what she wanted, for he never asked what she wanted, and she hesitated to broach the subject. She'd have traded all the floral bouquets and boxes of candy for a weekend at the Arts Festival in Sedona, but whether he didn't guess this or didn't care to she wasn't sure.

When she wanted to break a date to join the book club some of the other nurses had formed, he gently dissuaded her. "You don't need that," he'd said. "All you need is me." She supposed at the time that was right, for no one else had paid her the attention that Greg did. And though she did not love him, she loved the attention, and it seemed an unimportant distinction.

Valentine's Day came with a marriage proposal. For a moment her giddiness went flat like stale champagne. When she didn't answer right away he gave her a mock-hangdog look and said, "We can't leave this restaurant until you give me an answer." What was she to say? That it was too fast? That all their conversation had been on the surface and she felt she barely knew him? That she didn't love him? That his kiss was pleasant enough but not the thunderbolt she'd hoped for? If she said these things he would leave her life forever, and save for that time in California, these two months had been the happiest of her life. *And besides,* said the voice in her head—once her mother's voice but now her own interior voice—*it's not like anyone else is lining up for a chance. You'd better take what you can get.*

He didn't actually hit her until after they were married. There was the time he squeezed her left hand so hard that the stone on her engagement ring cut into her skin. The time he pulled her hair hard enough to leave him with a handful of red strands. And the bite on her shoulder—that happened on their honeymoon, and she rationalized it as passion and supposed it was all right, for at least one of them was feeling passionate. These things happened infrequently enough for her to write them off as by-products of the attention he still lavished on her from time to time, the attention she still loved. *I'm sorry. I got carried away. You shouldn't do that to me,* he'd say with a smile.

But it was different when she came home late from work one night. Some nasty upper respiratory bug was going through town. They'd been bogged down with patients, and some of the nurses were sick as well, so the hospital was short-staffed. Elaine dragged home three hours late, so tired she didn't even care about food; she just wanted a hot bath and a glass of wine. Greg's car wasn't in the condo's parking garage, which surprised her. She'd expected him to be sitting there, waiting for her and tapping his foot. She'd already learned he didn't like his meals to be late.

He walked in a few minutes later. She hadn't even had time to change out of her scrubs, just had her shoes off and was pouring herself a glass of pinot. "Sorry I'm so late," she said, "It's been a terrible day." Elaine glanced at the kitchen—it seemed as spotless as she'd left it the night before. "Did you have dinner already?"

"I had to go out," he said, his voice flat. "I went to Luigi's."

The hunger she'd been too tired to feel came to life. Luigi's was her favorite restaurant. "Did you bring me anything?" she asked, but could see that he hadn't. Not so much as a breadstick. "Thanks a lot," she said, and turned away. She didn't mean to be rude, but she was exhausted and stressed, and how much trouble would it have been for him to bring home some spaghetti carbonara?

"Elaine?"

His slap went across her cheek. He would hit her harder over the course of their marriage, but it was that first time that would stand out in her memory. It didn't hurt that much, but the humiliation went deeper than any physical discomfort. She'd always remember how he'd said, "You don't need pasta anyway, not the way your hips look these days." How her wine glass had gotten knocked over and how she'd cleaned up spilled wine and broken glass while she blinked back tears.

That first time seemed to give him permission. Pinches and slaps, pulled hair and rough pushes. And the insults. Aimed at her body, her intelligence, her art. Everything. Later she'd think those were what made her stay, rather than his occasional shows of attention or more-than-occasional physical hurts. They reinforced what the voice in her mind had said for years now: that she was too stupid, ugly, untalented to do anything but settle for what she now had. And even if that voice had fallen silent for a while, what could she do? Where would she go? She had no friends; her coworkers she kept at a distance lest they see her bruises. Her parents had never been a refuge, and besides, they were in Texas now, hundreds of miles away. And so she stayed. After all, he was still the courtly gentleman sometimes, and he didn't hit her that hard, most of the time. She told herself this was the best she could hope for, and after a while even convinced herself of this.

She'd been married four and a half years when she got to San Francisco again.

Three weeks earlier her supervisor had come to her, praised the job she did with the paperwork. Elaine had smiled and thanked him, wondering if he suspected the truth—that she took the paperwork because it was a refuge. It bored her, but it was safer than patient care—all those people needing attention, needing comfort, and while Elaine was a competent nurse she always felt like the patients were asking her for something she couldn't give. The walls she'd built from early childhood were higher than ever. Any damage to them during that time in California had long since been repaired. And over the years with Greg, she'd made those walls strong. Every so often, when her duties forced her to reach beyond them, she wondered if there'd come a day when she couldn't. And when that happened, would it be such a bad thing? She'd finally be safe then.

Yes, the paperwork bored her, but she was good at it, and she was rewarded with a time management conference in San Francisco.

Elaine hadn't believed she was really back until the plane landed and she looked out the window, saw the city whose streets she still walked in her dreams. Her heart pounded, not just from excitement. The conference was two days long, but she'd told Greg it was four so she'd have time to spend on her own. Even now, hundreds of miles away from him, her lie unnerved her. His job was stressful these days, and he took that stress out on her. She knew he wasn't on this plane or in San Francisco. She knew he wouldn't be there to bully her, pinch her, or break her nose the way he had a year ago. But being wary of Greg was a heavy load to carry. She hadn't noticed how heavy until the coastal fog caressed her and she breathed in the scent of the ocean. That night she went to dinner by herself and ordered what *she* wanted. She had only one glass of wine, but she felt drunk, so intoxicating was the freedom.

The first morning at the conference, she got her breakfast from the spread of juice, coffee, bagels, and fruit. But when she sat down and started to take her first sip, the coffee smelled wrong and sent her stomach roiling; she had to put it aside. It couldn't be the previous night's wine, could it? Just that one glass?

The nurse sitting next to her laughed and pushed the little basket of herbal teas over to her. "Try the ginger, that usually helps. You don't want the caffeine now anyway. When are you due?"

"Due?" It took her a moment. She fished her datebook out of her purse and did the math. *Oh my God.*

The other nurse laughed again, kindly. "Oh, honey. The look on your face. Here." She scribbled something down. "At the lunch break take this across the way to the hospital. Give it to Maureen in the lab and she'll bump you to the front of the line." She leaned in, pitching her voice low. "If I'm wrong, I'll eat my hat. I've worked the OB ward for thirty years, and I can always tell."

Elaine barely heard a word of the morning's presentation. She might have guessed it sooner. Her stomach hadn't been steady for the last week, but she'd chalked that up to nervousness over Greg and her deceit. And though she was less than two weeks late, she knew. The test result only made it official.

That night she begged off socializing. She ate in her room, and after the queasiness of the morning she was now ravenous. Without thinking about what she was doing she ordered the healthiest thing she could find and drank reduced-fat milk. After that she was wiped out, yet she couldn't sleep.

Greg wouldn't want the child—or any child, ever. Elaine hadn't learned this until too late; during their whirlwind courtship he hadn't brought up the subject and she hadn't thought to. But after the first year she'd begun to long for a child and tentatively broached the subject to Greg, who'd made his feelings clear. Very clear. Of course, he'd left all the responsibility for such matters up to her. She couldn't take the pill—it affected her hormones too badly—so she used a diaphragm, which was a chore. She'd asked him once why he didn't get a vasectomy, and it had been a week before the bruise he gave her faded and she could wear short sleeves again.

She'd told herself it didn't matter; she probably wouldn't have made a good mother anyway, considering what her own had been like. Yet during the conference she veered between telling herself that it would be best to end the pregnancy and drifting into daydreams of holding her baby, rocking it to sleep, reading *Goodnight Moon*. The next morning, at the museum, she couldn't concentrate on the artwork. She sat on a bench with her sketchbook forgotten in her lap, her eyes turned toward Picasso but her mind's eye seeing herself—not with a baby now, but with a child. A lively boy, perhaps, who'd ask for her help when he scraped his knee and who'd bring her clumsy bouquets of dandelions. Or maybe a girl, sweet yet strong spirited, whose hair she could braid, to whom she could read the *Anne of Green Gables* books. It wasn't until she was having lunch at the museum café that she realized Greg had not appeared once in these daydreams.

That brought her reveries to a quick end. Even if she somehow talked him into keeping the baby, he'd no doubt resent the child and treat it as poorly as—or far worse than—he did her. Did she want that on her conscience? No, but were her alternatives any better? Greg would want her to terminate; Elaine would never take that choice away from another woman, but she knew it wasn't a choice she could make and live with herself. If she killed the child, she'd be killing part of herself as well, and the thought made her shudder.

There was only one alternative: she had to convince Greg to let her give it up for adoption. Giving the child away would be the hardest thing she'd ever done, but at least it would live, and with people who would be far better parents than she and Greg.

Elaine pushed her half-eaten lunch away and made her way out of the museum. Her heart wasn't in it. Nor could she enjoy the city the way she'd meant to. Thoughts of the baby took over her mind and sucked all her enjoyment out of the day. It didn't help that the weather had turned gloomily oppressive even by San Francisco standards; she shivered as she stepped outside. As much as she'd yearned for freedom here, if she stayed, she'd go mad. Better to *do* something. She checked out early, canceled her plane ticket, and rented a car. Driving back to Arizona would give her time to think and help her feel like she was getting somewhere.

It was a mistake. The sky went dark gray, and before she reached San Luis Obispo rain was falling steadily. By then it was too late to go back. She kept on, hoping to outrun the storm. No luck. She'd always hated driving in the rain, and as night fell it only got worse. She finally gave up and stopped at a diner—at least she'd be out of the rain for a while.

She ran through the cold downpour and into a little piece of heaven. Heaven smelled like bacon and pancakes, it had Louis Armstrong on the jukebox, and most of all, it was dry and warm. Elaine took a seat at the counter, setting down her sketch pad and the time management book she was supposed to be reading. Her first inclination after reading the menu was that she wanted one of everything—the long drive had taken its toll, and she supposed she was eating for two. She ordered the evening breakfast special and tried to focus on the book but soon found herself doodling in her sketch pad. Drawing soothed her, as it always had. As the tension from her long drive eased, she found herself not drawing but jotting down names. A column for boy names and one for girl names. Nothing trendy. Something old-fashioned. Something Irish, perhaps? The list grew. The long drive had given her no ideas as to what she should say to Greg, but she had a fine list of names.

She glanced at her watch; it was getting late. How long was this place open? Only now she noticed how empty it was. No one here save for a few kids at one of the tables. She knew she couldn't stay forever, yet it was pitch black out and the rain still pouring. The diner owner assured her she could stay, and she was glad about that, but the thought that she was imposing took the enjoyment out of her doodles. She shouldn't do this. What point was there in coming up with names for a baby she couldn't keep? Elaine told herself to think about what mattered—how to convince Greg to let her give the baby up for adoption.

She was no closer to a solution when the door to the diner opened. Elaine glanced over her shoulder, saw some rain-drenched fellow in the doorway, and turned back to her sketch pad. Attend to the task at hand, she told herself. *Tara, Nolan*, she wrote.

A thud and a crash, and a call: "Hey, little help here!"

Elaine didn't recall running across the diner. It was like the stat cases at the hospital, when she didn't stop to think, just acted. The new arrival had passed out, the diner owner had caught him before he hit the floor. She took hold of the man's legs and lowered him to the floor, checked his vital signs. He wasn't just wet from a dash through the parking lot, that was certain; he was far too cold, and there was a pallor to his skin that she didn't like. But his breathing and pulse were normal. Hypothermia, but fairly mild. And that was good because the diner owner said there wasn't a hospital nearby. They'd have to get him warm here.

Together they carried the man into the diner's back room and got the cold, wet clothes off him. Elaine was grateful for the diner owner's calm competence and glad that her training didn't let her down when she was off the job. Still, it gave her a start when she saw the scars. It wasn't their presence but how recent they were, and how purposeful. Elaine had seen her fair share of sullen, sheepish teenagers in the ER with shallow cuts on their inner forearms. This was the real thing.

That didn't matter now. What mattered was getting this man warm and making sure there wasn't anything else wrong. Luckily he was soon out of danger, and even without a thermometer she could tell his temperature was back to normal. He didn't wake, though. She saw a bump on his head and worried about a concussion; after locating a flashlight on one of the pantry shelves, she checked his pupils, which dilated normally. Probably he was just cold and exhausted. She'd seen his backpack and his worn-looking shoes. A drifter of some kind, probably had no luck getting a ride and had walked in the rain for who knew how long. Elaine checked his pulse again, found it steady, then went to tell the diner owner and see if she could get something to drink.

The diner owner brought her a sandwich and milk, and she sat beside the cot. From time to time she doodled or jotted down more names in her sketch pad, but it didn't hold her attention the way it had. She kept looking at the man who slept on the cot. Ordinarily she didn't care to know much about her patients; she'd watch the other nurses make small talk and wonder how they did it; she'd seen nurses devastated when a patient died and wondered why they let themselves care that much. But she kept thinking about this man. What had brought him here? Elaine glanced at him, caught the glint of gold on his left ring finger. Where was his wife? What were those scars doing on his wrists?

A huge yawn interrupted her thoughts. Such a long day. And a longer day lay ahead—all those miles to Phoenix. Elaine turned out the light, found as comfortable a seat as she could, and closed her eyes, hoping for forty winks.

Sleep came more quickly than she'd expected and brought a dream much like the ones she'd had since learning she was pregnant. She stood on a beach that was foggy but bright, holding a baby in one arm. The baby was older than a newborn but too young to toddle. Elaine couldn't see the child's features or determine its gender, but she could breathe deep the aroma she knew from the hospital nursery—talcum and slightly curdled milk and the other warm, comforting scents of a baby. Usually in these dreams it had been her and the child only, but now someone held up a seashell for the baby to see; the baby laughed and clapped, and there was an answering laugh, a man's laugh.

Even in her dream, it didn't sound like Greg's laugh.

A sound like the wind's howl. But how could there be wind in her dream's still, foggy morning? She opened her eyes. For a moment she wondered where she was. Elaine leaned her head back, hoping to recapture the dream, and heard the sound again.

It was the man; he lay on the cot asleep and shivering. Not with cold, she somehow knew, but in the grip of a dream not nearly as pleasant as hers had been. Elaine sat up, started to reach out and wake him; his eyes opened, his hand reached out and caught hers. Before she knew it he'd sat up and pulled her close, clutched her the way a drowning man clutches at a lifeline. His voice was an urgent whisper, much of which she couldn't understand, save for a name: *Sarah*.

"I'm not her," Elaine said, and was instantly ashamed that the first thing she said was not a word of ease. Fear made her try to pull away; she told herself it was because of how he held on to her, but even in his desperation his hands didn't hurt her. It was the need that frightened her. Nothing she could do would help him. She told him he was safe now, that he was all right. He didn't believe her, and why should he? She didn't believe it herself.

It was the baby that helped her. What would she do for a frightened child? She sang—songs from the medieval and Renaissance music she'd been playing in the rental car. Almost instantly she felt him stop trembling. His head sank onto her shoulder while she stroked his hair and sang. Elaine wasn't sure how long it was until he let go of her, lay back down on the cot. Sometime later she paused between verses and heard his breathing, the slow and regular breaths of sleep.

Trembling, she found a can of ginger ale on the shelves and drank a third of it at once to ease her throat, which was dry from nerves and singing. She didn't sleep the rest of that night; instead she sat with two thoughts chasing each other, like the tigers going 'round the tree until they turned into butter. She thought of the man, what had brought him low and what was going to happen to him next. She thought of the baby and what she was going to do about him or her.

As dawn crept into the back room she stood up, stiff from her long vigil, and looked again at the man. He lay on his side, asleep. His profile was a good one, pleasantly angular. On impulse she reached down and touched his disheveled hair. So soft. Much nicer than Greg's hair, which always looked perfect but the gel and spray he used for that perfect look made his hair feel synthetic, and she didn't like to touch it. The man stirred. For a moment she wondered if he'd wake, and if he did, what she would do.

He didn't wake. Urgency gripped her. She had to leave now, before he woke and could make a claim on her. She could handle one claim now, but not two, and he'd be fine without her. Quickly Elaine gathered her things, and by the time the sun was up she was back in her rental car, heading down Highway 101. Toward Arizona, her home, but not for much longer. There would be a new home soon. A home with just two people in it—her and the baby.

Later she would wonder what misstep she'd made. She arrived well on schedule, and as far as she knew Greg never learned of her deception or her impromptu road trip. He was not the sort of husband who jealously checked her whereabouts; up to now he'd correctly gauged her as too afraid to fly, so he never worried about leaving the cage door open.

And it was no problem to gather the money she'd need for her getaway, nor to surreptitiously pack her suitcase with clothes and other necessities. She already did the bills, the laundry, the groceries. She even maintained her car, the little Honda she'd bought shortly before moving to Phoenix. In little bits and pieces she set aside what she needed. When she folded clothes each week she'd put a few items into the suitcase hidden under the bed. When she did the bills and banking she squirreled away cash—and always took it out of her own salary.

As for finding a new job in California, that was the easiest task of all. She told her supervisor, not mentioning the pregnancy but confessing about the bad marriage and that she needed to leave. Her supervisor nodded, and Elaine guessed that he'd long suspected something was not right in the Buchanan marriage. It made her wonder if anyone else knew and if so, why no one had said anything or questioned her lies about being so clumsy. No matter. She had her supervisor's letter of recommendation, and the résumés she sent to hospitals in California got replies. The worst of it was admitting that her mother was right about nursing being a practical career. But that was nothing—if she had to work as a nurse for a while longer, so be it. She'd do whatever it took to be free from Greg. It wouldn't be easy, but she'd had what looked like an easy berth for four and a half years now and couldn't leave it soon enough.

She gave herself a month. At times it seemed to go so easily she wondered why she hadn't done it sooner. Elaine could feel her secret inside her, growing even as the child was, and once in a while it would spark up, sending warmth through her. She would sing while she washed the dishes, ignoring Greg's yells to put a sock in it, she sounded like a wounded cow. She lost herself in daydreams while Greg watched TV. Her artwork had gone straight to hell, but she didn't mind. There would be time for it later. And she even had a date, given to her by Greg's casual statement that he'd be out of town on a conference for a few days in March.

That Wednesday in March she left work early. Greg had left in the morning for Chicago and wouldn't be back until Friday evening. Heart racing, palms cold and sweaty, Elaine drove to the condo and let herself in. She was seldom at the condo alone during the day and marveled at how still and quiet it was, not just in their unit but in the complex. All the young professionals had gone to work; there were few stay-at-home moms and kids to break the quiet.

Elaine set her purse down and went up the stairs. She changed out of her scrubs and then knelt, reaching under the bed for her case. It wasn't there. Frowning, she leaned in and swept her arm in a wide arc. Nothing but dust bunnies.

"Looking for something?"

Elaine made no sound but went stone cold inside and out. She wasn't aware of getting up but found herself standing by the bed, watching as Greg leaned amiably against the doorjamb.

"Did you really think I didn't know?" He made no move, threatening or otherwise. He wore a mellow smile, as if thinking about something pleasant. "You thought you had it all figured out, didn't you? A smart person would have checked to make sure I really was in Chicago. So easy to do that, but you didn't even think of it. So I guess this makes you ugly *and* stupid."

Elaine said nothing. He stood there, unmoving and smiling and making no threat, but he'd never scared her more.

He clapped his hands together once. She flinched at the sound, and it seemed his smile brightened a bit. "So," he said. "Got a name picked out for the rug rat?"

"What? How did . . ." Her voice came out in a squeaky whisper.

"Unlike some people, I can count to twenty-eight." Greg straightened up, looked at her coldly. "How do I know it's mine?"

Shock rendered her mute for a moment. Thankfully—her first thought was: *Aren't you bad enough? You think I want* another *man in my life?* "Of course it's yours."

He nodded. "That makes sense. God knows no other man would look twice at you. Think about that when you're living off ramen noodles in some shithole. You want to go, then go. I don't care as long as you don't take anything that's mine. But think about what you threw away. Not many men would have put up with your shit all this time, your mopey face and your crappy cooking and spending all the time with your head in the clouds doodling your little pictures. Not to mention you're boring in bed. Who else will have you?"

He'd said *go*. That's what she'd do. "I'll have me," she said quietly. "Me and the baby."

Greg shrugged. "Have it your way." He opened the closet and took out her suitcase. It was an old hard-shell Samsonite, left over from her nomadic childhood. He carried it over to the bed, set it down. For a moment he looked down at the suitcase, then glanced over at her.

"Like I said." He grasped the suitcase handle again. "You're not taking anything that's mine."

He swung the suitcase, slammed it into her stomach. The world went black, and when it reappeared she was on the floor, drowning in an ocean of pain, couldn't get a breath in even to scream. Elaine curled up into a ball, the same position as that of the child inside her. After an agonizing minute she was able to breathe, gagging little sips of air, but the pain was only getting worse, hot clamps ratcheting tight. Somehow she flung out her arms, hooked her fingers into the carpet, and tried to haul herself toward a phone. If she called 911 in time, they could save the baby.

Hands on her. Greg's hands. "Better make sure," he muttered, and dragged her out of the bedroom to the stairs. He didn't push, simply let go of her and let her fall down the stairs and into mercifully painless dark.

"Ma'am? Ms. Buchanan?"

Elaine looked at the man, then turned her face away. He seemed an odd choice for the police to send; though clearly in his sixties, he looked a far worse thug than Greg. A hulking, bull-shouldered fellow with his steel-gray hair in a 1950s crewcut. Scars on his face and on the hands that, despite his age, looked powerful enough to crack walnuts—or skulls. She saw the band of gold on his left hand and felt sorry for his wife.

She wanted to tell him to go away, but her throat was dry. Elaine reached for the cup of water; it was on the other side of the hospital bed. She couldn't reach it with her good arm, and it hurt too much to turn over. Before she could ask, the cop picked up the cup and with delicacy surprising in such a big, brutal-looking man, put a straw in the cup and held it to her lips. When she'd finished her drink, he set the cup down within easy reach for her.

"They said you could have visitors. I understand if you don't want to talk yet," he said.

She looked at him more closely this time. Lord knew she was no judge of character, but she saw compassion in this man's eyes. She'd have to take compassion where she could, it seemed, for she couldn't even expect it from her mother. *He wouldn't have done it for no reason,* Marjorie had said on the phone. *I'm sure you provoked him somehow.*

"It's all right," Elaine said. "You can stay."

The cop pulled a chair close beside the bed and sat down. "My name's Sergeant White. I won't be long. I don't wish to distress you."

She nodded.

"I wanted to let you know that you can press charges. Aggravated assault." Sergeant White looked away for a moment, seemed to regard the medical equipment nearby, the vase of flowers from her coworkers—and the flowers Greg had sent, now wilting in the trash can. "And manslaughter as well," he said as he turned his gaze back to her. "The district attorney is sympathetic to these kinds of cases. We could put him away for a long time."

It was appealing—in theory. Truthfully she hadn't the energy for justice or even vengeance. All she wanted was for Sergeant White to go away so she could sleep. Sleep, and forget. "I need to think it over," she said. Knowing how ridiculous it sounded, knowing that the cop would complain to his fellow officers about the stupid bitch who'd been hit and tossed down the stairs and had a concussion, broken arm, internal injuries, and bruises everywhere. Who lost her baby and still had to think about pressing charges against the man who'd done all this.

"I understand." No impatience in his voice. Perhaps he meant it. "I'll leave my card here. And please know . . . I'm very sorry for your loss."

Her loss. She could feel it, always. Not physical pain—she was doped up too well to feel much of that. The nurses knew her for one of their own and weren't stingy with the meds. But the emptiness inside. No sedative could take that feeling away. "Isabelle."

"Beg pardon?" The cop paused as he was putting on his jacket.

"They said the baby was a girl." The pain in her throat made it hard to speak. "I was going to name her Isabelle."

Sergeant White picked up his card, wrote something on the back. "My home number," he said. "Call any time."

He left, and though all Elaine wanted to do was to sleep, she couldn't She lay with her good hand resting on her stomach and thought. Later that night, she called Sergeant White's home number.

Sergeant White drove her to the condo. "Stay here for a few minutes," he said when he'd parked his nondescript sedan by her unit. "I had someone check out the area a little while ago. But I want to make sure everything's OK inside."

Elaine handed him the keys. He was gone for about ten minutes. She appreciated his concern, but she didn't think there was a need for it—not after what had happened at the hospital.

She'd let them know that Greg could visit. He'd tried to see her before, but on White's orders he'd been shown the door. But when she gave the OK he came, bearing flowers and an imploring look. He'd glanced at the curtain that hid the other side of the room.

"It's OK, we can talk," she said.

He started laying it on thick—*sorry* and *forgive me* and *I don't know what got into me* and *we can have another baby*.

When he stopped to take a breath she cut in. "I'm getting out in a couple of days. I'll get my things, and then I'm gone. I'll send you the paperwork. You keep the condo, everything. All I want is my stuff and my share of the money."

"What if I say no?"

"Then I'll see you in court."

It took a moment for him to understand she didn't mean divorce court. "You'd do that, wouldn't you?" His hand clenched. "After all I've done."

The curtain pulled aside and Sergeant White stood there. "Aggravated assault. Manslaughter. Care to add another assault charge? I don't mind. Neither will the DA." White's eyes never left Greg; his hands were clasped loosely in front of him, but anyone could see what big hands they were. "Let her leave in peace, and you walk away from it. If you so much as look at her cross-eyed, I'll put you away, and what you've done to her will look like a love tap compared to what will happen to you."

Greg had nodded and fled, as she'd guessed he would. He'd picked her because she was easy prey, and she knew he didn't have the guts to cross someone like White. Elaine didn't think Greg would be foolish enough to be waiting for her at the condo but let White check it out.

A tap on the window. Her heart jumped, but it was just Sergeant White. "I'm sorry to startle you, ma'am. It's all clear. I'll wait here, just let me know when you're ready, and I'll load the stuff in your car for you. Take as long as you need."

"Thank you," she said. Inside, it was cool and dim. There was no trace of the blood; the place smelled like carpet cleaner. Her suitcase with the clothes still in it had been tossed into the closet. She flinched at the sight of the suitcase, took everything out and put it into an old duffel. Clothes, toiletries, art supplies. It was surprising how few things she considered hers alone. Last of all she retrieved the portfolio case with all her best work in it, laid it down on the bed. As she took one last look in the closet for anything she'd missed, she heard the portfolio slide off the bed and spill pages onto the floor. She sighed. She was so tired, and her pain meds were wearing off. Perhaps Sergeant White could help—

She saw the drawings then. Saw what Greg had done to them. Ripped them to pieces. They spilled out of her portfolio like oversize confetti, impossible to salvage. Years of her best work, gone. Like Isabelle.

Elaine sank to the floor. Her eyes burned, but she could not cry. So empty inside, not just her womb but her whole body. Her spirit. A husk that would blow away in the breeze, like one of those kachina dolls they sold in the tourist shops. Too empty to breathe, let alone get up, get downstairs, start driving to who knew where.

She might have stayed there forever, but Sergeant White was waiting for her. Bad enough she'd disappointed him by not pressing charges against Greg—but how could she explain that none of this would have happened if she'd had the guts to walk away the first time he laid hands on her, or to refuse the proposal of a man she didn't love? She couldn't disappoint White again, not when he'd been kinder than her husband or her parents.

Downstairs she went, and waited by her Honda while he loaded her things into it. The last item he put in her car was something he took from his sedan's trunk: a small Styrofoam cooler. "My wife, Lynn, she put some sandwiches and drinks in here for you."

She thanked him, fighting back tears, for if she started crying now, she'd never stop. Promising to call him when she stopped for the night, and when she got to California, she got into her car. Once she was on Highway 10 it became easier. She let the highway drone on. After a while, hardly conscious of what she was doing, she began to hum the songs she'd sung to the man in the diner. How long ago that seemed. The melodies didn't comfort her as much as they had him, but they helped. A little.

For a year she did nothing.

She worked—first at a geriatric center in Palm Springs, and then at a hospital in Bakersfield. She ate and slept. She read fluffy mysteries in which the crimes were solved by cats or librarians. She watched Turner Classic Movies every night. She kept her head down and her mind on her work and never spoke to her coworkers or patients about anything other than the tasks at hand. She went to the coin laundry every Saturday morning and to the library every Sunday afternoon. She didn't take any art classes, and although she bought new sketch pads and pencils they lay untouched. She signed the necessary papers and changed her last name back to Cahill, for whatever that was worth.

She did not weep—not since the first night away from Phoenix, when she'd lain sleepless in a motel bed, had turned the TV up loud so no one would hear her, and cried into the pillow. Since then, no tears. And no laughter, either, save for an occasional chuckle at one of the movies she watched.

A year went by. There came a Sunday afternoon that was just like every other Sunday afternoon. The library was full of its usual quiet drone. Elaine held the new Janet Evanovich tucked under one arm. With her free hand she perused the music catalog, looking through racks of CDs. Music was like her art, something she hadn't indulged in since leaving Arizona. She'd had no interest. But she was tired of silence. Here was a new Mediaeval Baebes, some band called Faith and the Muse that looked interesting, a new recording of Saint-Saëns's *Carnival of the Animals*, a Tori Amos she hadn't heard in a long time.

And there he was.

Hands trembling, she set aside the Evanovich and the CDs and made a poor job of it—they tumbled to the floor, and she didn't notice. She grabbed the CD and looked at it closely. Yes, it was him. It was the profile shot of him on the cover, with his eyes closed. If the picture had been a full-face shot, she probably wouldn't have known him. *Winter Roses*. Daniel Whitman.

She didn't watch a movie that night. She didn't even eat dinner. She lay on her bed and listened to the CD over and over again. Elaine was a nurse; it was her job to help people. Yet it wasn't until she heard his songs with the melodies she had sung, listened to his lyrics, read over the news story about him she'd found at the library, that she felt like she had truly helped someone. He thanked her in the liner notes, but she needed no thanks. Hearing the music was enough, and it was so good to know that she had mattered to someone at least once in her life.

After that, she started drawing again, and her hands quickly recovered their old skill. She moved to Sacramento and took a hospital job there, signed up for an art class at the local community college. San Francisco was not far away, and there had been job offers, but she couldn't go. Elaine wondered if she'd ever be able to go back there, or if the city would forever be a reminder of what she'd lost.

Life was better in Sacramento, though she still kept her head down and kept to herself. What was the point in making friendships when she would just move on and lose them? When she found a place she wanted to stay, then she'd work on making a friend or two.

The next year saw her in Stockton; the year also made her an orphan. Her parents were on a charter bus, on the way to Branson, when the bus had a bad blowout and was T-boned by a semi. When the ashes were delivered, Elaine could think of nowhere to scatter them. Marjorie and Brian had been all over the country but if there was a place in particular they'd loved, Elaine didn't know about it. She drove down to Santa Cruz and waited till sunset, then poured her parents' ashes into the sea. She stood for a while on the beach, feeling far more pleasure at being on the coast than grief for the remains she'd just scattered. That night she sent out her résumés, to coastal towns only this time, and took an offer in Los Cielos because the name was pretty and sounded vaguely familiar.

Los Cielos reminded her a bit of San Francisco and soothed her. Here, finally, was a place she might be able to call home. But she couldn't.

She had more than three decades of life working against her—she'd always been ignored, sometimes even wanted to be ignored. Now that she wanted to be noticed, she had no idea how to be. Old patterns resumed but with a twist—loneliness weighed her down. Perhaps it was because she was an orphan now. True, she hadn't spoken to her mother since Marjorie had told her she was a fool to leave Greg. True, her father seemed to have forgotten about her since she left home. But they had been her only blood relatives save for some distant cousins she'd never met. Perhaps it was because of Greg. True, she never wanted to see him again and she hated him as she hated no one else, but if she had ever mattered to him, wouldn't he have tried to find her instead of signing the divorce papers without a hitch?

She'd been in Los Cielos six months when she wandered into the local record store, hoping to replace some CDs that had gotten damaged in her latest move. Blue Angel Records had a surprisingly good selection, new and used, and she was able to get some albums she'd had a hard time finding before. The place made her smile: next to the new releases was a life-size cardboard image of Britney Spears on which someone had put a cartoon dialogue bubble: "Don't shoplift, or I'll make another album." By the register a huge orange tabby snoozed, and there was a Hall of Fame wall covered with photos of local customers, most of them holding up their purchases and grinning.

As Elaine set her items on the counter, the music playing over the store's speakers changed. A soft wail of Irish flute—oh, she recognized it right away.

"You like this one? I do. Perfect for a rainy day like today." The clerk pointed to the far side of the store; Elaine saw a poster for *Winter Roses*, signed. "Dan gave us that when he did his signing here, couple years ago."

"You know him?"

"Heck yeah. He's a local, didn't you know? Go look on the Hall of Fame. No, little more to the left. There he is with his family."

Daniel Whitman was there with a pretty blonde woman and a boy who looked to be in preschool. The boy held a Raffi CD, and his parents were behind him, making bunny ears over each other's heads. Sarah and Jake. She knew their names from the liner notes. The picture gave her a chill although everyone in it was happy. Because everyone in it was happy.

"Did you know what happened? Terrible thing," said the clerk, who was apparently in no rush to ring up her CDs. "Dan took it hard. Even went missing for a while."

"When was this?" Elaine asked, and wasn't surprised to learn it was when she'd met him. "He still lives in Los Cielos?"

The clerk nodded. "He's a regular here. Come back often enough and you're bound to run into him. He'll sign your CD, no worries about that. He's a good sport." He looked at her closely. "Ma'am, you all right?"

She was fine, she assured him, just fine. Except she wasn't. Now she knew why the town's name had sounded familiar: her quick research at the library when she'd first seen the *Winter Roses* CD and wanted to know more about Whitman. Of all the places to come to. Why here? Why, when she'd finally found a town she liked? Because her first impulse now was to flee. She could not have explained why, save that she knew it would be dangerous to meet him.

Yet she stayed. Perhaps she liked Los Cielos nearly as much as she'd liked San Francisco. Perhaps she was tired of running and hiding.

It was on Christmas that she first went to the Chez. Elaine had never cared for the holiday: it brought back memories of dour get-togethers at whatever base her father was assigned to that year. Now it was the anniversary of when she'd met Greg and been foolish enough to fall for his attention. She'd meant to stay inside on the holiday and work on her drawings, but her apartment felt too small and stifling; there seemed to be a block between her brain and her hands, and she couldn't draw. That had been happening more and more, lately. So she took pad and pencils and wandered, looking for something she couldn't name. The sign on the Chez's door caught her eye: "Yes, we're open on Christmas! (Heathens welcome!)" It made her smile, so she went inside. Before long she was a regular. Here she could draw and no one would notice or bother her. Here she found peace.

A peace that was broken one Tuesday night.

She knew him at once, of course. There'd been a picture of him in the *Weekly*, just after Valentine's Day, in a write-up of some show at a local club. And once she was over the shock and felt assured that he didn't know her, she looked forward to seeing him and listening to him play. She liked the way he chatted with the woman who ran the place and the way he took requests agreeably. She liked to watch him at the keyboard, watch the way his hands moved and the play of emotions over his face. Late that summer when she took an evening class at LCU, she found that she missed the Chez and—to be frank—missed him as well.

She'd known something was wrong with him last Tuesday. It was clear that nothing he played pleased him. She found herself thinking that he should play something from *Winter Roses*, that it would help him. When he did, she realized one reason she kept coming back was because she'd wanted to hear him play it.

It was different from hearing the CD. Not just because of the unaccompanied piano, but because of the slight changes in tempo and mood she heard now. It was like the subtleties of light in Monet's paintings. She watched as he closed his eyes and gave himself over to the music; she supposed she looked very similar when she was deep into her drawings, those times she went into another world and afterward was dazed and disbelieving at the work that had come from her hands. Soon she'd forgotten all about drawing or even pretending to draw. Elaine sat and watched him, listened to the music, remembered those times when the thoughts of Isabelle had been too much, how she'd played this album and known that someone else had felt as she had, and how that had given her strength.

Elaine wasn't aware that she'd been singing along, not until the music ended abruptly but her voice continued on for a note or two. He sat with hands frozen above the keys, his face deathly white. He stood up, knocking over the piano bench, and for a moment Elaine felt sure he would faint. With the sense that history was repeating itself, she ran over to him, guided him to an armchair and sat him down. He didn't seem to notice, didn't even seem to see her. Ariel bustled over with a big glass of brandy, and Elaine was about to ask if something like this had ever happened to him before when he muttered the word *sparrow*.

She fled. But not fast enough.

"I'm sorry," she said now. He no longer sat across the table; now he sat next to her, holding one of her hands in his. When had that happened? How long had they been here? Had she really just blurted out her whole life's story to this stranger?

Except he wasn't a stranger to her, nor she to him.

"What for?" His voice was gentle, like his hands. She'd forgotten or perhaps never known that men could be gentle.

Where to start? For so many things. But what came to mind was that she should have stayed at the Shoreline Diner that morning. Maybe it would have changed nothing. But what if it had changed things, for them both?

Elaine tried to speak and couldn't. All this time her voice had been steady. It had helped to think that she was telling this tale about someone else. But she'd talked too long and was tired. Of running. Of hiding. Of herself most of all. Tears welled in her eyes.

He took his hands away from hers, as she'd guessed he would. But then he put one arm around her shoulders and pulled her close and with the other hand stroked her hair. As she'd done for him. Elaine tried to pull away but hadn't the strength. She laid her head on his shoulder and cried, felt the shelter of his arm and the touch of his hand on her hair, listened to his whispers that she should go ahead, let it out, let it go; she listened to the steady beat of his heart. What would happen later didn't concern her. What mattered was that she could let down the load and rest for a little while. Because she'd come home.

Chapter Twenty-Four

The garden was aglow in full sunlight; one could almost feel the warmth of the sun, smell the flowers. He started to lean forward and examine the painting more closely, but Elaine touched him on the shoulder.

"You won't see the details if you're close," she said. "That's the thing about the Impressionists. You won't see the whole thing unless you step back. Up close it'll just be a muddle."

Daniel stood next to her. Yes, it was obvious. When you were at a distance, the painting came into focus. "You're right," he said. "It's the light that makes it real, not the details."

She nodded. "Light was one of the most important things to the Impressionists. They'd paint the same thing viewed from the same spot at different times of day. Monet painted Rouen Cathedral twenty-six times, each at a different time of day. This one is his. *The Artist's Garden at Vétheuil.* And . . ." She stopped. Elaine's hair, which had been pulled aside, fell back over one eye in a look that was less Veronica Lake and more an animal seeking camouflage. "I'm sorry, I'm probably boring you."

"Not at all. I'm the one who should apologize, seeing as I know what I like but I don't know an Impressionist from an Expressionist. I'm one step up from just pointing and saying, 'Shiny' or 'Not shiny.'"

She laughed, and the sound echoed in the galleries of the Norton Simon Museum. It was a Thursday afternoon, and the place was nearly deserted save for a few senior citizens and an astonishingly well-behaved school tour.

It was Elaine who'd expressed the wish to come up here. She'd lamented the lack of Impressionists at the San Diego Museum of Art—no Van Gogh or Cézanne or Boudin, only one work by Monet—and wished the Norton Simon was in easier reach. She'd always wanted to go.

Daniel had asked her to keep Thursday free. He'd arrived, bringing along coffee and scones from Java Man, and it was worth every minute of the drive to Pasadena to see the look of delight on her face when he told her where they were going.

She stood in front of another painting, this one of a tree. He thought he recognized the style, though the painting itself wasn't familiar. "Is it Van Gogh?" he asked.

Elaine nodded. She drew her hair back again, and he could see her expression, pensive. "It's one of his last ones. He'd had himself committed to an asylum earlier that year." She glanced at him, not apprehensively but inquiringly. He understood and nodded. She went on: "When he was well enough, he'd paint. He liked painting these mulberry trees and thought this was his best one."

"I'm not sure how I feel about it," Daniel said. "There's something . . ." It reminded him of that session with Reg Fletcher, the one when everything he played came out sounding wrong. "Something fraught about it."

She nodded. "I don't like to look at it for very long."

Down the hall they went, touring the rest of the nineteenth-century collection. "Is this Monet again?" he asked of one sky- and seascape.

323

"Close. It's Boudin. He was a bit older than the other Impressionists and taught Monet some of his techniques. One person called him the 'king of skies,' and I can see why."

"It's not as real looking as a photo, but it still feels like you could walk right through and be there."

After the nineteenth century they had lunch at the café by the sculpture garden, then toured the seventeenth and eighteenth centuries, which were heavy on portraits. They speculated about what the people were like, based on their portraits. For a long time he stood in front of the Rembrandt portrait of the unnamed young boy, who reminded him of Jake. Then on to the twentieth century, which they both liked more than they thought they would. And then one last visit to the nineteenth century—this time he found himself intrigued by a painting he'd missed the first time around. Toulouse-Lautrec, *Red-Headed Woman in the Garden of M. Foret*. The woman in the painting reminded him of Elaine, not just the color of her hair but the way she was turned away, her face lowered, as if she wished to be unnoticed.

He turned and searched for Elaine; she was looking at *Low Tide, Berck* by Boudin—the king of skies. She seemed unaware of his presence; she had her hair away from her face, looked straight on at the painting, and wore a faint half smile. No, not as much like the woman in the painting as he'd thought.

It was late by the time they got back to Los Cielos. He drove to her apartment building—the Coral Villas, the same place he'd lived in for a while. It gave him a cold feeling inside to see it again, but that feeling vanished when Elaine smiled and said she hadn't had such a fun day in a long time.

"Want me to wait until you get inside?" he asked.

"If you don't mind. But—wait, I'll be right back." She got out of his car and ran into the complex, up the stairs. Her unit wasn't the same one his had been, and he breathed a small sigh of relief.

In a few moments she was back, carrying a book. *Boudin: Sky and Sea.* "Keep it as long as you like," she said.

Back in September, when she'd told him of her life and how she'd come to Los Cielos, he hadn't been sure what would happen next. After their talk, he'd gone back to the Chez every evening, but she hadn't returned. That Monday he'd wheedled a quick meeting with Dr. Levinson. It hadn't taken much wheedling, actually. Dr. Levinson had been fascinated by the whole thing. Yet he'd cautioned Daniel that Elaine might not come back. "She's been running and hiding for a long time," he'd said. "I think it would be good for her to stay, but don't judge her harshly if she doesn't."

Still uncertain, Daniel had gone to his other counselor later that same day. Beaditudes was closed Mondays, and the day off found Rachel sunning herself by the pool. The Kesslers had moved off the Hill and into a smaller but much more comfortable place; the ocean view was gone, but with a mere four-block walk to the beach, no one was complaining. He'd asked if he could have her advice, and he'd brought along a pitcher of sangria to sweeten the deal. ("At this time of day?" she'd asked. "Hey, it's happy hour. In Newfoundland," he'd replied.) By the time he was done telling her the story, the pitcher was empty and it was happy hour in Nebraska.

Rachel had said very little throughout, and behind her oversize, heart-shaped sunglasses her expression was impossible to read. "How do you feel about her?" she asked.

"I've been trying to figure it out." He knew he could be honest with Rachel. "I wasn't sure at first, I mean, because of how we met. Then and now. She seems like a nice person, and I want to find out what she's like when things are normal. See, I'm not sure what to do about that."

She sat up, peered at him over the Lolita shades. "God, you have to tell men *everything*," she grumbled. Then smiled, to soften her criticism. "If she's nice, be there for her. Lord knows she could use a friend. Just be that."

Is that enough? He started to ask but didn't have to. It was. Friends were the one thing that hadn't let him down, no matter that he'd let them down plenty. He'd be her friend, if that's what she wanted.

The next night was Tuesday, and he arrived at his usual time and saw her in her usual place. She looked at him, and he saw not a smile, but the promise of one. That was good enough for him.

For nearly a month they did little but have coffee and talk. About themselves. He told her about Jake and Sarah and about his lost wandering time; he told her how he'd come to stagger into the Shoreline Diner and how he'd come to write *Winter Roses*. Telling her this was comforting in a way that even talking with Drs. Howard or Levinson wasn't—Elaine had walked her own path on that road and understood it.

They talked about her drawings and his music, about life in Los Cielos. He liked the way she'd forget herself when she got enthusiastic about a subject, forget to hide behind her hair. And it was good to have another friend. You couldn't have too many of those.

The Monday after the trip to the Norton Simon, Elaine was getting ready to go on break when one of the other nurses flagged her down. "Elaine," Kimberly called out. "Phone for you."

Puzzled, Elaine picked up the extension. She could feel Kimberly's curious gaze—Elaine never got phone calls at the hospital. There was no one to call her. "Hello?"

"Hey, it's Daniel. It just occurred to me—is it OK to call you here?"

"It's fine, I was just going on break."

"Good. I should have thought of that sooner, but most of my friends own their own businesses. Or they're flakes. Or both. Are you near a window?"

"Yes."

"Look out toward the west if you can. Wouldn't Boudin have loved this day?"

The day was cool, and fat cumulus clouds loomed above the horizon. It made her long to go down to the shore and see the color of the sea and whether it was ruffled by whitecaps. "Yes, he would have. It's beautiful."

"I thought you'd think so. Anyway, I'll let you go. I'll be in LA the rest of the week, but I'll give you a jingle when I get back."

They said goodbye and Elaine hung up. For a moment she looked at the skyscape that begged to be painted.

"So? Boyfriend?" asked Kimberly, her eyebrows raised.

"Pardon? Oh no. Just a friend."

"Oh."

Elaine went on her break. She wondered why Kimberly sounded disappointed. Deprived of the chance for some good gossip, no doubt. Probably felt sorry for Elaine, that it was just a friend calling. But was there such a thing as "just" a friend? Maybe most people could take it for granted, that someone would call them up to say how lovely the sky was today. Or that she could show her latest drawing to Daniel and he wouldn't say, *Oh, that's nice* just to be polite. No, never could she take this for granted. It had been withheld too long, was too precious to her now.

One day in early November, she dashed out of Los Cielos General Hospital at lunchtime. As she did she got a quizzical look from Kimberly, who was used to seeing Elaine spend her lunches in the hospital's cafeteria, usually brown-bagging it and spending the hour with her nose in a book. But she'd read in the *Weekly* about a new restaurant just a block from the General, a Mongolian barbecue called Wok This Way. She hadn't been to one of those since her father had been stationed in California, and Daniel loved Mongolian barbecue and was eager to try it out with her.

As Elaine neared the restaurant her spirits sank. He was waiting for her outside, as he'd said he would—and he was even on time—but he wasn't alone.

The woman was dark haired and petite—probably five-foot-nothing at the most—very pretty in a long, wine-colored dress and with her jewelry glittering in the sun. She seemed the epitome of all those effortlessly confident girls that Elaine had never learned how to befriend. Despite Greg, Elaine found it easier to deal with men—if they didn't like you, usually they'd just ignore you. But in her school days there always had been girls who would whisper behind their hands and giggle as she walked by, who'd make catty remarks about her out-of-fashion clothes and her bookish ways. Those days were gone, but Elaine still got a queasy feeling when she met women her own age, and always wondered if she was being weighed, assessed, and found wanting.

Elaine considered heading back to the General. She could call Daniel later and tell him a stat case had come up and she couldn't get away. Then she told herself to go on—after all, was he the kind of person who'd hang around with a mean girl? She didn't think so, but . . .

Then it was out of her hands as Daniel spotted her and waved hello. Elaine waved back and went over to them. Daniel made introductions, and Elaine was surprised. So this was Rachel. She'd expected someone older, more maternal looking. What was that cliché line from the movies? *I thought you'd be bigger.* But Rachel was a tiny thing; even her hand, when they shook, was small. And Rachel seemed so genuinely pleased to meet Elaine that she agreed without hesitation when Daniel asked if Rachel could join them for lunch.

When they'd picked out their bowls of meat, vegetables, and seasonings and were taking them to the surly-looking cook, Elaine asked Rachel where she'd gotten her necklace. "I made it," Rachel said.

"Really? Was it difficult? It's so intricate."

"Not really," Rachel replied. "I've been doing this a long time. I run Beaditudes over on Sandcastle."

Elaine had been by the store a few times, had looked in the windows, drawn by the colors of the clothes and beadwork. She'd never been inside, even though the clothes were lovely and within her budget. Where would she ever wear them? "Are the red stones rubies?"

Rachel shook her head. "Garnets. They're less expensive than rubies, and I actually like the color better. And the other stones—wait, what am I wearing today?"

"There's gold-looking stuff and that clear stone you put in my bracelet," Daniel said, holding up his left hand.

"Ah yes. Brass beads and quartz—clear and rose quartz."

After they'd started eating and unanimously declared the restaurant a success, Rachel said, "I'm glad I ran into the two of you. I know it's early yet, but I need to talk about Thanksgiving. We're not heading up to the city this year."

"Everything OK with your folks?" Daniel asked.

"Oh yes, better than OK really. They're going to Florida for my great-aunt's birthday. Ninety-nine years old. The sibs and I are all on our own this year, so I figured Mick and I will put on our first Thanksgiving. Like to be a guinea pig?"

"I'll be there," Daniel said. "The Reillys won't mind."

Rachel turned to Elaine. "Would you like to come?"

Elaine was taken by surprise. She'd just met Rachel, she'd never expected to merit an invitation to Thanksgiving. Of course she had no plans for the day—hadn't celebrated the holiday since her married days, and those could never be called a celebration, not with Greg or her in-laws criticizing every dish she set on the table. Automatically she started to decline, then caught Daniel's eye. He gave her a slight smile; a look that said *It'll be all right*. She found herself saying, "I'd like that very much."

Thanksgiving was sunny and warm, a day to incite jealousy from those parts of the country that had actual seasons. Elaine arrived just after noon, bringing her contribution to the dinner. Rachel had asked that everyone bring something: "It doesn't have to be big. Even a two-liter of soda." Elaine had the idea Rachel was feeling the pressure of her first Thanksgiving dinner. She knew Daniel was bringing the dressing. As he put it, "Friends don't let friends eat Stove Top." Elaine had considered cooking something, but the only feedback she'd ever received on her holiday food was from Greg and his parents, none of it complimentary.

So she stood now with a loaf of French bread from the bakery, a bottle of wine, and a bag of coffee beans from Java Man. And she'd brought one other thing, as a thank-you to Rachel for the invitation. Daniel's car was already parked by the house, and as Elaine went up the walk she heard music playing and a loud splash. Rachel had said to bring a swimsuit if the weather was warm enough for the pool, but Elaine had left her suit behind in Arizona and had never gotten around to getting another one.

A sign on the door said "Come right in!" Elaine stepped inside and followed the scent of roasting turkey to the kitchen. Rachel stood with an apron covering her flowy dress (autumn red and gold), her hair in braids tied with feathers and beads, her arms folded, staring at the oven as if the turkey had done her a grave injustice. "Rachel?"

"Hey! Happy Thanksgiving!" She took the bag from Elaine, grinned when she saw the bottle of wine. "I should let this start breathing now. And who knows, perhaps we should sample it before dinner."

Elaine reached into her bag. "And this is for you."

Rachel unrolled the drawing. A cornucopia, but not one containing fruits and vegetables. This one spilled forth jewels and scarves, all rendered in oil pastels for their bright colors. "It's lovely," Rachel said. "Thank you. I should have it framed and put up in the shop."

"Thank you. For inviting me."

"Thank me after dinner, if you still want to. This bird may be a while, and it's my first, so I make no promises. Daniel's out back with Mick and Eskimo Sally."

Elaine headed out to the back, bringing a plateful of hors d'oeuvres. She stepped into the backyard to see Daniel and a blond man looking on bemusedly while a woman in a magenta swimsuit bounced on the diving board and sang "Carioca" until she lost her balance and fell into the water.

"Wow," said the blond man dryly. "Dinner *and* a show."

Daniel laughed, then saw Elaine and called out hello. The blond man took the hors d'oeuvres from her and introduced himself as Mick—like Rachel, he didn't look the way Elaine had expected. Then Eskimo Sally, looking not at all dismayed by her tumble into the pool, hauled herself out of the water and asked Elaine if she was related to some Cahills she knew in North Carolina. Before long they were joined by Eskimo Sally's friend Evie and her boyfriend Nate, and soon Elaine forgot to feel shy. Everyone seemed happy to have her there, and not just because she was Daniel's friend. They stood by the pool nibbling on treats; Evie loaded up the CD player with the Traveling Wilburys, Dave Brubeck, and compilations of eighties songs, and periodically someone would go in to see if Rachel needed help and would be kicked back outside immediately. But when Elaine went in, she and Rachel treated themselves to the wine Elaine had brought; soon they'd polished off a couple of glasses and were talking about San Francisco. Rachel called out the window to Daniel that he had mashed potato duty and that Mick had to help carve the bird. Soon it was a comfortable melee, with all the guests trying to help at once, but somehow they managed it and were sitting down to a feast as traditional as you could get: turkey, corn bread dressing, mashed potatoes, yams topped with gooey marshmallows, green beans, three kinds of pie, bread, wine. Eskimo Sally volunteered to say grace: "Some have food but no appetite. Some have appetite but no food. I have both. God be praised." And later on there were toasts, and some said what they were thankful for. Elaine didn't say anything; her shyness had returned, and she felt she couldn't say what she was truly thankful for. For meeting Daniel that first time and again here in Los Cielos. For not obeying her first instinct to run and hide. For joining his circle of friends. For the simple pleasure of a fine meal with nice people. For having a life that, for the first time in a very long while, seemed well worth living.

Heart of Light

Chapter Twenty-Five

All summer long the seats at Fulweiler Amphitheater were full and blankets were spread on the grass. *Saturday Under the Stars.* Every week brought something new. Concerts by local bands or an orchestra visiting from San Diego. One memorable night in July, a screening of *Jaws* and *Raiders of the Lost Ark*. Reggae Sunsplash was due to close the season on Labor Day weekend, and Rachel already had an outfit of Rastafarian red, gold, and green ready.

As for tonight, it seemed the local laser-and-music enthusiasts had gotten bored with recycling the same progressive rock tunes and had moved on to laser Bach—though it was not just Bach but Vivaldi, Debussy, Barber, Holst, Gluck, and Mahler. Rachel thought this could be a culture clash of epic proportions, and neither she nor Mick wanted to miss it. The rest of the town seemed to feel the same way, for the seats were full, and there was precious little space on the lawn not occupied by blankets and beach towels.

The Kesslers hadn't bothered looking in the seats, for they knew Daniel and Elaine would be up on the lawn. And there they were, sitting on a large striped beach blanket that Rachel recognized from past summer nights at the amphitheater and from beach outings over the years. As she had done all this summer, Rachel gauged their body language and the amount of space between them.

When they arrived Daniel was opening a bottle of wine while Elaine unloaded the picnic basket. "Can't wait to hear Miles Sanford's reaction," Elaine said, referring to the KLCU classical DJ. "This will offend him deeply. He still hasn't forgiven Wendy Carlos for *Switched-On Bach*."

"I'm not sure *I've* forgiven Wendy Carlos for *Switched-On Bach*," said Daniel.

Elaine saw them and waved hello, helped clear a space for them on the blanket. Soon they were all sitting comfortably with glasses of wine and beer, paper plates heaped with fruit salad and cold fried chicken, chatting before the show started. Elaine told them how her French classes in high school and college had finally paid off today when a family visiting from Martinique had gotten in a car accident and one of them needed to go to the ER. Los Cielos General had interpreters for ASL, Spanish, Armenian, and Chinese, but no French. "So I had to step up or we'd have had to wait for an interpreter from Oceanside. They were a bit banged up but nothing serious, thank goodness," she said. "They left just as I was getting off shift. Our dialects weren't quite the same, but I *think* they may have invited me to visit if I'm ever in Martinique."

"Sounds better than my day," Rachel said. "A woman came in, tried on twenty outfits, and didn't buy a thing. She had nasty BO, so I'll have to wash everything. Oh, and she asked if I had any necklaces that would make her butt look smaller. I just smiled and said no. What I wanted to tell her was that if I had something like that, I'd sure as heck be wearing it."

Elaine laughed. "I think retail's a lot like nursing. You can't say what you really think."

"Isn't that the truth." Rachel liked Elaine's hospital stories, and she liked seeing Elaine so relaxed. She seemed a much different person than the one who'd been so skittish at the Mongolian barbecue restaurant, the one who hid behind her hair and seemed startled when someone noticed her. She'd started coming out of her shell last Thanksgiving; from what Rachel had gleaned, accepting that invitation had been a bold step for her.

You'd never know that now, Rachel thought, watching Elaine as she talked with Daniel and Mick. She didn't hide behind her hair anymore; she wore a Beaditudes dress in midnight blue, and when she laughed it was a pretty sound. *Like wind chimes,* Daniel had said once.

After the sun had set and the show started, Rachel glanced once or twice at Daniel and Elaine. Looking, as she had all this summer, for hands being held, shoulders touching, for him to put an arm around the redhead.

And she looked when they said goodbye after the show and she watched Daniel walk Elaine to her car. She couldn't hear what they said to each other, but she didn't need to. Their manner and tone told her everything; it spoke of comfort and companionship and perhaps love of a sort. But nothing romantic.

Rachel knew she wasn't the only one who'd been observing Daniel and Elaine for any hints that they were transcending what Eskimo Sally called a "friendationship." More than once over this summer she'd caught mutual acquaintances looking sidelong at them to see if there was anything there. Last month, at the Reilly's Independence Day block party, Kate had sighed, "I wish those two would yield to the inevitable. I like her. I like her a lot. And they're good for each other."

Tonight as they got into the car Mick settled himself behind the wheel and glanced back toward the parking lot. "I'm glad I didn't take Eskimo Sally up on her bet. I thought for sure they would have gotten together by now," he said.

"When did she say it would happen?"

"Not until we knocked their heads together."

Rachel smiled ruefully. She'd have liked to have been on Mick's side, but it was looking more and more like Eskimo Sally was right. "Maybe we do need to knock their heads together."

"Not literally."

"No, just make them see each other in a different way."

"But they've known each other for a long while," Mick said. "I don't know if they can see each other as . . . Those things usually happen at first sight. In my limited experience, anyway."

"So you're saying you were instantly besotted with me?"

"Yes indeed."

"You're sweet. But their relationship isn't exactly ordinary." She looked out the car window, regarded the streetlights and darkened storefronts. "I think they're scared."

"What, you think she's scared that Daniel's going to be like her ex?"

"No. I mean, scared of losing what they have." Who could blame them? Not Rachel.

On a September Sunday Rachel closed up shop and drove over to the Episcopal church she attended once or twice a month. The day's last service had just begun when she arrived, and she discreetly tucked herself into a seat near the back. As usual she fell into a slightly dreamy state, half listening to the service and half musing on the way the late afternoon sun glittered in the stained glass windows.

But she snapped to full attention at the end, when the minister said he had an update on Mrs. Gresham. Alice Gresham had been the church secretary and all-around dynamo since time out of mind; she coordinated the annual Christmas tree decorations in the park, ran the Meals on Wheels program, and helped staff the bookmobile. She'd suffered a stroke earlier in the month, and though she was fine mentally she'd lost most of her sight. "By the end of the year Alice will be going up north to the Guide Dogs for the Blind campus to meet and train with a guide dog," Father Lewis said. "There's no cost for that, but we want to make a donation to the campus to help in these efforts, and we also want to help with Alice's rent and other expenses while she's away, not to mention helping get her place situated for when she returns." The church would put on a fund-raising party at the Marriott on Halloween: tickets were on sale starting today, and there would be auctions, dancing, catered food, and much more.

Like most of the congregation, Rachel joined the line for the tickets. Having what sounded like loads of fun, and for a worthy cause? Count her in. As she stepped up to buy tickets for herself and Mick, inspiration struck. "I'll take four," she said.

When Rachel got home from her book club, Mick was blasting away at zombies on the PlayStation. "Eat fire, nimrod! Ha. Oh, you're home." He quickly paused the game and looked up at her. "Is she in?"

"She is." Rachel sat down beside him on the sofa. "He invited her, and after book club tonight she asked if I could help her with something to wear. I didn't tell her the specifics, just said it would be nice and classy. She's coming in to get measured tomorrow."

"I can help out with some of the beading. Eskimo Sally says she'll pitch in, too."

"I'll probably take you up on that." Rachel slumped against him. "I'm beat. This matchmaking business is hard."

"Here, relax," he said, and began to massage her shoulders. "Do you think we need to get Daniel into a decent costume? Knowing him, he'll show up in his pajamas or something."

Rachel grinned. Daniel was the worst at Halloween costumes, usually showing up in something he'd tossed together at the last minute. Lucky for him, he had enough charm to make whatever half-assed ensemble he wore look endearing. But she knew what Mick was asking.

"I don't think so," she said after a moment. "She looks at him sometimes. I think she finds him attractive, but it's like ... like she's outside a shop window, looking at something she could never afford." She rolled her shoulders, turned to look at him. "What about him? Has he told you anything in guy talk?"

Mick shook his head. "He doesn't seem to notice her that way. But he doesn't notice *anyone* that way. Or if he does, he's keeping quiet about it, and that's not his way. It's like he's switched that part of himself off."

"He told Eskimo Sally he doesn't want to lose anyone again," she said.

He nodded. "Something I have noticed, though. He never asks if I know any guys she'd like to meet. He's always on the lookout for someone for Eskimo Sally, and before Amy and Carl got hitched he'd ask if I knew anyone right for her. But never for Elaine."

Rachel nodded. That was reassuring. But doubts still lingered. "Are we ... I mean, even if this works, is it the right thing to do?" It would be easier if Daniel and Elaine were unhappy. But they weren't. Who was to say that a change in their relationship was for the better? Of course, everyone wanted to see them together. But was it what Daniel and Elaine needed?

Mick was a long time answering. She took his silence for uncertainty until he said, "You've probably wondered why it took me so long to ask you out after we met."

She had. She didn't say anything now but waited for him to go on.

"I'd get out your number and start to call. Then I'd think about Gina. Even though I could tell you weren't like her, I didn't want to take a chance." He took off his glasses, polished the lenses, and went on: "But when I did, and when I knew that you were the one . . . Well, I didn't mind Gina as much. Because without her I wouldn't have appreciated what we have. What I'm saying is, if it works out with Daniel and Elaine, because of what they've been through it'll be something special."

She nodded. "Well then. Let's get to work."

Chapter Twenty-Six

A sign hung over the entryway to the Marriott's Cove Ballroom: *Welcome to the October Country.* Mick thought it very appropriate. The only thing he missed about Missouri was the leaves turning in the fall. California had no autumn to speak of—the state's only flaw, as far as he was concerned.

But autumn had come to this room. Orange and black streamers hung from the chandeliers. Party balloons in red, gold, and orange reached up, as if begging to be set free so they could fly up to the ceiling, somehow escape out into the sky. Each table had a jack-o'-lantern as its centerpiece. Real pumpkins, each with its own unique face—some were elaborately, painstakingly carved, others had crude triangular eyes and noses made by young children—and each with spare candles so the lanterns might be lit all night and fill the room with the sweet, nostalgic scent of slightly cooked pumpkin. And no one would regret missing out on trick-or-treating. Besides being laden with a huge amount of finger foods and appetizers from local restaurants, the buffet tables also boasted bowls full of candy: Milk Duds, Smarties, Pixy Stix, Tootsie Rolls, and Whoppers—all the classics, there for the taking. Adjacent to the ballroom was a darkened room where someone from the Bijou Theater would screen black-and-white horror movies all evening: *Dracula, The Haunting, The Phantom of the Opera, Murders in the Rue Morgue,* and ending with a midnight showing of *Young Frankenstein.*

Mick and Rachel stopped by the charity auction. Goods and services from local businesses ruled the table, and glass bowls filled with raffle tickets testified to each item's popularity. Mick was pleased to see how full the bowl was for the ensemble Rachel had contributed—scarf, earrings, necklace, and bracelet in autumn tones—and for the copy of *Winter Roses* with the CD insert signed by Daniel as well as all the session players and Reg Fletcher.

As for Daniel, he was here already, chatting with Rachel's friend Evie who was on DJ duty tonight and dressed like Alice in Wonderland. "Oh God," Rachel muttered. "We should have made him wear something nice. Look at that."

Rachel wasn't the only one vexed by Daniel's outfit. He seemed to be justifying it to Evie. "I *am* in costume," he insisted. "I'm a tourist. See? The shirt, and the ears?"

The shirt in question was Hawaiian, and lurid by any standard: gold with purple crabs. The ears were Mickey Mouse ears. Evie looked at the shirt with undisguised horror, possibly because her boyfriend Nate seemed to covet it.

"Where on earth did you get it?" she asked.

"Yeah! Where'd you get it?" asked Nate.

"At a 7-Eleven on Waikiki." He caught sight of Mick and Rachel. "Hey! You look great, but I thought you were doing *Star Wars*."

"Yes, well, we had a disagreement," said Rachel. "He says we should be Han and Leia, which is fine for him, but I wasn't going to wear cinnamon rolls on the side of my head."

"So I told her to go with the *Return of the Jedi* option. No dice."

"Why ever not?" asked Daniel.

343

Rachel looked at him as if he'd gone mad. "And wear the gold metal bikini? At my age?"

"I don't see a downside to that," Mick said.

"Nor I," said Daniel while Nate nodded in agreement.

Rachel sighed, turned to Evie for moral support. "Sorry, but I'm thirty-eight, and my gold metal bikini days are behind me. So I said, fine, we'll do the prequels."

"Wait, you'll dress like Sergeant Kabukiman, but you won't wear the gold bikini?" asked Daniel.

"She was going to make me say that line about the sand," Mick said.

"So we settled on this as a compromise." Rachel gestured to her gypsy costume and Mick's 1930s gangster outfit.

Mick was pleased enough; Rachel had offered to wear the gold metal bikini on their next romantic getaway. To be honest, neither he nor Rachel had given much thought to their own costumes, being preoccupied with making sure Elaine's was just right. Speaking of which. "Where's Elaine?" he asked.

"She'll be here," Daniel said. "They're shorthanded and she has to work a bit late tonight." He smiled. "I can't wait to see what she wears. She wouldn't tell me anything."

Mick felt Rachel's knee nudge his. Elaine herself hadn't seen the outfit until yesterday morning, when Rachel had taken it to Elaine's apartment to make sure it fit and make any necessary adjustments. Part of that had been strategic; they didn't want Elaine to give in to shyness and balk at the costume. And it had taken them that long to finish, even with Eskimo Sally helping out with the beadwork.

They said goodbye to Evie and went to get some food, then took their laden plates to the table where Eskimo Sally was already sitting. Or trying to sit—she'd opted for court finery, complete with powdered wig, and was having trouble with her skirts.

"Goddamn it," she muttered as she finally arranged herself. "I had to go all fancy, didn't I? Couldn't do something simple like you two, or just skip the costume altogether like Dan."

"As I keep telling everybody, I'm a—"

"Say, where's Elaine?" Eskimo Sally asked a shade too brightly. Not for the first time Mick wondered if it had been a bad idea to have her involved in Elaine's costume. Eskimo Sally couldn't keep a secret to save her life—telling her something was akin to taking out a full-page ad in the *Weekly*.

"Working late," Rachel said. "She'll be here."

Mick thought Rachel put perhaps a bit too much emphasis on this, and glanced Daniel's way, but he was staring across the room. "Holy shit," Daniel said, sounding dismayed.

"What?" Mick asked.

"I just saw . . . God, yes. That's Dr. Levinson and his wife."

Eskimo Sally shrugged. "Shrinks have social lives, too, you know."

"Yes, but I didn't expect to see them dressed like Frankenstein and the Bride and dancing to 'Suffragette City.' It's kind of a head bender."

"You think that's bad?" asked Eskimo Sally. "Wait till you see Dr. Hill and his lady friend. If she's old enough to drink legally, I'll eat my wig. Look, there they go."

They watched the May-December couple go by; she was drinking what looked like a Shirley Temple. Daniel chortled. "Between Dr. Levinson and that, I sense a conspiracy to get me back on Zoloft. I need a drink; can I bring back something for anybody?"

Everyone was set except for Eskimo Sally ("I'm happy with anything, as long there's an umbrella in it."). While Daniel went to get drinks, Eskimo Sally leaned over to Mick and Rachel. "Hey, guys, relax. It'll be fine. Their auras are good, and I read the tarot this morning. *Very* favorable. I even went and lit a candle at Queen of Peace."

"You're Catholic?" Mick asked.

"Nah. I think I'm a Methodist. Or Lutheran. I forget."

Rachel shot a quizzical look at Mick, who shrugged.

Eskimo Sally went on breezily: "Don't worry about it. Wheels are in motion, and all we can do is sit back and enjoy the ride."

But will they? Mick wondered. She was right, though; it was too late to do anything about it now. Rachel's hand stole over to his shoulders, gave them a reassuring squeeze. The evening lay before them, and he felt a thrill of anticipation; he and Rachel hadn't gone dancing in a long time, and she looked so gorgeous in her gypsy garb. He tugged on one of her scarves, brought her face close to his and kissed her. "You taste like Pixy Stix," he said, and they both giggled.

He turned back to the table to see Daniel and Eskimo Sally with their umbrella drinks. "Hey, now that you two are back," Daniel said. "A toast. Happy Halloween." The glasses rang together.

Elaine sat in her car; her damp palms left marks on the steering wheel. The Marriott's parking lot was close to capacity, and she'd had to park on the outer edges. She sat and watched passersby for a moment. A couple on their way out to a fancy dinner. A family just arriving, the mom and dad wrangling kids and luggage into the lobby. And a small but steady stream of partygoers.

She'd known about the event for a while—her coworker Kimberly, head nurse Connie, and Dr. Bradford all were members of the church and had talked of little else. She'd thought it sounded like fun—for someone else. Elaine was not a party person, never had been. Parties had been drab affairs in the halls of whatever base her family was stationed at, or they had been workplace affairs of enforced gaiety. She'd been surprised when Daniel had invited her. So surprised that before she knew it she'd said yes. It wasn't until later that she regretted what she'd done; she kept meaning to find a way to bow out of it gracefully, but every time she did someone waxed enthusiastic about the party or dropped some tidbit about it. Didn't you hear? All the top local restaurants would be providing food. Someone from the Bijou Theater would be showing movies—old-school horror, no blood and gore.

And so she'd found herself asking Rachel for help with a costume. She'd had to—Elaine was no good at coming up with a costume, and as for what you could buy in the stores ... well, the candy stripers didn't nickname the holiday Slut-o-ween for nothing. Rachel had been helpful— perhaps too helpful? Elaine had been a bit taken aback when Rachel brought everything over yesterday. She'd wanted to say no, this was too much, she'd never feel at ease with it.

But she'd wanted this more.

It would strike her at odd times. How much it had meant to have friends, to be welcomed, to know people enjoyed her company. Sometimes she wondered—had she really been planning to flee Los Cielos and resume her old vagabond ways?

Yes, she had, and if she hadn't met Daniel, she would have. But now she had friends—not just Daniel but Mick and Rachel and Eskimo Sally and others. It had changed her. She hadn't realized how much until she'd found herself going out for a coffee with her coworkers or talking with the others in her life drawing class instead of just going about her business with her head lowered and her eyes down. Just a couple of weeks ago she and Daniel had gone to the Tiki Terrace on karaoke night, and she had laughed herself into a stomachache when he sang "Wildfire." She hadn't sung, though, couldn't bring herself to do that. Maybe next time she would.

A year ago she'd never have come to this party. Would never have dreamed of it. And though, true, she was nervous about being in such a large crowd, about how she looked and what excuses she would make for why she couldn't dance, part of her was excited, too. To be a part of things. So long she'd been left out.

Elaine got out of the car, gathered the small clutch bag that held her necessities, and started for the lobby. She was aware of the cool evening air on her bare arms, of the faint jingle of her bracelets. Her walk was purposeful and carried her all the way to the ballroom's entrance, where she handed over her ticket and then stood, just inside the doorway.

So many people. Most of them she didn't know, and those she did were in disguise—no familiar faces in sight. For a moment she was the old Elaine again, wanting to run and hide like the little mouse she'd been. Would always be in some corner of her heart. For a moment she was back in school, standing on the side of the gym, unnoticed and half hating it, half cherishing it; pretending she didn't care when the boys' eyes went right past her and the girls looked at her and then giggled among themselves. For a moment she wanted to make excuses—she could do that, she was good at it—and go home.

"Elaine!" A blur of colors and a jangle of jewelry and Rachel standing there, looking delighted with her handiwork. "You look great."

"All thanks to you," Elaine said.

"*De nada.*" Rachel waved dismissively. "Did you just get here?" When Elaine nodded, Rachel said, "I'll show you around, then we'll find Daniel. I wouldn't tell him what you were wearing tonight, and he's anxious to see it."

Any thoughts of leaving the party or even hesitating vanished with Rachel's assurance and her arm linked with Elaine's, guiding her through the throng, saying hello to familiar faces and making introductions to unfamiliar ones. Past the charity table. Past the food table—Elaine was too keyed-up to eat but made a note to come back, it all looked delicious. They'd reached the bar and still hadn't seen Daniel; Elaine ordered a mimosa and had just taken her first sip when she saw him.

There was a taste in her mouth not of champagne but something tepid and unpleasantly bitter, like the coffee from the hospital vending machine. She felt cold inside, and yet her forehead was sweaty, and she was sure her face was flushed. She recognized him right away; no one else would wear a shirt like that. But she didn't recognize the woman he was dancing with, so elegant in a dress that could have been stolen from Madame du Barry, complete with powdered wig. He was smiling at his dance partner and looked as if he was having a wonderful time.

"Oh, there he is," said Rachel. "Pity about the shirt, but it makes him easy to find in a crowd."

"Who's that he's dancing with?" Elaine asked as casually as she could. After all, what did it matter to her if Daniel danced with someone? She ought to be happy for him.

"Eskimo Sally," Rachel said. "I think she's wishing she wore something simpler. Whoops, there it goes again."

Eskimo Sally had tossed her head a bit too enthusiastically to the music, and her wig tumbled right off. It landed on the floor between she and Daniel, and the two of them stopped dancing, stood staring at the wig as if they couldn't fathom where it had come from. Then Daniel picked up the wig and said, loudly enough for Elaine to hear: "Look, a tribble!"

Elaine took another sip of her mimosa. Now she could taste it. The unpleasant feeling was gone. She sighed and caught Rachel looking at her with an enigmatic Mona Lisa smile. Before she could wonder what that was about, she looked back at the dance floor—Daniel and Eskimo Sally were nowhere to be seen.

"They must have gone to our table," Rachel said. "Care to catch up with them?"

They navigated through the crowd. After a few moments they found the table. Daniel and Eskimo Sally were talking while Mick lit a fresh candle for the jack-o'-lantern centerpiece. "Hi, everyone," Rachel sang out. "Look who I've found."

Eskimo Sally put the wig down on the table and stuck umbrellas from everyone's empty glasses into it. By now she had quite a few umbrellas to work with. "I knew I should have dressed like Sailor Moon. It's impossible to dance in this get-up."

"Well, whoever designed the fashions of the time didn't think people were going to dance to Adam Ant," said Mick, obviously trying to add some sanity to the discussion.

Daniel was having none of it. "Are you apologizing for the *ancien régime* again? Damn royalist!"

"That shirt makes my eyes water, Dan. I still think you should have gone as Dudley Do-Right," said Mick.

"Yeah, you've got that lantern jaw thing going," said Eskimo Sally.

"Nell! I must save you from Snidely Whiplash!" Daniel cried out.

"Say, that's good," said Mick.

"Are you staying for *Young Frankenstein*?" asked Eskimo Sally.

Daniel shook his head. "Can't stay late. I have to be up at oh-dark-thirty tomorrow. Gig with Juliana Rael and she wants us in LA at seven a.m."

That offended even Mick's work ethic. "The day after Halloween? Is she nuts?"

"Not to put too fine a point on it, yes."

Eskimo Sally snorted. "Tell her to hire someone else."

"Can't. Too late to back out now, and she does pay well. I could use the income seeing as how I spent my last royalty check on Skee-Ball down at the pier. I kid, I kid," Daniel said to forestall one of Mick's tut-tuts. Daniel was fiscally responsible, for a musician anyway, but there was no telling that to the Professor.

Daniel glanced at his watch again. He'd have thought Elaine would be here by now. Surely she hadn't had second thoughts? It had occurred to him when he'd invited her that she probably wasn't a party person. Or she hadn't been when they'd first met. The change in her over this last year had been gradual and yet striking—it would hit him at odd times, and it was little things that did it. Getting a phone call from her, her voice enthusiastic and cheerful, no longer worried that she was bothering him or that he was tired of her. Seeing the way she no longer hid behind her hair or kept her eyes down; her voice no longer in muted I-don't-want-to-be-a-bother whispers. Her laugh, like wind chimes.

He hoped she would show up. He wanted to see what she thought of the October magic here tonight. Who knew, maybe *she'd* appreciate his costume.

"Anyone have a lighter?" Mick asked.

Eskimo Sally reached into some hidden pocket of her dress and fished out a Zippo. Mick busied himself with lighting a new votive for their jack-o'-lantern. Eskimo Sally settled her wig, festooned with cocktail umbrellas, back on her head. "I think you should stay for the movie anyway. What's a night without sleep?"

"I'm not as young and hardy as I used to be. Besides, it's not like I don't have the dialogue memorized anyway," Daniel replied.

Rachel's voice rang out over the music and crowd chatter. "Hi, everyone. Look who I've found."

Daniel turned to look. For a moment he didn't recognize that lovely creature there; he would have noticed that person before now, wouldn't he?

She wore a 1920s flapper-style dress, demure yet alluring, in a deep green that made her fair skin glow and turned her eyes to emerald. The dress was covered in beads that caught the light and fringe that shimmered and danced with her every movement. A feathered headband, the same deep green as her dress, circled her brow, and against the forest hue her hair was the color of banked embers. He saw her wanting to look down, away from his gaze—away from the gazes of everyone at the table, for they were all looking at her—and saw her instead smile and give her head a small, saucy tilt. He knew better than anyone what it had taken for her to do that.

Daniel wasn't aware of standing but was on his feet. Quickly he discarded the ridiculous mouse ears—what had possessed him to wear something so stupid?—and took her hand in his. It was slightly cool and damp with nerves but not as bad as he would have guessed. "You look . . ." He struggled to find a word that would do her justice, couldn't, and settled on the old standby. "You're beautiful."

"Thank you." She didn't believe it, he could tell. But it was true. There right in front of him all this time, and he hadn't seen. Now wasn't the time to wonder why he'd been so blind. What mattered was that he saw her in a way he'd never expected to; he'd always remember this moment, this night.

"Do you want to dance?" Daniel asked.

Elaine was about to reply that she didn't know how, but Eskimo Sally leaped into the conversation. "Dancing, bah! I haven't seen so much lame white-boy dancing since high school," she declared, plucking the umbrella out of her latest piña colada and sticking it into her wig. "I swear, just put the girls in teal butt-bow dresses, get Evie to play 'Hungry Like the Wolf,' and it'll be senior prom all over again. Sorry, I'll shut up now."

"And I'll try again," said Daniel with a smile. "Would you like to dance?"

"I don't really know how," Elaine said. But did that matter? She looked around and saw people dancing and no one caring if they were good or bad. It wasn't high school. No one was going to point and snicker.

"That's OK. Neither do I," he said.

That made her laugh, and the second mimosa had made her daring. Oddly enough the dress made her feel that way, too. She felt like someone else tonight, not boring old Elaine. And something else emboldened her: the way Daniel looked at her. Maybe it was only for tonight, and maybe only because of what she wore, but it hadn't been an empty compliment when he'd told her she was beautiful. He'd meant it. She could tell, because she knew him. What she hadn't known was that she'd hoped for some time now that he might look at her the way he had when he first saw her in the costume, the way he looked at her while they danced.

It was the fast dances that she'd worried about, but soon she learned to just let the music take over and move any way that felt right. No right or wrong way to do it. It helped that she danced with Daniel—for a tall man he seemed to be a good dancer, not stiffly lurching or a gangling tangle of limbs like some she saw. They danced until they were breathless and had to sit down and rest, and when they had their wind back they got up and danced some more.

A slow song came on. She started to head back to their table; after all, this was a dance for couples. But he caught hold of her hand. "May I have this dance?"

It was different than the fast dances. Elaine felt troubled in a strange way. Not by her worry of stepping on his feet, that vanished quickly. But the feeling lingered—not troubled but unsettled. By how close he was. Of course she'd been close to him before, often, but never with this awareness of his physical presence. Aware of his back, broad under her hand. Of his hands on her and his arms around her, their strength reassuring. She leaned against him a bit and breathed in his scent; she felt him stroke her hair. If only this dance would go on forever.

It didn't, but that hardly mattered. They danced and sat with their friends to talk and laugh. They applauded when Daniel's and Rachel's goods were auctioned off and when the party organizers announced how much money had been raised. At midnight they went into the room where the movies were being shown and sat down to watch *Young Frankenstein*. Elaine hadn't seen that one since those long-ago days after her flight from Arizona, when she did nothing but watch movies at home. It was much more enjoyable in a room full of people all laughing at the movie and reciting their favorite bits of dialogue, and with Daniel's arm draped comfortably around her shoulders.

When he walked her to her car, fog had settled on the parking lot. The streetlights had auras, as if they'd been painted by Van Gogh. She was more tired than she'd felt in years and more alive than she'd ever been, relishing the feel of her hand in his.

"Thank you," she said when they got to her car. "For inviting me. I had a wonderful time."

"So did I." He looked at her the way he had when she'd first arrived at the party. "You're lovely."

Elaine felt herself blush, automatically looked down. "It's the dress, I have to thank Rachel."

"No, it's not that. I just never . . ." He touched her chin with one finger, gently tilted her face up toward his. She'd never noticed how blue his eyes were—almost indigo, like the sea.

"Never what?" she asked nervously.

"Never saw you." He smiled. "I've been blind."

Before she could even think what to answer, Daniel leaned down and kissed her. A lingering, gentle kiss. Not a lover's kiss. Not yet. Sweeter than any kiss she'd ever been given before, and like a fine wine it sent warmth coursing through her veins. They said goodbye, and she drove home, and when she was finally in her bed she lay gazing up at the ceiling, remembering how he'd looked at her, how it had felt to dance with him. Remembering his kiss. Oh, how she'd wanted that, yet hadn't even understood until now how much she'd longed for it.

Chapter Twenty-Seven

"We'll take it again, starting from bar twenty. Have you sorted yourself out, James? Good. Ready on the beat of . . . Daniel? *Daniel.*"

"Yes, what?" He sat up straight and tried to look like he'd been paying attention.

Juliana Rael scowled. Her latest love affair had ended badly, and she was in an extraordinarily bad mood, even for her. "Get your head out of the clouds or your ass or wherever it is, and pay attention. Now then . . ."

Juliana turned away, and Daniel saw the bassist, Al Crawford, roll his eyes and make a face at Juliana's back. Daniel couldn't smile as much as he wanted to; yes, Juliana was in full-tilt bitch mode, but Daniel's head *had* been in the clouds. Or rather, back in Los Cielos. At the Halloween party. Which he didn't dare think about if he wanted to keep this gig, because this wasn't the first time Juliana had bawled him out for inattention. But as with any session, there were *longueurs,* and the chitchat of the other musicians held no fascination for him, not when he could be thinking about Elaine's kiss and . . . Juliana was glaring at him again. Daniel put his hands to the keys and somehow managed to keep his thoughts from straying to Elaine for a long time. At least half an hour.

At a nearby tavern, over much-needed after-session beers, he sat with Juliana and the engineer and a few of the musicians. Daniel wasn't sure what triggered it, but Juliana set down her glass with a clunk and eyed him suspiciously. "Dear God, Daniel. You're in love, aren't you?" She made it sound like an accusation.

"I think—um, I'm not sure?" Life would be so much easier if he could lie convincingly.

"It's a sickness." She shook her head pityingly. "I'll see you gentlemen tomorrow."

After Juliana left, Daniel asked Al, "Is it that obvious?" He knew he didn't have much of a poker face.

Al chuckled. "You keep getting this extremely serene look. I figured you've either had one of those near-death experiences or you're in love. Anyway, don't mind Juliana."

"I never do."

"She's not as mad as she acts," Al said. "She says your playing hasn't been this good in years. Even if you have been a bit of a space cadet. What's the lucky lady's name, anyway?"

"Elaine." On impulse he got out his cell phone and found the picture Mick had sent from his BlackBerry. "Here she is."

Al grinned. "You two look cute together." He polished off his beer, stood up, and clapped Daniel on the shoulder. "Well, congratulations. Bring her on up sometime so we can meet her."

Daniel lingered for a while, halfheartedly sipping his drink and wishing he knew how to feel. Everything had changed at the party. It hadn't mattered that he'd gotten no sleep that night, he felt so alive. And it was no surprise, what Juliana had said about his playing. He hadn't had this level of enthusiasm for the music since *Winter Roses*, and that had been an entirely different sort of passion.

But it wasn't that simple. If only it could be. Yet more than once his pleasant thoughts had been banished not by Juliana's admonishments but by a chill seeping into his blood. And by an interior voice that urged him to take it back, put things back the way they had been. He didn't listen to that voice—didn't want to listen to it—because it felt like the voice of reason, and why listen to that when he could be thinking about how they'd danced, and the scent of her, and how she'd smiled after their kiss?

He vowed that he'd stop thinking about it until he got back to Los Cielos. There was still a whole week of work to go, and Juliana's famously short temper would only take so much moony behavior on his part. Daniel vowed and was successful for the most part. But his brain had other ideas, and two nights before the gig ended he dreamed that Elaine was in his bed. He didn't wonder how she'd gotten to Los Angeles and found his hotel room; he took her in his arms, and they kissed and touched and made love. It was bliss.

As he woke the next morning he remembered the dream: *If the real thing is half that good, I don't think my heart will take it.* He instinctively reached out to the other side of the bed.

Cold and empty. Like always. For the first time in who knew how long, he did not simply accept it as part of his life. Yet he had to accept it. All his pleasant thoughts since the Halloween party and the night's sweet dream faded against the reality of the cold, empty bed. He remembered that first morning, waking up in the Kesslers' guest bedroom, reaching out for Sarah and not finding her. When he'd been on the run, sleeping rough in empty campgrounds, he'd sometimes woken and reached out, found no one. Daniel shivered, looked around the hotel room; it seemed gray and dim, though by now the sun was up. His waking thought had been correct—his heart couldn't take it.

For the rest of the gig he was attentive and professional. There were no more scoldings from Juliana. He ruthlessly quashed any daydreams about Elaine. When it was time to go home he spent the drive to Los Cielos thinking it over. Being logical. It had been a mistake. A moment of weakness on his part that he could chalk up to liquor. No, he couldn't, he'd only had two drinks and had been stone sober for hours by the time he kissed her. It was just because she looked so nice in that dress. Well, not just because of that. Elaine was lovely, especially now that she'd come out of her shell. It was their friendship that had worked that transformation. Not solely him, of course—it had been a treat to watch her befriend not just him but others, get past her fears that they would treat her like Carrie at the prom. But most of it was his doing. Why pretend otherwise? And she'd helped him as well. He couldn't think of another person he felt so at ease with, in spite of—or because of?—the fact that they'd seen each other at their lowest points, or close to them. The road she'd walked wasn't exactly his, but it was similar enough, and he knew that no one understood the way she did. That was a precious thing, and neither of them could risk losing it. They were better off as they were—or safer, which was the same thing, wasn't it? There'd be someone else for Elaine. She deserved some nice guy, and he really ought to start beating the bushes for a likely candidate. God knew why he hadn't done that before now. That would be best, for she didn't think of him in that way. At least he didn't think she did, though he'd caught her looking at him oddly once or twice over the summer, but he hadn't thought about what those looks meant. Hadn't let himself think about it. Hadn't let himself think about a lot of things.

He'd have to find the right place and time and the right way to say it. Hopefully he could tell her that he shouldn't have kissed her, he'd gotten carried away, and, dear God, how right it had felt, but that didn't matter. What mattered was keeping her as a friend. Keeping her safe. Keeping them both safe. And he'd have to do this alone, couldn't ask any friend for advice, for he knew they'd pitch twenty fits. Of course they were responsible for Elaine's Halloween dress—he knew Rachel's handiwork when he saw it. And when he'd returned from walking Elaine to her car, the Kesslers were sitting in the hotel lobby looking at him expectantly. "Well?" Mick had asked.

"Well what?"

"Did you kiss her?" Rachel cut to the chase.

"I don't see how that's any of your business," he'd replied, aware that he was grinning like a fool.

Rachel's laugh had been so loud it woke Eskimo Sally from her umbrella drink–induced slumber on a nearby sofa. "I told you he would! Ten bucks, pay up," she'd said as Mick cheerfully handed over the money.

No, they'd be no help at all.

His nerve failed him when he called Elaine to tell her he was back in town. Well, it was late, and he was tired, and it had been good to hear her voice, although it set off his subconscious, and he dreamed of her again, hearing her voice whisper to him in the dark. His nerve failed him a few nights later when they went out for dinner at Hokusai, the sushi place where the food went floating by on little boats; they were having such a nice time he hesitated to bring up unpleasant things, and it seemed only right to kiss her when he took her back to her apartment. It was even better than the first time, and though he knew he needed to stop this before it went much further, he was delighted to feel her returning his kiss with a confidence he wouldn't have expected.

Sunday, then. He made a pact with himself. That's when he would tell her. He invited her to a picnic, just the two of them, out at Lonely Point. No one to interfere, just the two of them being honest, because they were friends, and nothing was going to take that away from them.

The day was blue and warm—Boudin wouldn't have painted this sky, there weren't enough clouds. But he didn't care, and it didn't seem Elaine did, either. Nor did she mind the way her arms and face started to turn pink despite the sunscreen. "An Irish tan," she said and laughed. They had their lunch and went beachcombing; they walked and talked, and before he quite knew it, the sun was nearing the horizon. They sat on the beach, he leaning back against a dune, she leaning against his shoulder. Her hair seemed to glow in the afternoon sun and touching it was like touching a flame and not being burned. She settled closer to him and with no warning she murmured, "I love you."

All sound went away for a moment; all he heard was her words. Inside him it felt as though something had shattered or been made whole. Impossible to say which. He felt her body tense, looked down to see her hand white-knuckle tight on his shirt. She glanced up at him, then quickly looked away, but in that fleeting glance he saw that she hadn't expected to say it but wouldn't take the words back. As for his own words—he couldn't find them. Everything he'd told himself, all the reasons why, jostled in his head. He had to say it, now or never. It was for the best.

What he said was, "I love you, too."

Chapter Twenty-Eight

You drive, I'll take care of everything else, Rachel had said. Elaine drove to the Kessler house and found Rachel waiting and holding a small gym bag. "Was I supposed to bring something?" Elaine asked.

Rachel shook her head as she settled into the passenger seat. "Just extra swimsuits and towels. The mud can stain, so it's best to bring something you don't care much about." She accepted the coffee Elaine offered and gave directions. Just before San Juan Capistrano, a little spa Rachel went to "when I need to decompress."

The spa trip was Rachel's idea. She'd called Elaine the morning after Eskimo Sally's holiday shindig. That was no surprise. If she hadn't heard the argument, she'd seen both Daniel's and Elaine's early departures. *A day at the spa,* Rachel had said. *Mud bath, massage. This time of year, on a weekday, we'll have the place to ourselves. Just relax, get some perspective. What do you say?*

She'd said yes, surprising herself. But the thought of keeping her feelings bottled up just made her tired and more upset than she'd been when she left the party. Elaine had to confide in someone, and she couldn't turn to Daniel because he was what she wanted to talk about. Elaine glanced over at Rachel, who was examining the clay Kokopelli hanging from Elaine's rearview mirror, her one souvenir from Arizona. "Thanks for this," Elaine said. Now that they were on the road she was glad for this day away. Hard to not think about a person when everything in town reminded you of him.

Elaine hadn't meant to tell Daniel she loved him.

She'd loved him as a friend almost from the beginning. When she realized she enjoyed being with him more than anyone else. As for him being more than a friend . . . it had occurred to her once or twice. More than that, to be honest. He was handsome, all the more so because he didn't seem to know it and never took advantage of his appearance the way some other good-looking people did. The way Greg had. This past spring and summer she'd steal a glance at him and wonder. Then tell herself: *Oh no, that's not for the likes of you.* She'd be a fool to think he'd ever look back at her. If she was worth noticing, wouldn't someone have done so by now?

No, she hadn't meant to say it. But she'd been so happy ever since the Halloween party. Their first kiss she'd been too stunned to be more than the recipient of it; but after their dinner at Hokusai she took a chance and kissed him with a passion she hadn't thought she possessed and was delighted to sense by the way he returned the kiss that he was as affected by it as she was. And then the picnic—such a lovely day, and it wouldn't have mattered if it had been cold and raining, she was just happy to be with him. The words had spilled out of her, and she'd been as helpless to stop them as she was to stop breathing. Except she had stopped breathing for a moment, waiting agonized for his reply. And when he'd said he loved her, too, her relief and joy had been total, like coming up for air after a too-long immersion. It was a feeling she'd had before, that life was about to begin.

She'd been wrong about that before, though, and was gnawed by suspicion that she was wrong again.

The spa was tucked in the foothills, a low-key place run by earth mamas who sported chunky turquoise jewelry and carried a whiff of the burned-oregano smell Elaine remembered from the Reggae Sunsplash concert last summer. Elaine was relieved—back in Arizona Greg had once given her a spa day as a birthday gift. It had been one of those plush places where they gave you robes and you could order expensive low-calorie snacks; all the women there seemed to know one another, and they were all those groomed-to-the-hilt types whose glances made her distinctly uncomfortable, for she knew there were a hundred social codes and unwritten rules she was breaking. Hell, she hadn't even known if she should wear her bathing suit in the steam room or go au naturel, and instead had opted out.

While they checked in, Rachel turned to her and asked, "Did you want a manicure? I totally forgot to ask. I use my hands too much to make a manicure worthwhile."

"Same here," said Elaine. "I just look at the polish and it chips."

"And I can't do pedicures *at all*," Rachel said as they walked to the changing room. "It's literally torture for me. I can't even do foot massages. Poor Mick, once when I'd been on my feet all day with the holiday rush, he thought he'd give me a foot massage. I was supposed to be seduced, but all I did was spaz out and giggle."

"Mud and massage will be fine." Elaine was skeptical of the mud part, but she trusted Rachel, and was right to do so. They changed into their suits and went outside where there was a pool of clayey red mud and a stone grotto with showers and waterfalls. Nearby several mud-covered women were lounging in the sun.

"You just hop in, slather the mud all over. Don't be stingy with it. It's like being a kid again. Then you bask out here like a lizard, let it dry, then go to the waterfalls and let it all sluice off. We can lounge around in the grotto or go to the pool until it's time for the massage." Without further ado Rachel marched squelching into the mud, seized a handful, and slapped it on her shoulders and chest. Elaine followed suit, and once her skin was over the initial surprise, it did indeed feel good. Not just whatever it was doing for her skin but that childhood sensation of mud between your toes, to the infinite power.

"I feel so pagan," Elaine said when they were in the sun, letting the mud dry. She couldn't see how she looked, but Rachel looked like some savage woman out of an old Hollywood serial. She should borrow the Reillys' video camera, and they could make their own low-budget feature, *Captain Colonial and the Wild Mud Women of Los Cielos*. Get Daniel dressed up like Indiana Jones and he'd be a perfect Captain Colonial.

Thinking of him made her remember why she and Rachel were here. Elaine glanced around, saw they were alone. Somehow it was easier to talk about it now. Seeing a person plastered with mud took away the barriers; she wondered now if Rachel had treated Elaine to this day for that very reason.

The party had been at the Victorian that Eskimo Sally had refurbished into a bed-and-breakfast. A fun party, with food and Christmas music and a Secret Santa gift exchange. Yet there'd been a growing discontent in her, one that should have been assuaged when Daniel asked her to slip out into the back garden. It was dark in the garden, all overgrown vines and flowering shrubs, lit by Japanese lanterns. It should have been romantic, and a month ago, even two weeks, she would have thought it so. They kissed, but that was all they did. It was all they'd done since he'd returned from Los Angeles.

What am I to you? she'd asked after she'd pushed him away, after it was clear that tonight was not going to be the night. *Am I just a friend? You say I'm not but then why ...* She didn't finish, for what sounded reasonable in her head felt so crass as she tried to voice it. *Why won't you be my lover?* The first kiss she could have written off as an impulse, but after the second, and after their picnic, it had become something she wanted in an elemental way. No, needed, the way she needed food or air or sunshine.

But there was no way to say this. She couldn't say it any more than she could make the first move. *Pounce,* advised the magazines her coworker Kimberly brought in to the nurses' station. She couldn't do that. As she explained to Rachel: "I'd decide I should go through with it. Then I'd think, what if he gets a good look at me in daylight and doesn't like what he sees? What if it was just the dress that night and not me?" Elaine looked away, and said it in a hurried mutter to get it over with: "What if I'm not any good?" Because it had never been good for her. Mildly pleasant, the first year of her marriage, and after that it was mostly just another chore, like washing dishes. The same magazines that advised her to pounce said that if it was a chore, it was the man's fault—but Greg had said the problem was hers. After all, he'd had plenty of women, and they'd all been pleased with him.

Despite everything, she couldn't be as angry with Daniel as she wanted to be. She understood at least part of the reason he held back. He was afraid. *And do you think I'm not?* she said. *You know what this means to me. It has to be one or the other. You have to choose.*

"What did he say?" Rachel asked.

They were in the waterfall grotto now. The mud had sluiced away, and Elaine marveled at how refreshed her body felt, the silky smoothness of her skin. But though her body was relaxed, her heart was still unsettled. "He said he needed time," she said.

As for what his answer would be when he'd taken the time he needed . . . she had an uneasy feeling she knew already. She looked down at her hands, letting her hair fall like a damp curtain across her face. To her surprise, Rachel reached out and drew the curtain aside.

She was even more surprised when Rachel said, "I'm sorry."

"What for?"

Rachel shrugged. "For getting you all dolled up for the party. We—well, me, Mick, and Eskimo Sally—we wanted you two to be together. Everyone thought it was such a good idea, but I'm wondering now if we should have."

"Don't apologize. I'm glad you did." Even if he told her what she was certain he would—that he wanted to just be her friend.

By the time she got home that evening, Elaine felt like a rag doll—every muscle seemed to have been wrung of its tension, and even her joints moved more freely. Like the Tin Man in *The Wizard of Oz* after he'd gotten his oil can. She was calorically sated as well; at the spa they'd eaten organic salads, which were good to be sure, but on the way home the devil had gotten into them, and they'd stopped off for ice cream sundaes, giggling like naughty schoolgirls as they ordered the most decadent ones on the menu.

Her answering machine was blinking. Elaine pushed the button; she had a good idea who it would be, and she was right. "Hi," Daniel's voice said. "I was wondering if you were free on Saturday night, and if you'd like to come over. I'll make dinner. Let me know if you'd like that." A moment of hesitation, as if he couldn't think of what else to say. "Call me. Please. When you have a chance. Bye."

As she dialed to let him know Saturday was fine and should she bring a bottle of wine, she wondered. Had he made a decision, and if so what was it? Saturday was less than a week off but seemed very far away.

Wednesday night and Elaine reclined on the sofa. Her sketch pad was propped on her knees, her pencils in hand. From time to time she sketched but wasn't very diligent. The night was cold, the air full of a thick mist that never quite became rain—in the streetlight's glow it almost looked like snow. Reclining on the big velvet sofa—her one comfortable piece of furniture, bought when she'd decided to stay in Los Cielos—with an afghan over her, a Trader Joe's macaroni and cheese meal and a glass of wine in her stomach, music playing low. With Christmas-scented candles lit and what looked like snow falling outside her window, she felt very mellow and drowsy. If she could keep from thinking about Saturday and what might or might not come of it, she might have a relaxing evening. It did no good to think of what she should wear—maybe that Beaditudes dress she'd gotten for a suspiciously low price, the one with the matching jade necklace. Nor would she think about how she'd respond when he told her he wanted them to be friends and nothing more. No, better to let Saturday take care of itself and for now just relax and think about something else.

She was half dozing when the knock came at the door. Startled, she glanced at the clock. Just a little past eight thirty. Too late for even the most dedicated Jehovah's Witness, and her rent was paid up, so there was no reason for the landlord to come knocking. Elaine kicked off the afghan and went to the door.

Daniel stood on the welcome mat. A bit bedraggled, his hair damp and tangled as if he'd been out in the weather. "Hi." His voice a bit sheepish.

"Hi," she responded, feeling rather at a loss.

"Is this a bad time?"

"No, no. I just wasn't expecting anyone."

As he stepped inside she asked, "Is it raining hard? You're all wet."

He shook his head. "I biked over here."

"In this weather?"

"It was kind of refreshing."

He sat down on the sofa. She stood there, uncomfortably aware that the room was certainly not ready for company, with her dinner plate and the open wine bottle on the table, afghan bunched up at the end of the sofa, colored pencils scattered helter-skelter. "Can I get you something to drink?" she asked, half out of habit and half to cover her nervousness.

He didn't answer for a moment but sat wearing a faint smile and looking at her with a certain intensity that brought a flush to her cheeks. Then he asked for some wine, and Elaine went to the kitchen for a glass, glad to escape that gaze and the things it seemed to promise. Things she didn't dare hope for. He hadn't come here for that. If that was what he wanted, he wouldn't have come here now, when she looked like a frump in her sweats and socks with her hair in a scrunchie. No, he'd come here to say they should just be friends. And she was fine with that, really she was. Only . . .

She sighed, squared her shoulders, and went back into the living room. As she handed him the wine glass she felt his gaze on her. No one had ever looked at her like that before, had set her nerves atingle with a single look.

As she sat down he poured some wine, drank two healthy swallows. "Dutch courage," Daniel said with an apologetic smile. "I'm nervous."

Elaine wanted to ask but didn't dare. She watched while he set the glass down, ran his hands through his damp hair.

"I'm sorry for coming over like this, unexpected. I wanted to wait for Saturday. I had a nice dinner planned. I bought candles and everything. But I kept thinking, what if something happened before then, and I didn't get to tell you . . ." He looked down at his hands, took a breath. "You see, that's why . . . this last month, with you, it's like I'd been lost in the fog for so long, and now I'm in the sun and don't know how I stood being without it. And I was thinking, if I ever lost it again, I couldn't . . ."

Now it was Elaine's turn to look away. She would never blame him, but she had hoped.

She felt his hand touch her hair; one finger traced slowly down her cheek, under her chin, tilted it up. Elaine kept her eyes lowered for a moment, then looked at him; his face was very close to hers, his gaze so intense and blue it swept on her like a wave, shook her and left her breathless. *Let me have this.*

"But I love you. I want you. I want *us.* I think if we're together, we can take anything that happens. As long as that's what you want, too."

He started to say something more, but she caught hold of his shoulders, pulled him to her, and kissed him with a boldness she would never have guessed was within her. He returned the kiss, and she understood he'd been reining in his passion until now; the intensity would have been frightening in another man. When they broke apart, he said, "I take it that's a yes?"

She couldn't answer, just grinned and nodded. Daniel kissed her again, softly this time but no less passionate, gently pulled the band from her hair; as it fell free down her shoulders and back, he moved his hands through it as if he couldn't get enough of touching it. He kissed her neck, and she tilted her head back, her eyes closing as she reveled in the sensations. How could mere kisses and his hands touching her hair stir her so? But they did, and she heard herself sighing; his shirt was unbuttoned now—had she done that?—and she caressed his chest and shoulders and back, relishing the feel of his skin and the strong muscles beneath it.

His hands left her hair, and she felt him starting to lift her sweatshirt off; for a moment old fears returned, and her hands caught hold of his. "What's wrong?" he asked. "What is it, love?"

The endearment made her fears seem silly, but she voiced them anyway. "I'm . . . I don't want you to be disappointed. With me."

"I won't be, I promise."

Before she could argue that there was no way he could know that, Daniel cupped her face in his hands, kissed her softly on the forehead, then more deeply on her mouth. As they kissed he slipped one hand beneath her sweatshirt; she wasn't wearing a bra, and his touch, bold and gentle at the same time, made her gasp with delight. Soon her fears were forgotten, and she longed to feel his skin against hers. When he moved to take off her sweatshirt, she didn't hinder him but instead helped, once it was off he gazed at her as though she was something to be treasured. In a voice hoarse with emotion he told her she was lovely, so very lovely, and she believed him.

When he bent down to kiss her breasts Elaine no longer thought he might be disappointed in her; indeed, she scarcely thought of anything. No more shyness, not even when he gently pulled away the rest of her clothes. Passion had taken over her mind as she lay back on the sofa; she felt drugged yet exquisitely aware of the sensations—the plush velvet beneath her, his body against hers, his voice murmuring how beautiful she was and how much he wanted her. She shivered and sighed as his touch awakened every nerve, roused a feeling deep inside her that was warm and aching and was like hunger but wonderful in a way no hunger could ever be.

Daniel whispered a question and she said, "Yes, oh please, yes," for by now the hunger was like a live thing within her. He eased into her as she held him close and instinctively twined her legs around him; they moved together slowly at first, then as the pace increased so did the pleasure, until Elaine felt herself on the brink of something so powerful she almost feared it. Perhaps he sensed this, for he kissed her; she opened her eyes and saw the way he looked at her, saw the love and desire for her, and that was what sent her over the edge. Waves of pleasure swept through her, like a stormy ocean tide she was powerless to resist and did not want to subside, not ever. She held on to him, yearning to be even closer to him, hoping to make the divine sensations last just a little bit longer.

After, they lay on the sofa together. Elaine felt as if all her bones had turned to soft butter; if one of her Christmas candles had set the place on fire, she wasn't sure she could have summoned the energy to escape. Beside her Daniel sighed, stroked her hair. She looked at him; he lay with his eyes closed and a look of utter contentment on his face. Elaine smiled and closed her own eyes, basking in the afterglow and in the feel of his body against hers, the rough velvet of the sofa, the sound of the rain tapping against her window. And to think she might have lived her whole life without this. Without being loved. A miracle, and she knew that with the slightest turn of chance it would never have happened. She thought of the lonely past and what a different future might have been like, and without warning tears welled up in her eyes.

Elaine thought Daniel was asleep but instantly he was propped up on an elbow, regarding her tears with alarm. "What's wrong? I didn't hurt you, did I?"

"No, no. I didn't think this would ever . . . I didn't think anyone would ever love me."

Daniel reached down to the floor and picked up his shirt; with its sleeve he dried her tears. They kissed, slowly at first, then with rekindling passion. She asked, and he said yes but could they try it in a bed this time. She laughed and agreed; the sofa was comfortable but not *that* comfortable. He swung off, and before she could get up he deftly scooped her up into his arms and carried her to the bedroom. Elaine let out a delighted gasp; so wonderful that he should be that strong and that she did not have to fear he'd use that strength against her.

As he laid her down she told herself that it wouldn't be as good as the first time, nothing could be as good as that. In a way, she was right—it was better. The last thing she was aware of before she fell asleep was his arm draped across her, their hands intertwined.

Yet when she woke the next morning panic seized her. He was gone, she was certain of it. Greg's old insult was true—she was boring, and he'd tired of her. She was afraid to open her eyes and see for herself; afraid he'd be gone and she'd never again feel his body against hers, feel him inside her, feel his breath hot against her neck as he said her name, have him hold her afterward and tell her he loved her.

She heard an incoherent sleep mumble, and relief left her weak. Elaine opened her eyes. He was sound asleep; his hair was wildly disheveled, and he needed a shave; he was quite the most gorgeous thing she'd ever seen. He was here. Hers. There was the thought of waking him, but he looked so sweet asleep. Instead she laid her head on his chest and listened to his heartbeat, so steady and reassuring; she reveled in that sound and in the warmth and feel of him while she waited for him to wake.

Chapter Twenty-Nine

December.

Daniel meant to be home before four, but as he was leaving the university he made the mistake of stopping by Morgan Commons for a snack. There he was waylaid by Dr. Hill wanting to say hello and by a duo of artsy-looking students wanting him to sign copies of *Winter Roses*. It did sometimes boggle him, the way that album never really faded away, just as he was surprised by its fans, who were no particular demographic as far as he could tell; they might be fifteen or fifty-five.

No matter. He signed the CD inserts with a good will and made it home as dusk was falling, just in time to turn on the Christmas tree lights. He wanted Elaine to see those lights when she arrived home. He smiled at the sight of the tree, glittering and twinkling in the living room window. Neither of them had had a tree in years. They'd had to buy new ornaments, for she'd left hers behind in Arizona and his that had survived held too many memories.

Inside the house the tree gave off its spicy-sweet pine aroma. He had to tread carefully; the living room was still in disarray from the furniture they'd moved to make room for the tree, but also the clutter of boxes and pictures and other odds and ends—Elaine's things that she was moving in, bit by bit. True, she didn't have much. She'd moved too much over the years to bother accumulating many possessions. But there were still books and CDs and other items to be added to his. This weekend they'd enlist some help and move her sofa; into the music room perhaps, though how he'd practice without being distracted by the sofa and the memories of that first time was beyond him.

There was a message from her on the answering machine; she'd be home late, though no more than an hour. There was a slightly hesitant quality to her voice when she said it, and he felt a stab of raw anger. Not at Elaine but at that bastard Greg Buchanan and how he'd used the excuse of her working late to justify hitting her. Not for the first time Daniel thought he ought to get a posse together—Mick and Eskimo Sally and maybe Hugh Reilly. They could find Buchanan and pummel the crap out of him.

He pushed the thought away and set about prepping dinner—if he did the legwork now, he could have it on the table fifteen minutes after Elaine came home, give her time to change out of her scrubs and pour a glass of wine. Like the rest of the house, the kitchen was a bit of a mess with his possessions making room to accommodate hers while they sorted out whose coffeemaker to keep and where to put the wine fridge.

Daniel was stretched out on the living room couch listening to Dean Martin's Christmas album when Elaine came home. "Sorry I'm late," she said all in a rush. "I was so stressed I was on autopilot and started to head to the apartment. Oh." She looked into the dining room, and for a moment he saw it through her eyes. On the table candles were lit, wine was poured, and her Art Nouveau vase was filled with lavender from the backyard. No doubt she could smell that dinner was on the way. She looked at him, and he sensed her wonder that he'd done this, and it was both pleasing to him and curiously saddening. He'd done what any man with half a shred of romance should do as a matter of course, and yet it amazed her. Maybe one day it wouldn't amaze her. She'd expect it, as she should.

By the time she was out of her scrubs he had dinner nearly ready. "What are we having? It smells wonderful," she said, and when he told her it was his mushroom pasta called Eat Shiitake, she laughed. The sound rang through the house, and it occurred to him that in all the time he'd lived here, there'd been no sound of a woman's laughter. He'd missed that sound.

After dinner they retired to the living room, where he lit a blaze in the fireplace and bade her lie down so he could massage the work tension from her back and shoulders and legs.

"How did it go at LCU?" she asked. "Is that all taken care of?"

"I join the ranks of academia in January." Professor Andrews had been after Daniel for years to help with her music theory class and provide live demonstrations. Between the university gig three days a week and providing music lessons and tutoring the other days, Daniel figured he could keep a halfway decent stream of income while allowing him to spend more time at home. With Elaine. "Think you might want to join me?"

She glanced up at him. "What do you mean?"

"Well, I don't mean to speak out of turn, but I know nursing isn't really what you want to do. Why not see what all the classes you've taken amount to, find out how close you are to a degree. Maybe go part time on the nursing and try for your MFA."

"But then what?" Her voice was hesitant, but he could see the excitement in her eyes.

Daniel shrugged. "Teach, find something at a museum or a gallery? Don't forget there's San Diego close by, and Carlsbad or Oceanside if no one in town's hiring." He ran his hands along her back and shoulders. "Whatever you choose, I'm behind it. As long as it's what *you* want to do."

Strangely, he felt her tense. Then she sat up, picked up her wine glass, and turned away from him, looked at the fire. Had he said something wrong?

"I was kind of thinking about that. In a way. I mean, going part-time on nursing and doing something else. You see, I was hoping . . . and I understand if you don't . . ." She drew in a breath and said in a voice so low he had to strain to hear it: "Could we have a baby?"

Daniel had a moment of recall so complete it left him stunned. Jake at—how old? Three? Four? Old enough to have the occasional nightmare, and this one was about being chased by a dinosaur. Jake in his *Where the Wild Things Are* wolf-suit pajamas, his hair slightly damp with sweat, his sniffles easing and becoming the regular breaths of peaceful sleep. Daniel held his son and rocked him, singing the song that worked best as a lullaby—"Science Fiction/Double Feature" from *The Rocky Horror Picture Show*. And didn't put his child to bed right away but held him and rocked him, marveling at this person who was not just a mix of himself and Sarah, and no longer a baby, but a child with his own likes and wants and personality. In that moment Daniel had understood what it meant to bring a new person into the world and had felt a thrill of wonder—what would the future bring to this person, and what would that person bring to the world?

Seven years was all he'd gotten. But as he was readying himself to tell Elaine that he couldn't face the prospect of another such loss, Daniel knew that it was too late. If he'd wanted to keep himself safe, he'd never have befriended Elaine, let alone fallen in love with her. And while seven years was brief, so brief, it was more time than Elaine had with her own child.

In her face was resignation. She was expecting him to say no. He couldn't. He would never be able to say no to her, not for anything she truly wanted.

He reached out and drew aside her hair, which had fallen forward to hide her face, told her that yes, they could. Then he was flat on his back, Elaine on top of him and kissing him fiercely, much to his delight. It drove him wild when she forgot to be shy and let her passions have free rein.

When the kiss broke she looked down at him, smiled, but that hesitancy was back. "Do you like it? This way, I mean?"

He ran his hands along her thighs, settled them on her hips, which fit his hands so nicely, as if he were Pygmalion and she made to suit him. "I love it." No lie—it had always been his favorite for the view it gave him of his lover's face.

"It's not . . . weird or anything?"

Again that hot stab of anger, for he knew who'd told her that. To hide the anger and lighten the moment he said, "Not at all. Only please . . ." He did his best imploring look. "Be gentle with me?"

It was hard to laugh and kiss at the same time, but somehow they managed it.

January.

"An Epiphany party? That's unusual," Elaine said.

Daniel nodded. "It started when most of the kids left the nest, started getting married or going steady. Hugh and Kate figured that people would want to start spending some Christmases with in-laws. They decided Epiphany was close to Christmas but wouldn't conflict with the holiday itself."

"Plus it brings back the Twelfth Night tradition."

He laughed. "Stretch Christmas out as loooong as possible."

It was slow going to Torrance, for the weather had actually turned seasonal, raining all the way. Elaine both hated and cherished the delay.

She was nervous in a way she never had been when going to see the Reillys. Oh, that first visit nearly a year ago had been strange, for it struck her as odd that someone would maintain such close ties with in-laws who were no longer, strictly speaking, related. She had understood it better when she learned more not just about the Reillys but about Daniel's adoptive family as well. And her worries had been groundless; the Reillys had welcomed her the way she imagined they'd welcomed all new friends.

Would that change? For there was a ring on her finger now, white gold with a single emerald. It had been in her Christmas stocking, which in itself had been a surprise. She hadn't had a stocking since she was six, when a classmate had spilled the beans about Santa Claus and her mother had decided that with the myth debunked, there was no reason for stockings and the presents under the tree. It had been like being a child again, spilling out the stocking's bounty: candy and tea and a tin of gourmet hot chocolate and a couple of paperbacks. And then she'd reached deep into the toe of the stocking, found a small velvet box. For a moment she hadn't wanted to take it out, was afraid it wasn't what she thought it must be. But it was. Nestled in the dark blue box was the slender band of white gold with its bit of green fire. It was smaller and less flashy than another ring she'd once worn, the one she'd hocked at a Palm Springs pawnshop, but this ring would never leave her hand. Later that day, at the Kessler house, Elaine got to experience the feminine rush of being mobbed by girlfriends who wanted to see the ring *now*. Rachel, Eskimo Sally, Evie, and others all demanding to know when was the big day, was it going to be a church wedding or a visit to the JP, where would the honeymoon be, and so on. Elaine hadn't a single answer for any of those questions, but she hadn't cared. All that mattered was what the ring meant and that everyone was happy for her.

Yet the ring and what it meant weighed heavy on her as they drove. The misgiving had first come on her on Christmas night, when Daniel mentioned to Mick that they were going to the Reilly house on Epiphany weekend for the Feast of Fools parade. Elaine wondered for the first time: the Reillys had welcomed her as a friend, but would that change? Would they see her as an interloper, trying to supplant their daughter's memory? Her heart said no, and reason said that she and Daniel had been more than friends for some time and no one had said a word against that. Yet the habits of years and the voice in her head—silent most days, but it occasionally spoke up to tell her she didn't deserve what she now had—those told her that she could expect the cold shoulder.

Elaine said nothing to Daniel during their drive to Torrance, but she felt a queasy sensation as they walked up to the house and there stood Theresa. Then Theresa grinned and said, "Well, it's about time!" And flew off the porch despite the rain. "Let's see it. Let's see this ring. Oooooh! It's beautiful! Goes with your eyes. Doesn't it go with her eyes?" For Amy and Joanna were there, too, and even Joanna's oldest daughter, Belinda, all of them squealing over the ring as they walked into the house.

Then Kate's voice rang out, "Make way, make way." Elaine's heart sank, for if anyone had cause to be unhappy about this, it was Kate. But Elaine barely had time to register Kate's presence before she was caught up in the woman's embrace and heard a heartfelt whisper: "I'm so happy for you both." No sooner had Kate released her than the women began bombarding her with the same questions she'd heard at Christmas: when, where, all the rest of it. "For heaven's sake," roared Kate, "She just got here! Let her breathe and sit down and have something to eat, then you can all talk her to death."

And Elaine thought how silly she'd been to worry, when she had Reillys offering to help in any way. When Kate said that if Elaine needed a mom to talk to, she was happy to be there. When John Reilly (now Father John) called from Indiana to say that the next time he came out to California, he'd be happy to bless the marriage. "But we're not Catholic," Elaine said. In fact, she couldn't recall if she'd even been christened. "Oh, that doesn't matter to me," John said. "I just won't tell the Pope."

It was time for the parade. No one, it seemed, could quite recall how the tradition had started—different siblings wanted to claim credit for the idea. But every year a new King (or Queen) of Fools was crowned and led the family and any guests on a parade up and down the surrounding blocks before returning to the house for refreshments. Usually by the time the parade ended more than a few neighbors had joined it.

It was the job of last year's queen (or king) to decide who would be the new one; last year's queen was Belinda, chosen by her aunt Amy as a reward for rejoining the parade (the previous two years preteen Belinda had decided she was too cool for such goings-on). By parade time the rain had stopped—which was lucky, Elaine thought as she saw the crown on Belinda's head. Papier-mâché and cardboard, it was decorated with streamers, glitter, beads, pipe cleaners, and who knew what else. And there was a scepter, too, clearly fashioned from what was once a cheerleader's baton. "It's the same crown and scepter from when it all started," Daniel whispered to her. "The new king or queen adds something to it before they pass it on to the next person. Those happy face stickers? Those are my contribution."

"Well," Belinda said, "I guess it's time to go back to being just a common fool. What *am* I gonna do with these things? Oh, I know!" Belinda swiftly plucked the crown from her head and set it on Elaine's.

She stood there, knowing she must look a fool not because of the crown but because her mouth was agape in astonishment. Elaine wanted to ask how this could be, but the words wouldn't come, nor would they have been heard for everyone clapping and cheering. Elaine raised the baton high and sang out, "Let the wild rumpus start!"

Everyone cheered as the parade started, fueled by music pouring from a boom box Martin carried. Elaine held the baton in one hand, Daniel's hand in the other, felt the light weight of the crown on her head and the warmth of love and acceptance. Some might take such things for granted but not she; they'd been too hard to come by. She'd treasure this time always.

May.

They were married in a simple ceremony at the Los Cielos town hall, with a reception after at the Kesslers' house—very casual, a buffet with paper plates, and when dusk fell they lit tiki torches. Any friends and Reillys that hadn't been able to attend had sent cards and well-wishes, even the odd gift or two over Daniel and Elaine's protests that they needed nothing (and hadn't even registered).

No Whitmans were in attendance; no one had expected they would come. Certainly Daniel hadn't, not after what he'd said to his sister. He'd called the parental units back in January to let them know about the engagement. They were pleasant in a vague way and congratulated him and "Ellen." His call to his sister had been another matter entirely. "I'm a bit surprised to hear it," Victoria had said. "I hope she knows what she's getting herself into."

"Don't worry, I won't pop my cork and fuck shit up until *after* the honeymoon."

If he'd been thinking to get a chuckle out of her, he was mistaken as usual. "Oh sure, everything is hilarious to you. Please yourself, like always, but if I lost Les, I love him too much to get married again, ever."

Strangely, he hadn't felt angry. Just baffled that he'd ever spent time caring what these people thought of him or wondering what they felt for him. He should have just hung up, but his tongue had other ideas: "Is that it? Huh. I thought it was because he was the only man on the planet crazy enough to marry you."

It had gotten ugly after that, and Victoria was no longer speaking to him. The parental units weren't speaking to him, either, until he apologized to Victoria. That suited Daniel fine, though he had been strangely touched to get a phone message from Les a couple of days after the fracas. A hurried, whispered message, as if Les had been afraid Victoria was listening in: "Victoria was out of line. For what it's worth, I'm happy for you."

No matter. Daniel and Elaine lay together on one of the chaise lounges, a somewhat tight fit but neither of them minded. It was full dark now and everyone had left save for Eskimo Sally. She sat with a plate full of buffet food in front of her; nearby Mick and Rachel were gathering up empty cups and plates.

"Before I make myself useful, I have something for you guys. I know you said no presents, but trust me, you'll dig this." Eskimo Sally rummaged in her handbag, and after some fussing and a mutter of, "Licorice Altoids? How long have *those* been there?" she retrieved an envelope. "Didn't want you two to have to make a straight shot from Frisco down here, so I got you a room at the Madonna Inn."

Daniel felt his smile grow a bit fixed. He'd never stayed at the inn, but some years ago during a road trip he'd gone inside to use the restroom just so he could say he'd used the famous waterfall urinal. The whole thing had been so ridiculous he couldn't stop giggling and hadn't been able to pee.

He wanted to say that perhaps the inn wasn't their cup of tea, but Eskimo Sally looked so pleased with the gift that he just smiled and thanked her; so did Elaine. When Eskimo Sally got up to help with the cleanup, Elaine whispered to him: "Don't say a thing."

"Wouldn't dream of it."

"Where are you staying in the city?" Mick asked when there was a break from cleanup duties.

"The Saint Francis." He knew Elaine had always wanted to stay there.

"Oooh, I nearly got kicked out of that place," said Rachel.

They all turned to look at her.

"Hey, I've got my wild side. Well, not that wild," she amended. "High school grad night. Me and my friends were jumping on the beds. Really. We weren't even drinking. Anyway, management came and finger-wagged us."

"Ask for the Fatty Arbuckle suite," Eskimo Sally said.

"Who?" asked Mick.

"Never mind."

Daniel laughed. They'd leave in a couple of weeks, once the spring semester was done. It should be perfect weather and not too crowded with the spring break gang gone and the tourists not due until June. He hadn't been to the city in a few years and was surprised at how much he was looking forward to seeing it. They'd spend a week meandering up the coast first, and he was looking forward to that as well.

"Good Lord!" Mick was staring at his iPhone; he must have googled Fatty Arbuckle.

They made their way up the coast, stopping wherever they pleased and with their only timetable being their arrival in San Francisco. They stopped at state beaches to walk the shore and the trails. They spent a day touring wineries and stayed a night in Solvang, where the next morning they gorged on Danish pancakes and bacon.

On the 101 they drove past the Shoreline Diner; neither said anything, but Elaine couldn't help looking at it as long as it was in sight. Its exterior seemed not to have changed, and Elaine wondered if it was still the same inside. She wondered if the owner was the same fellow with the beard and the dog tags. Yet she felt no urge to stop; fortuitous though that night had been, the circumstances that had led them there and that had followed were too distressing. She suspected Daniel felt the same. He said nothing as he drove past the place, seemed not to have noticed it. Yet that night, which they spent in Rachel's family guest house in Carmel, she woke to hear him muttering in his sleep, felt his limbs twitching. Uneasy, she remembered the last time she'd seen him this way. The muttering became clear: *Now it's dark.* She shook him awake, and for a long moment he looked at her. "I couldn't find you," he said. She kissed him and stroked his hair, and he was asleep again in minutes; if he had more bad dreams, there was no sign of them.

He was fine the next morning, which saw them on the way to Monterey. At the aquarium they spent the morning touring and just before lunchtime caught a live show—actors in animal costumes explaining the importance of recycling and keeping the oceans clean. After the show they went over to the employee-only door where an actor removed her penguin head: under the disguise she had black hair and a crooked but pretty grin. He'd known Tamara was working at the aquarium and had asked Elaine if she minded him stopping to say hello to her. No, she didn't mind.

Tamara's good deed had saved more lives than just Daniel's. Elaine thought it might be awkward, and it perhaps it should have been, but it wasn't. Tamara took them to lunch at the aquarium's restaurant, told them how she was working her way through school, studying oceanography at Monterey Peninsula College, mentioned that her previous summers working at Great America had prepped her for the live show here at the aquarium ("At least the penguin costume is way more comfortable than the SpongeBob one."). After saying goodbye to Tamara they stayed the night at a bed-and-breakfast. The next day they arrived in San Francisco.

As in love with the city as she'd been, Elaine had seen very little of it beyond the art museum and its immediate environs. But with a week's freedom and Daniel's relative familiarity with the city, she was able to explore it to her heart's content. They visited Fisherman's Wharf and Alcatraz, walked along the Golden Gate Bridge, and visited North Beach. They spent an afternoon at City Lights and then walked to Caffe Puccini for dinner; they put ten dollars' worth of quarters into the jukebox, selecting Sinatra tunes and Italian opera.

But San Francisco seemed different in a way Elaine couldn't fathom. Not its appearance—it had never looked lovelier to her. Foggy mornings gave way to sunshine by noon, and around sundown the fog returned, not ominous or chilling but comforting, like a familiar blanket. The galleries of the art museums seemed to be just as she'd left them years ago. So good to see the paintings she knew and loved again. She smiled to see Daniel staring fascinated at Boudin's *Storm Over Antwerp*. On the third morning, as she stood at their hotel room's window, gazing out at the bay, she thought she knew. The city seemed less vivid to her, yet more *there*. More real. For a moment she worried this was a bad thing, that it had lost some of its magic for her. Then she understood: It was no longer a chimera, something to be longed for and glimpsed fleetingly but never something she could have. Now she could have it. It was hers. It hadn't changed—she had.

Daniel had to admit he was nervous as they checked into the Madonna Inn. *Not the Caveman room, not the Caveman room.* He was so relieved to find out it was something called Bridal Falls that he gave little thought to what the room would look like. With a name like that it was likely to be white and lacy and probably with a bed shaped like a swan or something.

He was surprised to see a room that was partially walled in stone, and what wasn't stone was green. Lots of green. It gave the room a peculiar, almost underwater feel. He could tell it wasn't what Elaine had expected, either. "It's named after Bridalveil Fall in Yosemite," she said, looking at a brochure. "I guess that's why all the rock." She looked around. "It's not as bad as I thought it would be. I kind of like it," she said a bit sheepishly.

As well she should. Green was her color, and he wondered if Eskimo Sally had put any thought into that when she picked the room. She might have, or she might have just picked a room at random—you never could tell with her.

Elaine explored the room while Daniel called Eskimo Sally to let her know they'd arrived. "Oooh, I was getting anxious," she said. "I thought you'd have checked in a while ago."

"Late start, that's all."

"How's the room?"

"It's a bit ..." He groped for a word that would be truthful yet wouldn't offend.

"Gaudy?"

"Yes."

Her hyena laugh resounded down the phone line. "I should bloody well hope so! It's the Madonna Inn, it's supposed to be gaudy." Her voice became softer, almost shy. "You guys having a good time?"

"Very good."

"The place isn't too tacky? I thought you'd get a kick out of it."

"We are. Elaine likes it. I'll give you a big old hug when I see you next."

They said goodbye, and he hung up in time to hear Elaine say, "There's a waterfall in our shower."

"I'd better call housekeeping."

"No, really, there's a waterfall in our shower. Come and see."

Daniel got up and went into the bathroom. Rock everywhere, even the sink. He hoped to God neither of them slipped and knocked their head against anything. He didn't fancy ending his honeymoon with a concussion. The shower was made of rock, too. Elaine stood, her hand on the faucets, grinning. "Watch this."

Sure enough, you could have a regular shower, or you could stand under a rock waterfall. They both regarded the deluge, and he said, "Niagara Falls. Slowly I turned . . ."

"Step by step," she said, "inch by inch." And they both dissolved into helpless giggles.

"Shower with me before dinner?" he asked.

"Love to."

He woke the next morning with the peculiar feeling of letdown he always had at the end of a vacation. The need for one more day, just one. It didn't have to be here. One more day in San Francisco would have been perfect. Elaine had loved being in the city; he'd loved her loving it. Just the look on her face when they'd gotten out of the car in front of the hotel had been worth every cent of the trip's cost.

He opened his eyes to find Elaine already awake, looking at him. She was shrouded in the bedsheets and looked pleasantly nervous. She said, "Are you awake?"

Daniel nodded. "Everything OK?"

She nodded, reached out and touched his hair. "It's all been so wonderful. I know we have to go back to the real world but . . . I thought we could make the last day memorable."

Elaine pulled away the sheets; she wore a lacy slip that was dark green, his favorite color for her, but sheer as well. It was demure yet left little to the imagination. Perfection. "No, no," she said as he reached for her. "Let me." She lay atop him, buried her hands in his hair, kissed him. Her kisses were like the slip she wore, shy and bold at the same time, burning pleasurably as she kissed his throat and chest. Before passion fogged his brain entirely in its delightful haze, he thought that with her fiery hair and fair skin and the green slip, in the room's peculiar underwater light it was like being made love to by a mermaid or a naiad. No, not those—a siren, for her sighs and soft cries of pleasure were a kind of song, one he'd happily fling himself into the sea to swim toward.

Later, he liked to think that was when they'd made Cecilia.

Cecilia Rose Whitman came into the world on a rainy February afternoon. Her birth was a scheduled C-section, and she greeted the world with a cry of protest that half the maternity ward could hear. "Good lungs," quipped the doctor as she handed the baby to Elaine.

Cecilia quieted almost the instant she was in her mother's arms. Daniel stared in fascination at his daughter: still red-faced from her howl, slate-blue eyes squinting against the light, head crowned with thick hair in a rich copper hue somewhere between red and gold.

The godparents arrived that evening. Cecilia had just finished a marathon nursing session, and now both she and Elaine were taking a much-needed rest. "Let's see, let's see," said Rachel as she and Mick walked in. "Oh, she's just precious. That hair!"

"You like the hair, you'll love the voice," Elaine said. "Loudest baby in the hospital."

"I vote for changing her name to Diva, but Elaine won't have it," quipped Daniel.

"Hey, I carried the baby around for nine months, I get the final OK on the name," she replied.

"Can we hold her?" Mick asked.

Elaine nodded, and Rachel bent down to lift up Cecilia, who fussed for a moment, then went back to sleep. Daniel watched Rachel as she held the baby, could already see Rachel planning outfits that would go with the hair. After a while Mick held out his hands, though he seemed a trifle uncertain at first—Daniel wondered if Mick had ever held a baby as new as Cecilia and doubted it; he'd been off in New York when Jake was an infant. But once Cecilia was safe in his arms he seemed quite content When the nurse came in with Elaine's dinner, Mick was the one who volunteered to stay and hold Cecilia while Daniel and Rachel went to the cafeteria for drinks and snacks.

"Care to catch a ride home with us tonight? You're probably wiped out," Rachel asked as they made their way down the halls.

"If it's no problem."

"None at all. Oh, Kate brought some casseroles by, they're in my freezer. Come on by and grab them any time." Rachel smiled. "She's a beauty, Dan. I'm so happy for you both."

"You won't mind the occasional babysitting then?"

"Are you kidding? It's my only hope of keeping you three from spoiling her rotten."

When he looked at Rachel to protest that he wasn't going to spoil Cecilia, there was a smile on Rachel's face, but her eyes were serious. Rachel understood, the way she always seemed to. She knew that the three of them had each lost a child. He gave her a clumsy hug as they walked. "What would we do without you to keep us in line?"

She laughed. "I'm sure you'd muddle through somehow."

"Glad you're certain of that, 'cause *I'm* not."

When they'd ordered some food at the cafeteria, Rachel said, "Go ahead and have a seat. I'll bring it over."

The dinner rush was mostly over, so Daniel had his choice of seats. He found a table over by the window and sat looking out at the rainy night. For the first time in a very long while, and without wanting to, he remembered the night that had brought him and Elaine together. He dreamed about it sometimes, though in his dreams that fellow Pete never arrived and night never ended and he was stranded on the beach, as alone as if he'd been abandoned on the moon. He'd told no one the whole story of that evening—not Elaine, not even Dr. Levinson. He feared they'd confirm what he'd always suspected—that Sarah had only helped him because she didn't want him to be with her and Jake. But now he wondered if she hadn't just been saving his life; she'd been giving him a chance to be happy again. The more he thought about it, the more certain he became that this was so. He remembered Christmas: watching Elaine show her ring to the friends, and Mick leaned close to Daniel and said *Sarah would have liked her*, and he'd nodded, not just to be polite but knowing that it was true. He remembered Dr. Levinson telling him once that the important thing was not to lose his ability to love; this was early on, and Daniel had said, *That doesn't seem very important now.* To which Dr. Levinson had replied, *Now, no. In time, it will be.*

"Dan? You OK?" Rachel stood there with soft drinks and sandwiches in her hands, a look of concern on her face.

"I'm fine," he said. He was better than fine; he was blessed, and grateful for it. "All's well." And he said it again, under his breath, when he returned to the hospital room to see his wife holding their daughter. *All's well.*

The Veil

Chapter Thirty

The sales clerk at Thalia Art Supplies looked like the typical university hipster: black clad, tattooed, and sullen. But his sullen look vanished as Elaine and Cecilia walked in. "Hey, Mrs. W. and Young Lady W.," he sang out. "Need a hand with anything?"

"Thanks, I think we're OK," Elaine said as she hoisted Cecilia into a cart. "Ooof, you're getting heavy." Cecilia was going to be tall, like her father, and at five no longer fit into the seat of the shopping cart. But as always, she was happy to sit in the cart itself, contentedly arranging the supplies Elaine placed into it, offering her candid opinion on frames and mattes or singing to herself with occasional breaks to chatter at passersby.

Elaine had long since lost count of how many times she'd been in here with Cecilia. Too many to number. Coming in for Bristol pads, pencils, pastels. An easel after they'd put the skylight and the track lighting in the workroom. They'd done that when they bought the house and put on the addition for Cecilia's bedroom.

She still came in to the supply store often, not just for herself now but for the gallery. Time and Tide usually needed mattes and frames, nuts-and-bolts items like that, and the owners liked to buy local and keep business in town. Elaine had been working there two years now and loved it. Oh, it didn't pay a huge amount, and there were always some annoying customers, the sort who were more concerned whether a painting would match their sofa than about the techniques the artist had used to create it.

But it was worth it when she could talk with a customer—not trying to sell anything to them, just talking about the painting or sculpture and how it was made—and to hear the customer say, "I'll take it."

More than once she'd seen Daniel watching her while she helped crate up a purchase. He'd stand there, often with Cecilia in his arms, and smile. When she asked him once what he was smiling about, he'd said, "It reminds me of that time at the Norton Simon. Remember, when you told me about the Impressionists?" Yes, she remembered.

"Mama?" Cecilia's voice interrupted Elaine's reverie. "When's Daddy coming back?"

Elaine smiled down at her daughter. Cecilia wore a sundress that came nearly down to her shins and paired with it a grubby pair of slip-on tennis shoes in checkerboard red and black. Daniel had a pair just like them. The dress was dusty from a hard day of tree climbing, and her fingernails testified that it had been mud pie day at the Kids Kamp Day Care. Her long copper hair flowed free, and she wore a necklace of bottle caps. A ragamuffin angel.

"Probably Saturday, sweetie. He'll tell us for sure as soon as he knows."

"Is he having a good time?" Cecilia asked. "He said he is, but his voice doesn't say that."

"He misses us, that's all," Elaine said, doing her best to sound both reassuring and nonchalant. Not much got past Cecilia, but she couldn't know about the discussions her parents had in the weeks leading up to the session. Discussions that hadn't been discussions per se—Daniel debating back and forth on whether he should go, she reassuring him that everything would be fine, the way everything had been fine these last five years. Finally he'd gone, but she'd heard the undertone of worry in his voice every time he called. She understood it, but there was nothing she could do to ease it. He wouldn't relax until he was back home.

"We should give him a fun surprise when he gets back. Whatcha think?" Cecilia sprang onto her knees, sending supplies tumbling from their orderly arrangement. "I want to make him a CD. Can I, Mommy?"

Elaine tried not to laugh. They'd given Cecilia unlimited access to their music collection from an early age—probably too early. Elaine still remembered when Cecilia was four and the day care teacher asked if Elaine could please explain to Cecilia why "The Lumberjack Song" was not appropriate for circle time. That one she could lay at Daniel's door, but she had only herself to blame for the time when she and Rachel were driving back from a shopping trip to Oceanside and heard Cecilia in her child seat, softly singing "At Seventeen" and then asking what "vague obscenities" meant.

The occasional inappropriate song aside, Cecilia loved music and handled the CDs and LPs with care. Before she turned five she'd mastered the technology and liked few things better than to make compilation CDs for friends and family, their cover art designed by Cecilia as well with her mother's colored pencils and pastels.

"I think that's a great idea. That can be your surprise. My surprise is, I want to make him some meringue cookies." Elaine was trying her hand at making egg tempera paint and had two dozen eggs that needed separating. Not for the first time, she was thankful for the Thatcher family at the other end of the cul-de-sac, who had a massive chicken coop in their backyard and eggs to spare. "Do you want to be my pâtissier?"

"Yeah!"

"Fantastic. Let's get this bought and make sure we're home before he calls."

They bought the supplies, Cecilia graciously thanking the sales clerk for the sheet of stickers he gave her. By the time they got home most of the stickers were either stuck to the car window or to Cecilia herself; this was nothing new. While Cecilia busied herself with raiding the music collection and singing along with the songs she chose, Elaine set about making dinner and waiting for Daniel to call.

"Well, I've had it. Care to cab it with me back to the hotel?" asked Reg Fletcher.

"Nah, think I'll loiter about for a while," Daniel said.

Reg laughed. "You're going to blow your chance to be the next Cliff Richard if you don't watch out. And after I promised Elaine I'd keep you out of trouble."

"Don't worry; if I get tossed in the drunk tank, I'll call Desiree to make my bail."

"Just make sure she bails you out in time for the session." Reg stood and brushed onion ring crumbs off his trousers. "Thanks for coming out here, Danny. I appreciate it a lot."

"No trouble," Daniel said. It was not entirely a lie. Just as he was not entirely sorry to see Reg leave. He had never been one for the bar scene in the past, but that's where he'd spent much of his time in New York. Not drinking to excess—three beers was his limit. He wanted not Reg's company but the bar's noise: strangers' chatter dissolving into a blur of sound, TVs and jukeboxes competing with each other. He didn't much like it, but it worked.

What didn't work: being in his hotel room, or even going to the movies. Too much quiet time that let his thoughts go back to where he should be. Home.

It'll be fine. They'd all said it. Elaine and Rachel and Mick and Kate and Eskimo Sally and Kenichi and Dr. Levinson. What they were really saying was that it wouldn't happen again. Of course they were right. It was just that when it was quiet and he was alone, he had time to remember that it was September. Perhaps out West the Santa Anas were blowing. And he'd left his family behind. Again.

And he was working for Reg again. Up until now Daniel had kept his session work within the borders of California—in Los Angeles mostly. But Reg had to stay in New York for legal reasons (another divorce), and Daniel couldn't refuse Reg's request to play on the new album. Without Reg, *Winter Roses* wouldn't exist. It would be a bunch of half-finished demo tapes gathering dust. He owed Reg a couple of weeks of his time.

But he did wish it could have been in Los Angeles.

"Daddy, *please*," Cecilia had said as he ran back from the airport shuttle for one last hug, one more reason to stay a bit longer. It wasn't *Daddy, please stay* but more like *Daddy, get going, you're driving us crazy*. But then, Ceel was such a self-possessed little girl. Not serious—she was as prone to the sillies as any five-year-old—but with a kind of confidence Daniel knew he himself had never had, not at that age.

He took out his wallet, opened it to the photo insert. His mind's eye summoned up the images of his wife and daughter very well, but he still needed to look at Cecilia's picture sometimes. How fast she was growing! It seemed no time at all since she was a tiny baby in Elaine's arms, staring in infant wonder at the lavender plants in the backyard. Now she was tall for her age. "Growing like a weed," Mick said, but Elaine said it was more like a willow tree, tall and slim and her long, straight hair indeed like a weeping willow, if willows had leaves of copper instead of green. The comparison ended there, for if trees had voices, they were of the whispery sort, and that was not Cecilia's way.

As a baby she didn't cry often, but when she did she seemed to be making up for her quieter times. "Definitely a coloratura," Rachel said the first time she heard it. Yet if those first couple of months had been hard, it hadn't been Ceel's fault. Daniel and Elaine had both worried that fortune would take away what'd they'd longed for, and not a night went by that one of them didn't jump out of bed to check on their daughter, who more often than not was sleeping peacefully and unaware of her parents' worry.

Finally Eskimo Sally had come to them. "You two need a night off from parenthood. Just look at yourselves."

Elaine had smiled ruefully. "Rachel said I looked tired."

"Tired? Pfft! You look like five kinds of shit, both of you. Which isn't all that big a deal for Dan . . ."

"Excuse me?" Daniel had said.

She blithely went on: "But you guys need more rest or you're going to crash. Look, I know you're nuts about Cecilia-girl. Who wouldn't be? And you've got new-parent freak-out times ten; don't try to tell me otherwise. You'll make *her* nuts if you don't relax. So, we've got it worked out. Rachel and the Mickster take care of the Infanta for a night, and you two get a comp stay at the B and B—take your pick of the rooms. Dig it?"

They did. Since then it had been good. When Cecilia was six months old they enrolled her in half-day care, and Elaine worked the nursing job three days a week and took classes at LCU the other two. They worked out a schedule that gave both of them time with their daughter and time to practice or study, and Cecilia seemed to have an affinity for her parents' callings. She was often content to roll on the floor playing with blocks and rattles and books for an hour at a time while Daniel played, or to make her own drawings or paintings in imitation of her mother.

Thinking of all this gave him a pang. He wished, as he did at odd moments, that somehow his own mother could know about Cecilia. His biological mother, wherever she was, if she was even still alive. Who might have helped give Cecilia her hair of gold fused with red. *There's a blond in the woodpile somewhere,* he sometimes thought, and Elaine said there were none she knew of in her family. He'd always assumed Jake's blondness had come solely from his Reilly genes, but perhaps not. And as he often had with Jake, Daniel wished he could tell his vanished mother: *You have a grandchild you'd be proud of.*

Before he knew it he was out of the bar and standing outside, flagging down a cab. Once he was in the quiet of his hotel room, he called home. "Did I miss bedtime?"

"No, your timing is impeccable," Elaine said. "We just finished dinner and were having some story time."

He wished his daughter good night and tried to follow her daily report from Kids Kamp: something about Zoe and some boys who were mean and who could build the better mud pies. After he said goodnight and sang "Puff, the Magic Dragon" to Ceel, he asked Elaine, "How is everything?"

"Crazy," she said. "Time and Tide's getting an early start on setup for the Christmas rush, and I had to make a run to the store for mattes. I'm wiped out." She sounded tired, yes, but happy in a way she never had been until she got her degree and finally quit nursing.

They talked and exchanged love-yous and goodbyes. Daniel went to his window and looked out. Mick had always insisted that New York had a kind of vibrancy you couldn't find anywhere else. Maybe so. It probably *was* so, but Daniel didn't want that. He wanted to be back in California. He

403

wanted to be back with his family, immersed in all the routines that took them through everyday life. He wanted to feel Elaine's arm across his chest as she slept, wanted to feel the silken touch of her hair. He wanted to hear Ceel sing in the bathtub and laugh at the way the tile's acoustics bounced her angel's voice back at her. He wanted to go home. There, he'd be able to lock the fears and the bad memories away, surround himself with the love of those who loved him. There he'd be safe. They all would be.

It was Reg who started it. After Daniel's final day of session work Reg took him out for a last round at the bar they'd all frequented the last couple of weeks. Reg said, "Danny, I've been meaning to ask you but haven't thought of how to go about it. So I'll just be blunt, if you don't mind."

Would it matter if Daniel did mind? Reg never had been known for his diplomacy, as countless people in the music industry could attest. Daniel just smiled. "Fire away."

"Are you ever going to do another record? You had something special there with *Winter Roses*. It'd be a shame to never do another one."

Daniel looked away from Reg, occupied himself with pouring a beer. The truth was that there never would be another album. Whatever it said about him, Daniel knew he didn't possess the creative gift to create his own work without some catalyst. His choice had been to make *Winter Roses* or go mad. Should the worst happen again, there would be no choice and no music; there would be only madness, which was silent.

"Don't know," he said lightly. "I've got a few things, bits and pieces. But nothing that amounts to anything." Daniel shrugged. "Guess one album is all I've got in me."

"Well, that's a bloody shame, but I suppose it's more than most can do. But if you ever do another, call me and I'll come running. And don't worry, next time I'll make it to LA."

"You don't have to—"

"Don't argue with me. I know you don't like to be far from home, and if I hadn't had Patti and her damn divorce lawyer after me, I'd have gone out West. Anyway." He clapped Daniel on the shoulder. "Safe journey, and give those lovely gingers of yours a hug from me."

"I will."

That night he tossed and turned and contemplated taking the sleep medication Dr. Levinson had given him for just this eventuality. But with his luck it would work too well, and he'd oversleep and miss his flight. So he gave up on sleep and channel surfed until he found a marathon of *Cops* (or what Sarah had always called *Lying to Cops*) and watched that until he didn't so much fall asleep as lose consciousness.

It started to go wrong in Houston, where the plane change was delayed. And it didn't get better when he finally got on the plane—first a thunderstorm and then technical problems. He'd accidentally packed his cell in his suitcase, so it was down in the baggage hold and no damn use at all. Daniel had a book but couldn't concentrate: he'd read a page, and then the feeling would come on him. Something was wrong. Not with the plane or the Houston weather but at home. Before long he couldn't concentrate on a word, let alone a paragraph. He gave it up and sat there. Waiting. Telling himself that everything would be fine when he got home and trying to believe it. After all, everything had been fine these past five years. In Los Cielos things were the way they always were. Friends were all well. As was the family—most of it. Daniel's adoptive father had passed away two years ago, and at times it bothered Daniel how little Tom Whitman's death had affected him. In fact, when Les had called and said *Dad's passed away*, Daniel had felt sickening loss tempered with bewilderment—why would Les call him about Hugh Reilly? Then he understood, and though he'd felt a bit ashamed at his relief, he didn't try to deny it, either. As he'd told Dr. Levinson, what good had it done to love someone whose feelings for him had been indifferent pleasantry?

So if Tom didn't count, not to Daniel, then he was well overdue for something to go wrong.

"Scared of flying?" his seatmate asked when they were—finally—airborne. Probably wondering why Daniel sat with his head back and his eyes shut, very still, but with his hands clamped together, fingers intertwined into a cold, sweaty knot. He nodded in reply; it seemed easier, and by plucking the air sickness bag from the seat pocket he was able to keep the seatmate from further conversation.

When they landed in San Diego—finally—he went to the nearest pay phone and called home. Voice mail picked up. No matter. They were on an errand. He was late, and they hadn't wanted to wait for dinner. They'd probably gone to pick up some nachos and quesadillas from Rodriguez Brothers. He was tempted to call Mick or Rachel but decided against it. It was fine, everything was fine, and he was just being an idiot to think otherwise. Besides, if he didn't hurry up, the shuttle would leave without him.

He didn't have long to look at the coastline during the shuttle's northward journey, for twilight dimmed to night before he'd gotten much past San Diego. Yet even his brief glimpse of the sea and sand soothed him, made his fears seem for naught. He'd get home and everything would be well, Elaine and Cecilia waiting for him.

The shuttle dropped him off; he grabbed his suitcase and carry-on, tipped the driver, walked up to the door. Where he found the lights off, the doormat askew, the main door locked but the screen door unlatched.

That cold sensation of free fall. So long ago—nearly a decade now but so fresh. Yet different this time because he should have known better. He stood frozen before his door and only when the screen door moved in the breeze, tapped gently against the doorframe, was he able to move, after a fashion. He fumbled for the keys he hadn't thought he would need—why would he, they'd be home—and grabbed them, dropped them, plucked them from the askew doormat, and began jabbing ineffectually at the lock, trying to get it open.

"Dan?"

Mick's voice but Daniel didn't turn around, because this time Mick was the bearer of bad news. But maybe if he didn't turn around or acknowledge, Mick would leave it unsaid.

"You OK?" Said with genuine bewilderment.

Daniel ceased his fruitless attempts to unlock the door and turned. Mick stood there by his fancy sedan, looking concerned and puzzled, but certainly not grim. "Did Elaine get hold of you?" Mick asked.

"No. I mean, my cell's in my suitcase." Daniel's voice seemed to come from somewhere else. "Where are they?"

"Oh, they're at the hospital."

Daniel wasn't aware of striding down the walkway to where his friend stood. Left hand clutching his keys so tightly the impression would linger till the next morning, right hand grabbing on to Mick's blazer. *"What?"*

"It's all right! Everything's OK. Really." Mick spoke in a rush. "Cecilia fell down, gouged her forehead. Elaine thought it needed stitches, so she took her over to LCU General." Mick's cell phone rang, and as

Daniel let go of his blazer, Mick got the phone and answered it. "Hello? Oh yeah, right here."

Daniel took Mick's phone with shaking hands. "Elaine? What's going on?"

"We're all right. We were making cookies, and Ceel slipped off the footstool, got her head on one of the cabinet hinges. They stitched her right up, I got Dr. Fine the plastic surgeon to do it. Everything's OK."

He had trouble speaking. He'd been so sure. "Can we come get you?"

"No, no. We already checked out. Ceel was a trouper—"

"They said I was a champ, Daddy!" Cecilia helpfully interjected. "I didn't cry one bit!"

"So I told her we'd get ice cream on the way home. She's fine, don't worry. Three stitches was all it took, and they're by the hairline. Dr. Fine says a year from now you won't even be able to see it."

"Thank God. I mean. I was . . ."

"I understand." Yes, she did. "Want some ice cream, too?"

"Chocolate. Chocolate to the infinite power. Bring some for Mick here, I freaked out and manhandled him. What ice cream do you favor, Professor?" he asked.

"Butter pecan, please."

"I'll see you soon," Elaine said. "I've missed you."

They said goodbye. Daniel hung up and handed the phone to Mick, who had already unlocked the door and turned on the lights, brought Daniel's bags in. Daniel walked unsteadily into the front room, where he collapsed onto the love seat. "I'm sorry about pitching a fit."

"Not to worry." Mick settled into a chair, loosened his tie. "Elaine said she couldn't get hold of you and wasn't sure when you'd be in, so she asked me to come by. You OK?"

"By the time they get here I'll stop feeling like I'm going to throw up." Daniel put an arm over his eyes.

"Why were you so upset?" Mick asked.

Daniel was dumbfounded. He sat up, looked at Mick, who sat there looking quizzical. Of all the people to ask that question.

He was about to say something, but Mick spoke first: "It's not going to happen again." Mick's face became still, almost stony, and his voice reminded Daniel of something he couldn't quite name. "Nothing like that is *ever* going to happen again."

This wasn't the assurance Daniel had been given before leaving for New York. This was a statement; no, it seemed to be an order issued to fate. And therefore a doomed order, because something always would happen, given time. Daniel had resigned himself to that. He would have thought Mick had as well . . .

Before he could think of what to say, the door opened, and Cecilia flew in, threw herself at him, wrapped her arms around his neck. "I have stitches, Daddy! Like Frankenstein!" He hugged her back, so tight she complained, then let her go so he could look at her. So precious to him, like Elaine, who sat down next to him and kissed him. So great was his relief that he was able to easily banish the fright he'd had. Shut it away in a dark chamber of his soul with the other dreads and bad memories. Something that could not be forgotten entirely but did not diminish the joy of being where he belonged. Home.

Chapter Thirty-One

In Cecilia's room was a desk, with cubbyholes for markers and pencils and crayons, with things stacked into neat piles. Coloring books, sticker books, her favorite chapter books, a year's worth of *Highlights*. And close at hand, next to the gooseneck lamp, was a journal. Like all the second graders at Saint Andrew's Episcopal school, she'd been given the journal at the start of the year and asked to make an entry at least twice a month. The title of the journal: *Things I Like*. And it had been no hardship for Cecilia to meet the minimum number of entries—indeed, she far exceeded it.

She liked her room: the way the sunlight filtered in though the purple bougainvillea flowers covering her window, and the lazy drone of bees she could hear on sunny mornings. The rest of the house pleased her as well. There was the workroom with Daddy's piano and Mommy's easel. Cecilia could not recall which was her first memory. Had it been sitting with Daddy at the piano, putting her chubby toddler fingers on the keys alongside his hands? She could see his hands so clearly in her imagination; they were tanned along the backs, and on one hand he wore a silver bracelet with pretty stones in it that he sometimes let her try on. Or had her first memory been at Mommy's easel, holding something? A paintbrush? A pencil? Cecilia's memory failed her on what the exact tool had been, but she remembered the color that had streaked across the white paper, a brilliant streak of turquoise.

No, perhaps her first memory was of her other favorite room: the living room, where the music was kept. Sitting in someone's lap. Mommy or Daddy? Or someone else, perhaps her Uncle Mick or Aunt Rachel? In a way it didn't matter whose lap it had been. What mattered was the memory of safety and happiness. Whoever held her loved her and rocked her gently as music played. Cecilia could no longer remember the exact music. At times she went through the collection, thumbing through the CDs in their plastic cases that went clack as they leaned to one side, or the vinyl records, so old some of them, in their big square sleeves and with a peculiar musty smell, and looked for the music that was from her first memory. She hadn't found it yet but felt sure that one day she would.

For she liked music as well—not just the Disney songs and the girl singers you heard on the radio, but stuff most of her friends had never even heard of. Ever since she was old enough to handle the discs on her own, she'd spent many hours listening. Sometimes her choices were based on an interesting album cover. Sometimes she picked a letter of the alphabet and started there, playing albums or artists beginning with that letter. Once or twice she picked up the light-up magic wand she'd bought at Disneyland, closed her eyes, pointed the wand at the collection, and let it guide her to what she should listen to next.

Cecilia remembered when she'd made her first CD. Grandparents Day had been on the way, and she'd wanted to give her Grandma and Grandpa Reilly something extra special. She loved them, and all her aunts and uncles and cousins, too. It was always so much fun to go to their house and play on the trampoline with the kids, or to have Grandpa Reilly spin Cecilia and her cousins on the tire swing until they got extra dizzy. And Grandma Reilly always had special treats like chocolate-mint brownies or cookies baked with M&Ms instead of chocolate chips. Cecilia didn't want to say anything to Daddy and hurt his feelings, but she didn't like her Whitman grandma very much. She never could seem to remember how old Cecilia was or what she liked to eat, and if Grandma Whitman gave clothes as presents they were always too small and *way* too girly. None of that princess stuff for Cecilia, those things were too hard to climb trees in. And her Aunt Victoria, whom she'd only seen once or twice, but who always looked at Cecilia as if she were some kind of bug. So it had been fun to make the CD for her Grandma and Grandpa Reilly, picking out music she thought they'd like. And they had liked it, or said they did, and soon that became what she gave people for Christmas presents—the CDs she made. She made them for her Mommy and Daddy, for her uncles and aunts, for her friends Zoe and Jack and Katrina, for her parents' friends like Eskimo Sally. Sometimes her Daddy even asked her to make CDs for his friends who lived far away: *Music for Reg. Music for Wayne, Beth, and Randall. Music for Tamara. Music for Dr. Howard.*

Today Cecilia stood in the line for pickup at Saint Andrew's; Tuesdays and Thursdays she went straight home after school, the other days she was at singing lessons. But this Thursday what arrived was not her family's car but something even better: Aunt Rachel's Vespa with the sidecar. Cecilia had a hard time waiting her turn in the line, for she loved riding in the sidecar. She got to wear a helmet and look like a big girl. It made her feel like a teenager.

"Your dad's still on his way from LA, and your mom has to work late tonight. Mind coming to the shop for a bit, and then we'll go to our place until she picks you up? Maybe take a swim?" asked Aunt Rachel once they were buzzing along in the Vespa.

"I like it," said Cecilia over the sound of the Vespa and of the portable CD player she held, which was playing her latest mix, a bunch of music by a man who had what Cecilia thought was the most amazing name: Ennio Morricone. As for the change of plans, Cecilia didn't mind. She liked her aunt's shop, and Aunt Rachel always let her use as many beads as she wanted to make necklaces and bracelets. It would be good going to her aunt and uncle's house tonight, too. Their pool was where she'd learned to swim, and they'd let her decorate the room she slept in whenever she stayed overnight. One more thing to put in her journal. She'd do that tonight when she was home with her mommy and daddy; she'd sit in her bed with the reading light on and write it down, singing to herself all the while.

Singing. Another thing she liked.

No, loved. It was not something she thought about much. It was *there*, like her parents and the smell of the lavender bushes and the way the sand was so warm under her feet at the beach. She never questioned its presence in her life. And yes, *now* she knew her earliest memory. Waking in the night—she must have been quite young still, for she could recall seeing the bars of her crib—to hear the sound of thunder and of rain on the roof, and being a little afraid. She sang to herself; she could not recall what melody, only that her voice seemed to come not just from her but outside her as well, and so comforting in the way that nothing else was save for her mommy and daddy. And Daddy must have heard her singing, for he came in and asked if she was all right, and of course she was, but she was still happy to see him, and he rubbed her back, and she forgot about the storm and slept.

When she was five she started her singing lessons. This was something she'd asked for. Cecilia knew about karate lessons, which Zoe took, and T-ball, which Jack did, and Spanish, which Katrina was learning. Her friends all liked their lessons—not like poor Brandon in the other

413

kindergarten class, who was in French *and* piano *and* soccer and who looked so tired all the time. Mommy and Daddy said one lesson was fine, but it had to be just one so she had to pick the thing she liked most—well, as if there were any choice? Cecilia knew she could sing, but even at five she sensed that for her voice to do what she wanted it to do, she needed a grown-up's help.

Ms. Caroline was her teacher, and three days a week one of her parents picked up Cecilia and took her to the studio where she practiced scales and learned to use her voice, make it go places she wouldn't have dreamed possible, without hurting her throat. And though her mommy or daddy always brought along a book to the lessons, more often than not when lessons were over she saw them with the book closed and knew by their smile and the look in their eyes they hadn't been reading but listening, to her.

She liked that most of all.

Today when she and Aunt Rachel got to the store, her aunt handed her three one-dollar bills. "Remember that bracelet you made last time? The one with the turquoise? I put it on the rack and someone bought it."

"Really?" It was the first money Cecilia had made that wasn't from household chores. "So awesome!'

Her aunt laughed and kissed her on top of her head. "You're going to put me out of a job, *chérie*."

They stayed at the shop until closing time, then drove to Aunt Rachel's house. Cecilia's uncle was already home; he picked her up to hug her, and the helmet she still wore bonked him in the chin. While the grown-ups got dinner ready, Cecilia took a peek at their music collection. It wasn't as big as her parents', but there were plenty of things to choose from. Aunt Rachel had lots of bands that wore their hair all up in the air and had silly, bright-colored clothes—bands with names like Dexy's Midnight Runners, the Rezillos, the B-52s, and Duran Duran. Uncle Mick had a lot of the same music she'd seen in her parents' collection, but he also had what looked like a hundred albums by some scruffy-looking guy named Neil Young. Cecilia was about to give one of those a whirl when she saw another CD.

She never liked to play *Winter Roses* that much. It made her too sad. Maybe if it was someone else singing it, and not her Daddy, she might have liked it better. And to make it worse, she knew why he sounded so sad on it. She'd asked him, and he'd told her about it, showed her the photo albums. She still looked at those photo albums sometimes; it was strange to see such a different part of her family's life and especially strange to think that she had a brother. Her friend Katrina had a little brother who was sometimes a pain, but maybe older brothers were different. Zoe's older brother was fun. He let them play with his Iron Man and Spider-Man action figures as long as they were careful, and sometimes he'd pretend to be a dragon and let the warrior ladies Cecilia, Zoe, and Katrina slay him with their lightsabers. Maybe Jake would have been that kind of brother.

As for *Winter Roses*, the only song she really liked was the last one, "Homecoming." Yet she'd always felt it was missing something. Maybe it was because it was music only, no singing. It needed a voice. She put it on now and lay down on the floor with her head next to the speakers (she could do that here—at home it made Mommy worry that she'd damage her hearing or something). She listened, and thought about what she'd sing if it were her song.

Daddy was the one who showed up first—Cecilia and her aunt and uncle had just sat down to dinner when the door flew open. "Hello, hello!"

he called out as he walked into the dining room. "My three favorite people in the world. Ceel, Rachel, and me! Oh, hi, Professor."

Cecilia smiled. Daddy liked to tease people, but it was never mean, and her uncle laughed the loudest of all of them. Daddy came over and hugged her. "How's my girl? I haven't seen you all day."

Mommy came in just as they were finishing up dinner, and she'd brought cupcakes from the bakery near the gallery. After the cupcakes, while the grown-ups were having coffee, Cecilia went back to the living room and put on the music again, her head by the speakers and singing softly to herself.

"So that's the excitement. Three hours to find one lousy invoice," Mommy said. "I earned those cupcakes. So how about you?"

Daddy laughed. "Troubadour wants to do a compilation album. A charity deal, in time for the holidays. They've been after everyone on the label for weeks now and won't believe anyone who says they haven't got anything new to give them."

"Including you," said Uncle Mick.

"Including me. Well, Reg suggested we just do a rerecording of something off *Winter Roses*, but that doesn't feel right."

Cecilia agreed. She closed her eyes and listened to the music. The music went on, the grown-ups talked on, and her eyelids were getting heavy when the music was turned off and Mommy said, "Wake up, sweetie. We've got to get you home. School tomorrow. Who you want to ride home with?"

In Daddy's blue car, Cecilia sat and ate the last of the cupcakes. She watched the lights of the town go by outside her window, and the sweet taste of chocolate frosting lingered. She was still a little sleepy, and she sang to herself without thinking of what she was doing. No words, just her voice. When they pulled into the driveway she was still singing, and she thought Daddy would ask her to stop, tell her it was time to get inside. But he sat, watching her with a strange look on his face. When she was done he said, in a quiet voice, "You are the most remarkable girl, Ceel."

"Thank you, Daddy."

"Do you want to be on a CD?"

"The one you were talking about?"

He nodded. "I always knew that song was missing something. And now I've found it. Had to come a long way to find it."

"What do you mean?"

He smiled, shook his head. "Just me being silly. We'll talk about it in the morning. For now, let's get those teeth brushed and get you in bed."

When her teeth were brushed and she was in her nightgown, after Daddy had read her a chapter from *The Magician's Nephew* and after Mommy had sung to her, Cecilia went to sleep. In her dreams, she heard song.

Chapter Thirty-Two

It was a sunny May Saturday, and Rachel had been at the shop since eight that morning. Lilah said, "Ms. K., go take a break. We can handle *las turistas*." Rachel's work ethic wasn't what it used to be, and besides, it was such a lovely day. She drove home on her Vespa intending to have lunch with Mick and maybe take a quick dip in the pool, and arrived to find Mick and Daniel drinking sodas in the kitchen.

"And if that's wrong, then crown me King Wrong of Wrongland," Daniel declared.

Mick bowed his head. "My liege. Lead us with wisdom."

They both laughed, sounding like high school boys instead of men on the dark side of forty. Rachel smiled, thought of asking what all that was about, then decided she was probably better off not knowing. "Hey, Dan. Want to stick around for lunch?"

He shook his head, took another swig of his root beer. "I have to get over to the gallery, be all manly and strong and help lift some things. But I wanted to ask—would you be able to watch Ceel tonight? Lara had to cancel babysitting, her mom's in the hospital down in San Diego."

"Is her mom OK?" Rachel asked.

"Broke her hip. Lara says her mom's in good spirits and she's got good insurance, so she's not too worried," Daniel said. "I know it's short notice, so if you can't, that's OK."

"I think that's fine," Mick said. "Let me check with my social director."

Rachel uncapped a root beer. "Yeah, tonight's fine. What have you got going on?"

"Taking Elaine to the Blue Lagoon for dinner. We haven't been since they reopened."

"How did that fire start, anyway?" Rachel made a mental note to get to the Blue Lagoon sometime soon. It had the best crab cakes, and it was right on the pier, just a five-block walk.

"I heard it involved flaming liquor shots, but my source is 'random student on the LCU campus,' so I could be wrong," Daniel said.

Mick shook his head. "Faulty crème brûlée torch. No kidding."

"Really?" asked Rachel.

"Huh. How'd you know that?" asked Daniel.

Mick shrugged. "Work friend did the insurance settlement. They got a bundle."

"Speaking of which," said Daniel. "They spent part of that bundle at Time and Tide. One of Elaine's pictures is on the wall there."

"Oooh, she must be excited," said Rachel.

"She doesn't know. They sold it while we were out of town. Evie was there for the reopening, and she told me about it. I've got the table right next to the picture reserved, I'm gonna surprise her." Daniel grinned in anticipation.

"In that case, our social calendar is definitely open," Mick said. "Bring Cecilia by any time."

"Awesome. Mind if I park the car here, and we'll just walk it? Shame to waste such a nice evening."

"Go for it," Rachel said.

"You're sure it's not a hassle?" Daniel asked. "It doesn't ruin a romantic evening with candles and Barry White music?"

Mick snorted. "I think I'm past the age when I can use Barry White albums as a tool for seduction."

Daniel looked stricken. "There's an age cutoff on that? Shit." He laughed and left for the gallery.

It was always crowded at the Blue Lagoon Bistro on a Saturday night, and even more so now that it was open again after its repair and refurbishment. But there was no wait for Daniel and Elaine; they arrived and were instantly guided to their booth, above which hung Elaine's picture: *View of the Pier from Lonely Point*. Her homage to Boudin—she'd even painted it outdoors, the way the Impressionists did it. Daniel remembered those days well, Elaine sitting at her easel at the very end of the point while he and Cecilia played on the beach below and he taught her how to ride a boogie board. Now he watched Elaine's face as she saw her painting: surprise and delight.

"You knew it was here," she said as they sat down. "Why didn't you tell me?"

"I only found out a couple of weeks ago. Evie told me. It took me that long to get a reservation and a sitter, and even then I greased the wheels to make sure we got this booth."

"It didn't cost a lot, did it?"

He laughed and shook his head. "The hostess is a fan. I just had to give her one of the CD singles, the charity version of 'Homecoming.' Ceel signed it, too."

"Let me guess, it took her twenty minutes to decide which color marker to use," Elaine said.

"Of course. She's *your* daughter."

Elaine looked at the painting again. He took the opportunity to look at her; there were a few silver threads in her red hair now, but she somehow looked younger than when they'd first met. She turned to look at him, and the simple happiness in her face made her look almost a girl, right out of college maybe. She leaned over and kissed him, and it was a sweetheart's kiss, still.

They lingered over their dinner and drinks and over the chocolate-dipped strawberries the hostess brought to them. As they left the restaurant and started walking down the pier, he heard something. A voice, he couldn't tell whose. Cecilia was his first thought, for it sounded like the vocals she'd done for the re-recording of 'Homecoming.' He stopped, listened, thought he heard it again. Thought it spoke his name. He stood still, eyes closed, trying to hear it again, but if it was there, it was lost in the tide washing against the pilings and the sounds of Skee-Ball and air hockey from the nearby arcade. "Nothing," he said to Elaine as she regarded him quizzically. "Just the tinnitus acting up."

"I didn't know you had tinnitus. How long have you had it?" she said as they made their way down Estrella Street.

He hid a smile. Elaine sometimes forgot she wasn't a nurse any longer. "If I don't, I'm lucky, what with all that time around loud music."

"You ought to get your hearing checked."

"Beg pardon?"

"I said you ought to—oh, I walked right into that one."

Daniel chuckled. "I've still got it. I can still reel 'em in."

"Reel *this* in, darling." Elaine walked away from him, over to the sidewalk across the street. She walked for three houses; after they crossed the corner of Estrella and Driftwood, she glanced over at him and giggled.

"I feel like we're in some corny musical. We should break into song or something."

"Get back here, then, or I'll sing the show-stopping number 'Across the Street From My Heart.'"

She dashed into the street to get to his side, and that was when the truck came around the corner, seeming to head right for Elaine.

Daniel didn't stop to think—if he had, it would have been too late. Nor was he conscious of starting to run. He heard nothing, saw only Elaine in the headlights, thought only of getting to her in time.

He pushed her, hard, and thought he saw her fall out of harm's way but couldn't be sure in the blinding glare. Before he could take another step he felt the shock of impact but no pain; heard bones break. He was flung up over the hood and onto the windshield. More sounds: breaking glass, screeching tires. And he was flying through the night. Not flying. Falling, and it took a much longer time than seemed possible. Time to understand that he wouldn't get up from this fall. Time to hope that Elaine was all right. Time for all this—and for a moment he seemed to be not falling but drifting, borne on a gentle tide. For a moment he saw not the asphalt rushing to meet him but brightness, distant and veiled. For a moment he heard not the wind rushing nor his heart's erratic pounding but something like music, strangely familiar. And laughter that he knew at once. Jake's laugh.

The asphalt slammed into him. A deafening crack at the back of his head, and black light exploded across his sight. A snap and a wrench in his spine and a sharp burst of pain that was gone so quickly he couldn't have screamed even if he'd had the breath for it. Twice he rolled and then lay on his back. His breath came in ragged gasps he could not control, and when he tried to move, his hands and arms would not obey. He could feel them, but they seemed to have lost all strength. Below his midsection he felt nothing at all.

None of that mattered if he could see Elaine. He tried to open his eyes, banish the black light, and felt that his eyes *were* open, wide. Blind. *Now it's dark.*

He tried to call for help but couldn't find the strength. Where was Elaine? Was she safe? He heard a babble of voices and the sound of feet on pavement. One voice rising above the others, made shrill and genderless by horror. "I knew you weren't OK to drive, and look at him! Look what you did!"

"Quiet!" Elaine's voice raised in a roar he nearly didn't recognize. It was the voice of the nurse now. She was giving orders: call 911, bring a blanket to keep him warm.

He had to know if she was all right. Summoning what was left of his strength he said her name. She was there, taking his hand in hers, telling him help was on the way. Her hands were so warm, he could feel the life in them; he breathed deep her scent. Yet he still needed to hear it. "You . . . all right?"

"Yes, love," she whispered. Not the nurse's voice anymore. "You saved me."

Yes, and that was all that mattered, not the blindness nor the numbing cold stealing through his body nor the feeling that the world was fading away. "Love you."

"I love you. Daniel." Her voice rose. Alarmed. "Stay with me."

I want to. "Ceel," he said, and a pain worse than anything the truck had done knifed through him. *I want to see my daughter grow up. Why can't I stay?* "Tell her." He fought for a breath. "Tell . . ." His family, his friends, all those he loved and would not see again.

"I will." She kissed his hand, clutched it tightly, and her touch seemed far away, as if it were happening to someone else.

"Hold on." Someone nearby said it, not Elaine. But there was nothing to hold on to. It was like grasping a handful of smoke. The darkness seemed to be inside him now, and he was afraid. There'd been another time much like this one, a time of fear and darkness. *Please. Sing.*

Daniel wasn't sure if he'd actually said it. But she kissed him, and she sang. Her voice was a trembling, reedy thing, unlovely to listen to, but it was hers. *Do way, dear heart, not so. Let no thought you dismay. Though you now part me from, we shall meet when we may.* Her voice and her presence, so close, kept fear at bay.

And he wondered why he had been afraid, for he could see now.

The light was not so far away as his first glimpse of it had been. The veil obscuring it was less substantial; like early-morning mist that both brightens and fades until it vanishes in the sun's warmth. Elaine's song merged with a sort of music he'd heard before, and the veil parted. Light shining on him, through him. Healing him—not his body, that poor wrecked thing—but his soul. Such peace came upon him. The old dreads and fears, the pains he'd borne so long he'd half forgotten a time they weren't there—all gone now. Freed of their shackles, he seemed to be lifted up, as gently and as lovingly as he'd picked up a sleeping child. Like one of those children, he gave himself over to what felt like an embrace.

Laughter again, Jake's delighted laugh. *I've missed you,* Sarah said. *Come home.* And other voices calling to him. Uncle Jacob. His mother, who *had* loved him, so much that she gave him to a family she'd hoped would give him a better life than he would have had with her. *Come home,* they said.

And yet Orpheus-like he looked back, saw Elaine kneeling over his body. The pain of loss was gone, but he could still recall it and wished he could somehow spare her that.

She'll be all right, Sarah said. There beside him, and oh, he'd never thought to see her again. She smiled, the smile he'd fallen in love with. *She's strong. Your love gave her that strength. Look. Do you see?*

Yes, he could see. See her soul, so beautiful and yes, strong. He'd watch over her, the way Sarah had watched over him. And when it was time, he'd welcome her home.

For that's what it was. Not an ending, nor a beginning. A homecoming.

Chapter Thirty-Three

The Whitman house's doorbell played the melody from "The Addams Family" theme; the juxtaposition of the merry tune with present circumstances was disconcerting, but Rachel had long since stopped noticing it. The doorbell had rung so many times these last few days. "I'll get it," she called out to whoever might be in the house now. She knew Elaine and Cecilia were here, and a complement of Reillys as well. Dr. Levinson had been by this morning, and Rachel thought she remembered seeing a friend of Elaine's from the gallery.

She opened the door and did not recognize the person standing there. This was nothing unusual. The many people who'd rung the doorbell included friends and colleagues of Daniel's and Elaine's that Rachel didn't know, and there had even been a few reporters. "May I help you?"

The woman was in her fifties perhaps, with an anonymous sort of prettiness. "Are you Mrs. Whitman?" Her voice was hesitant.

"I'm afraid she's busy now." This was the phrase they'd agreed on after their first encounter with a reporter. None of them had felt like talking to the press. "Is there something I can help you with?"

"It's all right. She doesn't know me. But I live where . . . where it happened, and today I found this."

The woman held out the silver bracelet Rachel had made for Daniel so long ago. Rachel took it, looked it over. The metal was scratched in places, one cabochon missing, another cracked. Not surprising. The force of the collision had knocked him out of his shoes. Rachel couldn't remember who had told her that little detail. It nagged at her, and she didn't know why.

After a moment she remembered her manners. "Yes, it's his. Thank you very much for bringing it."

The woman offered her condolences and left. For a while Rachel sat, looking at the bracelet. Black onyx to release sorrow. Fire agate for spiritual fortitude. Sodalite for peace and harmony. The onyx had cracked. She hadn't looked at the bracelet in a long time and for a moment had trouble remembering which stone was missing. Mahogany obsidian, that was it. For protection. A lot of good it had done. Should she give it to Elaine now or try to fix it first? Would Elaine even want it?

"You found it?"

Rachel glanced up guiltily; she'd dithered too long. Elaine looked pale and shaky, like a candle flame in a drafty room. Yet she had a candle's light about her, too. It was how she'd looked since they'd picked her up at the hospital. Rachel admired Elaine's resilience—the woman was bowed but not broken. At the same time she mistrusted it. Daniel had seemed strong at first.

She handed the bracelet to Elaine, who held it in both hands and regarded it with an expression Rachel couldn't fathom. "I was looking for it," Elaine said at last. "I'd forgotten he was wearing it."

"I can fix it. Tonight if you like." Rachel wondered if Elaine heard the unspoken question: *Do you want it to be buried with him?*

"It doesn't have to be tonight." Elaine slipped the bracelet onto her own wrist, but it was too large for her and hung loosely. She took it off.

Rachel shrugged. "I was going to swing by the shop anyway and check in on things. It won't take long."

Elaine held the bracelet still, looked at Rachel. "You look tired. Maybe you should go home."

"No." She said it a little more strongly than she'd intended to. "No, it's OK. Like I said, it won't take long."

Elaine sat down on the love seat, ran a hand through her hair. Rachel noticed how much Elaine's hands trembled. The abrasions on her palms were healing, but her fingers were smudged with charcoal. Elaine had been drawing. She'd spent a lot of time doing that. Rachel hadn't seen the drawings, and if anyone else had, she'd heard nothing of it.

Before she could say that Elaine was the one who needed some rest, Elaine said: "About tomorrow. I shouldn't have asked you. You've done so much already, I don't want to put anything else on you."

"It's OK," Rachel said. "I'll be back in a little bit. Call me at the shop if you need anything."

"I will."

As Rachel stood and was turning to go, Elaine's voice came again, so softly Rachel had to strain to hear it. "I keep thinking of this song Daniel liked. One of Reg Fletcher's called 'The Thing That Happens Next.' Do you know it?"

"Yes," she said, though she'd never been the Fletcher fan that Daniel and Sarah and Mick had been.

"It's like in that song. I see the thing that happens next, and I keep on going until I get to it. And then there's the thing after that, and I keep going. The problem is . . . I can't see after tomorrow, after the . . ."

After the funeral, Rachel's mind filled in.

"What do I do then? How do we . . . ?" Elaine's hands clenched tight, the charcoal smudges standing out like bruises.

Rachel started to sit down next to Elaine, but Kate Reilly was there. Kate put an arm around Elaine, who leaned into her shoulder and wept. Not loudly, but her quiet tears seemed more painful than any sobs. Rachel watched them and felt a sudden, sharp longing for her own mother. More than that—to go back to childhood somehow, surround herself with the love of her family. To be somewhere safe, someplace where friends weren't run down in the road like dogs.

"It's all right," Kate said to Rachel. "We'll be here. Go on, you look like you could use a break."

Rachel hadn't thought so, but as soon as she stepped into Beaditudes she knew it was true. Though she kept the place dark—the sign on the front door made it clear they'd be closed for the week—and went straight to her office, it was enough to look out at her racks of clothes and jewelry. The sight soothed her, as did the familiar textures of the works in progress she had at her desk. The pebbly feel of the beads, the whispery cottons and butter-soft silks. A sort of calm fell on her, and as she got to work the calm deepened. She polished away as much of the scratches as she could—they'd never come away entirely, though. She removed the cracked cabochon and found replacements of onyx and mahogany obsidian.

When she arrived back at the Whitman house to give Elaine the bracelet, she saw parked in front of the house a lemon-yellow Volkswagen Thing. She'd know that car anywhere, and sure enough sitting on the hood was Eskimo Sally, with an enormous bowl of nachos in her lap and Tom Waits growling out of the Thing's speakers.

"Hi, Sugar Magnolia," said Eskimo Sally. "Care to join me and have some nachos? I got the biggest order Rodriguez Brothers had. It's hungry work, getting your ass kicked at Go Fish by an eight-year-old. I should have taught Cecilia to play baccarat."

Rachel hadn't been hungry all day but now a bunch of gooey nachos sounded perfect. She sat down on the hood, hoping it wouldn't buckle under their combined weight. Not that Eskimo Sally would care; the Thing already sported plenty of dimples and dents. Rachel remembered when they were going for a ride somewhere, she, Eskimo Sally, and Daniel. After a parking lot incident, Eskimo Sally had declared, "Oh, look. Another ding for my Thing!" To which Daniel had replied, "You make it sound *so* dirty."

"You're smiling," Eskimo Sally said now through a mouthful of nachos. "Penny for your thoughts."

Rachel told her what she'd been thinking of; Eskimo Sally laughed. "I'd forgotten that. Me, I was thinking of how he told me that Mr. Waits"—Eskimo Sally jerked a thumb back toward the speakers—"learned his vocal stylings from Cookie Monster."

Rachel burst out laughing and couldn't stop. Every time she'd calm down she'd imagine Tom Waits singing "C is for Cookie" and start up again. Finally she calmed down enough to say, "He wasn't wrong about that." She stuffed several chips laden with beans and cheese and sour cream into her mouth so she wouldn't get the giggles again. Her stomach muscles hurt, but aside from that it was the best she'd felt in days.

They sat there for a while, gorging on nachos, sharing the margarita slushie and their fond memories. At one point Kate came out to join them; she respectfully declined some nachos but joined in the reminiscing. Kate went back inside, taking the bracelet with her and a message from Rachel to Elaine that she'd be there early in the morning.

Not long after came the sound of a familiar engine. Mick parked nearby but didn't get out of the car. He was on his phone. Rachel waved to him, but he didn't wave back; he seemed intent on his conversation, whatever it was. When he finally emerged from the car, he didn't stop to talk, didn't even say, "No, thank you" to Eskimo Sally's offer of nachos. He went straight on in to the Whitman house, his gait stiff as if he'd been sitting a long while.

"Was he like this the last time?" Eskimo Sally asked. "Because that would explain a lot."

Rachel shook her head. "No. I mean, he'd be quiet, but at night he'd talk. To me. Tell me stories about Sarah and Jake." There were no stories now. He said *yes* and *no* and *I'll take care of that*. He dealt with the things he needed to deal with, said hardly a word to anyone, and when he looked at you his gaze went past you, as if you were a stranger. Even Rachel couldn't get past his wall of silence. For a while she'd hoped Cecilia might, but that hadn't happened, either.

The sight of her silent husband killed Rachel's appetite. She thanked Eskimo Sally for the nachos and went home, where she had a quick bath and laid out her clothes for the next day. *I used to like wearing black.* Rachel went to bed early, for tomorrow would be a long day. She fell asleep almost immediately but woke early the next morning and found the other side of the bed cold. When she went in search of Mick, she found him in his home office, looking intently at the computer screen. Rachel knew what she should do—ask how he was doing—but the thought of trying to break through his silence was wearying; she wondered why she bothered anymore. Turning away, she went to get some more rest before the time came to bury her friend.

The shower poured hot water down on Elaine. Her scraped palms and knees stung, but only for a moment or two; they were healing. It was late, past eleven, and she'd turned on no lights. Thin moonlight slanting in through the window was her only illumination, all she needed. The darkness and the shower's white noise were a kind of cocoon. She stood under the near-scalding water and let it sluice down over her. After a moment a shudder ran through her; it was not unlike the way Daniel's body had trembled, at the end. Elaine leaned against the wall and cried, deep sobs that shook her so that she had to sit down. The relief was immeasurable. The shower was not the only place she wept, but it was the only place where she could let her grief have full rein, its sounds masked by the water's constant hiss. When others were around she had their sorrow to think of as well as her own. At night, she wanted to weep but not to disturb Cecilia, who slept next to Elaine; so she cried into Daniel's pillow, muffling her sounds the way she had in the bad old days when to cry audibly meant to risk her husband's wrath.

But here there were no such considerations. These shower sessions were like cloudbursts—intense but brief—and she was always done before the hot water had run out. That seemed appropriate, for it had all happened so quickly. That truck slaloming around the corner and seeming to aim at her, and she with no clue as to which way she should run. Then he shoved her, hard. She still bore the bruises. So strange. It was the only time his hands had been less than gentle on her. Elaine heard the first sound of impact as she was falling: that terrible sound of metal colliding with flesh and bone. The second sound she heard as she was scrambling to her feet. The sound, so loud and flat at the same time, so terribly *mortal*, had put paid to any notion that none of this was happening. Years since she'd worn a nurse's scrubs, but as she ran to him her mind ran through a litany of how she'd try to save him intertwined with a frantic prayer that it wasn't as bad as she feared. *A miracle. Give us a miracle. Please.*

No miracles.

Elaine allowed herself the luxury of another few minutes under the shower, then tilted her face into the spray, washing it clean. She stepped out and dried herself off, then put on her nightgown and robe. Her hair she left in a wet tangle; she'd deal with it in the morning. Daniel had always liked her hair most when she'd liked it least, when it was frizzed from the damp and flying out all over the place. How he'd loved mussing it, especially when they made love.

Much as she would have liked to revel in the memory, she pushed it away. If she thought of it now, she'd also think of what lay ahead. All that time without his presence. His voice. His touch. Without him.

Elaine sat on the bed for a moment, stroked Cecilia's copper-bright hair. Cecilia didn't wake but stirred and snuggled a bit closer with her stuffed bunny. Mr. Rabbit Trick had been drafted out of retirement. Elaine turned on the baby monitor, which also had been brought back into service: Cecilia had nightmares the first night after Daniel's death, but since then she'd slept well. Still, Elaine wanted to hear should her daughter call for her. Elaine took up her pencils and sketch pad, closed the bedroom door behind her, and padded through the house. It was empty now save for she and Cecilia, and its silence at night was eerie after the noise these days had brought. It was still a surprise to her how many people had been here for she and Cecilia.

It was not the number of the people that surprised her. She knew many would come. It was why they had come—not just for Daniel but for her as well. She hadn't thought they would. For the first time in ages her mother's voice spoke up in her head. Told her: *They'll come to pay their respects to him. He's the one they loved, not you.* That first morning after, she sat dazed at the Kesslers' dining room table with her hands cupped around a lukewarm mug of tea, shaky with exhaustion for she hadn't slept that night.

She watched the seconds creep by on the clock with agonizing slowness, knowing that soon Cecilia would wake and would have to be told. She listened to Rachel make phone calls; after a while Rachel came in, paused to light a cigarette, and told her the Reillys were on their way. Elaine hadn't known what to make of that. Already she was wondering if she'd been right to tell Mick and Rachel how it had happened, that Daniel had died saving her. Perhaps, she thought that first morning as she saw how Mick refused to meet her eyes or even look at her unless absolutely necessary, perhaps she should have lied. Yet she'd been too deep in shock. How could she lie about something she could barely believe had happened? Perhaps he blamed her; perhaps he wouldn't be the only one to do so. Certainly her mother's voice had plenty to say on that subject.

Telling Cecilia had been the hardest thing she'd ever done in her life. The girl's keening wail when she first absorbed the news was nearly as bad as those twin sounds of mortal impact, and had been so loud that the next-door neighbor had come by to find out what was wrong. By the time Cecilia's initial storm of grief had passed, Kate and Hugh were there—Elaine realized later they must have dropped everything and floored it to make the trip from Torrance so quickly. She heard them arrive and hung back for a moment, afraid of seeing blame in their eyes, but Kate held out her arms, and Elaine ran into them. "We love you, and we'll get you through this," Kate had said, and all Elaine could think of was that primal, comforting word: *Mama*.

And they'd come. More Reillys, most of them staying at Eskimo Sally's bed-and-breakfast. (She'd made arrangements at other inns for her guests. "Except for the guy in room four; he was a douchebag who always left the place a mess for housekeeping. I told him we had rats in the plumbing," she'd said with surprising cheer, though her eyes were raw-looking from crying.) Even Father John Reilly had flown out from Indiana and had made arrangements with Father Lewis at Saint Andrew's Episcopal to conduct the service. Dr. Levinson had come, and as always his presence and his manner soothed Elaine; she understood why Daniel had kept seeing him long after he'd needed the counsel. People Daniel had worked with—those she knew, like Reg Fletcher and Kenichi Hirota, and those she'd only had contact with through Christmas cards, like Daniel's old session agent Clive Smith. There was a kind-eyed woman named Susan Howard—Dr. Howard from up north.

And then there were all the wishes of condolence. Cards that made their way to the house, phone messages that got even to the unlisted number. Messages that all said the same thing, more or less. *You don't know me, but I loved* Winter Roses. *I heard what happened, and I'm very sorry for your loss.*

She was surrounded by friends and family and their love and support. No one blamed her. Yes, Mick was silent and distant, but he was that way to everyone. At the same time she knew how easy it could be to disbelieve that love and sympathy. More than once she'd thought of what Daniel had told her—how agonizing it had been, *knowing* that he was to blame and that everyone would soon understand that and blame him. More than once she thought that she could have blamed herself very easily.

Yet she didn't. And in a strange way it was Daniel himself who'd absolved her of that blame. She'd run to him, listening hard as she ran. For now that the two sounds of impact were gone she was listening for a groan, or better yet a scream. It would be a terrible thing to hear, but a man with strength enough to scream might have strength enough to live. She'd heard no sound from him, and when she saw him sprawled on the asphalt with his body bent at a slight but wholly unnatural angle, saw the way his head rested on the hard road's surface, saw his eyes looking blindly for her . . . She told Dr. Levinson (and only him) that was when she knew. No miracle.

But perhaps there had been a kind of miracle, for he'd been conscious and coherent. No blame, no reproach. Just relief that she was alive and safe. Love for her, for their daughter. There had been fear, but it had vanished as she sang to him. One of the songs she'd sung at the Shoreline Diner. *Whereto Should I Express*, composed by Henry VIII. And then . . .

Elaine sat in the workroom at her easel where the light was better. She opened the sketch pad. She'd made several tries. The most recent was close, but not quite there. Why she felt the need to capture that moment, she wasn't sure, for she knew she'd never forget it. For a second, no more than two, she'd seen the blindness leave him. She'd known he was seeing something, and she didn't try to look for what he was seeing because she didn't want to look away from him. Whatever he saw was of a radiant beauty and peace she could only guess at. It had been there for only a moment, and then he was simply gone, so quietly that it took her a moment to realize it. Until she saw that both sight and blindness had left his eyes. Until she laid her head on his chest as she had so many times before and heard only silence.

No, she could not capture that fleeting moment of sight in a drawing, not completely, but it soothed her to try. She could look at the drawing and her grief would ease, a bit.

For a while she drew, until her eyes were so tired she could barely focus on the work and her fingers ached from holding the pencil. Time to sleep, or at least try. After tomorrow she could sleep for a night and a day if she wanted to. And hard as it would be for her to face waking up to a life without Daniel, she would do it. For Cecilia. For all the friends who'd come to her in this time. For herself. And for Daniel. She'd told Dr. Levinson that maybe Daniel didn't resent laying down his life for hers; perhaps that was the end he'd have wanted, given the choice. A terrible thing to say, some would have admonished her, but Dr. Levinson said she was probably right.

Sound over the baby monitor. Cecilia's voice. Not raised in distress, but still Elaine put aside her papers and pencil, trotted down the hall to the bedroom. Only the night-light was on, and Cecilia lay there in the faint warm glow, looking up at the ceiling and singing to herself. "Mama," she said when Elaine entered. "I had a dream."

"A scary dream?" She brushed a long strand of hair away from Cecilia's face.

Cecilia shook her head. In the dim light her eyes were the same near-indigo shade as her father's. "A nice one. About Daddy." As Elaine got into bed Cecilia asked, "Mama, is it OK if I sing? Tomorrow?"

Today, actually. Elaine glanced at the clock. No wonder she was so tired. "Yes, love." She kissed Cecilia on the forehead, then lay down, closed her eyes, and drifted off to the sound of her daughter softly singing.

There was a feeling inside. His body or his mind, Mick wasn't sure which. Something tightening. If he'd believed in a soul, he'd have said it was that, being ratcheted tight. Too tight. It was hard to speak, and he was uncomfortably aware of his breathing. Might it become so tight he wouldn't be able to breathe? He wasn't sure, because every time he thought the feeling surely must have peaked and would lessen, it didn't. It just kept growing like Topsy, as they would have said back home in Missouri.

Home. He hadn't called it that in years, but that seemed appropriate. The place and its people had been much on his mind.

What made the tightening sensation so awful was that nothing seemed to ease it. He couldn't look at Elaine, let alone comfort her or share in her grief. He'd watch her sit with Rachel or Kate or Eskimo Sally or even some of Daniel's friends she'd barely even met (like that blond fellow who swore all the time, what woodwork had *he* crawled from?) and share memories—and all he could do was watch. He wanted to join in, wanted to mourn his friend, but whenever he did the sensation grew so that he almost couldn't breathe. For the same reason he couldn't meet Cecilia's eyes or put his arms around his wife or even talk to anyone. All he could do was the tasks he needed to perform to see Daniel into the ground.

Nothing helped. Not the food that already heaped the tables in the Whitman house. Not the liquor cabinet. Not the baggie of weed that Rachel kept stashed in her sock drawer. Not music—he could almost hear Daniel saying: *It's a well-known fact, Professor. If* After the Gold Rush *can't help, you are well and truly screwed.*

The other day he was driving on an errand and went past where it had happened. Just two blocks away. (They'd heard the ambulance go by. Cecilia had already been in bed by then, and he and Rachel had been watching *Animal Crackers*. "Yikes, that's close by," Rachel had said, and then "Hooray for Captain Spaulding" started, and they forgot about the siren.) One of those impromptu shrines had popped up, and he pulled over, got out to look at it. Flowers and cards and things. A bouquet of roses had fallen away from the rest of the pile, lay in the street. They were bluish-lavender roses. Winter roses. Of course. He meant to pick them up, arrange them with the rest of the flowers but instead ground them under foot until the blooms were mush smeared into the asphalt. He got back into his car and noticed that the tightening sensation had eased.

Mick began to understand some things then.

At the funeral, he sat in the front row with Elaine and Cecilia, Rachel, Daniel's mother and sister. He looked ahead without seeing. The tight feeling was bearable now, even though the priest was Sarah's baby brother, who of all the Reilly siblings looked the most like her. A memory bubbled up to the surface. Sarah giving his lived-in Chevrolet a token glance, then smiling and saying, *We've got a room. It's not much, but it's close to campus and the rent's cheap. Sound like a plan?* And he'd replied, *But you don't even know me.* She laughed, *Oh, don't worry, I've got excellent judgment. And you've got a kind face.*

Ruthlessly he squashed the memory. The constricting sensation receded a bit. No, he wouldn't think of that or the fact that John looked like Sarah who was gone like Jake and now Daniel, too. He focused on the words John said, which were meant to give comfort but brought Mick none, for they meant nothing without belief, and he had none, hadn't had any since all those prayers for his mother to come back had gone unanswered. His college girlfriend Holly, who never missed a Sunday at church (though she'd been known to go the afternoon Unitarian service if she'd overslept), asked him once if he believed in God. *No,* he'd told her, not adding: *Because God's a father, and I already have one of those.*

"Excuse me." Rachel slid out of the pew and went to the podium. Mick wondered what she was going to say. She hadn't told him. Or had she? Her voice made him feel worse, and he'd tried to hear it but not really hear it. Maybe he could do that now, if he weren't so damn tired.

She talked about the day he'd introduced her to Daniel, Sarah, and Jake. Yes, at the Independence Day festival at the park. He remembered the way their eyes had gone to her, shrewdly assessed her. *She's a keeper, Professor*, Daniel had said. Meaning: *Not like Gina.*

She talked on, and a sidelong glance showed how well everyone liked Rachel's eulogy. Not him. That tightening feeling was worse than ever; might it cave in his ribs and crush his heart? And if it did, would that be so bad? A crushed heart could feel no sorrow.

Nor was it any better at the cemetery. The ceremony itself was not so bad, he felt able to breathe again. Just when he'd thought the worst was over, Cecilia stepped forward and sang *Pie Jesu*. She'd sung it at her recital last year. Then, it had pleased him to hear her angel's voice soar. Now, he thought he might break.

The reception was held at his house—the Whitman place was too small to accommodate all the mourners. Mick stood off to the side. Tucked away in a corner, he was able to avoid some of the condolence-wishers. But not all of them, and every person who said, *I'm sorry for your loss*, or *I know what a good friend he was* only made that constriction worse, and he'd have thought he'd be used to it by now.

Through the murmur of voices came a sound—distinct, repetitive, and thoroughly irritating. Sitting halfway across the room was Annie Whitman, her daughter Victoria by her side and Theresa Reilly nearby. Mick glanced around the room for Victoria's husband, Les, saw him over by the food table talking with Rachel. That sound again. Mick felt a ripple along his nerves, inside things went a notch tighter. Annie sniffled steadily as she talked with Victoria and Theresa. He watched them and listened not to the words but to the sounds. Yes, it was like clockwork, that miserable little sniffle. Why couldn't the woman just get a goddamn tissue? Again the sniffle, and at the same time Victoria looked at her watch.

Mick walked over to them; along the way he bumped into a few people but made only token apologies. He stood in front of Annie, who sniffled again and looked up at him. She'd gone for full drama in the role of bereaved mother, even had one of those hats with the black net veil. Behind the veil her eyes were watery and weak looking, and she regarded him with mild interest. "Oh, hello, Nick. It's just awful, isn't it?"

He took a breath—it was hard going for a second—and said, "Why are *you* crying?"

His tone must not have been what she expected, for Annie looked at him with bewilderment.

"After all," he went on. "You didn't love him."

Out of the corner of his eye he saw Victoria's shocked look but paid it no mind. The tightness had eased, and the words came easily: "The heir and the spare. You know, for most people the second one's the spare, but I guess you decided to change that up a bit."

Theresa tugged on his arm. "Now isn't the time for this . . ."

"Why not? Everyone knows it." He felt relaxed, at peace almost. His hands itched, and he clenched them into fists. "If she'd given a tinker's damn for him, he wouldn't have had such a bad time of it when Sarah and Jake died."

"You're crazy, just like he was," Victoria snarled.

There was a jump cut, and he stood with his fists raised. Hands held him back—John Reilly and Eskimo Sally and Dr. Levinson. Before him Annie cringed while Victoria glared at him. Dr. Levinson murmured, "Don't do something you'll regret, not now," and Mick became aware of how many eyes were on him. What had he said or done?

He took a step back; his restrainers relaxed their grip but did not release him. "I'm sorry," he said because he had to say something. He took a few steps back, and they let go, though they still looked wary. He turned and walked to the patio doors, absently noting all the eyes on him—especially Elaine's. She stood with her hands spread to her sides, as if she was shielding someone, and peeking from around her he saw Cecilia. He looked for Rachel but didn't see her anywhere.

Mick walked out on the patio and stood by the shallow end of the pool. Everyone else was still inside, and he had it to himself. His hands stung; he unclenched them slowly and saw that his nails had bitten into his palms, deep enough to draw blood. Quickly he shoved his hands into his pockets, feeling guilty, as if he'd hit Annie. He hadn't—had he?

The patio door slid open and out walked Eskimo Sally. She wore a strange sort of half smile, and he couldn't read her eyes. "Well," she said, "that could have gone a bit better."

Mick turned away. "I'm sorry," he said again, knowing he sounded anything but.

"Care to tell me what the heck you were thinking of?"

"I'd rather not talk about it." Because he'd already turned away, the only thing to do was to walk farther out on the patio, toward the fence. Maybe she'd leave him alone.

"Hey," she said. "Want to get off that cross? I could use the wood."

He didn't answer. That tightness was starting up again. It seemed significant that it had eased when he'd confronted Annie and Victoria.

Eskimo Sally sighed. "Look, every word you said in there was true. But now's not the time, and that's not the way. Let's just hope John and Doc Levinson can talk Victoria out of bringing assault charges."

Dear God, had he hit them? "Did I . . ."

"No, but it sure as hell looked like you were going to, and that's all that bitch needs to call the cops." She chuckled without much humor. "Be a great way to end the day's festivities. If Dan's watching what's going on, I hope he missed that bit."

"Dan's gone," he said wearily.

She spread out her hands in a curious gesture, one which seemed to respect his opinion while at the same time telling him it was mistaken. "Even so, you had no call to say that to Annie."

"Didn't I?"

"Maybe she's realizing what's she's lost and regrets how she treated him. You don't know what's in her heart, so don't act like you do."

"Would you please leave me alone?"

"Not until I say this. I know what you're going through. I was there, remember? We were your first friends. Don't deny it. And now what are you doing? Threatening to punch out your friend's mother. Maybe you don't care if you end up in jail for assault, but what will Rachel think? She needs comfort, too, and you're acting like she doesn't exist. Did you see the way Elaine looked at you? Everything else she's going through, and now she has to worry you're going to be big man with his fists, like her ex? And there's Cecilia."

Shame flooded through him, hot and scalding. "What about Cecilia?" Remembering how she'd peeked at him from behind Elaine, who'd been protecting her daughter. From him. *Please, not that.*

Eskimo Sally's face, usually so merry, was graver than he'd ever seen it. "She thinks you blame her."

God, no. "Did she tell you that?"

She nodded. "You learn a lot during a two-hour game of Go Fish. If you hadn't agreed to watch her that night, Dan and Elaine wouldn't have gone out. She thinks that's why you won't look at her or talk to her."

"It isn't that . . ." But how would anyone know? Pushing them away because their comfort, their very presence, made that tightening sensation worse. But no one knew that. He hadn't let them know.

"I don't mean to be cruel," she said. "But you're hurting others and yourself. If nothing else, tell me: is this how you honor your friend?"

He said nothing. It was true, what she'd said. Every word of it. And the worst part was that at some level he'd known it all along. The pieces that had been falling into place while he hid from his friends and made his phone calls, came together.

A roar of an engine. He glanced up to see Victoria's car driving away; Les was at the wheel, Victoria and Annie were talking. *Looks like I'm off the hook.* "I need to take a walk," he said. "Can you let them know that?"

"Look at me." Once he'd turned to face her she gave him a long, level look. She reminded him of the way Dan's shrinks, both Dr. Levinson and that lady from up north, had looked at him. "All right," Eskimo Sally said. "Take your cell so we know where to find you."

He nodded, then made his way back into the house. Mick kept his eyes down so he didn't have to see the way people looked at him. In his home office he picked up his cell, and after a moment's hesitation he opened the bottom drawer of his desk, took out an envelope, and slipped it into his blazer's inside pocket.

Up and down the streets of Los Cielos, Mick let his feet take him where they would. He stayed away from the beach, for reasons he wasn't sure of. Besides, his mind wasn't on the beach now. It wasn't even in California. It was some 1,500 miles east, in Missouri.

He opened the cell phone and looked at the number he had saved. The Shady Rest Retirement Home, that's where the old man was. How old was he now? Mick had been a late child, and by his best calculations his father had to be at least in his early eighties. Still hanging on. Jake gone, Sarah gone, and now Daniel, too. And the old man kept clinging to life like a barnacle. Mick hadn't known at first why he was trying to find his father, but now he did. He wanted to call and say, *I understand now. You shut down after Mother left, and when you couldn't shut down you unloaded on me. It made the pain go away.* He remembered that feeling of calm that had come over him when he'd stood above Annie with his fist raised. *Yes, I understand now.*

Glancing around, he saw that his feet had carried him to MacHeath's. No wonder they ached so. Inside the tavern it was cool and quiet save for some chatter coming from the private party room. The main dining room was mostly empty—it was a weekday and not yet time for happy hour. Mick took a seat at the bar, and Eli came over to him. "Hey, man," Eli said. "How you doing?"

He didn't trust himself to speak, just nodded.

Eli seemed to understand. "Bombay and tonic for you?"

Mick nodded again.

In no time the drink materialized in front of him. "On the house," Eli said. "I'm so sorry about Dan. I'm gonna miss seeing him in here. He was a *mensch*."

"A *mensch*?" It hadn't been that long since he'd spoken, but his voice felt strange, probably because he had to force out the words through that tight feeling.

"A heck of a guy."

As if in agreement with Eli, there came a small chorus of cheers from the private party room. Mick glanced that way and saw people he recognized from earlier today, at the service. That blond fellow was standing up saying, "And then Dan the Man starts singing 'They're

Coming to Take Me Away,' and the guy laughs and comps us our cheeseburgers." The girl sitting next to him, a brunette with a big silver necklace, applauded.

"They've been coming in all afternoon," Eli said. "I can ask them to keep it down if you want."

"No, that's OK. In fact . . ." Mick dug out his wallet, tossed Eli his American Express. "Put the whole room on my tab. Tell them to get whatever they want, stay as long as they like."

Eli's eyes got wide. "You sure? They're racking up quite a bill."

"I'm serious." At least his money would do someone some good.

"You're the boss."

While Eli went to the private party room, Mick got out his cell and dialed. After a moment he heard a female voice with an accent he recognized immediately as southern Missouri, probably the Bootheel: "Shady Rest, this is Lori."

"Hello, Lori, I understand you have a Mr. Kessler staying with you. Is there any chance I could speak to him?"

"Let me see if he's awake. If he is, who shall I tell him is calling?"

"Michael." He only used that name for business, and it felt strange to say it. "His son."

Papers rustled. "Strange, I don't see a son listed on his paperwork. Next of kin is a nephew in Poplar Bluff. But here, let me see if he's still up."

"Bless your heart." When was the last time he'd said *that?*

He was put on hold and sat listening to some country singer—one of those new pop music ones, not old school like Johnny Cash. After a little while the singer went away and Lori was back. "I'm afraid he's asleep now. He usually is at this time. Would you like to call back tomorrow?"

No. "Perhaps I will. Thank you very much." He hung up, set the phone down, and took a long sip of Bombay and tonic. It went down cool and bitter. Yes, he understood his father now, understood that he'd been that way partly because it was his nature, and partly to assuage that feeling of suffocation. *Is that how it felt to you? Like a screw tightening until it might break?* Well, there was a way to get rid of that feeling without turning into a fist-wielding bastard. All he had to do was leave. Not to New York, he couldn't go back there again. But there were a thousand other places. Big cities where there was money to be made and work to lose himself in, where he could be just another cog in the wheel of business. He could leave his scruples behind and the money would come in hand over fist, and he wouldn't feel a thing.

It would be easy. No one would miss him, not really. Rachel might at first, but she didn't love him as much as he loved her, and she'd probably get over his departure pretty quickly. They wouldn't put lit candles in the window for him, like they had for Daniel. That was the one thing he'd never understood, really. Why Daniel had left, when he'd had so many people who cared and would have done anything to help him. He'd never understood, and now it was too late to ask. But maybe not too late to learn why.

It seemed very important to know. *You understand your father, now understand your friend. Do that before you choose.*

Mick took the note, the one Daniel had sent him so long ago, out of his inside pocket. Daniel had told him to throw it away, but of course Mick hadn't. It had lain in the bottom drawer of his desk, along with the unopened letters to his father and Gina's Dear John note. Pieces of paper that were deadweights to the past. He took the note out of its envelope; the ink had faded a bit over the years, but it was still perfectly legible.

Dear Mick,

By the time you read this, you'll probably know what's happened. And you know why—the main reason, I mean. It's all so simple really. My life's over, and it has been since I lost Sarah and Jake. But there's more to tell, and I need your help for this.

You see, by now you've probably all realized that I'm to blame. If I'd been there, it wouldn't have happened. I know this. I failed my family at the most basic level. I didn't protect them. I wasn't there when they needed me. And I know that I should have faced up to that. I should have been there when you all came to that understanding. But I couldn't face it. I love all of you too much to bear seeing that.

And so I left. There's no going back now. How's that line go? The one about heading out of the blue and into the black? You'll know the one I'm talking about, I'm certain.

I'm rambling. I'm sorry. This is harder going than I thought it would be. I'll only ask one favor of you, and I hope you'll do it. If not for me—I can understand that, you're probably furious with me—then for Rachel and the Reillys and everyone else. Please let them know that none of them are to blame for what I'm doing. I could not have asked for better people than they have all been. I wouldn't have gone on as long as I have were it not for them. And that's why I have to go. I can't lose anyone anymore.

I'm asking you to do this because I know how much everyone means to you. You never talked about who you were or where you'd come from before Los Cielos, but we all knew it hadn't been good. And then there was Gina. Most people would have let things like that break them, but you didn't. I admire that so much. If I'd had that sort of strength maybe I wouldn't be where I am now.

448

I know how distressing this is going to be, and you don't have to forgive me for what I've done. All I ask is that you accept my apology. I never wanted things to turn out like this. And please give my love to everyone. I miss you all so much.

Your friend,

Daniel

Mick crumpled up the note. No need to read it again. It was too late, anyway. Too late to tell Daniel that what had looked like strength was really cowardice, never letting anyone get too close. Not even Rachel. She didn't need him as much as he'd needed her because he'd always kept part of himself apart so she wouldn't need him. Wouldn't need things he couldn't give. As for his friendship, what had he done when Daniel came back to them? Mick had turned away. He'd been disgusted by what seemed like frailty; now he knew it was strength and knew he lacked even a fraction of that strength. After reading this note he understood how much of a miracle it had been that Daniel *had* come back; but it was too late for his understanding to do any good.

Running away, that's all you've ever done, Daniel had said once in the heat of anger, and Mick was getting ready to do it again. This was how he honored his friend.

Inside unbearably tight. He'd read somewhere that when a person drowned, as his breath ran out it felt like his chest was caught in a vise, so tight the bones might crack. It felt that way now, and like a drowning person he was tired of fighting it. *Go on, then. Break.*

He felt it happen. Heard it: a sharp sound like brittle stone cracking. And he was weeping, slumped forward onto his folded arms. He hadn't wept since he was six; all this time he'd been afraid to. But the longer it went on—for it wasn't just for Daniel; it was for Sarah and Jake, and his mother, for Elaine and Cecilia, and his own lost child, for Rachel, and the Reillys, and even for the wretched old man who'd helped make him this way—the more the tight feeling eased. He could breathe again. He could feel.

Felt a hand stroking his hair, then his shoulder. A voice said, "I'm here, it's all right. Let it go." He thought of lines from Dan's album. *Your voice calls to me. Your voice brings me back. Your voice turns darkness into light.* He raised his head from the bar.

Rachel looked at him with her beautiful hazel eyes. "Eli called me," she said. "Eskimo Sally brought me down here."

He could think of nothing to say, but she seemed to understand this wasn't his frozen silence of the last few days. Mick leaned his head against his wife's shoulder: it was small-boned, like a bird's. He smelled her perfume, felt the coarse silk of her hair. How long they sat there he didn't know, nor did he know how much longer his weeping went on. Only that when it ended, he felt so terribly tired and yet filled with a certain kind of strength, too.

"Are you ready to come back to us?" she asked.

"Do you want me back?"

"We need you. I need you. And Cecilia needs you most of all." She stroked his hair. "You're the only one of us who knows what she's going through."

Yes, fleeing would be easier. He'd feel no more pain if he did. But as incredible as it seemed to him, he was loved, and needed. "First, can we stop in?" He pointed to the private party room where the gathering was still going strong.

She smiled again. "I think Eskimo Sally's got chairs waiting for us. Now if we can just keep her from bogarting all the sweet potato fries, we'll be in luck."

As they got off the barstools he pulled her close, embraced her tightly. "For whatever it's worth, I love you," he said.

She returned his embrace. Not as tightly as his. It was an unequal love, and perhaps it would not last, but he would take whatever of it he could get. Already it was more than he deserved.

"I love you, too," she said, and they went into the room where the rest of Daniel's friends were waiting for them.

Winter Roses (Part Two)

Epilogue

The bus lumbered its way through the parking lot, then drew up to the front of the hotel. It came to a stop with a grumble of gears and wheeze of exhaust. Lights blinked on, and the Coastal Choral Ensemble closed their books, unplugged their music players, and reached for their purses and satchels. They filed off the bus, stood by the baggage compartment; already Ben was there with his ever-present clipboard while the driver opened the door and began handing out suitcases and garment bags. Not for the first time Cecilia mused that the group looked like any other bunch of tourists—a mix of men and women, all ages and sizes, wearing travel-rumpled sweats and jeans. Hard to believe they'd clean up nice for tonight's performance, but it always happened.

When she had her suitcase and garment bag in hand, she walked with the rest of the group toward the lobby. Her pace was slow, and she drifted to the back of the group, partly because she wanted to bask in the feeling of being home again.

Ben hailed from Pennsylvania and liked to make fun of California Christmas—how the lights and decorations were the only way you'd know what time of year it was, for the weather was the same as it always was. Cecilia conceded he had a point—she sometimes wondered what a Christmas would be like with actual snow—but there was no denying that Los Cielos got the holiday as right as it could. When the bus entered the town limits she'd been glued to the windows. Yes, the streetlight posts were wrapped in tinsel, and the trees on the business thoroughfares were strung with lights. Yes, the surrey bikes jingled with bells as tourists rode them up and down the streets. And there was more she couldn't see from the bus. No matter. Nothing much changed here, and when the group took its break between Christmas and New Year's, she'd have time to get reacquainted with the town.

Ben drew up alongside her; that was the other reason she'd dawdled. She was glad for the suitcase handle in one hand and her garment bag in the other, for she wasn't able to hold his hand. She wanted to, and knew he wanted to as well. But they'd agreed to wait. Until after the season, when the stress of the performances and the drama around who sang what and when subsided.

"Good to be home?" he asked.

She nodded. "I almost wish this was the last night. I mean, I'm really looking forward to the rest of it, but being back home, that would be the perfect way to end this."

The Coastal Choral Ensemble's holiday tour had begun the day after Thanksgiving. Up and down the southern half of California. Auditoriums, concert halls, town squares. The ensemble's mix of holiday songs both sacred and secular had resounded, and Cecilia knew she probably ought to be sick of the set list—certainly some of the other singers were—but then, this was only her second holiday season with the ensemble, and she hadn't tired of any of it yet.

They entered the Hilton's lobby; she hadn't been here since her high school senior prom, now some six years ago. At one end of the reception desk milled the group. Off at the other end of the lobby was their director, Russell Deane. Cecilia couldn't see him from where she stood, but she knew that voice, all mellow brass and bonhomie. She glanced around, but

Ben was already at the desk, speaking with the receptionist. By the time Russell had finished his conversation with the concierge, Ben had the group's rooms assigned, baggage whisked away, and instructions for the afternoon's rehearsal and evening's performance relayed.

"Everything in hand, Ben?" boomed Russell as he crossed the lobby. "Fantastic."

Cecilia knew she wasn't the only one repressing a smile. She might only be in her second year with the ensemble, but she'd figured out ages ago that while Russell was the director and the figurehead, Ben was the one who kept things going. Oh, she liked Russell tremendously ever since she met him at her audition. A former singer himself, he had an eye for talent. He also made an excellent figurehead for the ensemble with his still-handsome voice and the silver hair and beard that made him look like Papa Hemingway's distant, cheerful cousin. What Russell did not have was business sense, and his consider-the-lilies-of-the-field ways had brought the group close to bankruptcy in the past. (Cecilia had learned most of this before her audition, thanks to her Uncle Mick's research, and had it confirmed by the group's longtime members.)

The group's survival and growing success was attributable to Ben Sullivan. He might be only an assistant manager in title, but everyone knew that Ben ran the show. He got the gigs, set up the itineraries, coordinated the lodgings and transportation, negotiated the contracts, and helped out the members with whatever needed helping. Cecilia had seen how people concentrated on Russell because of his flash and good cheer, and then they were disarmed by the quiet young fellow with the glasses and the receding hairline who needed to have a word with them about this discrepancy in the contract, just a minor one they could resolve right now with no fuss.

Oh, you'll want to see Ben about that. That's what the older members of the group said to Cecilia when she had questions or problems. Not that she'd had many of either. For now she was just delighted to be making any sort of a living, putting her voice and that musicology degree to good use.

"You're rooming with Jackie, as usual. Here's your key," Ben said, handing the plastic card to Cecilia. She thanked him and for a moment wondered if she should say something more. No, best to let it wait until the tour was done. It wasn't much longer. Tonight's show in Los Cielos, two nights in San Diego, and the closing night show at Disneyland on Christmas Eve. After that they were free until after New Year's. No, not so very long.

Cecilia went up to her room to shower and relax for a bit until the afternoon rehearsal. Opening room 356, she found Jackie Choi's 1970s-vintage Samsonites on the other bed and Jackie's fine alto emanating from the bathroom in a dirty version of "The Twelve Days of Christmas" (a song the ensemble unanimously loathed and which Ben had persuaded Russell to drop from this year's set list).

"Four horny nerds, three felching men, two—is that you, Cecilia?" Jackie called.

"No, it's Norman Bates."

"Oh, OK. Before you stab me, Norman, could you score me a beverage out of the minibar?"

"Sure thing." Cecilia got a Snapple from the fridge and went into the bathroom.

Jackie peered around the shower curtain. Her sudsy hair was teased into Astro Boy spikes. "Thanks," Jackie said, then disappeared back behind the shower curtain, beverage and all. "You excited for tonight?"

"And how. I talked to Mom this morning, and she won't tell me who all's going to be there, which means it's everyone I know and she doesn't want that to make me nervous."

"Which of course only makes you more nervous. I have so been there."

Cecilia looked out the window. Maybe it was because she was home for the first time in over a year, or maybe it was that the tour's whirlwind of travel and performances had kept her indoors, but she had a longing to feel the sun and the wind on her face. "I'm gonna go take a walk around, Jackie. I won't be long."

"Knock yourself out. I'll be hanging out here with my trashy books. On the sixth day of Christmas my true love gave to meeeeee, six geese get laid. Fiiivvve golden . . ."

Cecilia left before she could find out what lewd spin Jackie had put on "five golden rings" and made for the elevator. The Hilton had a rooftop pool, and she went there not for a swim but to see what view the roof afforded her.

From there she could see most of Los Cielos. She could see few details from this height and distance but knew the places already. Los Cielos High, where she'd been in the choir, her friend Zoe on the drill team, and where she and her old flame Joel Harris had been homecoming royalty senior year. The university—by now it would be time for finals. Just north of that, home, as always awash with purple and magenta flowers. On the west side of town, near the beach, her mother's gallery and her aunt's shop. To the south, in San Diego, her uncle was probably putting money through the circus hoops. Over by the pier was her aunt and uncle's house, where some of her Reilly relatives were staying. They'd all be there tonight, she knew, and then there'd be a celebratory dinner out. Cecilia smiled.

It was not her favorite time of day yet—that was late afternoon, when the sun cast a golden glow over everything—but the sky seemed to give blessing to the day. It had rained just two days before, and the sky was washed clean. A scattering of small, puffy white clouds only accentuated the sky's deep blue. An Impressionist sky, Mama would say. The sky might send her Aunt Rachel running to her shop to see if she could replicate that blue in a scarf or shawl. Uncle Mick would call it another reason to never leave California—nowhere back east had skies like this, he would say. As for Daddy, he would have played something that matched the day.

Cecilia sat back in a chaise, tilted her head back. The December breeze was cool, almost chilly (for California anyway), but the sun was warm on her face. She thought of the dream; the day's beauty had called it to mind.

She seldom allowed herself to think of the morning she'd woken, somewhat surprised to find herself still at her aunt and uncle's house but suspecting nothing amiss, and had padded out to the kitchen. She couldn't recall exactly how her mother's and aunt's faces had looked; for some reason the detail that stood out in memory was that her aunt was smoking, which Cecilia had never seen before. The actual words Mama had used to explain what had happened were likewise lost. Cecilia recalled saying *Never?* Asking when she'd see him again. Had there been a reply? Surely there had been, but Cecilia couldn't remember hearing it. Mama's words had been drowned out in the roaring sound of loss, like wind howling through a hole in the world.

That night there were nightmares. Those she remembered with hideous clarity. In one of them she heard Daddy's piano playing and had been overjoyed, for they were all mistaken, and he was here. She ran to the room where the music came from and opened the door. He sat at the piano, but there was something wrong about the way he sat and the way he played. She called out *Daddy?* and he said *Ceel*, but there was something so wrong about his voice. She ran to him anyway, and when he turned to face her he looked like one of those ghouls from that *Dawn of the Dead* movie that she and Zoe had snitched from Zoe's big brother so they could see what a scary grown-up movie was like. The other nightmares were tamer but worse in their own way. In them she'd wake and find not just her Daddy gone and never coming back but everyone else: Mama, her aunts and uncles, Grandma and Grandpa Reilly, her friends, teachers, everyone. No one in the world left but her.

The next few days and nights after that were better, but only by comparison. She kept out of the way, spent lots of time listening to music, but it brought her no comfort. It was a way to pass the time. Mama asked if she'd like to go to Zoe's house for a while, and she said yes, but the girls didn't play. They sat in Zoe's treehouse and listlessly ate the snack Zoe's mom brought them; Cecilia had the feeling that, like her, Zoe now realized that death didn't just take old, sick people like Katrina's great-grandma. Time passed but didn't pass, those days. Everyone was so sad, so busy, and all Cecilia could think about was how she could possibly get through life without Daddy.

The night before the funeral she'd lain in her parents' bed, holding Mr. Rabbit Trick. Half of her wished sleep would come and last a very long time; perhaps she'd even sleep through the funeral. And the other half dreaded closing her eyes. What if the bad dreams came back? Worse still, what if she woke to find someone else had been taken away?

But eventually she did sleep, and when she heard music—not Daddy's piano, but a music she had never heard before—she went in search of it. Through the house she went, out the back door, and the lavender bushes were not their usual well-trimmed selves but very high, forming a kind of archway. She still heard the music, and smelled the lavender's bittersweet scent as she walked. Out of the archway and into a place that was not her backyard but someplace she'd never seen before. Later, she often thought of that dream and was never able to see where she'd been. She only had the sense of it being an in-between place, a safe place, so when he called out *Ceel* she turned without hesitation. He looked the way he always had, and so happy to see her. She ran to him, and he felt the same as always: strong arms around her, and the beard stubble on his cheek tickled her. He even smelled the same, like the outdoors and the Old Spice aftershave she'd gotten him for his last birthday. *Can't you come back?* she asked, knowing the answer would be *No.* Which it was. She wanted to turn away but didn't. *I'll be with you,* he said, *because I love you, and nothing ends that. Keep love and hope alive and no one will ever leave you.* He kissed her forehead then, and she fancied she caught a glimpse of the world on his side of the boundary. As the years went on whenever some moment of joy came to her or some particularly beautiful music made her heart soar, whenever some sight of rare beauty met her eyes, whether it was a painting at Mama's gallery or a sky like the one above Los Cielos today—those moments were like that fleeting glimpse.

Singing was like that. When she'd sung *Pie Jesu* at the funeral, she felt again his kiss on her forehead, that feeling of safety. That glimpse of another world. She didn't experience this every time she sang—far from it. But often enough.

"Mind if I join you?" Ben asked.

Cecilia opened her eyes and smiled at him. "But of course."

He sat down on the chaise next to her. "It's beautiful."

"I'll show you the sights when we're on vacation."

"I'm looking forward to that." It was a simple statement, but there was an underlying warmth to his words that pleased her.

For her first year with the group, he'd simply been Ben. As in: *Ben, I have a question about this. Ben, could you please help me with that? Ben, where the heck is my W-2?* She was struck early on by his grace under pressure and his competence that kept things running so smoothly it was easy to overlook. A few of the ensemble thought him a snob, for he kept to himself and wasn't one for idle chitchat. But Cecilia had her uncle as an example and knew that just because a man was quiet didn't mean he was stuck-up.

Shortly after the second year began, the ensemble's gig at a corporate party was canceled, and it seemed a shame to waste a perfectly good evening. Cecilia and Jackie consulted the local entertainment listings and found a nearby club with an Eighties Night. Cecilia quickly found scarves Aunt Rachel had sent her, fashioned them into headbands, and off she and Jackie went. As they dashed through the hotel lobby they saw Ben: he had headphones on and was scribbling something in a notebook, looking unusually intense. But he stopped at the sight of them and took off the headphones. "Uh, what's with the headgear?"

"Eighties Night at the Slow Club, just a few blocks away," Jackie said.

"Want to come?" Cecilia asked. It wasn't until later she wondered if that was crossing some sort of line to invite the management along, but Ben's whole face got a soft glow, and he smiled. "I love eighties music. Give me five minutes to run this up to my room."

That was the beginning of it. Jackie left early with one of her headaches coming on, so it was Cecilia and Ben. At first they just talked and ate bar food and drank fruity drinks. Cecilia kept trying to persuade him to dance, but Ben was having none of it until "Come On Eileen" started up. Even he couldn't stay still for that one, and they danced the rest of the evening.

"I didn't know you liked that sort of music," Ben said on the way back to the hotel. He seemed impressed by the way Cecilia had sung along while she danced, to nearly every song.

"I like all kinds," she said. "Between my folks and my friends, I don't think there's a genre I haven't heard at least once or twice."

"It just doesn't seem like you."

She knew what he meant. She'd seen the occasional notes in the press coverage: *Soprano Cecilia Whitman not only has an angel's voice but resembles one as well.* It was a compliment, she knew, but as she'd told Jackie and now told Ben, it made her sound like she should be decorating a Christmas tree. They wouldn't lay on the angel comparisons if they saw her on Saturday mornings, in her sweats, eating cereal doused with coffee instead of milk (a bad habit leftover from college) and watching *Army of Darkness*. Or dancing to Dexy's Midnight Runners and Haircut 100. "I like karaoke, too," she said.

"See, that doesn't surprise me as much. I love what the Ensemble does, but I guess it gets kind of limiting sometimes." Ben laughed. He had a very nice laugh, it was a shame she didn't hear it more often. "It's a good thing to go outside the box."

"What about you?" she asked. "How do you get outside the box?"

He hesitated so long she was getting ready to apologize for asking. After all, he was the group's assistant manager, and she was a rookie barely out of her first year. Finally, in a low voice he said, "I write my own music."

"Really? That's wonderful. What sort of music?"

"Oh, no genre really. Ballads and things. I don't really—oh, here we are. I have to go see Russell," he said, and left her in the hotel's lobby.

A few more months, a few times at karaoke and another Eighties Night, and he finally told her about the music. "Been writing off and on since I was a kid. I think I always wanted to, but I needed something to say first."

"You still have any of those songs? Or is it like my high school poetry?" she asked.

"Hidden in a box?"

"More like shredded and burned, put the ashes in the compost heap."

He laughed. "Not quite. More like, I've kept a few phrases and melodies. Most of it's half-baked rip-offs, but it's the people who inspired me, I keep coming back to their stuff," Ben said. He was much more expansive with her than he'd been before. "Gordon Lightfoot, early Genesis, King Crimson, Tori Amos." He paused, as if weighing what he was going to say. "Your dad."

It didn't surprise her, much. *Winter Roses* had been in and out of print a few times, but at least once a year someone found out she was Daniel Whitman's daughter and told her how much they'd liked the record; sometimes they asked her to sign it, which always made her feel strange, for it had been made before she'd been born. Once she'd met one of the session musicians who'd worked on the album. "You've got your dad's eyes, you know that?" Terry Apodaca said.

Ben said: "I was twelve when my folks split up. As far as I knew everything was fine, and one day my dad said, 'I've met someone else, I'm packing up to be with her. Bye!'" He shook his head, took a long drink of his beer. "My mom went to pieces. She did not see it coming. My older brother started acting out, got arrested a few times. Me, I just stayed in my room and listened to music a lot. Didn't help that I was just in middle school, you know, that real awkward time. It wasn't a lot of fun.

"I was listening to the radio one night and they were playing it. Your dad's record. 'Bitter Wine' was the song that hooked me. You could tell he was angry about what had happened. I don't know, it was like it gave me permission. To be angry about it, and write about that feeling, when your life's been . . ." He trailed off, looking at her strangely as if he thought he might have offended.

"It's a hole in the world," she said. And it never went away, not completely. How could it? But, she told him, if you had people who cared about you, it made the hole so small you didn't hear the wind rushing through it anymore; sometimes you would not think of that hole in the world for an entire day. Whenever she thought about those awful days, she always thought of after the funeral: lying on the workroom sofa while her mother stroked her hair, relatives in and out of the room, and then Uncle Mick had come in. She'd been afraid to look at him, for he'd been so strange during those last few days she'd wondered if he blamed her. But he'd changed. He looked at her and held his arms out to her, hugged her when she ran to him. *We're all here,* he said, *All here for you and your mom.*

"I understand," he said. "I've got good people in my life."

The way he looked at her then made her realize they were setting something in motion. No, it had been set in motion when she first asked him to Eighties Night, or maybe when she auditioned for the Ensemble.

They didn't kiss that night. That happened a couple of weeks later. He'd made her a deal—he'd give her his demos to listen to if she sang a duet with him at karaoke that weekend. She agreed and somehow managed to get through their rendition of "Total Eclipse of the Heart" without losing it completely. She shouldn't have been too surprised; his sense of humor was stealthy but could be wicked when he wanted it to be. Later she said, "You're lucky your songs are good or I'd never forgive you," and somehow they kissed. It felt so right.

Ben's practicality kicked in. They had to keep a lid on this, until after the season at least. She agreed, but now it was her turn to make a deal: he would come and have dinner with her family and friends on Christmas. If he didn't mind.

"Are you kidding? I'd love that!" Ben's eyes lit up.

It made her wish she'd asked him sooner.

It would be good, she knew. She hadn't made it home last year and longed for her old home. For the scents of the lavender plants and the ocean, and her mother's holiday feast. For the simple comfort of being with those she loved—friends, relatives, and now . . . well, maybe it wasn't love yet for Ben, but it might be one day.

Backstage at Stirling Auditorium, the Ensemble in their outfits. Those had been Russell's idea—velvet dresses for the women in one of four colors: basic black, midnight blue, deep forest green, or wine-dark burgundy. The men got formal wear with cummerbunds and ties in the same four colors. It had also been Russell's idea to give a singer, one from each gender, a solo song each performance (all other songs would be full chorus). Unfortunately this had left the jockeying for who got their solos at what gigs up to Ben to manage, and he also had to deal with people who didn't want to sing a song if someone else had done it. But he managed to get it sorted out, mostly because the levelheaded people outnumbered the prima donnas.

Cecilia had asked for her solo on the night of the Los Cielos performance, but now as she stood with the others, waiting to take the stage, she wondered if it had been a mistake. Her relative inexperience weighed on her, as did knowing that so many people she knew were out there in the audience. She'd even heard a group of voices call out: "We love you, Gingersnap!" and had to explain her high school nickname to Jackie and Ben. She fingered the corsage her mother had sent her— lavender tied with a ribbon that matched her dress. No, all would be well.

And it was. She took the stage with the rest of the group, and in darkness they began "Carol of the Bells," the lights gradually coming up as the song built—this bit of stagecraft had been Ben's idea, and it had also been his idea to toss "Christmas Time is Here" from the *A Charlie Brown Christmas* into the mix of songs.

The time came for her solo. Cecilia went down the steps to stand in front of the group, catching encouraging smiles from most and a discreet thumbs-up from Jackie. She wished she could see Ben but knew he was backstage. The lights made it too difficult to see the audience beyond the first couple of rows, but that was enough: Mom was there, looking so happy to see her and still so lovely. More faces she recognized. Family and friends. She had thought this turn in the spotlight was for herself, but it wasn't. It was for all the people who'd believed in her and loved her. *My whole family. You, too, Daddy.*

Her song was "Gabriel's Message," and as always when she sang well, she felt the song come not from her but from somewhere beyond her. She felt herself to be not the source but the conduit, and it was a feeling both exhilarating and a bit frightening. But the fright vanished quickly. She was home, after all, doing what she loved best. A gift she gave not just to herself but to those who heard her.

When her final "gloria" had faded into silence, the applause washed over her. Yet for a moment she did not hear it, nor feel the spotlight's glow. Instead there was a silence and light that felt like home. For a moment the hole in the world was gone. She'd sung for her family tonight—all of them. And she knew that all of them were proud of her.

The End

ABOUT THE AUTHOR

Photo © Loa Allebach

Kelly Cozy is the author of the *The Day After Yesterday*, *Undertow,* and the Ashes series. She is also the author of the movie guide *A Nerd Girl's Guide to Cinema*; volume two of *A Nerd Girl's Guide to Cinema* will be available in 2019.

She lives in California with her husband, son, and cats. When she's not at home reading, writing, or cooking, she can be found at bookstores, geeky conventions, or the beach.

Visit her on Facebook at: Kelly Cozy, Author

www.ingramcontent.com/pod-product-compliance
Lightning Source LLC
Chambersburg PA
CBHW071244250626
47163CB00002B/314